COLORS OF ATLANTIS

GOLDEN AGE SERIES: BOOK 1

DD ADAIR

Spiral Path
PRESS

CONTENTS

Copyright © 2018 by Spiral Path Press
First Edition

Published by Spiral Path Press
PO Box 1183 Divide, CO 80814.
Cover design by Susan Krupp at yuneekpix.com
Maps drawn by Dr. Jason Grundhauser.

For information about special pricing for bulk sales, please contact Spiral Path Press at ddadair2@gmail.com

ISBN: 978-1-7328055-0-7 (paperback)
ISBN: 978-1-7328055-1-4 (ebook)
ISBN: 978-1-7328055-2-1 (audiobook)
Library of Congress Control Number:
Please visit the author's website at www.ddadair.com

To the incomparable bond of sisterhood; by chance or by choice

and

To you, our beloved Reader
May you enjoy remembering Atlantis, as much as we did.

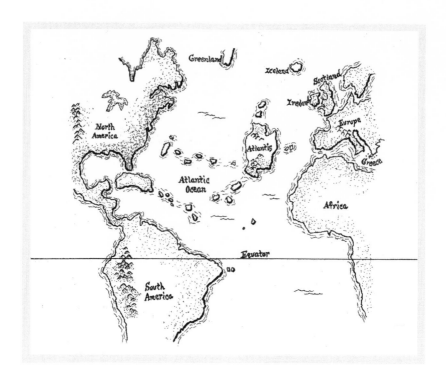

Placement of Atlantis in the Atlantic Ocean

Bourne of lightning and fire,
One shows the way.
Mark the hour of early birth with
crimson flower.
Darkness flayed in breast of men,
given now the way to mend.
Heed the two, follow one and
light prevails before
end.

One to come and turn
the tides, clear destruction
of evil minds.
Change the course and move
our race to fearless ground
on higher plane.
Be it so on mountains high
midst scouring wind and clouds
that fly.

Courses etched among the stars,
mirrored on earth in blood and flowers.
Salvation wove as dark and light
work together, ignite
a spark of endings to begin.

Birth causes death
and in between,
triumphs of time and sadness wing
to end unholy reign.
-*Atlantis Book of Prophecies:* Vol. Six

PART I

ORACLES

9,990 BCE HIGH CITY, ATLANTIS

"The stars move and tell you like a prophecy. Warn you of change, of opportunity... Stars are energy just like weather, like water, like the tide is an energy. Stars have messages. They are the oracle."

— "SACRED HIDDEN KNOWLEDGE" BY DOLORES CANNON

ZIEL

The Oracle burst into my private sanctuary, and the shadow of my death rode upon his back. Illusions of peace so tightly grasped within my fist for over a hundred years, shattered and fled the perfectly ordered room on icy wings. I shivered, drawing my meditation mantle tight over aged bones.

"*...and so the pendulum swings on through the point of balance, into the arc of chaos, destruction, and creation...*" My mentor's words came unbidden, and in this moment their meaning became experience.

"Ruler Ziel, most humble Leader, forgive me I implore you for interrupting rudely, but we have horrid visions you must know of. It is urgent. Imperative." The words tangled together in a clamorous tenor of trouble.

My nostrils flared; talcum powder. The pasty smell was a favored accoutrement of the 'earnest' Oracle. A contrived odor that sickened me, almost as much as the wildly colored plumage of the High City aristocrats. *Had we so lost our way that these were the brightest testimony to our advancements?*

He fell to his knees in front of me, blue sash askew, babbling like an idiot. All I could notice was the way powder smudged across his pudgy jaw in hasty, uneven blobs. A taint of white smeared the collar of his beige robes as his round, shaven head bobbed up and down. *A dying flower, fluttering in the winds of change.*

My heart began to beat a heavy drum of premonition.

"Oracle." I grasped his shoulder, breaking the frantic litany. He clamped thin lips and blinked at me with pallid, watery eyes. It was those eyes that got my attention, more than his shrill clatter of words. Powder or no, I knew this Oracle, and while he may be prone to vanity like any Atlantean, he was a talented and respected Seer, steady in his devotion and duties to his circle, High City, and me. "Take a breath." I inhaled slow and deep while he tried to follow my lead.

In the long span of years I've held this office, none have ever entered my private chambers without invitation. This, along with the fact that the weekly meeting for reports was in just a few short hours, elevated my concern.

"You needn't apologize. Your presence here tells me enough. Now, start from the beginning. Slowly. The facts, please."

Pawn, as named, having interrupted my customary predawn meditation, re-arranged himself on the brightly patterned rug to mimic my own cross-legged position. He rubbed his palms together in agitation, then wiped them on his robes. Sweaty. Fear.

I waited, willing my heart to slow its rhythm.

"Most humble Leader, my group meets every evening at the crest of night as we feel our senses to be the most open then. Our favored site for visioning is the south Rose Arbor, but the rains fell early so we met in the Blue room as is our assigned place. We lit the candles, said the prayers and joined our energies as..." he paused, his gaze nervously jumping around my simple rooms, then shifting to me and widening, as if he just realized where he was. "Well, you know the rituals well I am sure. Probably wrote them!"

Sensing his anxiety swell, I unfolded to stand. "It's alright Pawn, continue. I'll get water." I moved calmly across plush carpets to the pitcher and cup on my beloved rosewood table where I usually broke the night's fast.

But only silence answered. I turned to see Pawn hugging himself, attempting to still the trembling in his soft body. Slightly rocking forwards and backwards, he stared vacantly at some unseen horror, trapped in a mind that didn't know what to do with it. I sighed. *I was the one expected to know.* Yet this would likely end in unanswerable questions as so oft these visions tend to.

Pouring the water, I pressed the crystal cup into his hands. "Drink. It'll help."

He obeyed and I waited until he held it in his lap. "Tell me the image that bothers you most."

He nodded, taking another sip as I resettled on the ornate meditation cushion.

"They were ugly creatures, *very* large, with brutish heads and jagged teeth, *two sets* in some. Others had misshapen limbs or faces. There were rows and rows of them lining up. Their leader was shouting. Two fought each other and I saw one rip the arm clean from another." He shuddered.

"Human?"

I asked because I got reports almost daily now of bizarre and monstrous creations in Belial.

"Yes I, I think so, but much bigger. Mutations mayhap. Like a deformed army amassing to march."

Chills nettled my spine. The *Mutazio*. Habitually, my fingertip smoothed an eyebrow. The acrid tang of his fear was palpable—or was it mine? "Did you notice the land they were on? Was anything familiar to you?"

He shook his head. "Nowhere I've been. It was dry and... ragged. High desert with tall rock formations and small mountains. Little vegetation. It reminded me of something dying. Parched. But those creatures... the giants," he looked at me with haunted eyes, "they marched Ruler Ziel. There were men around them using whips—long, with barbs —driving them. Divided into sections they were, and spread as far as I could see. It seemed entirely... wicked." He shook his head—a quick jerk, as if to smooth away the scene, like the sand tablets children used for drawing.

Thoughts crowded in, vying for position. *The Sons of Belial are mobilizing their Mutazio. But to where? Atlantis? Mardu's built enough of an army to go to war!* I knew this was coming but so soon? Even more disturbing was the realization that the people of Atlantis, MY people, were entirely ignorant, naive, and unprepared. And whose fault was that? I suddenly felt old and tired—not pathos I usually allowed. Nor would I allow Pawn to see the inner turmoil his words were creating.

"Thank you Oracle. You were right to come to me. Ask your circle to document every detail, and bring it to me after midday meal." I stood and moved towards the door.

He scrambled to his feet, tripping over the hem of his robe as he placed his palms together at his forehead and bowed low; the respect due a mentor. With news this urgent and dire, his formality tired me.

But I returned the bow. "You are an effective Oracle, Pawn. I am grateful for your service. Let's not speak of this at the meeting this morning. We need better information."

He nodded emphatically, "Yes most Humble Leader. Peace be with you this day."

"And you," I replied as I shut the door, left with a horde of decidedly unpeaceful thoughts.

2

THE ONE I'VE BEEN WAITING FOR

9,990 BCE. HIGH CITY, ATLANTIS

The first domino falls, and before one can blink, a whole line, stretching long into forever, tips gracefully, inescapably, in one direction.

— ATLANTIS BOOK ON DESTINY

ZIEL

"... *I* want to tell Ruler Ziel, but I don't know if he'll listen...or believe that I've seen something far more important than any of *this!*"

I looked up from scratching dreary notes, scanning the packed benches of the report hall for the speaker of those small, breathy words. My hearing had always been my keenest sense. Oblivious, the Oracle next to me droned on, analyzing in wearying detail the dreams he'd had for the last six nights.

Speaking over a mill of voices filling the room, I interrupted, "Quiet! Who said that?" The startled silence stretched as a hundred confused faces swiveled around at each other.

Only one of them was looking straight at me.

"Come here", I commanded, " and explain what it is you have seen."

One of my small Council inserted a chair to my right as a young, sienna-haired girl crept forward from the end of the second row. Oracles gaped at her, and at me, in varied expressions of disapproval.

She sat, staring uncertainly down at fine-boned hands, while the Oracle-of-many-dreams on my left protested and I ignored him.

My sharp focus softened when I took in her shy round face, her mouselike trembling. "What is your name?" My tone dropped, privatizing our exchange. The rest of the Oracles would hopefully grow bored, and go back to whispering amongst themselves.

"Frond." She was tongue-tied, juniper eyes wide with fear at my undivided attention.

"Frond," I reflected her tone and relaxed back in my narrow chair. "Thank you for your service here. How long have you studied with us?"

"Just two moons Ruler Ziel." Chancing eye contact, her words began to flow. "I'm so sorry, I didn't mean to interrupt everyone else, but I've had a vision last night. It was the most...vivid and...real. Right when I was falling asleep so I got up and wrote it down—every detail—and I think it's important....maybe." Trailing off as her eyes rolled around the room at the hundred Oracles all still listening, her heavily freckled face flushed with the uncomfortable press of attention.

Two moons. This was probably the first weekly report hall she'd been to. Usually, Oracles studied a year or more, before braving any sort of report to me. She must be gifted indeed. Otherwise, none of the advisors would have granted permission to be here.

"Then I would be honored to hear it." I waited while Frond gathered her thoughts. Not easy, coming forward and speaking in front of a hundred of Atlantis' most experienced Seers, Astrologers, Dream Interpreters, Prophets and all manner of Diviners. Plenty of them currently displaying doubt baldly on their seasoned faces.

It was then that I noticed there was no one hovering nearby for Frond to look to.

"Where is your advisor?" None of them would leave a new student unattended at this meeting.

Frond looked down. "I don't know. I d-did not ask him, um, inform him that I was coming here..."

Hmm. Breaking protocol for a chance to tell me. This would cost her, once the missing advisor found out. I suddenly liked Frond. Young and shy she may be, but same as many vulnerable creatures, she had uncommon courage—born from necessity I suspected. I bowed my head to her, "Clearly you've great faith in what you have seen. Why don't you start at the beginning."

She pressed back in the chair, taking a deep, shaky breath as the room of Oracles strained to hear, expectations swarming us.

"There was storm, with lightning like I've never seen, striking an island over and over. I could *taste* it...the flavor of minerals, the scent of iron. It stripped the trees bare. Then I saw a baby born. Not in any Healing Temple either! In a tiny hut on the island right in the midst of the... destruction."

Here she paused, and I could see images seared in her mind, mirrored as shadows on a troubled face. I nodded at her to continue.

"I wondered then if the storm was trying to get to it. To the baby. She was tiny and the mother worked terribly hard to birth her. I saw the father too and he was helping—trying to at least. The odd part was that the baby changed... " Frond stopped speaking as the murmurs grew louder around us.

Oracles were wagging their heads, turning away in disinterest, muttering.

"A storm and a baby's birth on an island? What's important about that?"

"Probably just a dream."

"Somebody should teach that girl the difference..."

"Ruler Ziel will set her straight. He doesn't abide overeager time wasters!"

Their comments were striking at the heart of Frond's confidence. This wouldn't do. I stood—as though my small stature might intimidate. "Clear the room! Everyone will wait outside until we resume." The shocked, indignant looks I caused pleased me overmuch.

Our Oracle Hall was visually stunning, but then so is every part of Poseidon's Palace. With the same indigo walls and floor that comprise the rest of the second level, one entire side of the room was lined with clear doors. They currently stood open, allowing morning breezes to circulate. Abundant natural light showcased the beautiful colors of the stone, illuminating intricate carvings covering every surface, gilded with gold, silver, and orichalcum. The ceiling was inlaid with fist-sized diamonds, arranged like the Pleiades were in Atlantis' night sky during Poseidon's long life.

In moments, the room was vacant save my small Council, Frond and myself.

"Ahhh" Resuming my seat, I relaxed into the empty. "Much better. Oracle Frond, will you continue? I believe you said something was strange about the baby...?"

"Yes." She spoke slower now, unsure whether she was in a terrible mess of her own making, or if she had been right to come to me. "Yes... I saw the baby being born, I saw her suckling her mother's breast, I saw her sleeping and I saw her father carrying her around to soothe her squalling, but sometimes she had dark hair and sometimes it was light. I'm certain she changed...somehow...so I thought it very odd, and the first thing we're taught—about the only thing I've learned well so far—is that the grandest information can be seen in the tiny details."

I nodded. "Good! Wonderfully done! Indeed, the most useful bits can be subtle, common parts habitually overlooked." My solar plexus pinged excitement. *A highly unusual birth!* I needed more.

"Describe the island. Was it large? One of ours? Have you ever seen it before?"

Frond shook her head, unconsciously leaning away from my pummel of questions. "I've not. It was small, shaped like a... a stunted, waxing, crescent moon." She nodded, confirming her own description, but then frowned. "There was petals on the ground—no, that can't be right... anyway, I saw no other buildings or people, just the hut with the mother, father and baby inside. They looked like Atlanteans, healthy, strong, beautiful. The mother had tattoos starting at her temple, winding down her neck and covering her arm and ribs, even down onto her thigh—"

"Which side?" I interrupted.

"Her..." Frond pressed her eyes shut trying to recall. "Left side. All of them on her left side."

"And what were the tattoos of?" I was leaning forward now, could smell the nutmeg cream she used as a cleanser, almost able to see the images whirling around her mind.

Frond shook her head. "I don't know...I don't think I can make them out...oh! There was the divine feminine—the two connected spirals—taking up the entire side of her neck, and on her arm... " She opened her eyes. "I'm sorry Ruler Ziel, I couldn't make them out. There was only firelight."

"That's fine. You're remembering quite a lot. What else?"

"The lightning was constant, *persistent*, like the wind and the hail. I've never seen the like—maybe it's normal for sea storms? I just keep thinking it was trying to destroy something. At first I thought it was the island itself, but then when I saw the baby and she changed, I thought perhaps it was after the baby, maybe because she's different? Or has powers she shouldn't?"

Frond was falling into conjecture, that great trap all Seers navigate when we cannot explain that which we have seen. But I had an inkling of why she'd defied protocol to come to me. Why this inexperienced girl's inner guidance would not let her rest until she did. Exhilaration overtook me. This could be it, could be the birth of the prophecy! It spoke clearly of an unusual storm, and of fire. The petals on the ground fit perfectly but there was supposed to be red...

"Was there blood?" I asked abruptly. "Did you see blood?

Frond wrinkled her brow, "No. I'm sure there would have been, from the birthing, but no, I didn't see it."

Even without an obvious fulfillment of red, I was certain this was it. It had to be. I'd had thousands of births with unusual circumstances reported to me over the centuries, and none had fulfilled more than one or two of the seven specific details of the prophecy.

"Maya," I summoned the senior female on my small Council, "go and find out where there were storms last night with unusual amounts of lightning. I'm looking for storms over islands, and go back the last seven days. Wait, just have them start going back to find anything that fits. Also monitor the next several days. It possibly hasn't occurred yet."

Maya's lanky frame was already halfway across the expansive room, knowing full well what to do. She'd worked with me so long we thought more alike than different.

Turning to Frond I said, "Thank you for your bravery, reporting to me. I believe you witnessed a significant event. We must resume the weekly report hall now but will you kindly take supper with me tonight and bring any further details?" I nodded at my remaining two Councilors to let the buzz of Oracles back in while Frond replied.

"Yes Ruler Ziel, of course I will. Thank you for... listening."

As she rose I thought of one more thing. "Oh, and Frond, if your advisor troubles you, send him to me." I winked conspiratorially, and we bowed to each other as she slipped away through the crowd surging in.

A crowd of the most gifted Seers, Astrologers, Dream Interpreters, Prophets and all manner of Diviners who studied charts of the heavens from records of the last two yuga cycles, read dreams, past lives, and omens for scores of Atlanteans, and spirit journeyed around the globe and beyond the stars. These, plus two hundred more like them, reported to me all significant events in the metaphysical realms of Atlantis. Yet it was a fresh, timid student, probably with mediocre ability, that brought me the gold; the main event I'd been searching for; the reason I stay in this often exasperating position.

Here's one thing I know; the Universe adores irony, almost as much synchronicity.

My mind wandered during the rest of the long morning's reports. What are the odds of getting visions tied to my two primary concerns in one day—both from improbable persons?

"And you knew this would get my attention!" My out-of-context babble caused the current droning report to pause for a moment, then resume, and the day flowed along as though nothing of significance had happened.

By evening, Maya reported no lightning storms over any Atlantean islands in the last moon, and I hounded the weather people mercilessly, my excitement level soaring.

IT HAPPENED three days after Frond had come to me; a mother-head storm over a miniature island off the northwest coast of Atlantis. The biggest surprise was that I knew this place. Cherry Island, familiar only to the locals, was pounded into unrecognizable sticks by a collision of renegade storms, enduring for almost two days.

Finally, I knew what the red meant.

3

I AM ZIEL

9,990 BCE HIGH CITY, ATLANTIS

"Life can only be understood backwards; but it must be lived forwards."

— SØREN KIERKEGAARD

ZIEL

The problem with perceiving our future is the "when". Whether you have a vision, feel foreboding emotions that precede future happenings, or are informed by a helpful being, rarely does it come with a date stamp. No discernable timetable.

Same sort of problem with who and where. It's not helpful to witness events filled with strangers and places you've never seen before. When you are lucky enough to recognize someone or see a familiar place, you still won't likely know if it's tomorrow or next year or next decade. Even angels or higher beings trying to help, have difficulty telling you when.

Time is an anomaly only we humans live by, as ingrained in us as gravity and hunger. But outside the human experience, time is like trying to explain the succulence of a sun-sweet peach to someone who's never had taste buds. They won't get it.

So, you see the problem now.

I've known Atlantis is going to perish since I was twelve, and I've devoted my entire life to the *when* of it since that long ago vision. I know roughly how it could happen—if we don't change the course—and finally, now, I suspect who's involved. But is it next week? Or is it fifty cycles away? Will I still be around to do anything about it?

When I tell colleagues the things I see, they want answers to all the same questions that I have. They pester me endlessly about things I don't know.

It's maddening being a Prophet. Like assembling a puzzle when the pieces are doled out erratically over time and none of them fit until you have enough of them. And it's not like you have a convenient sample picture to go by. Probably you'll have twenty different puzzles going at once, and how should you know which event the pieces go to as they come?

There will in fact, come a day, when prophets are thought to be lunatics, and we will accept it, because that's what it feels like.

It's common to think that the psychically gifted have it better, that they have less need of faith. The reverse is actually true. We see the nature of humanity. We understand the powers and responsibilities of control. We have an inkling of things to come. And yet more often than not, we're powerless to understand the crucial questions; when? who? why? There-fore unable to do much about it.

Add to that being told endlessly that you must use your ability to somehow better things, as if there is some glorious objective that we must find and satisfy. I've not known a Seer yet who thinks they've fulfilled their life purpose. Like most people, they aren't even sure what that purpose is.

Without faith, our sad and empty "gifts" only leave us slumped again and again at the feet of failure. I refuse to accept that any bit of this is meaningless.

MY NAME IS ZIEL. Head of Atlantis' House of Oracles. Only male Ruler of the High Seven.

My childhood was as warm as it was long. I had visions from the beginning, but it was only when I started classes with other children that I learned this was abnormal. Mother listened carefully, taking notes, trying to help me piece together meanings, find possible ways to use the information.

She took me to High City at the age of twelve after I had the first vision of Atlantis falling. So soon after Lemuria's tragic sinking, she was terrified that Atlantis faced the same fate.

The House of Oracles was headed by a woman who seemed ancient to me at the time. She spent many days asking me questions, testing, determining how advanced my psychic abilities were. Then she asked my mother and I, if I would come apprentice with her. She had never taken an apprentice in all the years she'd been Head Oracle.

This simply confirmed what my Mother already knew; I was meant for great things. If she had known what those great things would cost me, could she have offered me so readily? Now that, I do not know.

Indeed, if my life has a mantra it is; "I do not know".

How can it be that I understand more of humanity's past, and foresee more of our probable future than perhaps any other living human, and yet most of my answers are truthfully the same four words?

I do not know.

4

CHERRY ISLAND

9,990 BCE CHIFFON, ATLANTIS

"I hunger for your sleek laugh and your hands the color of a furious harvest. I want to eat the sunbeams flaring in your beauty."

— PABLO NERUDA

TAYA

*S*he touched her bountiful hump of a belly, stiffened in one of those funny little contractions that came daily now. Taya carried twins but did not know yet what their sex might be. Waiting for Drey's return, to find out together, had been tougher than she'd anticipated. Tomorrow they'd finally know. And then there was only one moon left to prepare.

Despite a groaning backache, the muscular, tattooed mother-to-be, with hair like flashing wild blackberries, woke the father of her babies, at dawn. "Drey wake up! You're missing all the big ones." She pushed hair from his temple. Silky and fine as the arachnid web she'd once tried to weave with, it felt like harp music you could touch. "I've soft-boiled eggs waiting, and tea."

He flopped to his back and reached for her, eyes still closed. "Mmm. And what are we doing today?"

"Anything we please." Taya tugged at his hair, fingers trailing down across matching blonde stubble on his jaw. Even that felt soft as baby down. "Well, anything *you* please."

Drey always chose fishing. Taya was too incapacitated by her mountainous pregnancy for any of the adventures she would normally challenge him to.

She was happy just being together. Today was his first official day home from work. As was Atlantean custom, he'd taken leave to care for her until their babies were born, and of robust enough health that he could safely travel again to the far off lands that were his laboratories.

Yawning loudly, Drey helped her load their lidded basket;

-a packet of soft, freshly herbed goat cheese,

-two fragrant loaves of rustic grain breads,

-green snap peas from first harvest, thick as a man's thumb,

-large slices of crisp, mildly sweet jicama soaked in clementine juice,

-a log of dark, silken fudge; which Taya had bought at market yesterday, then rolled in chunks of toasted hazelnuts, turning it sultry and complex.

He stowed their feast basket by the door beside bottles of minted water.

"Aunt Sage made you a welcome home gift." She held out a generous jug of hempberry beer and kissed his cheek. "Let's bring it. It makes you entirely merry."

Hazel-green eyes still sleep-puffed, Drey planted a kiss on her lips. "Aunt Sage is an angel I think."

"Yes, well she's expecting a basket of fresh fish for supper, and maybe some early cherries if any are ripe yet." They'd drop anchor at the small comma of land, called simply "Cherry Island". It lay three miles off Atlantis' northwest coastline.

Inside their thatch-roofed cottage, Drey ceremoniously arranged his floppy fishing hat at a slight angle onto spiky, straw-colored hair; the hat he claimed brought him luck; the one Taya secretly thought looked ridiculous—but what good would it do to tell him? Reverently, he picked up a new fishing rod brought back from his trip.

"Odd looking contraption." Taya studied it. "Does it work?"

Drey's fine-boned face lit as he told her all about the extraordinarily tall, jungle man with skin like a cobra, who had gifted it to him. How the man had spent an entire afternoon teaching him how to use it, even though they understood not more than ten words of each other's language. "I hope I can remember how it all goes" he ended as they stepped out into the day's patchwork light.

Taya loved mornings. This sunrise glowed spectacular, torching a mirrored sky behind opaque clouds that were building an entire rainbow of corals and golds. She paused on the overgrown path that wound down the cliffside to a rather neglected pier. Faded and narrow, the pier stretched long over azure water in their small inlet, and ended at Drey's little white boat, tied firmly. "Look my love," she inhaled leaf flavored, new day perfumes, "Just look at our magnificent sky!"

"Dazzling, the colors of the light." He agreed, supporting her slow descent towards the water.

By late morning, with no sunshine left in the thickening day, Taya arranged extra cushions to support her heavy belly, and stretched out into the soothing rock of the wide little boat to relish a new book.

Drey's foreign fishing pole turned out to be both fun and lucky. He had caught such a bounty that he'd released two-thirds, and still had enough for a week of suppers.

Taking a break from reading, Taya contentedly harbored carnal thoughts, ogling Drey's sinewy tanned torso, enjoying his childlike exuberance at each fish that took his bait.

At first she had wielded the net, helping him pull in the exotically diverse sealife, listening to him expound on their names, the history of each species and how they would probably taste, based on the food supply they normally preferred. He was a library of encyclopedic information when it came to animals or plants native to Atlantis.

By the time they arrived at Cherry Island she was hungry and tired.

Drey tied them to the sturdy mooring dock built from varnished cherry wood, and helped her out. "We'd best make this a short stop my love", he grumbled, eyeing the darkening sky.

No longer colorful, the clouds from this morning's sunrise had risen along with the sun, continuing to mass and shadow all morning.

The sea breeze thickened on unseen cue, exciting the water into break-dancing to it's rhythm as Taya waddled onto the island, grateful for the prospect of a water closet. Her pregnancy allowed little storage of other bodily substances. She hadn't considered how awkward it would be; peeing off the side of a rocking boat, clutching Drey's hand for ballast. Raising her voice to combat gusts of wind, she called back to him, "You will bring the food? I'm beastly hungry!"

He was tugging the boat laboriously towards the sand, struggling against the churning water. "Go ahead, I'll catch up, with the food."

Taya lumbered up a slight hill towards shelter. Two small huts, used by orchard workers, hid in the middle of the island's southern end. No one lived on the island. The orchard keeper, pruners and harvesters came from the mainland; occasionally spending a few nights so their work days could be longer and fewer, especially during harvest.

The huts were almost a mile's trek inland. A well-used path, wide as a road, cut through the island's length, used to transport harvests of cherries to the dock, to be loaded onto boats and distributed across the mainland.

Taya thought how much she'd missed coming here when the trees flowered. Since she was a child, Spring had courted her, luring her across the water to come and sit in the magic of a thousand blossoming cherry trees. But Drey had been gone most of the past three months, finishing projects in preparation for taking this time away from his beloved work, and she had been too weary to make even this short trip on her own.

Already short of breath as she left the beach to enter the massive orchard, Taya stopped suddenly at the stunning sight of the orchids in bloom. She'd forgotten about the orchids.

Originally, this Island had been famous for a strange breed of native epiphytic orchids that grew wild. Drawing their nutrients from the salty moist air, they niched in between rocks along the craggy cliff sides of the roughly three by five and a half mile-land spit. Used to be, the orchids ruled the old ferny floor of the sparse forest right up to beachline. Many nuances of purple, white or yellow, they bloomed in the early summer and late autumn, avoiding the tropical summer months and rugged winters.

Over a century ago, some botanist theorized that the island's loamy, acidic soil was just right to grow cherries. He'd proven right, and every square foot of land that wasn't beach or rock was cleared of it's random growth, and planted with cherry trees. After that, the orchids were considered backseat to the crimson fruit. But no one told the orchids. They bred and scattered and re-infiltrated the new cherry tree forest, coexisting happily, creating a fairyland that the local mainlanders enjoyed.

Now, the exotic flowers were a spotted carpet of angelic royalty, bowing and waving to Taya in the currents of stormy air, and she forgot her uncomfortable bladder and grumping hunger. Stooping awkwardly to sniff their citrus and sunshine sachet, she caressed their velvet faces.

"Just look at you, perfect, glorious little things! How graceful and regal you are..." Unable to hold it any longer, she anointed a nearby patch of earth and hiked upwards.

Spying an orb of peeking crimson, she stopped. A branch near the hut clearing had ripened its bite-sized globes into shocking red earlier than their neighbors. "Yes!" She whooped, plucking the first one straight in her mouth, cramming the rest into pockets of loose, breezy pants.

Just then, the layered masses of silver-plated clouds overhead decided to drop their load. A stinging rain began, forced ahead of the whining, erratic wind. Taya picked faster, straining to reach higher, balancing her unaccustomed weight, as droplets pelted her from every direction. Drey arrived, juggling food basket, fishing pole and net of fish, with his lucky hat and her book crushed under armpits.

"I think... we might... be waiting out the squall here.... it's much too choppy to risk going back....likely be over in an hour or two." Drey panted between breaths. "Oh! You found cherries!"

Taya popped one into his open mouth and grinned suggestively, shouting slightly over the loud jingle of water spattering leaves, "We're stranded here in paradise? Whatever wicked things shall we do?" She teased him with a brief touch of rain-wet lips, placing one hand precisely and not at all lightly, onto his crotch. "Come lover," she turned towards the huts that promised dry warmth, "I will have you now."

Taya could feel Drey's eyes on her backside, extra curvy with fertility's pronounced shape. He'd been away from her a moon and a half this time; his need most likely blinded him to any extra shapes she'd grown since the last time they'd made love.

Taya knew men. Almost as well as the patterns of knots, and kaleidoscopes of color she wove daily into tapestries, offering comfort and pleasure to so many people all over her homeland. She knew perhaps too much about the human male's baser instincts and how the slightest hint of sexuality could eclipse vast amounts of accumulated wisdom. They were like a wolf once it caught a beguiling scent.

Lightning arced fitful splits end to end across the sky, and thunder rent the water-laden air so close Taya jumped and squealed, pulling a thoroughly soaked Drey into the largest of the huts.

Built of peeled cherry logs standing vertically, and lathed smooth on two sides to fit snugly against each other, the space inside was octagonal and thirty foot across. Capped with a slanted roof thatched with hemp reed, the hut was dusty and basic inside but provided all the necessities of human comfort. The smaller one was full of bunk beds, a single water closet and a fireplace, while this one housed a cooking area with a long trestle table lined with benches; enough to feed twenty workers at a time. The large hearth with old-fashioned roasting spit took up one wall, and a small booth built off to the side hid two toilets.

"I'll go see if there's bedding in the other one before it gets worse out there." Drey said, dumping his dripping load onto the table. "We can get out of our wet things, wrap in blankets at least."

Taya headed towards the neatly laid wood in the fireplace. By the time Drey returned with armfuls of blankets, she had the fire crackling, snapping heartily as it ate into tiny air pockets nestled in the bone-dry wood.

They stripped away clothes, shivering at wet cotton's touch on chilled skin, and Drey grew quite instantly distracted at the naked sight of her. Spreading his hands wonderingly onto her swollen belly, he traced the maplines of blue veins webbing this way and that under thinly stretched skin, pausing at the belly button fully popped out in a little pucker, "They have grown so much, our babies". He dropped a little kiss onto the top of her enormous protrusion. "I've worried about you this last moon. Worried that it will be too uncomfortable or painful while they get bigger. I don't see how your poor body can stretch any more!"

Taya moved his hands to each side of her extended belly and pressed them in firmly so he could feel the stirrings that she felt.

The babies were moving slowly, constantly, as if swimming. Cozy in their dark, underwater womb warmth, their feet and elbows and bottoms drew graceful geometry onto the inside of Taya's skin, just as our species have drawn meditative art onto dim cave walls through eons of time.

"My back hurts like the devil." She spoke quietly as their hands followed the wondrous stirrings. "Could you massage it? After we eat?"

But his eyes were on her chest, taking in her bare fullness. She watched desire shoot through him even as he tried to control and detain it, and she forgot about food and backaches and storms.

Slowly, his hands slid upwards to cup the full weight of her newly lush breasts. "It's like you're blooming." His thumb traced the pale blue, tattooed branch that wound from under her left armpit to flower around her nipple.

She kissed him hard, expressing the longing and desire of this last lonely moon. An urgency, some unnameable need, exploding upwards inside of her. Her desperate openness undid him, beckoning like a bonfire draws wandering nighttime teenagers to its mesmerizing heat.

Their lips and tongues and hands danced with each other, greedy with lust's eloquence, while the fire slowly licked its warmth throughout the round room.

Drey stepped back abruptly, wrapping a blanket around her. She watched him arrange a pallet of blankets on the floor planks; scarred with decades of fire sparks, gouges of workmen's boots, and misshapen, simple pictographs carved by those who were perhaps trapped here by a pounding storm, as they were now.

She settled with a sigh onto the blankets as Drey brought the basket of food to her, pausing to empty cherries from her wet gaucho pockets. "We've plenty of time love", he murmured.

So they prolonged their pleasure by feeding each other cherries; dripping tangy scarlet nectar. Licked it off each other's skin, rosy with passion's expectation and fire heat.

Drey threaded the largest of their fish onto an end of the spit, to roast slowly into pale pink, while they settled into the soft centers, the most secret places of their love.

Taya marveled yet again at how Drey could be carried away by his pure primal need, yet translate it into paying passionate homage to her body. As if she were a holy, much-beloved shrine; a sacred altar where he worshipped, single-minded and fervent.

He didn't last long and Taya followed him into her own hard waves of orgasm; their private empire of tremulous ecstasy; a boundless sea, tided with sensations of connecting this intimately in body, mind, and spirit.

Afterwards they whispered, drowsy and marvelling at their ability to create such pleasure. As the fire dried sweat and satiation from their bodies, they drank minted water and ate smoke-crisped fish, sucking its salt juices from their fingers while the storm's noise assaulted the land outside.

5

MARDU

9,990 BCE TEMPLE CITY, BELIAL

"Power changes everything till it is difficult to say who are the heroes and who the villains."

— LIBBA BRAY, THE SWEET FAR THING

MARDU

"*T*HIS TASTES LIKE PISS!"

The attack of words echoed back a harsh garble from polished walls, and he reduced his volume to menacing.

"What can *possibly* be difficult about bringing me a decent cup of wine?" Mardu waited a beat—until the servant hovering just outside the doors of his cavernous, opulent suite came scurrying in—before flinging the crystal glass of plum wine across the room at her. It missed her head, leaving dots and dashes of sticky liquid across the gleaming, black-marble floor as it flew. Shattering against a life-sized painting of two men and a woman, naked and copulating, wine dribbled down pale flesh.

"I'm so sorry Master. It was the only plum wine in the house, but I will go to the markets immediately, and bring you something better. What would you like while you are waiting? We've the excellent cherry blend you favor? Or perhaps a warm apricot brandy?" She was hurriedly mopping wine off grossly oversized genitalia in the painting, eyes cast down to avoid the faces twisted in depraved grimaces; something extreme, pleasure or pain. All the same to Mardu.

"Are you really so stupid? It's too hot out for brandy! I want something light, chilled—not bitter..." He bent his swarthy head over today's messages littering the mahogany shine of his ornate desk. A perfect replica of the desk that should rightfully have been his as the Head of Foreign Relations in Atlantis' High City.

His mind was preoccupied with welcome news, delivered just moments ago;

...our Anubis friends speak highly of you Dominus Mardu. They eagerly invite your visit to discuss terms of a mutually beneficial liaison.
     -R

He leaned against silky high-backed cushions, satisfaction softening his blunt features. Buried in thought, he stared out the window while the pretty servant girl finished mopping up splattered wine and crystal shards.

"Go away." Mardu's curt murmur hastened her exit. "I want Orja."

Light-skinned, with exotic upslanted eyes, Orja had been bought halfway round the world when she was twelve, by one of Mardu's merchant Captains. While most Belials used their conrectus, animals engineered with human "upgrades" to be used as servants, Mardu allowed only full humans into his home. Requiring lavish beauty to surround him at all times meant the servants he used were physically stunning, the most exquisite to be had from the world's slave markets. She'd been serving him the longest, and oversaw his household. Mardu favored her unfazeable nature and quick thinking.

"Orja, I've changed my mind, bring me cold meat, something smoked, and beer. Send up Balek as well. I've need of him. Then fetch the plum wine—you're the only one who finds anything palatable. When you return I have more writing for you." He pointed to the codex.

The use of her name communicated his good mood although Mardu didn't look at Orja when he spoke. She might be useful to him in myriad ways, but she was still beneath him. He acknowledged the house servants only by giving orders or unleashing his rage on them.

"Yes Dominus." She left the room swiftly.

For early summer, it was too warm this cloudless mid-morning in

Temple City, Belial's capitol on the southwest coast of the Atlantis Continent.

Mardu felt an exceptionally high mood filling him, as he savored the herbed boar, thinly sliced into moist layers that melted in his mouth. Washing the tender meat down with a thick black ale, robustly malted and icy, he sped through the rest of the messages; all good news furthering his plans.

"I'm here. Whaddya want?" Mardu's teeth grated at the squeaky voice of his eldest son, and he narrowed his eyes, studying the fourteen-year-old's skinny frame and shaggy, dirty hair. "You look like a weasel." He wrinkled a great gladiate nose, turning his broad, heavy features into a snarl. "You smell like one too! Bathe and put on something befitting a son of mine. And don't talk like an imbecile!" He stabbed a forefinger at Balek for emphasis. "You'll come with me. Be ready in one hour."

Balek's voice turned whiny, "But I'm 'spose to... er, due at my fighting lessons *now* and I'm to meet my friends at the arena later. They just got a new lot in."

Mardu scowled, tossing back the last of the ale. "You can watch misfit creatures butcher each other anytime. Today, you learn how to secure an army."

Balek's narrow-set eyes took on a dark gleam of interest. "Oh?" He sniffed. "Sounds important. Are we planning to attack somebody? Take over Atlantis and rule it like we should? Finally have land to spread out? We're strong enough, and they're just a bunch of old weak farmers and *meditators!* I know lots of battle strategies, I can help you plan—"

Mardu cut him off with a rare indulgent tone, "Today will be a step forward, but we must be certain of victory before attack. Now go and do as I told you. No more questions."

"Yes Fath—uh, Dominus." Balek left, his sharp odor following him out intricately moulded doors.

Mardu finished eating, plotting the day ahead.

The boy was right; finally they'd balanced the scale. Several hundred years after Onus Belial's glorious rise to power, there were more Sons of Belial than Atlanteans—many more. And, the Belial's mean average age was thirty to forty years younger. More importantly, the majority of the Belials were male, and trained for war.

Proliferating in such great numbers, however, had brought a host of problems. They now lived layered on top of each other, in one continuous over-crowded city.

The portions of Atlantis land granted to Belial long ago, accommodated them well at the time, but currently, had grown to roughly half again the population of Atlantis. They lived in less than a quarter of the space Atlantis citizens enjoyed. This brought food shortages, forcing them into dependance on Atlantean growers and herders. The Belial nation simply did not have the land to produce enough.

An agreement was reached long before Mardu took power; the Atlanteans provided food in exchange for conrectus to grow it, and a share of the metals Belial mined in other lands.

Atlantis' Law of One held it morally and spiritually wrong to mutate animals with physical and intellectual human characteristics, yet these creations proved quite useful. Since Belials made them in droves for their own servants or pets, and since Atlantis needed to produce more and more food, it was agreed to allow farms the use of conrectus to labor in fields and orchards. Used as the elephant, ox and horse were before technology took over, conrectus were productive, even more than the machines Atlantis had developed.

By the time Balek returned to the suite, smelling and looking a different boy, Mardu was anxious to go. A scribbled note fluttered on his writing table, weighted by a knowledge stone; a six-inch, smoky crystal pyramid crouching beside his enormous codex book.

> *"Orja, always write my words exactly.*
> *I was up half the night so there is much to add.*
> *It needs strict organization of course.*
> *~Dominus Mardu"*

Moons earlier, Mardu hatched the brilliant idea to write a better history of the Sons of Belial.

In his youth, he'd studied and served in Atlantis' High City, aiming to become Head of the House of Foreign Relations, which oversaw its military. But he'd been betrayed by the traitors that called themselves the High Seven. Determination to one day take revenge, fueled a rage continually stewing just beneath the surface; an energy Mardu clung to and hoarded. He had utilized this darkness to assassinate the longtime Sons of Belial leader and take over the Belial nation, assisted only by a handful of hired murderers and thieves.

He'd been schooled in the Atlantean version of Belial's national history, but now he understood how balefully slanted it was; tainted by their high-minded morals. "I will tell the truth of our rise. It is fitting that I—Onus Belial returned—be the architect of what every child in our land from now until the end of time shall know of their heritage." Mardu had pronounced grandiosely to Orja.

He planned to surprise his entire nation with their written history. Hence, Orja's involvement. Many nights he put himself to sleep speaking the stories of the Sons of Belial into a crystal keeper, embellishing, manipulating or subtracting at will. Then Orja, who wrote well, would transcribe it into the massive codex, bound inside its jewel-studded orichalcum covers, organizing his ramblings into subject matters and time periods. Mardu imagined it would someday be the most precious treasure Belials had. Certainly, they'd honor and revere it forever. Copies would be made from it and textbooks presented to every learning hall in Belial.

One day, all of Atlantis too.

FERMENTED GRAIN SCENTS lingered in delicate glasses scattered down a long table. Clamor from several million lives filtered up from the endless, close-fitting city that lay below the Grand Council room.

Mardu wore silk. Its tyrian red hid the layer of armor he never left home without. "General Pompeii will not be present today. He is in Greece as we speak, searching out those sympathetic to our cause, plotting a path for our invasion." Thunderous applause prevented Mardu from continuing as several dozen assembled Generals pounded the polished table in frenzied approval.

Mardu waited until it died away. "He expects it will take one year. Less, if the border soldiers pledge allegiance to increasing their wealth as readily as our own soldiers do!" Laughter rolled around at this truth. Mardu continued, "So, warriors of Belial, we must be ready! In as little as one year we may start phase one of our plan to increase and expand the Belial Nation!" He was shouting, but the hearty stomping and pounding and cheers of his men drowned him out. Patient with their enthusiasm, he went on. "And still more good news... General Rogan communicated from Anubi. They are eager to meet. I will go there when the time is right and begin our alliance... "

General Hercule spoke into Mardu's pause, "Pardon my question

Dominus Mardu, I've only just returned from the muta camps. Why an Anubis alliance?"

Mardu swung his head towards the voice, annoyed at the interruption. "Ah. Hercule. I await your report on the Mutazio. The Anubis are loyal Sons of Belial. Chased from their homes unfairly, yet they still practice the Belial ways of freedom and power. We created them and they are ours to use." Broadening his gaze, he looked slowly around the room at each man as he spoke, "We will mend the rifts, right the wrongs done them, and they will become our ally. Known only to you, my chosen Generals, they will be a secret army-in-waiting, should we have need of them. Now, I will hear each of your reports, after which I will present my orders for those of you being reassigned."

Their meeting room spanned the topmost floor of Temple City's tallest building. Over a hundred floors high, it housed Mardu's Generals and other elite government heads. They lived in spacious luxury with extravagant indoor gardens and spas. No expense was spared in their food, entertainment and comfort.

The building extended below earth's surface as far as it rose above. These subterranean levels housed Mardu's more secret laboratories and activities, as well as hidden histories accumulated by those who had led before Mardu. Few had access to those deeper levels. Mardu was the only person alive who knew all of what those depths told, shown to him by his paranoid predecessor, whose trust Mardu had worked hard to gain—right up to the day he slit the man's throat.

The meeting ended but several lingered to speak privately with him.

It was late and Balek had fallen asleep sprawled across an upholstered bench in the far corner.

"The Lady Councilors are again, raising the issue of you choosing no female Generals. They are concerned at the ill-treatment of women and girls across the city, and blame it on a growing majority of men in Belial positions of power." A General spoke. He oversaw Belial's Lower Council, which governed the day to day affairs of the people.

Mardu snorted. "Women have no place in war—or leading for that matter. Their emotions rule them and they use their hearts more than their heads! Always concerned with spiritual things when we live in a *physical* world. I've had my fill of arguing with females in power. They see things too disparate. What good are they to me, save giving me pleasure and raising my sons?" Emptying his glass, he slammed it on the table, perturbed at its sudden void.

The General bowed an apology, "I know it seems a bothersome detail.

Still, Dominus, I must tell them something. Fewer and fewer women care at all about power, but these ones do..."

"Then take it away! Convince them they are powerless and they will be. If they want tender-hearted leaders whose greatest goal is to make everything *fair*, they should move to Atlantis!" Mardu held up his empty glass in impatience, and a serving girl ran to fill it.

"Yes, alright, but there's just one more matter. Councilor Vara is still missing. Her mate is frantic, with no idea what may have happened to her, and I don't know if I should go ahead and replace her Council position or wait, out of respect."

"Councilor Vara..." His forefinger drummed against the table. "Red hair, young for a Councilor?" *Voluptuous for a Councilor?*

"Yes. She's been missing nine days now, with no clues to her disappearance."

It was her own fault. She'd flirted with him constantly, finding reasons to see him, talk to him, invite him to all her dinner parties. Flashing that saucy secret smile, she teased, playing coy games. And then—had it already been ten days ago? —she came to him. It was late. She'd drunk a little of everything and worn nothing beneath her gown. He gave her what she wanted, what she'd been begging for. Only—part way through, she'd suddenly wanted to stop, played a little game of "no" after moons of "yes". It angered him, as it would any man. So he took all he wanted anyway. Her resistance pushed him a little farther than usual. Too late, he realized that she wasn't just some slave or throw-away girl nobody cared about. She could become a problem to him. He'd been forced to preempt that problem. Unfortunate, but the fault was her own. She'd invited it. And who was she to resist him?

"Replace her. If she turns up, we'll decide what to do next. Probably went off with some Atlantean boy she wooed. You know women, constantly changing their minds." He shook his virile, well-groomed head at the folly of females.

"Why're we taking Greece a'fore Atlantis?" Balek yawned as Mardu's guards piloted the aero to his palatial home.

"Do you never listen? I brought you so you'll learn, not fall asleep!" Mardu snapped. "And stop speaking like those dregs you hang out with! We need the Greek army with us—not coming against us as Atlantis' ally. If we war with Atlantis, we stand to lose our lands, homes, food, everything! We must be absolutely certain of victory and the Grecian army is the third most powerful in the world." Mardu's barrel chest expanded with his diatribe. "And it's not just armies I'm building. My scientists are hard at work on newer weaponry, controllable diseases, mass mind control... those things take time."

Balek yawned again. "Are all your meetings that long and boring?"

6

CHERRY ISLAND BIRTH

9,990 BCE CHERRY ISLAND, ATLANTIS

"Then the sun and moon shall rise together, restoring balance to Earth. Ruling over Atlantis to blaze forth justice and finally, peace"

— ATLANTIS BOOK OF PROPHECIES:VOL 4

TAYA

*H*er low back pounded earnestly.

Drey massaged the phantom-bruised tissue, intuitive fingers digging out insistently lodged aches, then falling still, as they both dozed despite the exaggerated sounds of the storm outside.

Much later, by the glow of a wriggling body of coals and a racket of hail attacking the walls in great curtains, broken by regular searing explosions of lightning, Taya rose to stir the fire. She stretched, felt the slight sensation of a fluttering release deep inside, and then hot fluid streamed down her slumber-warmed legs.

"Drey, Drey, DREY WAKE UP!!" Her volume rose, ambushing the sprawled form, and he came to his feet, sleep-confused and startled, blinking in the dim.

"What??? What is it?"

"I—my waters just broke I think. Drey MY WATER JUST BROKE!" and she started crying and mopping at the gush of thick wet, down both legs. She babbled things that made no sense. "I don't know what to do. We're stuck here and I can't have the babies here. I don't know *how*. I CAN'T HAVE THE BABIES YET....!" She stopped then, going very still, closing her eyes to the panic.

Drawing in slow intentional breaths as if inhaling all the chaos swirling around her into her center, she imagined transmuting it into manageable calm.

Drey was still standing naked, helplessly watching her. Stupefied. Statuesque.

She opened her eyes when the first strong contraction dropped her to her knees.

Placing both hands underneath the great bulk of her rock-hard belly, she moaned, a long, humming sound of dread and disbelief. As the contraction released, she reached up to tug Drey down with her.

His eyes were fixed wide in a stare of fear transcending hysteria. The frozen kind. Like ambushed rabbits who pray for invisibility because they literally cannot move.

Sitting back, Taya cupped both sides of his face, drawing his forehead to hers. Speaking gentle now, words fringed in tears. "Drey the babies are coming. You *must* help me. I need you. Please....please, don't be so scared. I can't...you have to find a way through. It's you and me love. We have to do this."

Her hands returned again to the tightening belly, words falling from her bowed head, fading to another low moan. "I can't bear this alone..."

He blinked, eyes trying to focus. "I'm sorry. I'm here now. Of course you're not alone." Drey tentatively touched the upper contour of this living, breathing, flesh-mound that seemed so suddenly to have a mind of its own. He looked surprised at the taut strength. "Oh! It's....so hard! Does it hurt? Is it supposed to do that? Nevermind, of course it is! Oh Tay, our babies are coming!" Drey rattled on, soothing her until the pain passed.

Again and again, contractions tightened her belly tissues into a mountain of rigid proportions, as if some unseen taskmaster was condensing the flesh into a stubborn unyielding shell. She surrendered to the pain, to the absolute, uncompromising takeover of ancient, animal instinct.

Drey's fascination for all of nature's mysterious processes transformed him back to the scientist persona he was famed for. "Just breathe love, first of all, you have to breathe. I will find more blankets and dry towels and, let's see...would you like something behind your back? Tell me what will make you comfortable. Water? You should sip water. It's going to be alright you know. All is well. Animals and people give birth all over the world, every day, in every imaginable situation. If they can do it, so can we."

Drey finished his pep talk and Taya heaved a sigh as the contraction released again. He really was back. Thank heaven, earth and the inner deep! She watched him crashing around the hut, banging cabinet doors, actions just this side of panic. He looked very determined.

Sipping water, she rearranged the pallet and pillows and tried to remember everything the midwives had told her during her visits to the birthing spa in the Healing Temple.

HEALING WAS CONDUCTED in magnificent pantheons called simply, "Healing Temples". Healers were trained in the ancient arts of alchemy, metaphysics, and endless new experimental sciences.

The Birthing Spa, thirteen miles from Taya's village, was on the seventh floor pinnacle of that Temple's soaring edifice. Built by an architect with a love of combining rose quartz and illumin (a soft metal blend, flecked a very pale gold and used to coat stronger but less attractive metals), the structure was a monument to both sacred geometry and relaxation. The Spa itself was comparatively small, but felt spacious with more glass windows than solid walls. A Master Botanist grew tropical fruit trees and flowering plants. Drey usually brought some exotic, gorgeous specimen from his overseas travels for the Spa's healing plants collection.

Sparkling green crystals lined the ceilings, capturing and directing the universal energies swirling in and out of earth's atmosphere. Low stone walls divided steamy mineralized soaking pools, each with different healing properties. Distilled essences of flower blossoms, herbs, even trees, could be added for treatment of everything from skin conditions to undesirable emotional states. Originally meant for underwater birthing, the pools and tubs were the most used area of the entire Temple, enjoyed more often by the rest of the population than by pregnant women.

Births had been declining for several generations. Less people were willing to give up lives of exploration, experimentation, and utter freedom to care for little ones. It was custom to sterilize all children at age ten; a completely painless procedure that could be reversed at any age for any reason—resulting in no accidental pregnancies, where once there were many. Conception was always intentional now. Births were blessed news, marked by ceremony and rituals that celebrated the couple who desired to parent together. It was considered a holy honor, this miracle bestowed upon frail mortals; the ability to procreate.

"ALL OF IT no good to me now!" Taya muttered miserably coming back from remembered luxuries so far away, as she braced for another clenching of her womb.

"What's that love? I wish we had something for the pain....please, please tell me what I can do for you." Drey begged, wiping the perspiration from her face and chest.

She swatted his hand away, panting out each word. "Don't...do....that.....now!" She felt mutinous and surly inside her pain. "I'm sorry! I don't mean to be awful. You can...will you wipe my face now, it's soothing." Her moods bounced back and forth with dizzying violence.

Drey dabbed away her sweat. "What else should I be doing to prepare for.....for when they come out?" His voice edged into desperation.

She rushed her words, unsure how long the space before another contraction.

"How much beer is left? Is it enough to dull me some? Can you look for anything else here? There might be some schnapps or essential oils or something to rub on my perineum to numb me. Do you think it's alright if I drink that? Could it damage the babies?"

Drey was already at her side with the beer. "I think it'll be good for the babies. This can't be pleasant for them either." He held the jug of yeasty, hempberry ale to her lips. She gulped as much as she could before the next gripping came. And then she forced her mind to go to the waterfall.

TAYA'S favorite part of the Birthing Spa was the waterfall. Designed so the shallow pool at its base flowed away in a miniature river, it circled the entire floor before recycling into the waterfall's summit. Scented oils were mixed in the waters that misted fragrance up into the air streams, delivering tranquility through the entire Temple. It was sitting there, lost in the singing of the waterfall, trailing fingers in its gentle current, that Taya had met with the midwife, just days ago.

Healer Jayne, the eldest of the healers here, had talked Taya through the process of birthing. "There will of course be massage to relax and stretch your muscles as they labor. We'll use reflexology to aid your internal organs and systems, help the entire body focus on delivering the babies. And of course, hypnotherapy will keep the pain at a minimum—in fact, most mother's report no real discomfort. We'll have music, singing bowls, harps or perhaps some drumming—whatever works best for you—that welcomes your babies with serenity. We'll use herbal teas and whole fruit blends to fortify and energize you and the assisting father, ah...Drey. He will be back before the birth?"

She had ended their appointment with a reminder, "Though many choose not to, giving birth is still considered the most joyful, blessed service possible during a human lifetime. In the rare event of complications, right over here is our room for emergency procedures. We've the newest technology—fascinating for me—but I'm sure you will not need it."

ANOTHER VIOLENT CONTRACTION HIT, pulling Taya back into this "blessed service" her body was struggling to perform. Focusing on something pleasant distracted her from the pain—and helped her not be so mean to Drey.

"Describe the pain, maybe I can figure out how to ease it some." Drey hovered at her side.

Taya gulped the last of the beer, "Uhhh...it's like my organs and muscles and tissue—pretty much every cell of my body between here and here (she cut one hand below her breasts and the other at the top of her shapely thighs) is being simultaneously pinched, pierced and set on fire. But I think the beer is helping." She was already slurring very slightly. "And? I think you should stretch my perineum now. Do we have anything oily? Something slick? Healer Jayne said she would have to massage me, help it enlarge before....so the babies heads won't tear me." She trailed off as another contraction pulled her focus inward.

Drey held her hand. She clenched him unmercifully, jerking him close to pant "The butter. get. the. butter."

He nodded his understanding. Of course. The creamy coconut butter they'd brought for their picnic bread would make a perfect massage oil. He moved between her knees and tentatively began to work with her tender pulsing flesh.

"Have you even seen a birth before?" Taya wasn't sure she wanted to know the answer.

"Of course! I've assisted two cats and a monkey. Once I watched a camel being born. That one didn't go at all smoothly."

He mostly worked in botany. Right now, Taya wished he'd spent more time with the animals, or better yet, the humans.

The storm turned deafening. Lightning crashed at reckless intervals and the rain, or hail maybe, sounded an audacious whacking against the hut.

Drey worried briefly about the boat he'd pulled only part way onto the beach. "I'm not sure that rope's thick enough to hold, the waves must be monstrous in this wind. And no one knows where we are....how will you know when to push Tay? Did the midwife say?"

She rolled her eyes at him wailing. "I don't know! I've never done this before!" Panting into this new height of pain prevented further expressions of outrage. He was calmness itself, while she was being shredded from the inside out.

And the storm bore down as if hungry for something.

She shrieked when something brutal ripped inside. Switched from panting to weeping. "I think I need to push...it hurts so much!" Violently shaking her head, she moaned "I can't do this. What if I can't do this?"

"Of course you can. I will help you. Look at me, look at my eyes, listen to my voice, I will talk you through it alright? Trust me. You're the strongest woman I know, of course you can do this! Now a deep breath in.....and push!"

Her face felt like it might burst with it. Just spontaneously implode.

"I think I see a head Tay! They're coming, yes.....you're doing it......keep breathing.......and Puuush!"

Unhinged thoughts about splitting in half. Right up the middle starting at her vagina. Rib cage separating neatly into two equal halves. Would it stop at her chin?

She bore down twice more.

"Its head is out Love!" Drey was nearly shouting, wild with wonder. "Tay, I wish you could see this, breathe my love, breathe. Another big push! That's it. This is simply amazing!"

She tried to see, to watch, but her belly stubbornly humped out, contending for the precious view.

In-breath.

Wicked pain.

Lightning grabbing at the hut with tremendous ear-splitting force. Puuuuuuush! Had she just moved her bowels?

Drey danced up into view holding a small, messy, straggle of human. Tears tugged from his unnaturally bright eyes. "It's a girl Love, we have a girl and she has light hair like me. She's breathing! Can you see her breathe you did it! and its a girl what shall we call her...."

"FIRE! THERE'S A FIRE IN THE ROOF!" She pointed at the smoke billowing down from a growing, ragged gap. Thrust her arms out for her baby.

His triumphant litany faded as he searched frantically for a bucket. At least it was raining. Murderous bolts of electricity crashed from outside, where he'd gone, trying to see if the fire was being adequately drowned.

Meanwhile, Taya was;

-Birthing the other end of the fat pulsing vine connected to her tiny daughter's navel. It hurt overmuch for just being a slimy formless mass.

-Gag coughing as the smoke found her, shielding the baby's face with a cupped hand.

-Trying to arrange baby and bloody afterbirth beside her, since her still-occupied belly didn't leave much room for holding just yet. Unbelievably awkward, amniotic sac steaming warmth, with a strong foreign, pungent scent.

-Darting worried glances towards Drey, still outside dodging lightning.

-Registering smoke and rain both crowding their way in through the hole in the roof like uninvited, overeager relatives vying for importance. (Wasn't hemp supposed to be fire resistant?)

-Overcome with awe, staring at the solemn face of her teensy child whose eyelids slit unevenly and moved, trying to open but caked with blood-flecked something.

-Breathing her way through more intense waves of tremendous, suffocating pain. Did this end??

-Wiping whitish gray mucus from her daughter's nose and mouth. Was she breathing alright? Was this a bad dream? Had she just lost all touch with reality? Oh gods! She needed to push again.

"DREY!!!" She croaked his name again until he came back.

"I'm here, I'm here. I think the fire's out......enough." He was coughing as he took position between her legs. "Breathe Tay." He watched her push mightily, as she screamed the agonizing notes of her suffering into the rain spattered, smoke-fogged room.

Another head popped out. This one dark, trying to burble noise already.

Taya didn't even wait for the next contraction. Just sucked in some smoky air and heaved again, slurping out the rest of another daughter.

Drey held the baby as close to her face as the hot wet cord would allow, tears sliding through cold rain on his cheeks and gritty sweat on hers as their eyes met and stuck. Locked into a desperado pact to survive this madness. Unwilling to succumb to the odds standing in line against them.

Her voice was overused and raspy. It felt as if she'd birthed searing shards of crystal. "The sac—last thing. I don't know if I can...."

With aching tenderness he laid their baby girl down beside her sister. One with dark hair painted onto a perfect miniature skull, squalled in tiny mewls of surprised misery. The other one waved scrawny limbs, still trying to swim in this new chilly loudness, mouth moving, soundless.

He pushed Taya's sweat-soaked hair off her face and leaned close to her ear. Her eyes were closed and she slumped like something utterly wrung out. "I love you Tay." He said, "You're a Mama now...and I'm a Papa. Let's finish this so we can play with our babies, yes?"

She blinked open to look at him. Two silent tears leaked out the corner of each eye. One long, lung-bruising inhale and her face went purple when she pushed. For the last time.

Neither of them remembered much of tying off two cords with fishing thread and cutting them with Drey's thin, fish-gutting knife.

Or how exactly Drey managed to carry all three of them at once into the other hut to escape the splashing chill of the storm. It hadn't given up trying to force itself through a smoldering gash, slowly burning wider in the overhead thatch. Only the rain kept it from combusting into all out flames.

It seemed like hours before water warmed up over the smaller fireplace and babies, seeming too tiny to touch, were sponged off, and Taya roused enough to drink and clean herself up with Drey's help.

The first attempts at breastfeeding were a blur, as was the entire night-long vigil of banging wind, fire-minding, babies unhappy with this uncomfortable new world, and extravagant attacks of exhaustion.

ALL IN ALL;

-The storm romped for fifteen more hours before dribbling away into their second morning. Waking in the smaller bunk hut, all four of them were piled together on mattresses dragged close to the hearth.

-The cherries Taya had picked would be the only ones harvested that year. Every cherry, leaf and small branch was stripped from the trees. Many of the tallest trees had been twirled and split by lightning strikes.

-Every last orchid was decimated down to its roots.

-The babies were ridiculously brilliant, judging by how quickly they learned to eat.

Drey and Taya could literally not stop staring at their tiny faces or touching the dainty lacework of fingers, ears and toes of their twin girls. It took them half the next day to settle on names.

-Nobody told Taya that a baby's first bowel movements are black, like boar mud or tar. She sobbed shuddering earthquake-esque wails, believing something was terribly wrong with them. Nothing Drey said could console her. He gave up and let her release all the trauma from her body.

-The large hut ended up roofless when the smoldering fire in the thatch eventually ate all of it.

-Drey's boat disappeared, leaving not one trace it had ever brought them here.

-It was Aunt Sage who finally found them, bringing with her a cargo full of rescue.

Taya found that the scent of childbirth lingers, its odor distinct like dirt and rain, unique as horses, or autumn's leafy deadfall, or the ocean. The womb's peculiar smell is round, a cloyed metallic musk, the scent of dense nutrients and cell divisions, and the very beginning of decay. For as soon as life begins, decay begins as well—at least in this world it does. This world that relentlessly repeats the same two themes over and over:

Birth.

Death.

With varying degrees of life in between.

7

JAYDEE VISITS

9,990 BCE TEMPLE CITY, ATLANTIS

"Equality is a lie...a myth to appease the masses. Simply look around and you will see the lie for what it is! There are those with power, those with the strength and will to lead. And there are those meant to follow—those incapable of anything but servitude and a meager, worthless existence."

— DREW KARPYSHYN, DARTH BANE: STAR WARS

MARDU

She stopped not more than twelve feet away to greet their host. Her hair was frosted a belligerent shade of blue and styled to resemble the plumage of a peacock's fanned tail. Tall, like most Atlantean women, her features had perfect symmetry, as if engineered.

Mardu could hear her high-pitched titter over the cacophony of guests drinking and mingling, their energy high and tongues loquacious from the stimulating pre-dinner refreshments.

Already, a steady stream of Temple City's elite visited a discreet corner filled with smoking pipes, fine lines of snorting powders and wafers that melted instantly under the tongue. They would partake only a bit now but by the time the night was over, they'd have to be carried to their aeros by servants come to fetch them home.

Tonight's dinner party was hosted by the Head of the Temple of Mind

Power; a man Mardu judged vain and ridiculous. But he could affect, even control, a person using only his mind, making him much too dangerous not to keep close as an ally.

Their Host claimed the peacock woman's hand, eyeing her large, jiggling breasts exposed to barely above the nipples, held high by her gaudy gown. "Jaydee, I'm flattered you are here! And so marvelously attired tonight! I shall mix you a special delight myself but first, let me drink you in…"

They moved closer and Mardu watched the Host position her against the wall and begin mixing from carafes, bottles and pitchers. His movements flowed languorously, fingers slow-tracing the glass vessels as if moving through honey and Jaydee began to writhe subtly against the wall. Mardu could hear her gasp and moan just barely over the party swirling around them.

The Host stopped mixing for a moment, focused fully on her body as it stiffened while her eyes closed. She spasmed visibly once, twice, and again before a sigh flowed from her as her orgasm released and she sagged into a nearby chair.

The Host smirked, placing the glass of lime-green sweetness in her hand. "Welcome to my home Jaydee. You are a delight. I do hope you enjoy this evening". He kissed her parted mouth, fingers skimming her puffy breast tops as he brushed past her to greet another guest.

Mardu rolled his eyes muttering under his breath. "Pompous ass."

Regaining composure, Jaydee looked straight at him, startling when she realized he'd witnessed the entire episode.

He raked his gaze over her, knowing the sleek wet between her legs was chilling with fear. Then he turned away, towards a large group of men arguing politics to his left, dominating the conversation smoothly.

Barraged much too long with questions and concerns from highly stupid people, Mardu was simmering when they were finally seated for dinner. He took the top of the head table.

"Having a good time Dominus Mardu? I'm terribly honored you joined us tonight. Is there any way to add to your enjoyment?" The Host was seated to Mardu's right.

Mardu shook his heavy head as the first of ten courses was served. "Just food… and here it comes…"

Scantily-clad teenage girls paraded in with platters so huge, it took two to carry each. The platters held fruit, cut and arranged to resemble vignettes, scenes from Belial culture. Here was a multi-level marketplace, there the temples of City Center. A harbor scene even had merchant ships docked. But the party favorite was Belial warriors sparring on a battle-field. Guests clapped in delight at the colorful details, before picking and nibbling at their favorite pieces.

The second course arrived, large cheeses carved as life-sized birds of prey, each clutching some small dead thing in their talons. Conversations became boisterous again as guests shaved off pieces at their leisure.

The third course was chilled sweet soups, spouting, trickling and pouring from ornate tabletop fountains, served alongside the fourth; loaves of hot bread shaped like breasts. Much commenting and laughter from the half-drunk crowd led to contests contending for the browned buttery nipples.

Meats came next, first a rainbow of seafoods, then tender elephant trunk and reindeer veal, then a pause before the seventh course, tradi-tionally the grandest.

The serving girls in unceasing motion, removed half-eaten servings and kept wine glasses brimming. When all else had been cleared away, the final meat course was served; un-born piglets, roasted whole, ranging from two to four pounds each. Posed suckling from teats holding creamy herbed sauces, the tiny pigs looked tender, pink and moist. Guests took their time savoring this delicacy, full to bursting by the time the Host called for entertainment, before dessert.

The girls returned, this time wearing transparent gowns that flowed and swirled around them, thinly veiling their naked bodies underneath. Four drummers struck up heavy beats from the corners of the room, fulminating in a frenzy of introduction, before settling into deep, rever-berating tempos. The girls danced, twirling and bending round the guests, stepping or crawling along the tables to writhe in dark colors of gossamer. Each dancer chose a guest, seducing him or her with practiced eye contact, whispered words and subtle movements intensely honed.

Mardu chose this moment of distraction. Sliding his way from the room, he climbed quickly to the second floor in their host's five-level apartment. Finding a room that would suit his purpose, he waited.

Jaydee crept by, checking every nook and doorway, looking for him.

Mardu yanked her into the room, flinging her halfway across it. She landed in a heap of surprise. Locking the door, he turned, clouded in rage, his voice low, controlled, as he walked towards her.

"What are you doing here? I explicitly told you never to be seen with me. NEVER!"

Stooping, he backhanded her across the face when she tried to speak into his tirade. "Silence! Whatever you're here for, it is not important enough to risk being known, being reported back to High City. You stupid stupid whore!" He turned away, huffing his disgust.

She crawled to kneel in front of him. A breast had spilled out from his roughness, her eyes held tears. "I've missed you so, Dominus, missed your touch, your strength....I will do anything...what I have to tell you can wait. Will you let me give you pleasure? Please..."

Her desperate desire for him, never failed to arouse him. As she stood, his eyes were on the exposed breast, rust colored nipple overly large and hardened.

"Why are you here?"

She fondled his face. "Ruler Ziel has found the One of the Prophecy."

"Which prophecy?" Mardu jerked his head back impatiently. There were thousands of them.

Jaydee quoted a portion:

> "Bourne of lightning and fire,
> One shows the way. Mark
> the hour of early birth with
> crimson flower.
> Darkness flayed in breast of men,
> given now the way to mend.
> Heed the two, follow one and
> right prevails before
> end."

"I memorized it exactly—after I discovered which prophecy Ruler Ziel was so intent on. I was almost cau—"

"Who is it? And don't call him 'Ruler.'" Mardu paid little attention to prophecies. Certainly, he'd never heard of this one.

"I...I don't know that...yet. I will find out for you, of course, but I thought if it's as important to Rul... uh, Ziel as the rumors say, I should come to you, give you the information myself and ask what exactly you want me to do about it." Jaydee was caressing his chest now, rubbing her body against him, trying to be seductive but coming off as insistent. It irritated him.

The drumming and voices thundered and blared beneath them. Mardu calculated he had plenty of time without being missed. These kinds of parties ramped up, ending with lewd sexual displays on the dinner table. Plus, the dessert courses were still to be served. With one hand he grasped the large breast still hanging free of Jaydee's gown, his other hand shoving down her bodice to free the second.

She gasped, leaning in to his touch, ending in a squeak of pain when he squeezed. Hard.

His low growl was threatening as he emphasized each sentence with another savage squeeze. "I *want* you to never be in a public place with me again! I *want* you to stop being ignorant and get me some information I can use! What I really *want,* is for you to be worthy of me. You look like a buffoon and if I knew who did that to your hair, I'd run her through with my blade."

He had pushed her backwards towards the bed during his tirade. Turning her around, he bent her over across the high mattress and roughly shoved up her skirts. "Instead, I will run *you* through for letting that be done to you….." He laughed at his own witticism as he slammed hard and deep inside of her. "Let's see what else you will let be done to you…."

IT WAS some time later when he finished with her. The party din had risen to raucous levels and he refastened his clothing as Jaydee huddled, shivering and raw on the bed. Rage temporarily spent, Mardu's voice was friendly, belying the vicious ways he'd used her. "Go away. Do not come back downstairs. Find a discreet way out and be gone. Send word when you have something more. We'll meet at the usual place."

Satisfied, ready for dessert, his dismissive glance took in the fingerprints darkening to bruises on her breasts. Branding his things brought pleasure. Perhaps he should mark her permanently as his. Just the thought made his low belly tingle. Better to wait until her usefulness as a spy wore off.

He left her there like that. It did not cross his mind to care.

8

ZIEL MEETS THE TWINS

9,987 BCE CHIFFON, ATLANTIS

"We know nothing until we know everything"

— ST CATHERINE OF SIENA

ZIEL

The morning was still dark when we departed High City. They chattered in bursts, my own personal council of advisors, plus a representative of every other self-important body in our overinflated City. Too damn many.

I learned as a teenager to keep certain prophecies and visions to myself or at least to my own small council. Our esteemed House of Oracles has many gifted Seers who get overly excited when they finally piece something together. Then the whole world knows. Then they all come to me yammering for solutions. "What shall we do? How can we fix it? Tell us all that you know about this..." And next come the ad nauseum discussions. Everybody has an opinion—each sure they've divined the best course and the talk goes in endless circles for weeks and moons, until I want to cut out their tongues so I no longer have to listen to their egos.

It becomes my dearest wish; a giant bouquet of dry, deflated tongues that are finally finally still.

As if my wish had been granted, fifteen voices faded into blessed quiet while my entourage napped or studied the landscape below.

Hours later, I roused for arrival into Chiffon, the village of my birth on the northwestern coast of Atlantis.

The village proper was a cloister of whitewashed, patchwork buildings, tall and architecturally curious. To the south and east of the village stretched fields and orchards that we'd been flying over for some time now. To the north grew a forest, small but dense and pushing right up to a cliff edge that dropped abruptly into the sea. There were stretches of beach further up the coast, but here, the cliffs ended in grey limestone and water sprays. The sun was high overhead by now with midday meal approaching.

Children flowed into the village around the Temple, stretching and playful after a morning of lessons. They shaded their eyes, pointing up at our bright, royal gold Aero as we dropped onto their landing site. Some of them started running out towards the village edge where we were exiting the Aero, but calls from their Teachers brought them back inside for their meal.

Beside a pond crammed with enormous blue lotus flowers, waited ten village Elders to greet us.

I sighed inwardly, offered an outward smile, and returned their bows and formal greetings. They were eager to have us, gushing about the meal waiting and prying for the purpose of our visit. I had spoken once to my fifteen en route. A stern decree that I would be the only one to answer questions about our visit here today, and probably, the only one to speak to the ones we are seeking. Word would leak out, rumors would inevitably grow to fill in the absence of information, but I planned to do my utmost to deal well and truly with this family.

"Welcome Most High Oracle." A prolonged, low bow. "I am Nardin. It is our great pleasure to receive you into our humble village. I trust your journey was pleasant and that you find our sea beautiful?"

Nardin, the village elder, was perhaps, the most neutral man there is. Taller than I (of course), with thin brown hair, he had a completely forgettable face and manner. Very dutiful. Dressed in soft blue silks that moved constantly in the sea breeze, he was undoubtedly loyal and kind.

"Nardin, I miss Chiffon's tranquility more than I realized. Thank you for this welcome. This is an informal visit, and rather private in nature. We have no need to disrupt your day. As I said on the Comm, I only require the use of a trolley for a couple hours. There is a family I am here to speak with. Nothing very important...although by the size of this entourage you'd think it is!" I examined this lie before it left my lips but judged it necessary. I'd need to tell a few more to weave a web of protection around the little ones. It might make only a small difference but I owed them at least this much. "My people would have a bite to eat in your market, we need nothing fancy. I will go on ahead to my errand."

Nardin looked perplexed. "But we have prepared a great meal for you! Surely you are very hungry after coming so far. Won't you pause to rest and nourish before continuing on your....errand?"

For the first time, I smiled with true pleasure. How perfect. A formal meal would keep everybody busy and I could do what I came for in peace.

"So very good of you. Really. All of these will gladly join you." I waved my arm expansively, beaming at the fifteen wagging tongues. "You will all go with Nardin. These generous elders have prepared a meal for us and I'm sure they will enjoy hearing the latest news from High City. As well, it will be good to hear how this village is faring and to enjoy this rich beauty they live in. You may rejoin me after you eat, but please take your leisure."

Turning to Nardin as the exchange of introductions grew loud between my Fifteen and his Ten, I produced a small pouch of dried fruits and nut bars. "I've adequate sustenance. If you will kindly point out the trolley I may use, then I will be on my way."

"Certainly, yes, and I will take you myself, wherever you require Most High..."

"Ziel." I interrupted, letting the displeasure I felt show plainly on my face. "My name is Ziel and no, you will not accompany me. As I stated earlier, this is a private matter."

Nardin's eyes went wide and I felt the rush of offense he took at my sudden dropping of proper pleasantries. "Ah, yes I-I-I see." He stammered. "Right over here then. Is there anything else you require?"

"No." I bowed deeply. "I am grateful for your assistance and the food and company you generously offer. Farewell, kind Nardin, until we meet again." Climbing into the small cart alone, I steered it away as the large group moved slowly, walking towards the village center.

Chiffon was named, as many villages and cities are, for its primary occupation. The Atlanteans who settled here found an abundance of silk worms which they learned to cultivate for their finely-spun filaments. Weaving it, those early villagers produced a new generation of fabric wonders. Additionally, cotton and hemp were grown here, and cloth produced for all manner of household uses.

Built since I'd last visited, were large, outlying buildings where many weavers transformed a plethora of material from the earth, the sea, and the creatures of both, into a wide variety of textiles.

The woman I was going to see was, in fact, responsible for expanding Chiffon from a small, mostly agricultural community into a thriving industry that trades not only across Atlantis, but across the world as well. Long considered the leader in weaving, many apprentices still come here to study the growing and harvest techniques, the developing of new materials, or the designs of weaving and fashion. It has easily quadrupled in population over the last ten years and I wondered if they struggled to keep up with the growth.

Chiffon was my hometown for the first thirteen years of my life—ages ago when silk was a fresh discovery. But there is only one other who likely remembers that.

Nostalgia bloomed bright and sharp in my chest as I rolled slowly over forest paths towards the sea cliffs. Not much looked familiar from so long ago, but the feel and smell of the air, that unique melding of sun warmth and salt mixing into the moist black soil, was enough to bring it all back. Something deep inside wanted to find the little cottage I lived in with my sweet, intellectual Mother, see if any of it still stands, and who might live there now.

But I did not. The surliness I'd displayed all morning vanished, revealing an anxiety that's kept me persistently away, uncovering the pain of an old regret. I wished now that I had walked instead of driving, that there was time, that I would be here long enough to go slowly and absorb all the feelings.

Their chalet was surrounded by roses and heather in a shaded edge of the forest, the back of it overlooking the sea.

I brought the trolley to a quiet stop in a clearing that held a small garden. Half a dozen llamas and sheep, widely varied in colors, grazed between trees. Two dragon-looking reptiles about the size of a large foot, basked, intertwined, on a sunny pathway that cut through rambunctious groups of vegetables. Squinting at the odd, sunning reptiles, I followed a stone path towards the charming home, startling when a skinny, tan monkey ran in a limping gait straight for me from the nearest tree. Its long tail dragged unmoving across the ground and it screeched loudly, baring its teeth and flinging its hands in the clear gesture of "go away!"

The front door of the sand-washed home glowered a shocking, purplish blue and a half-dead looking flamingo lay in front of it as if it collapsed there, legs skewed out in unnatural angles.

Something else streaked through the air and I only saw it was a flying squirrel as it landed squarely on the shrieking face of the monkey, bringing abrupt silence. As they tumbled around together, I continued, somewhat cautiously towards the door. Stepping over the bird, a bright shade somewhere between orange and pink, I rang a bronze bell that was shaped like a half moon with a girl sitting on its lower curve, hands cupped around her mouth, howling up at it.

The flamingo raised its head, one eye blinking at me.

The monkey had pried the squirrel off its face, again coming towards me in its awkward limp with more hair-raising screeches.

I rang again, louder, and I'll admit, urgently.

The door opened and an exotic, dark-haired woman grabbed my arm, yanking me inside and slamming the door behind me, just in time. The monkey thunked off the other side and must have bounced into the flamingo because we heard a bird squawk and then the monkey shrieks turned to a sort of howl fading off into the distance.

She snickered at me. "You look like you've just been pushed off that cliff out there and don't know how to swim". There they were, the tattoos. In ghostly silver-blue ink, swirling vines started from her left temple, winding behind her ear and down her neck. Completely covering her bare shoulder, her arm and a sylph-like hand, vines morphed into the seven moon phases and sacred symbols so elaborate I barely recognized them. Even her left foot bore bedizened designs. Transfixed by Frond's vision come to life, my heartbeat surged. She was whispering, at the highest volume I've ever heard anyone whisper.

"And who are you?"

Bowing, I blinked to compose myself, whispering back. "Lady Taya, I am Ziel. I see now, that perhaps I should have told you I was coming, but I thought it easier this way...I need to speak with you and your mate about an important matter."

A lavender-grey snake, big around as my bicep, dropped into view from a rafter overhead, hovering beside Taya's head and flicking its forked tongue at me.

"Well, *that's* a relief!" She stroked the underside of the snake's head. "This is Sila...I thought for a minute that you were here to give me some horrible news about Drey. Ziel?.....from where exactly?" She was muscular and sort of dangerously intelligent looking, despite messy hair and dirty hands trying to smooth out wrinkled clothes. Her stained knees indicated she'd been kneeling in the garden a good part of the morning.

I took a breath, stepping back slightly from the impertinent snake.

"From High City. Head of the House of Oracles. I do apologize for just dropping in like this. I won't take up much of your time...."

"*Ruler* Ziel?!" She shout whispered, sounding unsettlingly like a hiss. "You're Ruler Ziel and you came—did you come all that way today? What...I don't....Drey is not here. What in the world do you want from us??"

I smiled my best calming smile. "Taya, might we sit? Everything is fine, let's just take a moment. May I have a drink of water please? I haven't eaten since very early and if it's not too rude, I would like to eat the things I brought, then I will tell you exactly why I am here."

"It's alright, go back to your nap." She muttered to the snake, then gestured for me to follow towards the back of her home into a bright eating room. Two pieces of polished driftwood held a beautiful thick slab, crafted from twisted cherry wood. Round, plump cushions surrounded this low table and I sank my ancient backside gratefully into one. The entire back wall of glass panels folded open to a stone patio. Beyond was only sky until it met the sea. It looked a mirage almost, hues of cobalt and cotton so perfectly painted.

Taya set before me a fat, pottery cup brimming with minted water and I thanked her profusely before gulping it. We sat in silence for some moments as I chewed dried pears and a bar made from hemp hearts, coconut and toasted black rice. Taya studied me, taking frequent small sips from her own cup of chilled honey wine. "You should know, Ruler Ziel—"

"Just Ziel." I interrupted through my full mouth.

"You should know, Ziel, that my morning has been rough. I'm perturbed that I look like this and that my house is a mess and that you just *showed up*. Some warning would have been preferable. I don't receive my own friends like this and here you are, the most important person in all of Atlantis! Not to mention—I'm scared to death of why you're here. It can't possibly be good."

I nodded in understanding and sympathy, pleased she spoke so honestly. How long had it been since anyone scolded me? "I apologize. Clearly, I did not think this through well." A total lie. I've thought of little else for the last three years. "May I ask, why are we whispering?" It rather amused me, an entire whispered conversation between two strangers.

"My children are napping and I desperately need them to. They've been like wild animals today and if they don't get good naps, they're like to make me insane before bedtime. I can't believe they slept through Monkey's noise."

"Ahh yes, your children. Twin girls I believe? And they are almost three, yes?" I sought to keep my tone light, nonchalant.

Her eyes twitched narrow in suspicion. "Yes...Ahna and Aiela turn three at the next full moon..."

Putting down the remainder of my food, I leaning forward, deciding to level with her now before her patience was strained further. "Taya, I had hoped to speak with both you and Drey together. Forgive me for intruding and worrying you. Your girls are gifted, are they not?"

She nodded slowly, began running all eight fingers and two thumbs up and down the ridges of her pottery wine cup. "They are...different from the other girls their age. Now that they're talking, we are trying to find out exactly why. It's not been determined yet, we're not sure what all is happening within them, but at least we know they're not mentally ill. The opposite in fact, indications that they are quite advanced."

I looked her straight in the eye, "I believe they are psychically gifted. There are ancient prophecies foretelling a birth. The birth of one with the power to save the world, using the seat of Atlantis. I have spent the last fifty cycles of my life monitoring birthing stories in our land and beyond, none of which have even begun to match the prophecies. Until now. I knew, three days before you birthed your girls, that one of them is the one. I have brought you the prophecies. You may keep these."

I pulled the rolled parchments from my shoulder bag, placing them on the table. I'd brought not only a copy of the original Prophecy, but also every vision on record at the House of Oracles that related to the prophecy. Neatly piecing together the picture I needed them to see, and believe. "I have sought to keep this very quiet, to protect your family so the girls may grow up normally until they're ready to come to me. Perhaps younger than usual since we know who they are?"

Taya took on an expression of challenge. "You're assuming a lot. That is not for you to decide—prophecy or no. The girls will choose, when the time comes, what they will do with their lives." Tossing back the rest of her wine, she refilled it. "This is too much to take in right now. I appreciate you came a long way, but we should talk another time when Drey can be here."

I nodded, expecting this gentle doubt. It felt unbelievable to me too. How much more to an unsuspecting parent, already struggling with the challenges of small children, and the worry of those children being inexplicably different. "Of course we can talk another time. I was unwise in coming unannounced. I do hope you'll pardon me. I am intrigued though, what is the story of the monkey, the flamingo and I believe there were strange reptiles as well as a flying squirrel? It's quite a menagerie."

She relaxed back into a proud smile. "Those are Aiela's patients. Drey started it by bringing home a crippled goose. Aiela wasn't even talking, but she calmed and nursed that mangy bird back to health. Now, she and Ahna seem to find broken animals on a regular basis, or the neighbors do. Drey brought Monkey back from his last trip. The poor thing was paralyzed except for its head when he found it. It's a terrible bother but the girl's love it so. For sure the most territorial creature we've ever had, which isn't all bad."

I chuckled with delight, asking more questions, hearing more stories, putting Taya at ease in safe and familiar territory while learning their ways of life.

"The wooly pets are all mine. I'm a weaver, among other things, so I breed them to improve the quality and colors of their wool."

"And the snake?" Plenty of Atlanteans kept them as pets. I'd never liked them.

"She's been with me since before I was born. We still don't know what exactly she is. Even Drey, hasn't found another like her. She tells me when an earthquake, or sea storm is coming. She even predicted the last volcano—you remember the one so near Atlas?"

I nodded, genuinely happy to listen to this remarkable woman, more interested than she would ever guess in the small day-to-day happenings of her little family. Taya seemed content to tell me amusing stories, for as long as I would listen, about the daughters and mate who were her world.

She forgot for a time, the purpose of my visit. It barged unceremoniously back when my communique spoke from my pocket, breaking our careful quiet. "Ruler Ziel? Ruler Ziel? Are you there?"

I jumped, then rolled my eyes muttering "Damn tongues. I forgot about the tongues." She looked alarmed as I fumbled to switch off the sound. "Taya, I didn't come to Chiffon alone today. There are more High City 'importants' than you want to know, here with me. Nardin has conveniently distracted them with a meal but it seems they are finished and seeking me now. They were hoping to meet you and your family. You must understand, they are all convinced of the importance your daughters play in our future. Pardon, for a moment..." The comm vibrated continuously. Fishing it out, I touched a button, speaking brusquely. "You will all stay there in the village. We're coming to you. Patience until we arrive."

Taya began protesting and I let her. I had already seen it happening.

She broke off when they padded in barefoot, to lean against her, staring glassy-eyed at me, both sucking their thumbs. One with long, thick tangles surrounding her miniature body, hair black and shiny as a stallion, the other with choppy, fine, golden strands that kept falling into her sleep-brightened green eyes.

My heartbeat skipped and everything inside me softened. Children undo me with their purity and beauty. I regret, that I will never be a parent.

Trailing behind were more pets; a brindled dog, taller than both, followed the dark haired child. What looked like a panther cub sat licking its paws by the golden-haired one.

Taya caressed their heads, looking a fierce, otherworldly mama. Her voice sounded loud after an hour of whispered conversation. "Girls, this is Ziel. He came to visit from far away. Monkey tried to eat him."

They chortled impishly around their thumbs.

"Ziel, this is Aiela, our midnight moon, and this is Ahna our little diamond."

I wished I had thought to bring toys or sweets, something that would please them. Instead I bowed to them from my seat. "Your Mother saved me from Monkey and I am most *most* happy to meet you!"

Aiela sidled over to stand boldly close between my knees. "See-wah howd stiwa now." She spoke commandingly, placing her chubby hands on my cheeks. They were sticky and her sucking thumb left traces of wet beneath my eye. She peered intently, squinting into my pupils as if looking for something. We were of a height with me sitting on the floor cushion still. I could smell her sleep-sweet breath and I was holding mine, afraid to move a hair—more unsure of myself now than I had been during Monkey's attack.

"Yew awe *good* See-wah." She finally pronounced with satisfaction. Turning to Ahna then, "Come hewa Ahna. Come see See-wah."

Ahna stepped obediently closer, pushing the dog out of her way, leaning against my leg to eye me solemnly.

Aiela reached over and pulled Ahna's thumb out with a moist pop. "Tehwa him Ahna."

I glanced uncertainly at Taya but she seemed to be enjoying her cubs interrogation.

"We see'd you." Ahna spoke with the quiet dignity of a much older child. Aiela nodded in agreement as Ahna continued. "You come'd now."

Aiela left suddenly, chubby bare feet pounding back into the room they'd emerged from. She returned quickly with paper. On it were odd-sized partial stick figures with round unclosed circle heads drawn in thick colors.

"That's you." Ahna pointed to a giant stickman, "an this is.....wots of peopow." She shrugged, unable to explain the people further. "We had cake! and sometime....we were big!" she flung her arms wide to demonstrate their bigness, "and you tow'd us a story."

"Momma, we want cake today!" They chorused. Psychic or not, they still had the attention spans of any three-year-old. Taya sighed with the air of the defeated.

"Yes. As it happens, we will go into village with Ziel and you can get cake, since you took such nice naps. But you must get dressed quickly, wash your face and hands, both of you." She shooed them back towards their room. "Ziel, give us some minutes and we will come with you to meet your people."

IN THE END, Monkey was docile and obedient to the commands Aiela garbled as they each took my hands and led me through their gathered menagerie.

It seemed Flamingo had taken a turn for the worse, so that required some extra moments to sort out.

I took the three of them, (no less rumpled, just in different mismatches of clothing—with less animal hair clinging to it) into the village and introduced them to the Fifteen. They would boast later of having met the One of the Prophecy, even though we didn't know exactly which child it might mean. The village ten looked on in bewilderment and I offered no explanations. Let Taya decide who should know what.

The girls seemed entirely comfortable crawling into my lap or holding my hands, but didn't talk except to inquire about their cake.

Sending my group off to find food for the return trip and make their farewells, I was finally alone again with the delightful little sisters and their mother, at their favorite bakeshop. Today's choices were a dense hazelnut spice, spongy cherry lemon, and buttery lavender vanilla cream.

The girls wanted some of each and I was firmly on their side, the three of us wheedling shamelessly until Taya gave in.

I would have given them the moon, had they asked.

Taya promised Drey would contact me when he returned—which was to be before the girls turned three. I'd come just a few days too early.

But this was no accident.

9

TAYA'S ART

10,016-9,995 BCE. CHIFFON, ATLANTIS

"I know a cure for sadness: Let your hands touch something that makes your eyes smile."

— MIRA

TAYA

*H*er childhood had few boundaries. Not many don'ts.

Standing outside naked in the tropical drizzle? Totally acceptable. At home anyway—not so much at school where they frown and raise perplexed eyebrows. Dipping hands and face in slippery warm willow tallow to let it dry into buttery smoothness and crackle off when you move? What could be more fun?

For Taya, the world was primarily textured. Sure, she enjoyed colors and scents and music. But they were a lot of backdrop, merely complementing the exquisite mosaic, the glorious palette of *touch*. Her foremost impression of any given object was how it felt to her body.

Take for instance, the primal rumble of coastal crags close by her home, all granite, that she could climb to the top of, and then lay on her belly feeling the bite of the rock against her tender cheek. Or collecting smooth brittle nuts shaped like little smashed thumbs, fallen under Brasil trees in the deep woods. She needed to experience how it felt to sit on things, clamber over them, kick, lick, hug and poke them. Drifting duck feathers caressed her, chocolate's elegance anointed her tongue, velvety beach sand caked gritty warmth onto her feet, which, she'd explained to Auntie Sage at four, was the ocean's way of loving her. Forest floors thatched with long spidery pine needles happily pricked between bare toes. She knew a thousand ways to touch her world.

Auntie Sage intuitively surrounded her with multitudes of touchables even as a toddler, fascinated with how Taya interacted with them. Sila, her pet snake, was by far her favorite texture.

Taya illustrated stories by touch instead of pictures before she could write. Entertaining her friends and neighbors, she blindfolded them, spinning a tale that they could feel. It might include blowing lightly on their lips or a thimble of water thrown into their ear. Most times you got something squirmy placed in your hand, or were asked to take off your sandals and let unknown substances be feathered or perhaps slimed between your toes. It was always an experience and the other children begged for her stories. The more adventurous adults loved them too and like a magician, Taya never revealed her secrets.

By the time she was twelve, almost everyone in the village, and many beyond, had bartered for a piece of Taya's art. She created irresistible feasts for the fingers, each one unique. They might look like some talisman of unidentifiable forest and beach and field rubble, but if you closed your eyes and touched, they became like objects textured with heaven.

Auntie Sage was from Taya's maternal family. Theirs was a long line of girls—orphaned girls actually. Auntie was very blunt that there were many reasons she'd chosen not to have children. Number one on her list was the fact that all the parents seemed to die young in their family branch—as far back as you could trace it.

Grow up orphaned. Make babies. Orphan them.

Sage preferred a different life plan. "I didn't choose to mother, but motherhood chose me and that has been best." She told Taya.

That was when Taya was seven and very philosophical about things. "Motherhood sure knew better than you Auntie. We are happier together than all the other girls I know. Their mothers have too many rules. That's why I have to play with the boys. They can't remember the rules their mamas make."

Auntie Sage had laughed and hugged her for a long time. "I hope so Tay, I hope so. You are better than any other plan I had."

. . .

TWICE TAYA ASKED how her parents died. The first time was right after she'd begun to grasp the concept of death and then some helpfully heartless child asked what happened to her regular parents. When Taya repeated the query at home, Auntie stared into the evening sky for a long silence with watery eyes and then told a story of twelve words.

"I don't know how they died. Their last thoughts were of you."

The second time tho, Auntie judged Taya older enough to know more and so elaborated a little with words and a lot with the gift. "I really don't know. The people they worked for told me some dog-shit lie that your parents *both* ate something poisonous and it killed them fast. Pah! I taught your mother too much about poisonous plants for that to happen! And I *know* when someone is lying. I wanted to find the truth and I tried for a long time." Auntie paused with a far-away look in her eyes. "But what does it matter really, except to make us sadder?

You were not quite two and traveling with them across the water in Merika. They died—however it was—and I was summoned to come get you when the Seacruiser docked back in Atlantis." She shrugged, "Then I brought you and Sila back here to your home. There were two things they told me that felt true; your parent's last words were of you, and Sila was found curled around you, hissing and striking at anyone who tried to remove her. They gave me this and now is the time to give it to you I think." Auntie went to her huge chest that filled an entire wall space, holding teas, essential oils, trinkets and memories in endless drawers, shelves and tiny cupboards. She took out a coconut-sized leather pouch.

Taya rubbed the old suede scent onto her lips and cheeks and eyelids, reveling in the feel of it, before Auntie Sage told her that the bag wasn't the gift and to look inside. Taya opened the drawstring at the top, pulling out a thick, jagged peel of bark and a large, round, gritty white sand dollar. Both had writing on them. Four baroque letters were carved onto the bark's sap-stained smooth side; **Taya**

Charcoaled onto the white sand dollar in a spiral of fluttery script;

Taya~My most precious part of life. I love you like the ocean.
Deeper than you'll ever see. Without pausing. Eternally. ~Moma~

Taya had cried for her parents then, for the first time. "I wish I could remember them" she heaved inside Auntie's comfortable arms.

Auntie's tears lacquered her own tanned cheeks. "Me too, Tay, me too. But I can tell you about them. Oh! they were so in love, those two. With each other and with you..."

Perhaps it was due to her childhood village being rooted in the art of weaving, producing the finest textiles for longer than anyone could remember, that no one was surprised when Taya became obsessed with fabric. The day she learned to weave was the day she found her calling.

Next, she began making her own yarns and threads, weaving cloth from all manner of things: Wild silkworm spinnings, hemp bast fibers, cotton, bamboo, sheep and llama wool, coconut husks, flax stalk, reeds of palm and papyrus. Mammoth and Yak hair, as well as the mucous from large, bottom-dwelling sea eels were useful for waterproof items. Although many of these materials had long been used in Atlantis, Taya invented prize-winning blends for clothing, household goods and even armor.

Instead of a traditional teenage apprenticeship, she sought out engineers, working with them to devise better weaving looms and sewing machines than her village had conceived before. Three new textile factories were organized and efficiently producing the results of her inventions before she was eighteen.

Some of Atlantis' best designers moved to the village to work close to the factories. Chiffon's outlying farms grew enormous fields and forests to supply them.

Although she was the catalyst behind so much successful growth of the village's long-time livelihood, Taya chose to live quietly, spending her time creating and searching for new substances to weave.

Taya was fourteen when the first odd request came down.

One day, after returning from a short trip to "see an old friend", Auntie Sage gave her a thin bamboo board with cracked and broken edges. In its center was several series of bumps, divots, scratches and random marks. "This is a system of communication. Do you think you could learn it?"

Taya instinctively closed her eyes and ran her fingertips lightly over the board. "I can feel the patterns... But how will I know what they mean?"

"Turn it over".

There was the key. This entire side of the board was taken up with translations into letters and common words. Taya was instantly engrossed.

"Why are your hands purple?" Sage exclaimed. Taya's fingers were dark as eggplant up to the knuckles.

"Grinding murex shells. Makes pretty purples..." Taya muttered, distracted by the board.

Sage left her alone and went to fix their meal. It would be awhile before Taya came asking what this was about.

When she did, later that evening, they were watching the sun sing itself to sleep in colors. Their forest, wrapping the little cottage, faded into uncommon stillness as if the birds and small animals were watching the sun's stunning bedtime ritual as well.

Aunt Sage looked at Taya for a long time, blinking thoughtfully, before she answered. "Well. If I tell you about the board, next you'll want to know how it came to me. And THAT story has threads that reach all the way back into my girlhood. It has other threads attached deep into ancient power struggles of Atlantis. It's a big big story. But. There are things that we've been asked to do and it's fair that you understand why. So. Let's make tea."

Much like Taya used all manner of living things to weave, Auntie Sage used flowers, roots, grains and unusual herbs, barks and even sea plants for concocting her healing teas. Tea was Auntie Sage's emotional balm for anything. Boredom, events hard to comprehend or accept, fatigue, frightening times....they were all dealt with, balanced or perhaps cleansed, with rivers of tea.

She prepared their tallest pot.

Wrapped in light blankets and nestled side by side in the big tree swing, holding spiraled pottery mugs of sweetly pungent tea, Auntie began. Speaking softly as the forest shifted towards sleep, "Do you know how old I am?"

Puzzled, Taya shook her berry-black head. She'd never thought to ask.

"Well neither do I really. I stopped counting seasons long ago. It doesn't matter where I come from but it is important what was happening back then. Hmmm.....where to begin? Ages and ages ago, in the great motherland of Mu, scientists started using plant cells and then DNA from animals to create better physical bodies. The problem with tampering in DNA is that there are infinite variables. They couldn't regulate the outcomes—even doing the exact same process with the exact same substances every time. They succeeded in making many subspecies, even of humans.

You know that our Atlantis history begins with strange Beings that had unearthly power over elements, who were revered as gods. Stories were told that all these gods came to us from other worlds. The truth is, Mu bungled and barged through experiments like spoiled toddlers with the ability to create new toys. Too late, they thought to fear the power some of these Beings had. And what if the Beings procreated? Spawned new races that would overrule them? Or eventually dilute humanity so much that our DNA would end up a giant mess? So they shipped them all off to this continent—what would become our Atlantis. Literally the opposite side of the planet. Mu even built these miscreants a city to live comfortably in. It was presented as a privilege. An opportunity to colonize a new world, live in a place where they wouldn't be so starkly different. Really tho, it was banishment." Auntie paused to sip her tea. Letting Taya's mind catch up.

"So.....we've had no visitors from other worlds? What they teach is all a lie?" Taya's mind spun. This was a very strange story compared to what was in the history books. And why did it concern her?

"Oh we've had—still have—visitors from other worlds for sure. Poseidon really did come from the Pleiades, hence our revered symbol for Taurus the Bull in which his home planets shine. It was eons after Mu was gone that he took a beautiful land full of wild, warring miscreants and turned them into a nation. But our Atlantean heritage doesn't begin exactly the way you're told. Omissions were made. Some of those original.....creations, were thought immortal. But the generations following them, the offspring and children of their offspring, were not. It's probable the immortals went into hiding, or left for another world sometime during the first epoch, where they didn't have to watch everything they loved, die from this physical plane.

Ten kingdoms were established and ruled by the mortal sons of Poseidon. That was when Atlantis wrapped halfway around the planet spanning what are now separate continents, and Lemuria ruled the other half of the world. You know the rest. How every last remnant of the royal families died when volcanoes destroyed Lemuria and much of humanity worldwide. How Atlantis civilizations rose again and were destroyed again in ensuing Epochs, each earth calamity reducing our continent's size to what it is today. So here we are, in this 'Golden Age' where we've learned to honor Lemuria's sacred Law of One."

Taya's eyes were glazing over. "I don't understand. What does this have to do with you? With that board?"

"Too much time passed. Eventually, no one remembered the disasters of those Mu experiments. Lemurians destroyed Mu's records so no one else could work from them. Yet still, during each Epoch, Atlantis science progressed in much the same way, attempting to improve the health and lifespan and powers of the human species. Each time, we've outlawed it at some point. But Belial scientists answer to no one. Lots of people and their children looked perfectly normal but had been altered so that their psychic powers, mental powers or physical powers were stronger. I am a result of those experiments. I'm aging much slower than normal. I don't know exactly how old I am. I don't know much about the time and circumstances of my birth or even who my parents were. As you're figuring out right now, I'm not a traditional 'Auntie' to you. I am your spiritual relative though. Your ancestors are my only family." She stopped here to gauge Taya's reaction.

Emotions clustered inside Taya, like abandoned orphans. "I don't understand! Why haven't you told me this before? If you're not my Aunt, then how come you said you were?"

"I AM your Aunt! I love you as much as anybody has ever loved a child. I was an 'Auntie' to your Moma and Grandmoma. I'll be an 'Auntie' to your children someday. Blood ties don't run as thick as everyone believes. Love ties—those precious ones our Soul chooses—remain, long after blood dries up and decomposes. Our love bonds go with us into the great beyond and these relationships become our forever treasures, sweet girl, not blood, not power, not things. Only who we loved here, and who loved us."

Taya felt teary, softened by such powerful truths. She ran her fingers up and down the sides of the mug strumming the ridges, self-soothing, much like small children suck their thumbs. "I guess we're just two orphans..."

They smiled at each other. A smile pocked with hollows that only orphans know, and Auntie held her tight.

"And the board? What has all this science and ancient history to do with the board?"

"Well. I loved a boy once, a boy who was like me."

Taya raised her eyebrows, perking up at the hint of romance.

"Oh but he was dreamy! We were children together and he was my closest friend. Then when he got handsome I started feeling new things for him. He said he loved me. He acted like he loved me. But then... well, then he left me."

They swang in silence for a beat, absorbing the sad.

"He was psychically gifted so they took him away to High City to apprentice in the House of Oracles. He said that he would come back—

but he never did. It hurt quite a lot for a long long time." Auntie sighed. Gulping lots of tea.

"And after all this time, he contacted me with a request that I 'meet one of his people and consider their message'. That's where I was on my trip. I didn't tell you because I had no idea what it was all about. I was so shocked to hear from him. I met two of his 'people' and they gave me this board because I live in a village of weavers. He needs information from scientists who have been blinded. It's a terrible story.

The Sons of Belial know no limits with their experiments. A group of scientists, working for Belial, refused to continue some sort of atrocities. Apparently, the scientists were captured trying to escape, and blinded as punishment—you've heard how cruel Mardu is. They're being held hostage. Kept alive only because the information they possess is needed, still relevant to whatever Belial wants from the experiments. I was asked to devise a way to send messages by weaving items—clothing, sheets, towels-—for the prisoners. They say all else has failed. Even the Oracles attempted to communicate, but the scientist mind doesn't trust what's not physical. An Atlantean spy recovered this board from the prisoner's trash. They say it's a note from the prisoners on how they can communicate. And their key of course."

Taya had leaned in conspiratorially. "Ohhhh, I *understand* now! The note says. 'We soil clothing and sheets often. Request cheap replacements'. *That's* the message! I thought it was just a practice note. But that's how they can get messages. Ohhhhh, this is EXCITING! I get to be part of something *important!*" She bounced beside Aunt Sage.

Auntie laughed. "Yes, well Atlantis already sells items made of simple materials to the compound holding the prisoners. Now, they just need someone trustworthy to weave their messages into the textiles. Messages that those poor blind souls can read. And that, darling, is where you come in. I know the best weaver in all of Atlantis."

Aunt Sage gathered their tea things. "I'm tired. You must be too. We'll work out more of it in the morning. I've shattered too much of what you believed tonight. Let's sleep it off, shall we? We've much to contemplate..."

MARDU'S ANUBIS ARMY

9,983 BCE ANUBI, EGYPT REGION

"I'm not a leader now. I'm a whole damn army."

— JOSS WHEDON

MARDU

T wenty-eight of his best men accompanied Mardu when they landed their Aeros in the fertile lowlands, referred to as simply Anubi. And Balek.

"It stinks like a slaughterhouse." Balek whinged as they debarked. "Is it the dogs or their livestock?"

"Both probably" growled Mardu, displeased no one waited here to meet them. "Now shut up. You're here to learn, not run your ignorant mouth. Your only talent is consistently saying the wrong thing."

Created under the reign of Onus Belial, the Anubis were accidents in a search for immortality. Mutating slowly over the last five centuries, these half-canid, half-humans were meat-eaters and grazed goats, sheep and reindeer. Their lands for hundreds of miles around were long ago hunted to extinction.

Shortly after murdering the previous Sons of Belial leader, Mardu decided to believe the rumors that he was Onus Belial reincarnated— minus the psychic abilities, which was terribly unfortunate. Still, he'd already accomplished much and would complete what Onus Belial, or any of his successors, failed to; he would become the first king of Atlantis, since Poseidon. He'd reunite the Atlantean continent.

From there, he would rule the world, prosper them, set them free from the small-minded tyrannical leaders they served. He had two hundred and fifty thousand Belial soldiers, and of course the muta army—but he'd learned the hard way not to wholly trust any one scheme. Many sources of power meant the plan would go forward even if one failed. The Anubis were another branch in his plan.

The large Belial party traipsed slowly, grumbling about the heat, funneling between tightly spaced, single-story structures that formed a large niwt. Flat topped, they were built of sand-colored bricks, no doubt formed from river clay and baked in the relentless sun-heat that harassed them now. Two repugnant faces peered from the shadows of a low doorway. Otherwise the town appeared deserted, until they arrived at its center. Here were several thousand inhabitants, squatting on their haunches, facing a twenty foot statue of Onus Belial. Gilded with at least a dozen different metals hammered together like patchwork, the towering statue gleamed, contrasting the wood and clay around it. Offerings of bleached animal skulls, pelts, wilting flowers, wineskins and trinkets from wood to gemstones, littered it's pedestal, as big as the aero Mardu arrived in.

A female that looked human, except for a slight snout protruding as her nose and mouth, noticed them first, leaping up to point, making sounds deep in her throat that caused a path to magically clear before him.

The Vizier and his Ruling council poured forth from the crowd in welcome, prostrating to the ground before Mardu. They barely spoke, using gestures to escort him to a large hall. A ripple of excited whining sounds and short gruff words accompanied his exit from the squatting bodies packed around their statue.

Blessedly cool inside the Anubis hall, the entire Belial party were directed to crude mats of reed, presented with meat and water, urged to rest in the windowless dim.

Disconcerted, seeing these half-humans up close in varying degrees of mutation, Mardu did not waver, determined to make them loyal to him. Anubis were reportedly hard to kill. A disposable force that didn't die easily was exactly what he needed.

He began with gifts.

"I bring to you, as an offering of good faith, armor and four armorers who will outfit your warriors. A whole cargo aero of wild animals—which you can release and hunt for your sport—and four dozen slave girls. These will entice or amuse you—or at least be useful as servants." *If you no longer preferred fully human women.* He kept this thought to himself.

After a queerly silent feast of roasted meats, Mardu conducted a formal meeting with the Anubis elders. He assumed their obedience. "I require that you begin drills and training at once. Next time I come, I will expect to see an army. Let's talk of weapons and how many shipments you will need. We've developed excellent armor made of a light metal—an alloy our scientists have perfected. I think you will like it, black as onyx and strong as diamonds, yet wholly flexible. Of course we'll need to customize it to fit your...ah...shifting shapes. Hence the armorers." He eyed their tall, pointy ears and disfiguring snouts. These elders were most fully mutated into dog form, retaining the ability to stand upright, the torsos and thankfully, arms, of men. Pink skinned, ranging from hairless to fully furred, Mardu found them disgusting.

"I assure you, joining the Belials, fighting for me, will ensure you a place of honor in the new Atlantis; the new world formed after I, Mardu, ascend the throne as High King."

He did, in fact, already have the throne. Molded as a gift for Onus Belial, from a huge chunk of meteorite iron that had travelled untold distances through the universe before impacting earth, it was an original Belial treasure. Mardu didn't use a throne yet, relishing the day he would install this icon in Poseidon's Palace, and from it, subjugate the world.

"We am loyal peoples. You do see." The Vizier assured Mardu in a nasal voice with the syllabolic cadence of yips and barks. Little wonder they rarely spoke. "Do we accept your offer, you have not stauncher subjects. I am attended Onus Belial as boy and we am worship him yet, is our true lord. He create us, he honor we sacrifice, and now he return for claim us, reborn as Dominus Mardu." All six elders bowed low, chanting words Mardu could not make out.

"Your allegiance," Mardu flashed a benevolent smile, "will earn my highest favor. Serve me and you shall regain your Atlantean status. Our alliance pleases Onus Belial. Let it be your act of ultimate worship."

He let the Anubis confer. It took only moments.

"We am accept Dominus Mardu for rightful master. We pledge loyal Anubi people for Belial service." The Vizier intoned, bowing before Mardu. "Our people am not stop yearning for lifeways and lost lands. Long we do dream of day we return home from sad exile."

. . .

"Stupid dogs." Mardu denigrated to Balek once his entourage was enroute back to Belial. "So *loyal*. I tell you, it's a mark of lesser intelligence, this supposedly honorable trait of staying true, holding steady, just for the sake of *loyalty*." He spat. "I am proven right once again. And pay attention son, to this religion they've developed—not that I'm complaining, after all they worship me—but religion aims to preserve. It's nature is tradition so it resists new ideas, other ways. Religion and loyalty shows us the Anubis are more comfortable not thinking for themselves—making them infinitely more usable." He snorted, closing his eyes to get some sleep. "Pay attention son. I'm teaching you how to rule."

The flight home would take hours.

ZIEL'S CRYSTALS

9,983 BCE HIGH CITY, ATLANTIS

"Any fool can know. The point is to understand."

— ALBERT EINSTEIN

ZIEL

Today I begin arrangements to secure my secrets, and to pass along all that I hold dear. At last the Crystals will be awakened to their purpose for Atlantis, for the day is coming when I will go beyond this life.

Some days I look forward to that—or just not being a Ruler. No one envies the job of the High Seven; day after day of difficult decisions.

Atlantis is governed by Seven Rulers, typically all female. Why? A general consensus that women tend towards balance and their regions have proven to thrive; perhaps it is the innate mothering sense to provide for needs and cherish peace. Down through our carefully preserved history, male rulers consistently valued power and wealth over peace. It's true Atlantis controlled much of the world during those times, but the cost was interminable warring. We don't *require* female Rulers, as evidenced that I am one. It's merely become tradition.

There have seven areas of governmental focus called Houses; Education, Justice, Agriculture, Economics, Sciences, Foreign Relations, and then there is the House of Oracles; both the complement and the counter-balance to the High Seven.

We advise the other Houses, and provide practical spiritual support. We are composed of those born with metaphysical tendency such as prophecy, telekinesis, clairvoyance, claircognizance, and other psychic abilities. In other words, we study, expand and wield powers unseen.

But we are a dying breed. Literally. Metaphysical powers thrive in monastic conditions with focused training, no distraction, food and activities of high vibrations. Our best and brightest Oracles rarely marry or have children, so fewer and fewer babies are being born with these kinds of gifts and in those that are, the powers are ever more difficult to revive.

Then there is another disturbing trend of late. We've lost several efficacious individuals because they choose to dishonor the Laws of One. Control—using any power against others—is strictly prohibited. But it is intoxicating, this ability to influence, or even totally control. And the Sons of Belial are only too happy to laud and elevate these gifted individuals, even offering an esteemed place in their society, where there are no expectations of the disciplines of self-control.

The Sons of Belial nation was born from such an individual. Onus Belial was perhaps the most powerful psychic the House of Oracles has ever seen. He lived and died during my childhood but I have studied his writings. He made hundreds of prophecies, many of which have unfolded. Indeed, the very prophecy that I am following for our hope was given by Belial himself.

He was an extremely insightful prophet who practiced mind control over many. Attempting, at his height of power, to take over Atlantis, he planned to become the first king since Poseidon. Expelled by the Rulers, he was still backed by a portion of our armies. He had plotted well his rise to power. It came within a scant wasp wing of outright war because his followers *wanted* him as their leader. There were many of them, and they were Atlanteans, so their desires could not be ignored.

Onus Belial was the first to teach individualism; that some humans were better (wiser, stronger, pleasanter, more beautiful) than others—therefore more valuable and should be treated accordingly. He also taught that Atlanteans were far superior to other cultures and races of the world, and the proof lay in our wealth, our abundance, our ever-expanding technologies.

Belial thought the Law of One held Atlantis back. He argued that everyone deserves only what they earn. His followers began demanding ownership of homes, land, crops, and goods.

Eventually, as an offering of peace, the Seven gave a portion of Atlantis to them, with the understanding Belials would now rule themselves. They would be separate from Atlantis in everything, since they chose to no longer adhere to the Law of One.

The major difference between us today is perspective. The Law of One makes decisions based on what is best for the whole, and honoring free will. The Sons of Belial make decisions based on what is best for whoever's in control at the moment.

At least we of the sometimes rigid Law of One can see clearly what happens when our practices of self-control and spiritual purity are abandoned.

Ultimately, who is to say that it's better for Atlantis, or the world, to only have the Children of the Law of One with its light and goodness, instead of offering the darker and often fuller counterbalance of the Sons of Belial. If there is only one way to live, then it's not much of a choice is it?

But I am just an old man of many failures. Older than most. More failures than most. And in the grand scheme, I know so very little.

THE CRYSTALS. You're probably wondering about the Mega Crystals. They can provide almost unlimited power at the center of our grid. No longer will our energy need to be enhanced, dispersed and reflected by the Sound Eye.

While that is true, it is not the only reason I've had them unearthed and brought here. It's not the reason I've had half the underside of our most sacred City dug up and reconfigured into a maze that circles for hundreds of miles.

These Crystals are the second-to-last task on my list to complete. My hope is that they will survive to someday power the globe. But with such power, comes great risk. There are dark times ahead and I do not know who will triumph. It is during these dark times that I will finally perish, so I must prepare. I must equip someone else to stand between the power of the Crystals and anyone who seeks to use them for harm. As it happens, I know exactly who this is to be.

There are two of them. I secretly think of them as granddaughters. If I had followed another path presented in this lifetime, they would have been. I love them as if they were my blood.

Ahna and Aiela, the One of the prophecies.

TAYA AND THE CRYSTALS

9,982 BCE HIGH CITY, ATLANTIS

"It is not in the stars to hold our destiny but in ourselves."

— WILLIAM SHAKESPEARE

TAYA

*D*usk had claimed the ground below as Taya approached.
Hovering in the aero a little longer than necessary, she watched High City glow, brightening in perfect concert with the fading sky. Bursting with colors, the spired towers and pyramids, the canals with their web of bridges, even the pathways and streets laid out in complex geometric patterns, came rapidly alive, light-dusted in sparkling hues.

The Sound Eye, hanging two hundred miles up in space like a second moon, glittered a luminous afterthought of the sun's rays.

Taya's trip had taken longer than she'd planned, due entirely to too many forays of fancy. More than once she went far out of her way for a closer glimpse of something curious. Most of all, she had revelled in complete independence.

Now she was here in Atlantis' capital, greatest city ever built. Tens of thousands of years old, inhabited by nearly seven hundred thousand souls, it was a metropolis dedicated to manipulating energy, elevating beauty, recording the endless expansion of knowledge, transmuting history into wisdom and the worship of creative powers. It was home to the Seven Rulers, the House of Oracles, the World Library and Poseidon's Palace. Not to mention the Sacred Temples, and the Aades of Sacrifice. Most of Atlantis's youth came here, at one time or another, to apprentice in their chosen pursuits.

Please Ziel, be here to get me. And please please please have food. Gods, could there be a prettier city? Here for a whole moon. What bliss.

Thoughts ricocheted inside Taya's mind as she settled the aero on a bright triangle lit in customary orange. This one was numbered 531, in giant, white, glowing letters, according to Ziel's detailed instructions.

What could I possibly be needed for, here, that will take an entire moon? And why all the secrecy?

He was indeed waiting, alone, rushing to greet her as she stepped out of the metal, triangular transport. Smaller in height, Ziel wrapped his arms around her. "A thousand welcomes my dear, I can't tell you how much it means to me that you have come. I will explain everything now that I can look into your eyes—I could not risk your purpose here being known. But come! I've a lovely supper laid for us and you must be travel tired."

They'd talked frequently after the long-ago visit he'd made to Chiffon, becoming unlikely friends. He'd visited every six or seven moons thereafter, always jocular and tender with the twins, captivated by their maturing charm. By now, she and Drey thought of him as family.

Taya relaxed into his affection. "I'm so curious I can barely stand it. But supper first. It didn't occur to me this morning to bring food."

Ziel gestured toward the city that flowed away below them, "So you are enthralled with our night lights. I watched you hovering."

"I haven't been above the City at night before. It's quite something." Taya crawled halfway back into the aero, handing one of two small bags back to Ziel. "I don't remember colors—but it has been, what... eight years since I was here?"

"It's a recent indulgence. Some creative genius has added hues to our light paint so that they glow any color you could imagine. The latest fad."

Ziel was referring to the paint-like substance Atlantis used. During the day it looked like any finished surface might, but at night, trillions of tiny solar grains illuminated. The streets, walking paths, buildings, even fences, trees and artistic adornments lit up in the night, seeming to mirror the galaxies above. This allowed the city to continue to work and play long after the sun went down.

High City was where the first Atlanteans had settled, centered by Holy

Mountain which rose from the plains like some god-formed fountain-head. Near its peak, natural springs—some hot, some cold—gushed with artesian force from the ground. Mist wreathed its summit of tall rock "fingers" every morning and evening when the the air was chilled.

Legend told that Poseidon had searched long for a place of perfect beauty. He built his palace upon this mountain, in a spiral ringing it in ascending layers, each story stepped perfectly one atop the other. Spreading out from the base of the Palace he dug three concentric circular canals, cut through with four straight channels pointing to the four directions of the world. These flowed out into the surrounding plains, irrigating vast fields that grew bountiful crops, and orchards that supported a panoply of creatures. Beyond the city, the four straight canals became rivers, meandering through all the continent, rejoining the sea on four sides of Atlantis.

Now this ancient City—partially destroyed in each earth calamity that had ended preceding epochs—was fully restored. Grown far beyond its original boundaries, Atlantis' capital is home to a large portion of her population. The wide, curving strips separating the canal rings support a metropolis including temples, apartment-style homes, centers of business and manufacturing, academic spaces, markets and various gathering places for the people. The surrounding plains house all the overflow, stretching wide, surpassing every horizon.

Taya and Ziel stood on top of the great stone wall that Poseidon had built to protect his empire. Butting up against the outside of the third canal ring, it rose a gigantic twenty stories high and was some fifty feet thick. It was a fixture for eons, although Atlanteans no longer worried about attacks and hadn't for generations.

Sections of the wall were used for a variety of purposes, one of which was to serve as an Aero lot where the cross-country transports could come and go safely without bothering the flow of life in the city below.

Ziel led Taya towards the staircase that zigzagged down the wall's inner face, "I would have had you fly directly to the Palace but we allow such few arrivals and yours would have attracted attention. Better to stay anonymous. You're simply my niece, come for a long visit with your adoring uncle. A trolley waits below to take us home. It would be quite a walk and I'm sure you're tired from travel, yes?"

"Not tired so much as famished." Taya replied. "A walk sounds nice after traveling so long—perhaps after we eat."

They finally arrived at the bottom of the staircase. "*That* must have been a climb for you!" The glowing wall seemed to lean over them.

"You're inferring that I'm aged?" Ziel teased. His hair, shot with three shades of silver, was unbound tonight, reaching almost to mid back. "It *is* slower going of late. I once could run up these steps without stopping. I can assure you, I stopped a bit tonight!"

Canal boats and trolleys were used to traverse High City..

Trolleys were little more than a square box, with seats set between four wheels, it had a roof to protect from rain and was powered by a small solar engine that was whisper quiet. A driver maintained each one and transported people and goods around the city during his or her daily shift of service. The city's orderly congestion meant they travelled no faster than a person might run. Although walking was still the main transit, trolleys were used for those very young, very old, disabled, or travelling greater distances. Canal boats were for transporting cargo.

Their large, shy driver leaned against the trolley, watching people walk by. Bowing the traditional Atlantean greeting, she took the bags from both Ziel and Taya to stow under seats, then quietly drove them across the high-arching, outer canal bridge.

Ziel pointed out where things had been torn down recently, modern buildings erected, or perhaps an empty space awaiting someone's plans to be realized. "There's quite a focus of work to build more bridges traversing the middle and inner canals. More bridges will allow for better traffic flow in and out of the central rings."

"It does worry me." He admitted. "The complacency. No one thinks of threats anymore. It's as if they've forgotten even the word 'danger'. Dark forces gather Taya, I feel it. Even now they move against us, underground and I fear, from within. Our people grow more innocent—no that doesn't describe it exactly—more *naive*. There are few who remember the last threat of attack and even fewer who remember why. But I have not forgotten. Every day those memories are coming back to life. It's as if they're *awakening*."

Winding to the heart of this indelible psalm of a city, they climbed to a side entrance of Poseidon's Palace, talking all the way.

Taya paused, gazing at the froth of colors that seemed to billow out below in all directions. "It's all quite...removed from up here isn't it?"

Ziel nodded. "Oracles require a careful balance, seclusion from the energies of so many people, overwhelming to our sensitive psyche. Yet we must stay available to this nation we serve".

"Ahna doesn't like being around people much. Even school is a struggle. Could it be the same sort of sensitivity?"

"Likely so. Shyness or introversion indicate sensitivity. Human instinct is to connect, so intentional disconnect indicates some level of discomfort."

"Hmm. I'll have to explain that to her. She thinks she's abnormal. Goodness this is big up close!" Her neck craned, taking in the enormity of Poseidon's Palace.

"Our topmost, or Summit ring, just above the Oracle level, houses the other six Rulers and their supporting staff." Ziel pointed. "The third ring is divided between the Old World Library and areas where the Seven and the Oracles do their work. The bottom levels are used for many things including palace staff quarters, learning spaces, meditation halls and public areas used for performances, ceremony and festivals. You'll find the entire palace richly decorated with ancient artifacts and art dating from the times of Poseidon. I hoped you would enjoy staying here."

Taya merely stared in wonder at huge lit statues, molded from bright gold, adorning the entire exterior of the Summit rings.

"Come dear, plenty of time to gawk and explore in the morning light, let's get you fed and settled." Ziel bowed thanks to their girl driver as she left them, still silent as a backdrop. He carried both of Taya's bags and led the way under an open archway, to an elevator that slid soundlessly up.

On the Oracle level, the floors and walls gleamed smooth indigo marble, ornamented with astronomy themed carvings. Nooks cut into the marble walls that once had held candles or perhaps oil lamps, now held large stone balls that glowed with stored solar power. Like perfectly spaced moons they lit a pathway that seemed as if one were traveling through midnight, so dark was the swirling indigo color of the walls. They walked for some time turning this way and that until Taya lost track of where they were. Then Ziel opened a door into a small, yet lush, suite of rooms.

"Here we are at last. Welcome to my home." He set down the bags, leading her to a low table, surrounded by high-backed cushions and laid with food. "Sit, eat, and after, we shall put away your things. Then it will be time to tell you all that I have held from your knowing."

Taya smiled, taking in the fact that Ziel had brought her here, into his private space. She hadn't been expecting it. "You have a guest room then?" She sank into the cushions, mouth watering at a platter mounded with fresh vegetables and chilled goat meat, bathed in an herbed white sauce.

Ziel's eyes lit with childish excitement. "I never had before! But my project for you requires it. I had one made—never used that space anyhow. This task we undertake is... sensitive. You will see."

Extending his hands over the food, he said, "I bless this food with gratitude. May it nourish our bodies." Then passed her a platter. "Here try the meat, it is one of my favorites." Ziel began eating, apparently as hungry as she was. He spoke with his mouth full, loudly crunching crisp vegetables. "You will need tools and probably other things I have not foreseen. Tomorrow, we can go into the markets and find all that you require. Oh! you must try these figs, they're perfectly ripened..."

It was only a short time later they both leaned back from the table, having eaten their way through an impressive amount, and talked through the highlights of Taya's family happenings in recent moons.

"I'm *too* full now." Taya groaned. "That was delicious! Why is it that someone else's cooking always tastes better than my own?"

"Ah, this is good, we're *both* prone to gluttony. And now, my dear, it must be time, because I cannot wait any longer. Come, I think without ado or preface, I shall just show you why you are here." Ziel said, rising.

He led her across the main room to a small bedroom made comfortable with tapestries on the walls depicting the four seasons of Atlantis. He brought her bags, setting them carefully on the bench at the end of the bed, then turned and shut the door, locking the oversized bolts at the top and bottom of it. "You must always lock this before you go down." Ziel touched her shoulder. "Remember... always."

Pulling aside the winter tapestry, he fit a small key into a lock that blended perfectly with the dark marble swirls. "The keyhole will take some practice finding. It sits directly behind the winter sun." Ziel pushed on the wall just under the key and a slab became a short and narrow door, pushed inward, opening a portal into darkness. "Ah, yes, we shall be needing lights." Ziel reached under the bed and pulled out two light spheres, fashioned into lanterns, handing one to Taya. "Follow close my dear. Please go careful... and quiet until we are below." His voice dropped to a whisper as they started down a long, winding staircase that smelt of earth and all the things that dwell in it.

Angling in towards the heart of the mountain and slick with moisture, it took careful concentration to navigate the rather crude steps. And then they were done with stairs, and in a tunnel, perhaps four feet by six. They walked along in blackness, angling ever downwards, sometimes at rather steep inclines. They passed other tunnels leading off in both directions and stairways that went both up and down at intervals.

Ten minutes of walking, brought them to a small cart in the fashion of a trolley but half the size so that it barely fit the both of them. "It takes half an hour to get there." Ziel drove through a maze of utter blackness, the small hum of the cart and Taya's thrumming curiosity accompanying them. They spoke of small things, but Ziel seemed alert, wholly focused on navigating this tangled labyrinth that she could not see.

Taya's eyelids grew heavy until suddenly Ziel turned and stopped.

"Just one moment more, I beg, and you shall see the fruits of my work." Ziel hopped out, his light floating away, swallowed by a void. A grinding lever echoed across the space and the lights came on in a colossal cavern around them.

Taya gasped, awestruck. Climbing from the cart, she went straight to the giant Crystals that clustered like three solemn sentinels in the middle of the cathedraled cave.

Intense, bright lights nestled beneath each eighty-foot crystal, with more lights beaming down on the peak of their pyramidal points. They seemed to glow from within. The cave walls that should have been earth, were instead a whitewashed stucco and the floor was white marble tile. At intervals along the walls were more lights so that the entire cavern was lit as bright as day. With the glowing Crystals at its center, it felt as if they stood in a holy space.

"Ziel, they are… incredible. So beautiful, I can't even describe this feeling of…of first seeing them. The heart of Atlantis. That's what these are. You've found the heart of Atlantis!" She felt like weeping, and dancing with a strange joy coursing through her.

Ziel gazed at the Crystals with quiet pride. "Yes, this is the work that I've brought you here for. I didn't just *find* the heart of Atlantis, I brought them here and designed it. Mother Earth has gifted us with her treasures. What you're feeling right now is the effects of their immense energy. You'll get used to it. We won't stay long these first few visits, but I wanted you to see them so that you can picture the work. So you'll know the enormity of what I'm asking of you."

She was touching them now. Both hands wandered the Crystal's clear surface. She felt even higher as their energy responded to her, intensified at her caress. "You want me to program them." She breathed this new understanding reverently. As if it were her dearest dream coming true.

Ziel chuckled. "I'm going to remind you later how giddy you were."

Taya grinned happily, moving onto the second Crystal, stroking and examining with palms, fingertips, and even the back of her hand.

"Yes, I do want you to program them, focus or direct their energies. More importantly, I want you to carve them."

"But I'm a weaver. I don't know the first thing about programming crystals…" She spoke dreamily, eyes closed, cheek resting against the Crystal. "…or carving them." It was humming to her.

"A crystal matrix resembles fabric. Your intentions as you carve, combined with your thorough understanding of things interwoven will program them. You must create a map of sorts for future generations, in case our knowledge is ever lost.

We'll bring in trained programmers at the end to ensure your intentions are fully configured. But you can start by etching designs onto their surface. Perhaps it will be with sequences of touch, combined with the correct mental vibrational state, or intention of the will, that they become activated. Perhaps something else. It'll come to you, and the Crystals will help you know what to do. The whole point is, their programming needs to be something entirely new. You're here because of your endless creativity and your great proclivity to think in ways outside the usual." He let this sink in, watching her press her lips against the third one.

"Come. Let's go back above where we can speak seriously of all that I have done by bringing them here." Ziel pulled her gently away from the Crystal where she was stroking its surface and telling it fervently how perfect and gorgeous it was. He guided her to the cart, shut down the lights, and drove them back to the tunnel that led up towards her bedroom. Taya chattered animatedly the whole way, planning her designs in flamboyant gestures.

"Only two wrong turns—excellent!" Ziel crowed. "This maze still confounds me."

Their hike back up took substantially longer than coming down and sobered Taya completely by the time they arrived, breathing fast, into her little room.

"This one is yours, I strongly request you keep it on your person at all times. I've one of my own," Ziel held out the lacy metal key to the secret door. "You must be thirsty. I will make tea. Please settle in and call to me if you think of things that could make you more comfortable."

"Why must I bolt the door before going down?" Taya studied the heavy, primitive bolts.

"Because you and I are the only ones who know this way to the Crystals. Apprentices help with household chores and our meals so they will be in our rooms during the day at suitable times. I've spread the lie long and often there is only one entrance to the maze. If anyone discovers the passage from this room, I would need to obliterate it for safety. Then we'd have to take the long way 'round. This little shortcut will be quite a convenience. When you are working below alone, the bolted door will be a signal for me to know—and to come find you, should you lose your way.

If your door is not bolted, I will assume you are at market, or otherwise out experiencing life in our City."

"I will lock the door *every* time I go below." She swallowed, trying to dislodge the lump of uncertainty. "But if I do get lost? How will you find me?" The thought brought a chill. She'd seen only a bit of the maze and it was intimidating, as if it had been designed with the purpose to confuse and lead someone astray.

"Your key is a beacon. I can find you anywhere as long as you have that key. I've other ways if that fails—only they could take longer. Next time we go below, we'll mark the way together. We won't lose you my dear. Join me for tea when you're ready." Ziel took his leave, shutting the door behind him.

Taya examined her amenities. A cedar wardrobe, inlaid with flowers made of jewels, to store clothing, books or other items she might need. A low bed, made up with beautifully embroidered bedding with a padded bench at the foot. She knelt and peered under the bed to put away their lanterns. There was a large wooden tray, its compartments empty except for half a dozen of the little lantern spheres. Perfect for her tools, she decided. Fatigue settled in. She left unpacking for the morning, changed into fresh and comfortable clothing to sleep in, and went in search of her tea.

She found Ziel nestled in ample high-backed floor cushions that ringed his little table. A pot of tea waited, with fragrant steam wisping from its spout. He appeared to be meditating so Taya slipped into a cushion opposite him and quietly poured hot amber liquid into a tiny teacup carved from jade. She'd only just curled up to sip, when Ziel opened his eyes and smiled.

"Taya, thank you *ever* so much for coming here. For agreeing to do this work before even understanding what it is you've agreed to. Your trust is overwhelming and humbling. Truly, you've no idea how desperate I've become for someone to trust. You helped me when you were young— though you may not have known it. Do you recall weaving messages into sheets and blankets and such?"

Taya nodded. "Aunt Sage made it into a game. We had such fun imagining the rest of the story. I'd forgotten all about that!"

"I haven't. That concerned one of the gravest dangers we've faced from Belial's madness—a story for another time. Your talent served me well then and it is what's called for again. I want you to understand the truth of what is happening in Atlantis and I pray you'll forgive my bluntness, my refusal to shield you from it."

Taya said nothing, sipping her tea. It was a smokey chocolate, decadent and enlivening.

"I suppose it's inevitable for corruption to creep into any society when we no longer have to depend on each other for survival. Prolonged ease and abundance offers addictions to pleasure, a cycle that is unquenchable and destructive. The irony is that we walk the same path towards destruction as the Sons of Belial—approaching from two opposite directions. For so long I've judged them for their dark desires, their lack of self-control, their cruelty and debauchery and contempt for all that we consider sacred. Yet now I see that all of our striving for perfection, our aspirations for enlightenment, our rigid views of holiness, these are just another form of extremity. Our Law of One has been good to us Taya. We've progressed farther and sustained harmonious culture longer than any nation that has come before. Yet we've thrown off the balance. And so we come to the end of the Golden Age."

Ziel paused to pour himself tea. His tiny cup carved from obsidian, steamed blacker than coal in his wizened hand. "All of my striving, all of myself, I've poured into prolonging this Eden where I hoped...well I guess I hoped that we all could live happily ever after. I thought we'd evolve into higher beings that honored Creator." Ziel shook his head sadly. "But I failed to consider motivation. Why would anyone want to grow or change when they're surrounded with everything they could ever want? We're a spoiled bunch of children. And there is nothing more dangerous or destructive than spoiled children with unlimited power in their hands —power they did not earn and so will not use wisely. A shift is coming Taya. I've foreseen oh so many ways it could play out—some of them humanity won't survive."

Taya considered this in stunned silence. "I-I guess I thought all was well..."

Ziel looked doleful, smoothing one bushy silver eyebrow with a forefinger. "We've misused the evolution of our ancestors, the knowledge of those who've come before us to deliver us to these heights. Instead of teaching, sharing it with all who are open, we've created inequality, wide ranges of wealth and privilege, divided by miserable, deathly crevices. We've become intolerant. Mostly, we've been arrogant, taking the best as our personal spoils, unwilling to contribute our own comforts to improve the entire planet. We do not live the concept of the greater good outside our borders."

Taya poured them both more tea, "And so... what can be done?"

"There must be catalyst. I'm trying to get the Rulers to approve widespread programs of aid. Requiring everyone to participate somehow. The poor people across the water who slave in hot fields of misery to fill someone else's belly, who are beaten and outcast, these ones are learning what they came here to learn, while we are stagnating. Don't you see? It is very rare, very difficult for someone surrounded by only goodness to seek or gain wisdom. 'So the first shall fall into ruin, and the last shall be first.'"

His bright cerulean eyes were distant. "My visions have shown many possible futures: I've foreseen the Sons of Belial overtaking High City and from here, taking control of the world—drowning it in violence. I've seen us going to war to prevent that invasion, losing massive numbers of lives. Alternatively, I foresee us continuing on in the same rut we're in now, which brings increasing malcontent, division, and eventually civil war, setting everyone at odds with those they once counted dearest. That war escalates to destroy the planet. The best future I've foreseen is where we transform into a nation that spreads across this globe, working alongside those in need and those in bondage, teaching them how to live free. We power the world with our crystals in that version, providing technology, healing and light to all who want it." He sank back into his cushion and sipped tea with troubled expression.

"I am unsure these days Taya. I've lost my sense of direction except for two things—the Crystals, and your twins. They're the common denominator in the positive futures." He paused, rising to go to his food cupboard, and returned with a plate of cookies.

"How did you find the Crystals? And where?" Taya asked, not yet ready to discuss Ahna and Aiela's role in all this.

Ziel brightened. "It was quite an adventure! I first had the idea while contemplating the harmonizing power of crystals. If it is right and fair of us to expand this harmonious technology to the rest of the world, we needed more—and bigger. I began to wonder, just how large of crystals has this wondrous earth created? So I asked. In deep meditation I communed with our great pachamama and inquired about her larger crystals. I was shown unbelievably huge ones growing in caverns. But of course mere visions are not helpful in knowing *where* to locate them on the planet, so I used a map of the world to narrow it down by body-testing." Ziel paused for a sip. "The closest cavern to us, is in the south of Merika, west of Atlantis."

Tea forgotten, Taya leaned in. Ziel's excitement was contagious.

"I took a team of experienced miners to this place—far inland with rather forlorn mountain ranges abruptly sprouted where I'd least expect them. The landscape changed drastically and often, from lush valleys to gigantic trees that rivaled Old Forest. We finally found the area where I was sure the crystals were buried, halfway up a mass of craggy peaks, but they lay so deep beneath the surface I almost gave up hope of reaching them.

I had a hundred more miners brought in and then left the team to their work. Ten or more shipments of supplies, and several moons later, they called me back to see what they had found. It was spectacular. An enormous water-filled cavern housing a veritable jungle of mega crystals. Steam filled the tunnels they'd carved, dropping almost a thousand feet down from the surface. The temperature was 110 degrees inside a space large enough to fit two of Poseidon's Palace! They had pumps running continuously to keep the water level low enough to explore. It was all lit up and I wept when I first entered."

He beamed at her. "So unexpectedly exquisite. A treasure that we would never have known existed had we not begun seeking it. I'd asked for one or two crystals that exceeded our single, long used "mega" crystal in size and purity. I was led to *hundreds* that absolutely dwarf the one we used."

Taya smiled, feeling his wonder.

"Getting them out was another project entirely. I ended up bringing over our best telekinetics. Working with crystals proved a whole different puzzle than their usual metals, or the lower frequency sandstone, granite or marble stone that they move around and build monuments with. We found a way of using the power of the crystals themselves. Projecting their minds inside the crystal columns, the Telekinetics moved them as if they were an extension of their own body. A partnership between human and crystal. They were ecstatic with their increased powers around and in the crystal cavern.

Indeed it was a holy sight to see; crystals measuring eighty feet in length and seven feet in diameter, moving *up* one thousand feet of tunnels and coming to rest on the surface, introduced to sunlight for the first time. It felt like innocence being born. All in all, it took us thirteen moons from the time we started mining, to when our three mega crystals were in High City, awaiting the final move into their new home.

It seemed a sin to hide them back underground, away from the sunshine. But a necessary sin. Just being in their presence for very long, made one giddy with their power. I would not risk that power being used by foolish people."

"And so you created the maze." Taya said.

"Yes indeed. You might know that throughout the epochs of Atlantis, a catacomb of tunnels, caverns and underground buildings has been built for many purposes and protections, under Holy Mountain and High City. There are mysteries and legends that all blend together into compelling stories that we who live here, love to tell. And so I felt more than a little guilty at having this historic underground collapsed. I brought in miners and engineers and literally had every space beneath our mountain filled in.

Then, starting over, the Crystal's Cathedral was hollowed, built and decorated. Once they were placed in their new womb-like home, I began the long arduous work of secrets. Layers upon layers of them. I used different workers from all parts of Atlantis, to tunnel the maze. I alone held the layout, no other person laid eyes on it. I gave each team only a tiny part to complete, rewarded them well and sent them home, before they understood what it was they were participating in. At times I drugged their food or drink to help them forget. No one caught on how massive the maze was they were building."

Taya swallowed. "How massive is it? Exactly."

"Over two hundred miles of tunnels on three levels. Big enough to wander until you die."

Unnerved, Taya shook her head. "I believe it! And you had those carts specially made?"

"I did. Of course the other six Rulers have all been in to marvel at these 'columns of power' as they call them." A mischievous smile crept across his face. "They know bits of my secrets but they don't know it's mutable; the maze has stairways and false walls that can be moved."

Ziel leaned back against his cushion and spread his hands out palms up. "So now you know the whole of it my dear. Yes I've brought you here, hoping you'd become the Crystal's Keeper. No I can't promise you that this is the right path. But this choice—these visions and understanding of the crossroads we've come to—for better or worse, this choice has been given to *me*. So this is what I have chosen." He sighed then, long and deep, rubbing droopy eyes. "I know it's a lot to ask."

Taya had never felt her limitations so strongly. She wished Drey were here. He could help her sort it all out. The depth she'd walked into the earth tonight to meet those Crystals which she didn't understand but was supposed to program. The philosophical depth Ziel had opened before her now. Twice in just three hours, he'd plunged her into a world that she felt unprepared and ill-equipped for. "I think I need to go to bed—before I blurt out how mistaken you are in me." She strummed the sides of her little mug. "I'm having terrible fears. What if I'm the wrong person to help you with this?"

Ziel chuckled then, a cheerful warmth that sounded like hope. "*That,* my dear, is precisely how I know I've chosen well. You are everything that is needed." He yawned. "No, no, don't get mired in effort now. You don't need to have it all figured out." Rising and stretching, he cleared the teapot and cups and saucers to the small basin in the corner. "I've kept you up past midnight! Sleep as long as you like in the morning. There's many exotic tea blends here for when you rise and we can break our fast in the markets if you like."

Hugging her firmly, Ziel said. "You do still—and always—have choice in the matter. I won't ask you to stay, to help me against your will or better judgement. Rest well Taya."

AFTER TOSSING and turning in her desperate clutching for sleep—to escape the maddening circle that her thoughts seemed bent on, Taya was surprised to wake early.

Chimes rang in the distant interior of this vast building. Pitched in the upper octaves yet not brassy or invasive, they played for what seemed like several minutes. All sleepiness fled with the ceasing of the chimes and Taya rolled up to stretch, yawning. Not bothering to change from loose, cotton night clothes, she wandered out into Ziel's main area and commenced making tea. Sniffing various tins and boxes and jars she settled on one pungent with aged tea leaves and sage, tinged with the sweetness of blackberry. It was strong and she welcomed the jolt of caffeine a few minutes later as she gulped. Sunrise was just beginning to lighten the sky outside Ziel's single window.

Taking her mug, she stepped out into the same indigo hallway that had brought them here yesterday, headed in the opposite direction from where they'd arrived. Her hopeless sense of direction would likely mean she'd need help to return. She didn't care, too excited not to explore. Waving on orb lights, she walked on in the silent hallway that curved ever so slightly, and was soon joined by a sleepy-eyed oracle.

He stepped out from a doorway not far from Ziel's and startled to see her but then bowed wordlessly and walked in the direction she was headed. She noticed doors standing ajar a few inches here and there and soon there were three more oracles traipsing in front of or behind her. All male. All somewhat surprised to see her but pretending not to be.

She squashed a giggle at the absurdity. With no idea where they were actually going, she kept walking, turning a corner and descending several flights of stairs before commencing down another long hallway two stories below where she'd started. This hall was as smooth and cool as the indigo upstairs but these walls were jade. Their carvings told fifty-thousand-year-old stories.

More and more people were joining the wandering procession, female now, all silent, moving in one direction as if sleepwalking.

Taya lost track of the turns and staircases and connecting hallways, but after walking what seemed like a mile, they descended one last staircase into a vast circular room. Rich satin fabric padded these walls and patterned carpets quieted the floor.

It was half full of people already perched on little cushions, meditating. Some of them with blankets draped around their shoulders, others in their night clothes like her, and some fully dressed in the robes of their profession. They faced the central altar, a huge, white-gold pedestaled table that held a flickering congregation of candles and fresh roses. Clearly, a sort of communal alter.

She found a cushion and a blanket piled on the fringes of the room and settled into her own meditation, a welcome respite from the troubles and joys crowding her mind. Connecting deeply to the vast wisdom and peace, the wholeness each of us carries in our being, she sat until her tea was long gone and her bladder announced its fullness. Giving thanks for renewed inner contentment and spiritual strength she rose, glancing around at the emptying room. Now to find her way back to Ziel's apartment—or at least a water closet.

She started back up the wide staircase, walking for awhile before she knew for certain she was very lost. "Excuse me, I need to get back to Ruler Ziel's apartment, and I'm turned around. Can you help me?" Taya spoke to a mousy looking girl with intelligent eyes in a face full of freckles. She had the most beautiful sienna-colored hair.

"That is in the men's area and we don't cohabitate really….so I'm not exactly sure… where are you staying? Perhaps I could help you find that?"

Well. It seems Ziel forgot to mention that important little fact.

"Oh, but I am to break fast with Ziel and I'm to meet him at his apartment." Taya knew she was a bad liar even as the girl replied.

"You said *get back to Ruler Ziel's apartment.* So which is it? Are you meeting him or getting back to him?"

Taya narrowed her eyes. "I am his *niece*—not that it's any of your business—here visiting for awhile. And yes, I need to *get back* there and meet him for a meal!" Taya had squared off, indignant with this over-curious Oracle.

The girl eyed Taya's tattoos and her demeanor changed promptly. "Oh! I ask your pardon. I did not mean to offend you. Of course I will show you the way. Anything for Ruler Ziel's family! She scuttled off, glancing often at the silvery blue designs on Taya's skin, and Taya followed, mollified.

"It's alright. I'm sure you have to be careful to protect his privacy. It's nice that you all look out for my Uncle. What's your name?"

"Frond" the girl replied with a small courteous bow.

"Frond, I am Taya. You're the first Oracle I've met other than Ziel. You are an Oracle I assume? Tell me, how do you navigate in here? It must take time to learn this building!" Taya chattered, trying to distract herself from the discomfort of a full bladder.

"I have apprenticed here since I was sixteen and this building isn't hard to learn. It's laid out in mathematical proportions so once you understand that, it is easy. Just a pattern repeating itself. I feel as if we've met before, where are you visiting from?" Frond was smiling now. Eager to please. They talked until reaching Ziel's door and Taya gave profuse thanks.

"I will look for you again Frond. Enjoy your morning."

Ziel was nowhere to be seen, so after using the tiny water closet Taya set about brewing another cup of tea. She would wash, dress, and begin making a list of the tools and supplies that she needed.

TEMPLE OF MIND POWER

9,982 BCE TEMPLE CITY, BELIAL

"The question is not, 'Can they reason?' nor, 'Can they talk?' but 'Can they suffer?'"

— JEREMY BENTHAM

MARDU

*L*ooking neither right or left, Mardu stepped onto the moving walkway, a ramp which carried one between buildings in the Belial capitol. The walkways formed a patternless web. Inter-structure connections spidering every which way, including up and down.

Regardless of size or purpose, every structure in Temple City's center was built in the style of a temple. Even apartment buildings, business centers and shops were miniature monoliths, each one glittering more than the last. Every new architectural design sported more columns, was gilded with wider arrays of metals, or finer details of mouldings with intense, sometimes clashing, color combinations. Visually oversaturating, it had no blanks, spaces or pauses.

Atrocious, that's what is was. Mardu could barely stand to look at it as he stalked through this cramped city of excesses so extreme, they were redundant.

His bodyguard spread around him as best they could, ever alert for those who might come against him. Mardu's enemies outnumbered his allies many times over. He paid elite warriors, the best he could find, enormous sums to protect him. He used only those men who had mates, parents, or children that they cared about. Insurance was prudent. Yes, it required constant vigilance to stay ahead of the plots being made against him every day.

As a clump, they hurried into one of the largest edifices of the city. This one an actual Temple, but the only indication was its outrageous size. The Temple of Mind Power, originally meant for healing, and training the focus of one's mind for many useful purposes, now held more laboratories than healing rooms and employed more scientists than teachers.

"Stay where you are! Continue working." Mardu hurled orders at workers as he cannoned through echoing halls and rooms. He didn't want any of them to run ahead and warn the priests and priestesses that he was en route. This level was used for the latest body fashions. Currently it was enlarging the nipples and genitalia of both genders to ridiculous proportions and dying them garish colors.

He headed his entourage to the lower levels. An electrical odor, biting and chemical, gave way quickly to the distinctive stench of burnt hair and flesh. Then the finale, a malodorous cloud of feces, dense, unmoving. Mardu swore, covering his mouth and nose, wishing he'd remembered to bring the impregnable perfume blends that he used when visiting the Muta camps.

Finally his entourage reached the areas, where theories were put into practice. Judging by the sounds, he'd chosen an excellent time to pay a surprise visit, to see what might be going on that wasn't reported to him. It kept everyone a little more honest.

They followed intermittent yelps, howls and screams through concrete tunnels to a set of oversized double doors, motorized, too heavy to open.

Lit in brilliant hues, the Creation Room gaped a hundred and fifty feet across. It looked square at first glance but was actually an octahedron, as if two four-faced pyramids were stacked, base to base, one pointing up, and one pointing down. The floor was sheets of glass spread on a grid so that nothing very solid separated the pointed apex above and below. Red, yellow, blue, orange, green and white lights beamed down from above and up from underneath the floor, creating pools of intensified color. The walls were of a quartz that had the unfortunate side effect of reverberating every sound in the barren room. This shape, these materials and lights, were all necessary to amplify the energies needed for the work being done. Mardu paused just inside to watch. Disruptions could easily cause death in this wretched place.

Perhaps twenty-five large, rolling carts were scattered around, each bearing an animal. The animals were so heavily sedated, they looked dead, but wide straps secured them anyway. Mardu noted several bulls, goats and horses, a giant bird, two jaguars, a serpent so big that the cart could barely contain it, and a giraffe. A control screen jutted from the top of each cart, projecting images.

About eighty priests and priestesses, worked in four groups. They were hooked into quantum machines which focused the power of their minds, refining and magnifying until it changed the molecular structure of the animal, putting human faces, arms, perhaps whole torsos or legs onto the animals. Consciousness of combined mindpower created what-ever image emitted from the crystal screen attached to the cart.

After a group finished with an animal, it was wheeled to rest in the light pools, strategically sequenced to aid the healing and integration process.

Mardu felt oddly fascinated, watching the slow, steady morphing from animal to human. Body parts transformed more easily than faces. Entire head changes took the longest.

A blond priestess glanced up after her group finished giving the serpent a human face and two sets of arms. Detaching her head from the machine, she came over to stand next to him and his guards, smiling at the wonder on their faces.

"Welcome to our little temple of creation Dominus Mardu. Is there something I can answer for you? Shall I get one of the Overseer Priests? Or are you just observing today?"

Mardu smiled back at her, "I always have questions but I'd rather talk to you than an OS. Let's start with who or what these particular creatures are being made for."

She stood close enough to brush his arm, talking low and fast so as not to disturb the work. "We fill orders from many people, usually merchants or wealthy families. Most of these here will become a pet or a house servant. Some, like that bull over there and one of the jaguars, go to foreigners who will take them back to their lands and make plenty of money just showing them. The snake and the bird are experimental. We're always seeking new exotic blends that can be of more service to humanity, even if it's just to entertain us! It is fascinating to see what each of our unique creations is capable of with their hybridized body."

"I see." Mardu shifted closer, fancying her easy manner and bright blonde hair. "What will happen after the sedation wears off?"

"Well, I'm sure coming in, you heard some of the complaining that goes on, as well as the smell! We keep them here during their initial adjustment period to monitor and teach them a new way of being. We enhance each animal's brain during the transmutations. Not only do they have new body parts, their intelligence is higher. They can learn many tasks to serve humans, and come to understand us better. Some will even be capable of basic speech, which makes for wonderful pets. We found that increasing brain activity shortens their adjustment period. Many are ready to go to their new homes in a week, others, we take to the farm for further adjustments and training. Sometimes, there is one which cannot adjust. Those we send to the arena's, as you know, to at least provide entertainment."

Mardu did know. Combat arenas were disposals for these creatures. Those pets or servants who grew too old, got sick, or just weren't wanted anymore, all ended up sold to the arenas for their popular killing games.

"Tell me about the farm, I've not been there." Mardu was lying. Of course he'd been there, and suspected they were hiding things from him. But he wanted to see what all she would tell him. He found her pleasant.

"Oh! You should visit. I don't know why it's called a farm when it's a floating complex—I'm sure you know that!" She blushed. "Of course in our water labs, we do transform fish and reptiles. Mermaids are captured and brought there for training and breeding. Very popular as they fish for their human family and can bring back sea food we humans know nothing about. I have a pair myself. They are so happy, seeming much more free than the land dwellers...." She registered the boredom on Mardu's face. "...anyway, the farm also serves as a collection point for the animals. Those placing an order can view and select which beast they desire. Of course it's a much better facility than here for training the creatures, some of the newly created are taken there for submission protocols before being given to their owners.

Next up today, we have an entire batch of cows for Atlantis' gardeners and orchard keepers. We mold their top halves into human form. With the brain enhancement, they become well suited to grow, harvest and prepare food. Cows have such placid natures you see...they make good nursemaids and you know that we trade them for our nation's food..."

Mardu was shifting back and forth, impatient with being told things he already knew or didn't care about. "Are there any other batches that are particularly interesting? Or for different purposes?" He was thinking of aggressive beings. Surely there were Belials who ordered creatures for dark purposes. He could envision several combinations that would be very useful.

She shook her head, puzzled at his probing. "No, not that I know of. I'm here almost everyday lately. We've such a long waiting list for creatures, see, and the Temple Heads pay us quite well....but no, just lots of pets and servants. The most unique conrectus are the prototypes we ourselves dream up. Of course we'd love to recreate the fantastic beasts of ancient times—many keep trying. But there's just not enough oxygen in our atmosphere today, to support the sort of gigantesque growth in creatures of lore. We've tried using special chambers with enriched oxygen levels, but at some point, the beasts outgrow it and die."

Mardu nodded, accepting that perhaps the Temple Heads had been telling him the truth. There seemed to be no schemes to overthrow him with a private army of creatures. He invited the blonde-haired priestess to accompany him to a dinner party tonight and she accepted. She'd be a good one to keep close, and she was unusually attractive. He needed a new plaything, all the usual ones were irritating lately.

14

ZIEL

9,982 BCE, HIGH CITY, ATLANTIS

"I want a life that sizzles and pops and makes me laugh out loud. I want to sleep hard on clean white sheets and throw parties and eat ripe tomatoes and read books so good they make me jump up and down, and I want my everyday to make God belly laugh, glad that he gave life to someone who loves the gift."

— SHAUNA NIEQUIST

ZIEL

*T*oday is glorious. I'm fully aware that having Taya here is *the* contributing factor but also the weather is that perfect balance of sun warmth and shade neutral. To be fair, our weather deviates only slightly from this "perfect balance". We long ago figured out how to control it. Year round, only slight adjustments differentiate seasons so that crops flourish.

My meditation very early this morning was extra gratifying, returning me to the Great Center; that blessed balance where calm and clarity live— which I spent years trying to stay in all the time. I learned I cannot handpick my states of being or emotions—like we handpick the weather. Humanity's gift and curse is a constantly changing kaleidoscope of every possibility of experience.

The chimes had not yet sounded when I emerged to brew morning tea before taking some exercise. I joined a group of younger members of the Houses jumping around in tandem to a variety of drumming. It was terribly early for such an energy output. I left halfway through.

My exertion of climbing the wall to meet Taya's aero yesterday convinced me my lungs are suffering from long spells of inattention, hence the drum-dancing decision. Also, I'd like to keep up with Taya in the markets, not to mention the trips we will make back and forth from the Crystal cavern.

After my exercise, I enjoyed a mineral soak before meeting with my small council to break our fast. These three will be acting for me while I'm occupied with Taya and our duties, so I will meet them most mornings for updates and questions. They are my brightest proteges, two women—one of which will replace me as Head Oracle—and a boy who I'm quite sure I've known in another lifetime, so quick was our bond and deep affection for each other. Rumors abound that we are lovers but the sad truth is we're both in love with women we can't have.

Homosexuality is no longer frowned upon, nor applauded. Our ancestors bounced between believing it angered the gods, and believing it made you a god. Thankfully, we've progressed to the realization that our souls are genderless, and except for reproduction, why does it matter whose sex chemically attracts you?

Nearing noontime, I hastened back to my apartment to fetch Taya. Hopefully she'd slept in to refresh from yesterday's travels, after my rudeness of keeping her up so late, not to mention, piling rather intense concepts on her. I would make it up to her.

She was curled in my floor cushions with tea and a book from my extensive collections. "If I'm interrupting, say so and I will leave you to read as long as you like. But I thought you might be hungry?"

"Famished!" Taya beamed up at me, snapping the book shut decisively.

So vivacious she was with her strange tattoos. Her left arm was a study of symbols that I meant to inquire about someday. Her hair, a color that hovered between black and blue, even purple in some lights, was done in a hundred tiny braids which showcased the exotic long angles of her facial structure. Eyes that slanted up a bit were ringed with dark lashes, her irises colored a light lavender-grey, gave the impression of looking into me.

"You're staring at me." Those eyes narrowed a bit.

"I know. Just thinking how uniquely magnificent you are. If I had a daughter, I'd want her to have as many layers of intrigue as you do."

She blinked a few times, not expecting my honest compliment.

"If you're ready, let's go forage in the markets for food." I moved towards my door.

"Oh wait! I made a list of the tools I'll need. Would this be a good time to get it all?" At my nod, she fetched her list and we made our way out to the courtyard, setting off down the mountain towards sprawling market streets.

The markets were crowded with noonday traffic. Taya kept hold of my arm and I walked slowly so she could take in all that we passed. It was hot with the press and sounds of hundreds of people in the food stalls, ordering fresh-made salads stuffed inside tomatoes, melon halves, peppers or oranges. Sea foods came prepared at least twenty different ways. Grain cakes, breads and puddings turned the air sweet and yeasty. Exotically spiced nuts, new fruits and teas always had crowds of samplers. Spying a shaded stall I favored often, with cheerful cheeses that were crumbled, cubed, curded or rolled with fresh herbs, dried fruits, vegetables and even thinly shaved meats, I steered us to it.

My choice was a slice from a roll the girth of my thigh that combined a mild white cheese with tiny diced tomatoes, cucumbers and herbs crushed in fresh olive oil. Taya chose one with lemony pesto, pine nuts and feathery slivers of salted clams. Carrying generous servings on crisp lettuce leaves the size of our heads, we slid through the throngs, already nibbling. Under a laurel tree, we enjoyed our lunch before diving back in for tools.

We got distracted often. Taya fingered the newest clothing designs and finally succumbed to the merchant's urging to try some on. The hauls of gemstones found and brought back from far flung places 'round the world drew her in. We sampled the newest batches of wines made from fruits I couldn't name. This last distraction was mostly my fault, but Taya matched my enjoyment of the tastings, both of us entirely merry and quite giddy by the time we found the last item on her list.

Weighted down, we staggered to a spot where I could hail a trolley to take us the short distance back to the Palace.

I could not stop humming, could not remember the last time I'd had so much fun. Telling Taya as much, she agreed.

"We are well-matched shoppers." A tinge of guilt crept in as she eyed her bags of lovely new things. "Maybe we can go back another time and find gifts for the girls and Drey."

"Anytime you like." I assured her.

Nearing evening, after unloading our baubles, tools and wine, we decided to take another jaunt down to the crystals to deposit three large, heavy tools.

Going slowly, we marked the way with reflective stones. Taya explained her preliminary plans for programming, asking my opinion often and sketching a bit of her inspirations on the crystal's surface, designs that were exactly perfect. I had not even realized the full extent of her artistic talent and inwardly, I gloated. I had chosen well, too well, for me to take much credit for actually. Already, Taya reacted less to the Crystal's immense energies.

She wanted to drive the tiny cart back and caught on quickly, enjoying rather high levels of speed, for a beginner, through relatively tight tunnels.

Over a light supper of chilled beet soup and grain salads, I proposed we attend a concert.

Taya couldn't resist donning one of her new style of garments purchased earlier. Quite a stunning gown, it was made of gauzy material, clinging to the body until mid thigh where it flowed, long and sparkling to a few inches above the ankle. Solid fabric underneath covered the breasts and pelvic regions but the beautiful shape of the body shone through the rest. This material was of the latest fashion craze that changed colors when it moved. Fine threads comprising the cloth were manufactured to be three-sided. This material's thread was colored blue, green and purple, so that it appeared to phase from one color to another depending on one's angle. The effect was a shimmering constant display of colors. She looked like a brightly colored tropical fish maiden. "Drey will insist you wear this often I think—and now we must go." I coaxed her away from admiring herself in the mirror.

We arrived just after the concert had begun in the great square of the eastern courtyard. Perhaps three hundred people came to enjoy the music on this warm night. A family group of twenty musicians sat in formation, playing harps of all sizes strung with finely spun crystal. They played classical pieces composed purely to beauty, melancholy songs, and fast songs that aroused the crowd to great bouts of twirling, breathless dance. Traditional garlands were brought out for the final two numbers. Used for synchronizing groups, heady scents from the flowers uplifted us as we danced, intertwined, full of the joy of life.

15

DREY

9,982 BCE. AFRIKA AND ENGLAND

This then is the mystical experience of the "dark night of the soul"; when old convictions and conformities dissolve into nothingness and we are called to stand naked to the terror of the unknown. It is only in this place of absolute surrender that the new possibility can emerge.

— CHRISTINE VALTERS PAINTNER

The woman lay on her belly in a sleep so sound she might have already been dead. Her mate sprawled on his back snoring gently. Black-skinned, in their late twenties, they were Afrikan scientists that lived and worked at this facility, assisting Drey in his research.

Six men, silent and strong, crept 'round the floor pallet where the couple slept. Four of them held the man down while the fifth wrapped hands around his neck, crushing his windpipe.

He tried to thrash, or scream, but no noise passed the crumpled throat or the meaty hand covering his mouth. And then there was simply no more air.

The woman would not have noticed anyway. Her head lay at a grotesquely awkward angle, eyes still closed, long, swan-neck snapped. Dead a full three minutes before her mate, she had never woken.

Drey

They came for him when the night had bottomed out, and could get no darker. Soon, the earth's face would seek the sun's warmth like a drunkard who wakes, searching desperately for his next bottle of comfort and pseudo-life.

Drey woke to a quiet, rough voice in his ear. He sat up groggy to a circle of hairy faces obscured by shadows from the lanterns they carried. "What? Who are you?" He rubbed his eyes and then his face briskly, mumbling into his hands "What's happened?"

"You are Drey." The same medium-pitched raspy voice. Coming from the leader of their group Drey assumed, blinking away the blurred shock of lights flooding his pupils.

"Yes, I am Drey. What do you want? This can't wait till morning?"

"You need to come with us. Get dressed. My men will gather your things."

"What? No! Your men will kindly keep their hands off my things!"

Hands seized him then. Roughly pulling him from bed, half carrying, half dragging him outside into the cool desert sand, while Drey struggled and protested.

An aero was waiting.

"Get in." The leader spoke from behind him with a nudge towards the aero door.

"No. Not until you at least tell me where we are going." Drey was afraid now. What had they done with his assistants? Who were these men to be so bold as to take him against his will? And what did they want from him?

One of his escorts moved to shove Drey through the aero door but the leader deflected it, squaring off toe to toe with Drey, speaking softly into his face. "I will explain all of this to you while we travel. If you cooperate, you will not be harmed."

Drey considered a moment. "If you're not returning me here, please bring the bag under my bed and the small wooden box just inside my lab door to the right. They're important to my work." He was Atlantis' leading botanist. This hostile abduction had to be related. He stepped around raspy voice, climbed into the aero, and settled into a seat. Clearly, protests were futile.

Of the six, all but their leader laid back into the plush seats, preparing to sleep. Whatever mysterious destination they were headed for, it wasn't nearby.

The leader sat across from Drey. His bony frame was large. Chestnut hair pointed down his back in a single braid, and a substantial bush of beard masked his face. About the same age as Drey, he seemed a quiet man, the kind who has confidence in his own abilities with no need to prove himself. This was what convinced Drey to cooperate. Someone had sent this big man to bring him...somewhere, and this man would do it however he had to. Of that, Drey was certain. He sat calmly waiting for the big man to speak again.

"I am Nico of Belial. We have a problem that needs a scientific solution. I cannot explain the nature of the problem and I don't know why you were chosen. I was sent to fetch you. Beyond that, I have no answers."

Drey nodded, replying evenly, "I appreciate the explanation. Where are we going?"

Nico considered before answering, "England. We're headed to England."

Drey nodded again, pitching his voice amicable. "How did you know where to find me?"

Nico shrugged. "I was told you'd be at a desert lab in South Afrika and given coordinates. I do not know how this information was obtained. I do know there are those who keep record of whomever could be useful. You must be on that list."

A chill ran through Drey. Who else was on that list? Did they monitor Taya and the girls too? Taya was in High City for an entire moon, on some secret task for Ruler Ziel. He had no way of knowing how she was. No way to check on the girls who were staying with Auntie Sage while both their parents were away. The communication grid did not extend outside of Atlantis yet.

Strangely, something inside of him wanted to admire Nico's obvious intelligence. His plainspokenness and lack of posturing seemed out of character for a Belial soldier.

The Afrikkaan couple will miss me very soon. Probably go get help when they can't find me by the end of today. Unless something's been done to them...

"How long will I be away do you think?" Drey inquired, watching Nico lay back in his seat as if settling down for the remainder of the night.

Nico's heavy shoulders lifted in a shrug, "How would I know? I don't even know what we need you for." Then he shut his eyes and turned to face away.

Drey eyed his bag stowed in compartments by the hatch, thinking through their contents. He had arrived at the desert lab just two days before, planning to spend an entire moon there. Except for the assistants, no one would miss him for at least 27 days....

Mostly he worried about Ahna and Aiela. Could they be snatched away as easily as this? Surely not in Atlantis. He had only been threatened when he'd resisted their demands. Perhaps they meant him no harm as long as they got whatever they were after.

Drey groped for the lever that laid his own seat back. Might as well rest while he could. Who knew what lay ahead and when next he'd have the chance?

◎◎

DESCENDING THROUGH A STORM WOKE DREY. His captors sat up around him as the wind caught the aero, tossing it about. He couldn't make out the terrain they bounced towards, through forbidding clouds and slapping rain.

Nico flashed him a sardonic smile. "We're there. Welcome to England. Thank you for not trying to kill us while we slept. For that I will make sure you return home."

Drey swallowed. "I'd be grateful Nico."

They bumped and warped their way slowly down, landing hard on sloppy ground. The men, who'd spoken only in occasional, low-pitched grumblings to each other, took Drey's bags. Nico took Drey. They stepped out into a ruined courtyard of sorts surrounded by broken stone buildings. Rain-soaked walls bled a soft black, their mortar cracked and crumbling with age. That is all Drey saw before a rough bag was hauled over his head from behind and Nico's grip tightened on his arm.

"Just precautions. Nothing more. Best not fight." Then a softer tone close to his ear. "I keep my promises."

Right, Drey thought darkly, *and what power do you actually have? Best not make vows you can't keep.*

They walked awhile, turning three times. Door. Right turn. Thirteen steps up. Left turn. Eighteen steps up. Slight left. Door. A chair pushed into the back of his knees.

"Sit down." From Nico and the hood was removed.

Drey gasped a little before he could stop himself, facing a creature he knew not of. She was foreign looking, though he couldn't explain what seemed so immediately different, and exceedingly—even shockingly—beautiful. A girl, perhaps late twenties, with short, red-gold hair and very white skin, watched him. Her deep-set eyes glowed amber above high, hollow cheekbones and would have struck him as feral if it weren't for the overwhelming sadness pooled within.

"I am Nadya and you are Drey." She spoke in a heavily accented monotone, as one reciting lines. "I am a scientist specializing in neural pathways of the brain. I have failed to find an organic compound suited to these one's needs. This is why you are here. To assist me in creating this compound. Then you may return home." She stared at him for some moments as if waiting for protests or questions or demands.

Drey simply nodded and commenced examining their surroundings, an attempt to stop himself from staring at her. The room was small and bare except for the chair he sat on and a small bed she perched on the edge of. A cell, Drey decided. Her cell. *She is a prisoner like me. I will have to find out why. Perhaps when there aren't four Belials crowded around us in a small space.*

Finally Nadya spoke again. "You have many questions I am sure..." She trailed off as if unsure how to begin answering his unasked questions.

"I'm actually very hungry. Might we talk over a meal? Perhaps?" Drey asked hopefully.

Nadya's eyes swung immediately to Nico. *Ah, so he is in charge here too.*

Nico nodded at the man to his left. "Go to the kitchen. Bring food to her workroom. We'll meet you there."

Then the bag went back over his head and Drey lost track of the turns, doors and stairs this time.

When the hood was removed again he was seated at a long wooden table in the middle of a crude laboratory. It was antiquated compared to an Atlantean Lab, with hundreds of clay vessels, pots, jars and beakers of all sizes lining floor to ceiling shelves around the room. Three narrow, rough-hewn tables took up much of the floor space, one of them filled with stacks of codices and scrolls, the others littered with crystals, scientific tools and containers holding various sized brains suspended in liquid.

One of the nameless men set in front of Drey a platter of boiled eggs and root vegetables. Bland, but steaming hot and filling. Nadya sat across from him watching, hands folded on the empty table in front of her. "You're not eating?" Drey spoke through a mouthful.

The two men on either side of Nico chuckled as if Drey had made a joke.

Nadya shook her head. "I have dined already."

"Perhaps next time then. Sharing a meal is the fastest way to form bonds of trust and friendship you know..." One of the men behind him snickered again.

Nadya looked down into her lap. "You are....kind. But we will have to bond another way."

Drey started to ask why but Nadya kept on. "Let me explain to you what I have been working on and where I am stuck."

She talked for a long time, telling Drey of her progress in developing a method to train and control large animals. "They think the enormous reptiles and mammals that prey on humans so many places in the world can be, not only tamed, but useful for hunting or labor, by the very humans they now hunt. They want to experiment also, with the giants rumored to live in some lands.

Their theories have been sound so far. By placing a tiny bead in the frontal cortex of the brain, it can be activated, producing any level of pain sensation desired. They want it to also be capable of detonation, to produce instant death. I have found there is strong activation during the induced pain at a second site in the medial frontal cortex, the caudal part of the anterior cingulate, an area implicated in controlling our so-called motivational behaviours or how we act to meet our 'needs'. This activation is directly related to perceptions of the unpleasantness of the pain, and is accompanied by activity in several subcortical sites, such as the amygdala, cerebellum and striatum."

Nadya paused when a Belial man gathered Drey's empty plate and utensils and started shuffling with the other two guards toward the door, clearly overwhelmed with boredom from the scientific liturgy.

Nico nodded his permission at them saying to Drey and Nadya, "Knock when you are finished." And then they were alone.

They sat examining each other and then Drey leaned in close, low voiced, deciding to take a chance on her. "What is going on here Nadya? Why did your people snatch me away like this? It seems to me that you may be in trouble. I can help you—"

She spoke fiercely, "These are NOT 'my people'! I am Lamia." She paused for reaction. But Drey's face remained blank. "Banpiro may be the term you are familiar with. No? I come from a small village in northern England. My people have been here for hundreds of years and most of us are at least that old. We regenerate at will. We do not die unless burnt to ashes. We cannot digest most human foods, but we do hunger for blood. And thrive on it. We *hunt*."

Drey's face showed his internal shock. "Your people...you, are results of the genetic modification experiments?"

She nodded, bitterly, "From the carnage of Onus Belial—when he first sent his scientists across the world to create new species. Specifically, species that do not die. They controlled us then as their test subjects. They seek to control us again. These nodules I am inventing, I suspect they are meant also for my own people! I am told they are not. I am promised they are to be used only on animals. But I do not believe it. I think the Belials will use them on whomever they please. And my people would be especially valuable because we rarely die. Imagine what we could be used for!" She was hissing, frantic at the possibility.

He glimpsed long, pointed canine teeth when she spoke and her eyes burned a paler yellow. She was so very entrancing. In the way that a lioness is. He felt the zing of warning shoot up his spine. *Danger! She is powerful and predatory.* "But why are you helping them? Why aren't your people rescuing you? Surely you are stronger?"

A heavy lock clanked on the door and one of the silent men entered. Looking annoyed, he settled on a stool in the corner of the room. "Shouldn't you be working?" He snapped darkly at them.

Nadya spoke as if interrupted. "As I was saying, I am looking for a substance that will protect the brain tissue from the electrical pulses of the metal node. The problem is that it slowly cooks any tissue it touches. Our longest surviving test subject underwent some sixty pulses before the brain tissue was so damaged that it began to die. Most of them survive half that. I have tried several plant compounds but I cannot find one that all the subject species will not react allergically to *and* will not dissolve over time *and* does not act as a conductor in the nodes dormant state. My knowledge of plants or other organic substances is too limited. Let me show you my attempts..." Nadya led Drey around her lab, explaining, orienting him, guiding him through each failed experiment shown in the preserved brain tissues. All documented neatly and thoroughly.

He barraged her with questions and together they began to list possibilities, drawing on Drey's lifetime study of biological substances. It must have been close to three hours before he stopped long enough to ask the guard for a drink of water.

The rest of the day continued in the same manner. A guard was always with them as Drey examined every phase of Nadya's research and experimentation. When he asked for food or water, it was brought immediately.

Needing to relieve himself, he was directed to a door at the back of the laboratory. It led into a tiny room with a pallet on the floor. Beside the pallet was his clothing bag, but the box he'd requested brought—containing tools and knowledge crystals—was nowhere in sight. The crude toilet was a hole cut into the splintery wooden stand in the corner.

Wet, unpleasant smells drafted from the hole. The walls were of the same stone and mortar he'd seen coming in and there was no window.

Drey had no idea how late it was when Nico came in to take Nadya away, only that he felt very tired.

Nico inquired if there was anything else Drey wanted. "I assume you will be needing supplies? Give me a list. Then get some sleep. Tomorrow you will have to give a report to the big man. The one we all answer to."

Drey shivered on the thin pallet which lent scant comfort to the unevenly planked floor. Trying to warm enough to fall asleep, he wondered what in the world he was into. Fear wasn't something he'd encountered much but now it reached for him. Circling. Penetrating his thoughts, pointing only towards despair. Questions swirled tight cycles inside his head, about Nadya, the Belial's plans for this project and for him. Finally resorting to meditation to soothe his fearful mind, he slept.

Trapped inside a perfectly seamless, crystal-clear box he was banging his fists, kicking at the invisible walls and ceiling. It sank into the earth so slowly its movement was imperceptible, like the moon's movement across the night sky. Soon he'd be buried alive. Sensing that to escape the box he must solve its riddle, he was frantic because no one had told him what the riddle was. His brain pounded, straining and reaching for answers. But he didn't even know the questions yet. His riddle box was deep inside the earth, the top few inches level with weeds surrounding it when they started shrieking at him. He woke with a start. Echoes of screams, faint but unmistakable were coming from the corner of his room, drafting out of the sewage hole.

He sat up, head throbbing, slowly realizing he wasn't still dreaming. The chilly pallet, the ache of travel and fear convinced him fully. He fumbled for the lantern and match, dragging himself up to relieve his bladder once the light was flickering. Had he dreamt that scream? Probably. Restless dreams were to be expected after this dark day.

Deciding he'd take the light into the lab and explore escape possibilities, Drey was standing at the toilet when another scream sounded. Piercing, guttural, drawn out, it raised every hair on his body. Nadya? Or someone else? It sounded female, agonized, with a volume of deep anger.

Wide awake now, he hurried through the crowded darkness of the lab to its door. Locked as expected. He searched slowly around the long room's perimeter, examining each bit of wall not blocked by the ample shelving—which wasn't much. The ceiling was wood beams. Two windows, little more than slits high in the stone wall, ran just under the beams. Perhaps three feet long, they were barely tall enough to fit his arm through. Yesterday he had glimpsed only gray sky and fog through the few inches of space, but at least he knew this one was an outside wall. That was something. He kept knocking into things, exploring midst the night, stumbling against crates and barrels sitting in places his tiny flame couldn't reach.

A pair of beady eyes glowed behind one of the barrels containing grass scented herbs, before skittering away into the shadows. Marvelous. Mice, rats and who knows what else. More to be wary of while sleeping on the floor.

What if the Belials planned to never return him? Would the Afrikaans be able to help? Would they even bother telling anyone in Atlantis? What would Taya do if he didn't come back at the end of this moon? How long would she wait before looking for him? Auntie Sage would certainly get help from High City. Probably go to the region council first, and report him missing directly to the House of Sciences for whom Drey worked. With her connections, she could get an entire army out looking for him, but the world is an awfully big place. An army could look for years and never find him. Drey fought the despairing thoughts. Too soon for that. He barely even knew why they'd brought him here, and certainly, he'd not yet met enough of the people.

Taking a piece of paper, he returned in the darkness to sit on his pallet, back propped against the jutting stones and made a list of ingredients he would need, noting where to find them, letting his orderly mental processes quiet the fear storm brewing. He already had a pretty good idea of what might work as a coating for the capsules that Nadya had invented, but it would need to be tested, he supposed. They would want proof before they would consider letting him go home.

Rolling the list into his shoe, Drey finally blew out the light and curled up as small as possible under his threadbare blanket. Using his extra pants for a pillow, he fell back into a restless sleep where his memory kept replaying the terrible scream. Dreamland took him back—though no refuge from waking life.

He was trying to hide from the screams in an ongoing maze of thorny cacti grown high over him, which he felt an urgent need to harvest and take home. But they pricked his hands, drawing blood at the slightest touch and he had no idea how he was ever going to get back home if he couldn't harvest even one of these giant, obstinate plants.

16

TAYA

9,982 BCE HIGH CITY, ATLANTIS

"I like to see people reunited, maybe that's a silly thing, but what can I say, I like to see people run to each other, I like the kissing and the crying, I like the impatience, the stories that the mouth can't tell fast enough, the ears that aren't big enough, the eyes that can't take in all of the change, I like the hugging, the bringing together, the end of missing someone."

— JONATHAN SAFRAN FOER

TAYA

By the third week, Taya missed her girls intensely.

Beguiled by High City's glitz, and Ziel's fascinating lifestyle, she had adapted quickly to a pace exactly opposite her gentle, slow days at home.

But the dazzle wore off.

Wistful images played randomly across Taya's mind as she swung high above the floor in the cathedral cavern, carving patterns onto the Crystal's surface. Splashing with five-year-old Ahna and Aiela in the sea surf, tracking astonishing amounts of sand back into the cottage, caked to miniature arms and legs. Bedtime, when they begged for Drey's stories and her songs, clamoring for "just one more" before settling into light little snores—made even sweeter when they snuck off for some "snuggles" as Drey called it.

Drey had been so excited to spend the first week at home while she came here. "I'm overdue on bonding time with my daughters." He'd enthusiastically plotted a hundred things they'd do together. Ahna and Aiela would go to morning classes, molding a galaxy of planets, mixing new colors of paint, or dancing to learn form and design. Drey would be there to take them home for midday meal, then the afternoon was theirs free. Usually the girls took naps still but Drey had probably let them skip it so he could take them to Ahna's giant tree for stories, or to the beach to build sandcastles, or fishing, or to Aiela's rock caverns to build toad forts and tiny fairy houses. His list was long. With only a week of afternoons and evenings, Taya doubted they would get to everything.

Last week he would have left for his Afrikkaan lab and Auntie Sage was with the girls until Taya returned.

She wondered how they had fared with meals. Drey wasn't much of a cook. His food concoctions were fairly strange. But the girls would eat anything for him—unlike when Taya made something new or not an absolute favorite and they devolved into picky eaters.

She sighed, then laughed at herself. Just a few weeks ago she'd complained of too much time and energy sucked up constantly by the demands of mothering twin seven-year-olds. Here she was now, almost in tears because she missed them fiercely. Instead of reveling in the solitude and total freedom here in the greatest City in the world, she was clinging to memories, trying to recall the fresh smell of them after evening baths, the feel of them pressing into her when they encountered someone they didn't like.

"Why do we always want what we don't have, more than what we have?" Taya's question to the grandly lit Crystal echoed softly in the white underground cathedral, as she swung gracefully in the ropes that suspended her while she worked.

She had taken to rising early for tea and meditation. Shocking, because at home, she could barely drag herself from bed to feed the girls and get them to their morning class on time.

One of Ziel's students brought early breakfasts of millet porridge sweetened with coconut nectar or sometimes teff porridge turned almost black with cocoa powder. The hot grains were accompanied always with fresh fruit. She packed all this food and brought it here to the crystal cavern, etching and carving for hours, taking small breaks to eat and stretch, usually not returning to her little room until mid-afternoon. She'd spend the day's remainder exploring.

Sometimes she would wander to the markets for some exotic snack or other, maybe find a new garden tucked somewhere, or visit one of the Temples, learning a little more of this endless city. Every few days she'd have a healing treatment or an herbal-infused hot water soak to stay in balance and ease the aches from odd positions and muscles ill-used while carving.

Once a week, she met her cousin Charis for tea, and one evening she stayed the night out in Charis' charming and sprawling tree house in Old Forest.

Charis' lifemate Bren had died suddenly just eight months ago. Charis was consumed by mourning still, steeped in bitterness at her great loss. She seemed fueled by a loneliness that she refused to let go of, unable or unwilling to move on in her own life. Taya did not know how to reach her. They argued the morning after their "sleepover" as they'd flippantly called it, ending with hurt feelings and a less than amicable parting.

Evenings were spent with Ziel. They would dine together, perhaps join a dinner party in the lavish home of some Ruler, Priestess, Merchant or Head of something-or-other. She'd lost track of all the people she'd met and who they were in the complexity of High City society. Good hearts, most of them, but she had no interest in forging bonds with these privileged, complicated people she'd likely never see again. So she listened and asked questions, pushing away the unbidden feelings of her own inadequacy, determined to enjoy this taste of extravagant living. Secretly, she was glad it was only for a short time.

Sometimes Ziel took her to a concert or a storytelling performance. They enjoyed showcases of drawings, paintings, sculptures and every art conceivable. Or evenings of poetry, magic and acrobatic performances, along with music of any sort you could imagine, each a study of new sounds, movements, colors and techniques. There was no limit to the innovations created by Atlantis' talented citizens. The push for "new" and "expanding" seemed almost frenetic. Although entertained, Taya always left with two questions in her mind. Where would it all end? How much would be enough?

She mostly enjoyed the late night discussions with Ziel. It became their habit to take tea together before bed. She would tell Ziel of her day's progress with the crystals, usually straying at some point into a memory she'd had of the girls or even from her own childhood. Her mind had much free time for thinking during the long hours below. It was as if Ziel were a long-lost friend who happened to miss most of her life until now. He seemed to deeply desire catching up on who she'd been and what she'd done, always listening intently, responding with uninhibited belly laughs or even tears, coaxing out details as if to collect every nuance of her experiences.

Taya noticed he became especially sentimental when she spoke of Auntie Sage raising her, or grandmothering the twins. His ears literally perked up whenever Sage was mentioned and he admitted once to being from Chiffon. Sensing this was a delicate subject, but much too curious to let it pass, Taya waited until a night they stayed in. Marvelling at her own brazen conniving, she suggested they open a bottle of the exotic wines they both loved. Chatting turned to deeper sharing and she opened a second bottle before judging the time to be right.

"Don't you think it's time to tell me of you and Sage? Clearly there is history between you..." Taya spoke nonchalantly, chin resting on her hand, fiddling with the book lying next to her and trying not to look too intently at Ziel.

He hesitated, caught by surprise at the sudden probing. "Why? Does she speak of me?" His tone was hopeful.

But Taya couldn't lie to him. Not about this. She shook her head, "No, she has never spoken of you. Not that I can remember."

Ziel looked so crestfallen, she wished she'd never asked the question.

"I see. Then I shall not speak of her either." He rose abruptly from the table, draining his wine cup between mutters. "I did what I thought was right at the time. That's the best any of us can do. What else does she want from me...?"

Taya's curiosity burned even brighter. If Ziel wouldn't talk, she would apply her schemes to Auntie Sage when she returned home. *I know you better Auntie, one way or another I'll get the whole story out of you.*

Sometimes during their conversations, Ziel would present yet another concern."The Sons of Belial have become so strong they could conceivably overpower Atlantis, yet my fellow Rulers refuse to take my fears seriously. They've too much faith in our long-dormant army." He smoothed an unruly, silver eyebrow. "Always, they ask what intelligence or visions I base such dark forebodings on, but nothing I tell them is enough. They are determined to sweep it away, inventing carpets under which they can safely hide any dirt I bring them. They refuse to experience fear in any form, forgetting that fear, like all unpleasant emotions, offers a gift."

Another time they plotted at length how the Crystals might help protect Atlantis while making power available to other nations. Eventually, they even devised a plan to program in a hidden function, a way to use the Crystal's inordinate power destructively, in the event it was ever needed.

"If the balance were to shift and the Children of the Law of One were no longer in control of Atlantis and her armies and weapons, this may be the only recourse we as Rulers would have. A failsafe. Of course the Rulers would never approve this...." Ziel eyed Taya for a moment, pausing to let the enormity of what they were planning sink in.

But Taya was accustomed to living by her own code. She raised her tiny garnet teacup to him, "A toast then; to our rebellious inclinations. They'll probably save the world some day."

17

DREY

9,982 BCE ENGLAND

"Do you not see how necessary a world of pains and troubles is to school an intelligence and make it a soul?"

— JOHN KEATS

DREY

*N*ico nudged him awake with a booted foot. Setting a jug of water on the floor beside a bundle of cloth he spoke in his peculiar rasp, "There's food on the washing barrel. Sorry about the chill. I will return soon, the big man wants to see you."

"Thank you." Drey blinked at the soft-spoken man already retreating through the lab. Sitting up to drink deeply from the jug, he puzzled once again why Nico was being kind to him.

A steaming bowl sat on the lid of a small water barrel. Drey opened the bundle beside him which turned out to be some washrags and towels of sorts, wrapped in another thin coarse blanket. Appreciating these small comforts, he ate the hot, gritty porridge. It didn't taste like anything much but it warmed and filled his belly.

Washing and dressing, he wandered into the lab where more light than yesterday already filtered through the window slots, enough to sit at the table and try to decipher one of Nadya's experiment journals. Written in her native language, he could only extract meaning from the graphs and pictures that she included every few sentences. This particular journal showed detailed maps of the three main parts of the brain. It seemed a normal human brain he decided, but then he was no expert. For all he knew it could be animal.

They shrouded his head again, before beginning a long walk. This time going outside, he could feel the sun warmth reaching through the air still drugged with moisture.

Nico spoke very softly by his ear. "Be quiet except to answer questions. The big man is volatile. Unpredictable."

Back inside, he felt the distinct difference of walking on carpet and the air was warm and drier. Distant shouting grew louder until a door was opened and closed and they were in the room with the shouter.

An adolescent's voice, partially changed, screamed insults petulantly. It stopped abruptly, and then Nico spoke from Drey's right side.

"This is the one you requested brought, to solve our little problem. This is Drey."

Unsure what etiquette is when meeting someone while hooded, Drey bowed slightly.

Silence for a bit and then the same pubescent voice spoke close in front of him. "You know what I want you to do?"

"Yes, I believe so."

"How long will it take you to fix Nadya's problem?"

"I have several ideas of what could work. I've made a list of the things I will need and where they can be found. As soon as you get them for me, I will begin experimenting. It shouldn't take too—" Something hard hit him violently on the side of his head. Sharp pain shot through his ear, down his cheek. He curled over with a howl. Nico's hand on his arm kept him from falling, straightened him back up.

The voice laughed at him. "No no *no*, see you have no power here *Atlantean. Never* tell me what to fetch for you! I could kill you. And now I don't like you much so I probably will..."

Drey cowered inside startled pain. His head throbbed sharply.

Another impact rocked him. On the same side, vicious, especially traumatic with no warning, no way to see it coming.

"What do you say to me idiot? It's polite to answer those better than you. I can do this all day, beat the proud right outta you." The voice squeaked, mean and taunting.

Drey was reeling, even with Nico trying to hold him steady. He felt dizzy, terrified. "I'm sorry....I did not mean....to offend you sir. Certainly,

I can gather my own supplies. Will gladly do what you think is best to complete your, uh, project. We've a good start and I will work day and night to hasten it along." He bowed again, inwardly cringing, praying there would be no more blows. He heard a snort.

The voice retreated a safer distance away. "Do that. I expect you to finish very soon. And keep your hands off my little bitch while you're working for her. Remember, you work *for her*. She is my lover. All mine. Oh—if you try to escape, I will bring your entire family here and butcher them in front of you. I know about your little twin whores. I promise you they will scream for days before they die if you even think about leaving before I'm done with you. Now get out." The bored flippancy of the voice raised tiny chills on Drey's body.

They escorted him back to his room where he wetted a rag in the cold water barrel and held it to the swelling side of his face. It did not soothe away the shock. This was the first time in his life to be struck in anger, or treated cruelly, or have his life so maliciously threatened.

Nico left with the list and instructions from Drey on where to find the requested items, saying "I'll get these to you today and we need to talk. There are things you need to know."

When Nadya came to start work in the lab, her eyes flicked across bruises blooming on his cheek and around his eye but she only inquired about the ideas he had, and the ingredients list he had sent with Nico. A guard was with them the entire morning as they examined the nodules Nadya had used and dissected the fresh brains of two monkeys and an elephant, all killed by too many pulses from the node placed within them.

IT WAS during another bland meal with Drey eating and Nadya watching, when they were finally left alone again.

"You have met that *sheitan* Balek I see!" Nadya commented bitterly, gesturing to Drey's colorful eye and cheek. It was swollen and sore, still trading sharp pains back and forth across the inside of his skull.

"He struck me! I said only what he wanted to hear, still he hit me twice while I was bound and hooded! I don't understand why." Drey had not encountered such people in his life, and the shock was evident in his ragged voice.

"The pleasure centers in his brain activate when he causes pain." She shrugged as if it was obvious. "He needs no reason but that. The drive for more pleasure thrill causes him to do such things. Probably he learned it as a child, received attention or had another need met that he connected with inflicting pain." Nadya stated this in a clinical monotone.

"Who is he?" Drey asked.

Nadya leaned closer, speaking fast and low, glowing eyes constantly on the door. "Balek is the eldest son of the Belial leader. I have heard his father is a vicious, cruel man who takes any and everything he desires. But the son—pure evil. We must hurry and finish Drey! I cannot take much more." Her golden eyes held a desperate plea.

"What is he doing?.....I heard screams last night, was it you? He says you are his lover." Drey didn't want to know, felt all his inner defenses rising at once to block the knowing.

Nadya leaned back, stared away into the stone wall, swallowed twice, wrapping her arms around herself, shrinking from the memory. "There is not love in what he does! He ties me....he does what he likes.....and mostly, what he likes is to hurt. He speaks of my 'power' constantly. Believes he somehow *absorbs* it from me by complete domination over my s-sex." She wouldn't look at Drey. He sensed her shame and how foreign it felt to one so fierce.

"Nadya," Drey made his voice compassionate but firm, "you must fight. You are *powerful*—not helpless! I will help you any way I can, I promise you. But you must make a plan to save yourself in case I can't...what do you know about this place? What opportunities do you have to get away? What are *his* quarters like? I'm certain he doesn't come to yours..."

She met his eyes, despair parting for a moment of hope, blinking out as quickly as it came. "You do not understand, they have Mahlia too—my sister. If I fight, they will hurt her. If I leave, they will kill her. Or worse, *he will keep her*, use her instead of me for his sadism. I would kill her myself before I let that happen! When I am with him, I am always chained and...muzzled." She bared her teeth at him. "Why do you think I have not already gutted him? I am a *predator*. It would be nothing to me." She was back to angry hissing now. A good sign Drey thought. Her rage is what would save her.

A guard returned, eyed them suspiciously before snapping. "Do what you're s'posed to be doing".

When Nadya defiantly snarled, Drey got another explicit look at the neatly pointed canines, fluid beaded at their tips.

The guard, enraged at her unspoken threat, grabbed her arm, yanked her against him. "Maybe I'll have Mahlia tonight." Then speaking louder to ensure Drey would hear, "Lunatic bitch would enjoy it."

"Nico will not let you." Nadya spat, shoving away from him. But her hands shook when they resumed their work.

Just before evening, Nico returned with bundles and bags of the requested plants and substances. Dumping them on the table, he sent their guard to his supper. Speaking fast and soft to Drey, "Can you finish the nodes tonight? How certain are you they will work?"

Drey glanced at Nadya, confused by Nico's conspiratorial tone.

Her eyes shone feral as she whispered, "He cares for Mahlia. Wishes us to escape as soon as the nodes are finished. If Balek can return to his father with success, he is less likely to spend time hunting or punishing us. Nico will help us...you understand?"

Drey studied Nico before answering. "Yes, we can finish them tonight and I am certain they will work."

Nico nodded. "Good. But we still have to test them, prove it to Balek. When we go to the animals I will bring along the men who pose the greatest threat. Their death will be blamed on you which will give me a reason to imprison you next to Mahlia's cell. Once I ensure Balek is satisfied with the nodes, I will make it look like all three of you escaped. Do you trust me?" He was looking at Drey.

Drey sighed. "Seems like I'll have to. There was never a plan to let me go."

Nico shook his shaggy head. "Only in my plan. You must find a way to ensure your survival, and your family's once you're home. I cannot help you with that—there is nowhere to hide if Dominus Mardu believes you're a threat."

They worked long past midnight mixing, grinding, melting, coating, cooling, recoating, preparing the nodules for experiment. Finally, the tiny balls were ready for insertion into test subjects, first thing in the morning.

Midway to dawn, fatigued in every aching part, Drey was desperate to fall asleep when the screams came. Three of them. He lay shivering, wishing he didn't know what those terrible sounds meant.

Finally, getting up to pace, finding anger, he let it build, formed it into resolve. They would escape no matter what it took.

NICO BROUGHT them to the test subjects midmorning. Drey was led unhooded, beside Nadya out of the compound. It was a fair walk across gently rolling hills covered with wild grasses, woodlands ringing the horizons. The sky was clouded with a chilled wind pushing into them, but still, Drey gave thanks to breathe fresh air, thanks for the hope of going home.

Two other men accompanied Nico, carrying the supplies and tools needed.

On the far side of an irregular, pointy hill was a lean-to guarded by a wolf. Constructed hastily of rough-cut wood, the lean-to led inside the hill. Chained to a rock the size of two men, the skinny, demented-looking wolf growled ferociously and lunged as they approached. Nico threw it a hunk of some bloody carcass and they slipped inside while it tore at the fat and gristle.

The shallow cave had been divided into cells, low cages made from green-wood, bound at the junctures with heavy rope—as much to protect the occupants from each other, as to keep them in, Drey decided.

Half a dozen monkeys of varying breeds, lethargically draped across each other, dozed even through the din from the wolf outside. Three apes of various colors and sizes were caged separately. And by itself, well away from the primates, was some feathered descendant of the Reptilian Dinosauro.

Lying down, its chest rose and fell weakly though its head had turned at the sounds of them entering. Heavy lidded eyes watched them. Drey estimated its length at nine feet or more, not including a powerful looking tail.

More cages sat empty then occupied and he wondered just how long Nadya had been at this. The place reeked of sour feces and rotting blood. Stacked against the far wall were carcasses in various stages of being hacked up. Unrecognizable, save for paws, claws or toes protruding from the heap, they seeped a pool of gore, floating hair clumps and hosting swarms of flies.

"Feed them." Nico commanded the two men who had dumped their loads of supplies near the entrance. Pausing to tie strips of cloth over their mouth and noses, the men obediently picked up machete's and proceeded to chop at the carcasses, tossing chunks of dead flesh inside each cage. Drey fought the urge to gag as the monkeys lazily reached out and started gnawing on decomposing meat of their own kind.

"They are heavily drugged." He realized aloud, turning away.

She nodded. "It is the only way to work with them, since we have few people and no adequate restraints. Twice I have been bitten and that thing there," she gestured towards the reptile, "almost killed the men who brought it. It is smarter and stronger than us. They underestimated the amount to sedate it."

"Where did it come from? I've not seen anything like it." Drey helped Nadya mash up some fermented substance which the men added to water bowls inside the cages. Recognizing the bittersweet smell of the cicoidal buds, fermented with sugar to increase their narcotic power, Drey understood the animal's lethargy. This drug would relax them to the point they would have little awareness of their surroundings, their muscles would respond very slowly when they moved.

"Merika most likely, uninhabited parts—where monsters still live."

Drey knew where she meant. Deep jungles in central parts of the Southern hemisphere continents harbored species unexplored by recent generations of Atlantean scientists. Glaciers and cliffs in remote places around the globe preserved remnants of this species that had once ruled the earth. Created millions of years before humanity, these highly evolved creatures nearly obliterated earth's first tentative human civilizations. Mu struggled and failed, time and again, to outsmart the giant predators, their technologies causing more harm than the predators themselves did. Lemurians considered them part of earth's trials. During an early epoch, Atlantis hosted a meeting of nations to devise a way to rid the world of the man-hunting giant reptilians. Using atomic weapons contributed to a polar shift, tipping the balance in humanity's favor when it wiped out this stubborn population which had worked its millennial way to the top of the food chain.

Humankind burrowed underground, building entire cities deep in earth's center with help from the "star people", surviving for generations until the dust had cleared, and the sun could revitalize and nourish earth's surface once more.

Drey had examined two Dinosauro skeletons, carcasses of unimaginable size, often well preserved under layers of volcanic dust, or frozen inside glaciers. He'd wondered if any of them still lived to hunt those vast spaces where humanity had not yet spread.

Nadya was already injecting two of the chimps with a node. The long needle didn't faze them even when it sunk carefully into their freshly drugged brain through the eye socket. Guided by a holographic imaging crystal, Nadya carefully deposited it in a very precise spot. "We will do the reptile next—it will not live much longer. I have to keep it paralytic from the neck down. We try to give it the other drug but it refuses to eat or drink. Like I said, it is smarter than we are.

Nico," She turned towards the large quiet man, "we will need the mouth bound shut." She nodded towards the watchful creature, hands busy loading the longest needle with another node.

115

Nico took thick ropes and the two men with him.

The large predator lay still in its cage, eyes tracking their every move. It waited until an arm reached to wrap its long beak-like mouth in rope, snapping viciously closed as the Belial guard screamed in pain.

"Help me finish it!" Nico commanded the other guard and they wrapped the rope around and around the protruding mouth—which still trapped the wild-eyed man from fingertip to inches below the armpit.

Beside Drey, Nadya had calmly filled two giant syringes with a clear liquid. She handed one to him saying "Empty it into the neck. You take the armless one."

Drey hesitated. He had never killed before. Sure, death had been part of his world. Family and friends had accidents, or died of old age. But not this. Not intentionally killing another human.

"It is them or us!" Nadya snapped at his reluctance. She ran towards the three men still tussling with the beast.

Drey followed, filled with dread and disbelief that his choices had come down to this.

The men had just enough time to register shock at being stabbed in the neck, with Nico looking on, before their bodies started spasming, eyes bulging, teeth mashing lips and tongue. Churning blood and foam spilled out, dribbling onto their chests.

Nico waited until they went still, before using the huge machete to cleave the arm, still trapped between the beast's jaws, from the shoulder it was attached to. Blood ran as the man's body fell heavily beside his companion's.

Nadya was already back with the node, movements fearless as she wrestled the beast's huge head, thrashing this way and that, trying to escape what it seemed to know was coming.

Nico stepped in to help her while Drey, feeling numb and mindless, watched as Nadya placed the node. Its skin looked like a jungle lizard but it had feathers where a human scalp would be. Its body was shrouded in them down to the dangerously clawed feet. It was, Drey thought, like a pieced together ostrich, crocodile and kangaroo.

"Almost done." Nadya announced, studying the holographic image of the brain before releasing the node. Pulling the needle out in one swift motion, she stepped back.

"Now we use this." Nadya handed a black box to Drey, roughly the size of his palm. She held a second one. "They are programmed to the nodes. This knob turns right to increase charge strength. At its highest, the node will burst and... instant death."

Drey nodded, feeling like he was in a dream, or underwater, wondering how Nadya could act like they weren't surrounded by filth and suffering animals, as if they hadn't just killed two men in painful, hideous ways. He fought waves of trauma and surreality.

"Here," Nadya repeated, touching the dial on the side, "Are you listening Drey? Here you tune to the frequencies of the different nodes, enabling you to control many separately with one controller. Every node shares also a common frequency as backup. The very bottom of the dial will control every node at the same time. You understand?"

Drey nodded, hoped he would retain what she was saying.

"The previous subjects died from tissue damage at sixty pulses and less. You will pulse a hundred times while I monitor the brain tissues for damage." She set Drey's controller to the bottom frequency which would control all three of the injected nodes at once. "Press this button, wait five seconds and again. Keep count for me."

The monkey bodies twitched and the beast's head jerked the first time Drey pressed the button. By the twentieth time, the beast was twisting its head violently, trying to escape the repeated pain and the monkeys were thrashing slowly against the far wall of the cage, emitting sounds that were unmistakable wails. "How much pain are they feeling?"

Nadya paused from studying the brain image of the monkey closest to them. "About the same as the worst stomach ache you have ever had."

"I don't have stomach aches."

"Never?" Nadya was disbelieving.

"Our bodies are healthy. Most physical problems are accidental injuries." His voice was very flat.

Nadya stared at him. "What sort of pain *have* you experienced?"

"Umm... accidents with plants. Rashes, poisons, small chemical explosions sometimes. I've been bitten more times than I can count. My head still hurts from Balek striking me...." He shuddered at the memory.

"Keep pushing the button Drey, we must finish this before we can leave."

Drey cringed each time he pressed it, imagining the relentless pains to be like cutting an open wound. The animals were writhing, shrieking, unable to comprehend what was happening to them or why.

"That's one hundred." Drey felt nauseous. His body trembled uncontrollably as if from cold, trying to release the shock of being taken and threatened and hurt, trapped in bloody surroundings, the agony he was causing, killing another man to save himself.

"The tissue is normal. No change at all!" Nadya was actually smiling, rejoicing at their results in the midst of this nightmare.

How can we be so different? Drey thought, watching her steady hands, her eyes filled with relief at their success. *Is her culture so inundated with violence and killing that she is immune?.*

"Nico," Her sharp call jolted Drey from his thoughts.

Nico returned from waiting outside the cave.

Drey envied him the fresh air.

"It is done. One hundred pulses and no tissue damage at all. There are hundreds more coated nodes in the lab and instructions for everything we did. I have developed the exact placement in the brain and charge strength needed to control the subjects. We know for certain Drey's substance will protect the tissue for multiple use. We are done here."

Nico nodded, eyes landing on Drey. "Finish them and let's go."

Drey stared at his own hand, paused on the controller.

There's nothing you can do for them.

He twisted the knob until it wouldn't turn anymore.

This is mercy, compared to any other fate.

He pushed the button, saw only slight movements as the animal's bodies sagged, carcasses easing mercifully into death.

"I need to hit you." Nico announced, smearing blood down the side of Drey's face.

Drey nodded, understanding the farce must be played. Thoughts of whose blood it might be, collided with the blinding pain from Nico's fist. It split the skin of his eyebrow, catching the side of his nose hard enough to start his own blood flow, dripping steadily onto his shirt. He turned and vomited against the wall.

"I'm sorry. Come on, let's get you back." Nico was helping him straighten, guiding him outside the cave.

He retched again seeing Nadya's face buried in the wolf's throat, draining its blood. So much death, and it wasn't over yet.

"I *hate* the taste of dog blood!" Her disgust dripped along with the red flow on her chin.

"Better than the other's drugged blood..." Nico was practical. "Here is the plan. Back at the fortress I will put you in a cell next to Mahlia where you must eat and drink and rest." He spoke mostly to Drey. "There is a pack to take when you go. I will gather the important things from the lab and present them to Balek where I'll tell him you were successful and the nodes are operational. That you murdered two of our men and attacked me in an escape attempt. He will rage and plan to kill you but will want to present his success to his father more—who will want them tested immediately on the Mutazio.

Drey stopped walking at this. "What Mutazio?"

"It's the primary purpose of all this, controlling Mardu's Mutazio."

"Tell me about them." This would be valuable intelligence to take back.

Nico shook his head. "Not enough time. There will be weapons and matches with the food in your pack as a backup, if my plan doesn't work. The only thing I ask is that you let Balek go, unharmed and with the work you've done."

Nadya snarled and hissed at this. "You do not know what I have endured from him! I will take vengeance!"

"Then what we are doing now is for nothing!" Nico faced off with her. "If Mardu's eldest son does not return to him untouched—with the completed nodes, all of this will start again and Mardu will not stop until you both have paid according to his satisfaction. Do you know what that means? Not just your sister and family but your entire village—perhaps all of your kind will be punished as brutally as possible. Is that worth avenging one boy's evil?"

"We are not that easy to kill!" Nadya seemed more animal than human in her anger.

"*You* don't know the massive amount of resources Mardu has." Nico retorted.

After that they walked in silence until with a sigh, Nico bound their hands and hooded Drey. Dragging them roughly through the winding stairs and hallways, he left them in the tiny stone cell he had promised. "If I'm not back before morning something has gone wrong."

Drey drank, though it worsened the pounding in his head. Chewed and swallowed the crumbly, tasteless food even as it curdled in his stomach. Forced himself to rest on the urine-reeking mat barely three feet away from this animal-like woman. "You will let Balek go?" The fear and unending shocks to his system made his voice quaver.

Nadya turned her pale yellow eyes slowly to him and stared, unblinking. He noticed for the first time her eyeshine. Tapetum lucidum, the glowing eyes of nocturnal and predatory creatures. Not present in humans. Disorienting him even further were very human tears leaking from those round glowing blanks. She sniffed and wiped at them.

"Yes. This time I must, but it is not the end. Someday I will find him again..." She sounded defeated, more weary even than he felt.

"DREY WAKE! THERE IS TROUBLE." Nadya was pushing at him, jostling him from incoherence, her voice agitated. "They took Mahlia, I heard them, it has been too long. Something is wrong."

Every joint rebelled as he forced his body up, fumbled at the little pack Nico had left for them. "How...how do you know?"

"Nico would not have let them separate us, we were to go together. We must find a way out of here. *Now!*"

"Yes, alright. We've these two knives...." He urged his mind to work.

Nadya was pacing the edges of the small cell, tension jerking her eyes this way and that. When he turned up the lantern, they landed on him and she stilled. "Yes. Fire."

He understood instantly. The door was wood just like the ceiling and floors. "Wrap your nose and mouth in something and the sleeping mat round you." He doused the lantern oil around the hinges and latch, letting it run down to create a trail for the flame to climb. "We may be running through flames, and will surely breath smoke. No, wet that first. And one for me too." She'd torn the sleeves off her tunic for face masks. Obediently, she soaked them from their small water jug.

The door was old and very dry as Drey had hoped but the room still filled with enough smoke to burn their eyes and lungs, enough heat to start blistering as they ran together, crashing their bodies against it again and again, expecting a guard to come and stop them any moment. The ceiling caught fire, hot splinters raining on them before finally, the charred wood gave way.

A door stood open to an empty cell just across. They ran together down the smoke-filled hall, too dark for Drey to make anything out away from the blazing door.

"This way!" Nadya pulled him towards the left. "Hold onto me. Step where I step."

He followed her up long winding stairs, stumbling on portions turned to dust and rubble in many places.

"Shhh." She paused at the top, looking around at things he could not see in the forbidding night. He smelled the smoke following them, heard cracking, then increasing groans as the ceiling of their cell no doubt began to give way and the fire found more fuel to consume.

"I must find Mahlia. You should go. Hide and wait for us or get as far away as you can, it is your choice. Go north, if you go. We will find you and my people will help you home."

She pushed him out the door and Drey could see again. Stars by the billion twinkled prettily overhead and the smell of burnt meat was so strong, his stomach growled. A huge mound of dying coals across the courtyard breathed orange sparks at every ruffle of breeze, lapsing to heavy smoke columns in between.

"No, no, *oh please no!*" Nadya rushed towards it, seeing things he did not yet, instinctively understanding its significance.

Nico's mighty body lay in black wetness, hands and feet bound, his throat cut from ear to ear. He had been kneeling, some detached part of Drey's brain deduced, and they'd left him where he toppled, bleeding out. Nico's wide staring eyes concreted an expression of horror and despair. When Drey knelt to feel for any sign of life, he found only the eerie luke-warmth of a body dead perhaps an hour.

He jumped as Nadya began a high keening noise, making as if to walk right into the mound of coals. "No! Stop Nadya!" He leapt to grab her around the waist and dragged her back, collapsing on the ground beside her, trying to cover her mouth with his hands to stop her growing wails. "Shhh, they will hear us, we must go!"

Shouts came from inside the fortress and Drey knew Belials would be spilling out to escape the fire any moment.

He saw then, the object of Nadya's agony. A charred skeletal lump, still smoldering heavily, coals mounded in a perfect ring around it—toppled in much the same position as Nico. "NO! Oh no, How could they?! I'm sorry my friend...so very sorry." He held her shuddering body for a moment before speaking firmly into her ear. "We *must go* Nadya, there is nothing left to save." He stood but she did not move. Pulling her up, slinging her over his shoulder, he loped off into the night, panting under the weight of her.

They were barely away when shouts and coughing became loud and three men, carrying a fourth, pushed out of the door.

"To the aero! Get him in the aero! I will get the nodes!"

"What about the others?"

"Not worth our lives. We got Balek, let this hellhole burn!"

Drey had dropped them both flat against the ground lest someone spot their moving forms.

Nadya didn't speak as he pressed her to the dew-soaked earth while they watched the aero lift off. She uttered no sound when he forced her to stand, marching her, numb with grief, across the fields in the direction he guessed was north.

Hours later, the rising sun washed gold through scattered clouds and Drey knew he was right. They were headed directly north.

Nadya's voice came small and detached. "Somehow they knew of his betrayal, of his plans...that Nico loved her. They made him watch her b-burn. She was the last blood family I had." She stopped to sob then, curled on the ground while the sun continued to rise, turning the sky fresh and lovely with colors of new blossoms, indifferent to the gruesome night they'd just passed.

He wondered if any others had survived the fire. "Your instincts are quite something." He pulled the water jug and a crumbly cake from their pack.

She sat up to accept the water he offered. Sipping, she watched him eat with golden eyes, gone dull under the quiet sky.

All day they walked through thick forest, pausing to fill the water jug at a small pond Nadya had smelled from far off. Pushing through rushes abloom with delicate pink flowers, Drey broke off bits of hornwort and cotton grass, his pockets half full from mindless gathering habits before he remembered he wouldn't be able to examine them, had no collection to study. Keeping the watermint and hawthorne to eat, they walked on, seeing no one and no roads—save the trails of animals.

Nadya had wept most of the morning, silent tears that faded by after-noon as she slowed, overcome with exhaustion. "I need to lie down and sleep—just a little while." She begged him over and over but he insisted they keep moving, afraid still that Balek might be searching. Finally taking her hand, he pulled her along behind him like a small child.

"Do you need to eat? Is this why you have no energy?" The thought came late in the day when his own stomach started audibly gnawing at him.

"Yes. I need to hunt. Is better during night, but I am too tired..." Her tears had started again.

"Alright. Let's look for a place. Sleep awhile and hunt later."

He gathered sticks, built a small fire as the dropping sun left the forested floor cold and damp. Searching in widening circles, he found various edible greens, sharply bitter, and a handful of late, wild berries to supplement the tasteless grain cakes in his pack. Only one left after tonight—still, he could survive just fine on the things that grew here. There should be nuts around too.

Nadya slept as if dead, seeming to barely even breath as she lay curled on her side against the rock face he'd chosen. They had no blankets, nothing but the clothing they wore.

Drey scooped together forest debris, cutting branches of thick leaves until he had fashioned a nest of sorts. With the leafy branches layered over top, he hoped to pass the night in relative comfort.

A WELCOME SMELL WOKE HIM. Nadya glanced over her shoulder when he stirred, her eyes a sore red but her movements quick and sure again.

"Good, you are awake. I brought you meat. The smell makes me ill, perhaps you can finish the cooking?" She held out a stick with strips of unidentifiable flesh wrapped around it. Drey forced himself to wait until he was sure it was cooked enough before devouring it, as if he hadn't eaten in days. Nadya had gone to find water—and escape the offensive roasting meat. He wondered if it was her banpiro preference, or the scent memory of her sister being burnt to charred bones.

The days bled together, indifferent, except more were rainy than not. Drey shivered and shook, walking faster to generate more body heat. Most nights were short with misery and wet chill as they huddled together under the dryest covering they could forage.

"How much longer?" He tried not to ask it too often. The answer was always the same.

"I do not recognize anything yet, so I do not know."

They talked of their families and homes the most, although Drey had many curious questions about her species, how they came to be, the uniquities of living among humans versus staying to themselves, how many there were, how they procreate, how exactly their digestive system worked.

In return he told her much of Atlantis life. The never-ending greed for knowledge, the extreme beauty and pristine order that felt exhausting so that it was a relief when he traveled to other continents for his work.

She seemed dazzled by his telling. "It is the homeland of my kind you know. Long long ago, but we have not forgotten. Though it sounds more splendid in your telling than ours."

"You should come for a visit. My mate and daughters would love you..."

Her face showed pain. "I fear seeing you will always remind me of these terrible deeds. Of my lost Mahlia. You are kind to say this, that I may come meet your people. You are a very good man."

"But surely you will have healing? From all that was done to you?"

She shrugged. "Like what? It is too shameful. I will not even speak of it! And I am the healer for my kind. Though it is more a scientific understanding that we use than human healing practices. Our bodies know how to heal themselves."

"There is nothing that will help you? But you have been hurt...terribly!"

Again the careless shrug. "My body is fine. The hurt is only in my mind now."

"We have restoration for all of it. To neutralize the memories and release the trauma at least. If you have no remedy, come to us. We will care for you."

She considered this is silence for awhile. "Perhaps...I will see how it is, after some time."

IT WAS THIRTEEN DAYS LATER—OR maybe fourteen—when she stopped very still, turned in circles and sniffed the air, nostrils flared. "We are home. I know this place, smell the deer herds? We breed them—our continuous supply of blood, so we do not hunt our lands empty."

Drey shook his head. "I smell only the forest."

She laughed for the first time since he'd known her, golden eyes seeming lit from within again, her whole body coming alive. "It is this way. Come. If we hurry we may be home before night."

They lived around the shores of a large lake, in sprawling homes as well built as any in Atlantis. Hundreds of years of loving craftsmanship showed in the lines and shapes of their wood and stone architecture. Perhaps two thousand humans and banpiro called this town home. It had a thriving market and a temple, "Where the humans worship their strange gods. Banpiro revere only the earth, the nature." Nadya explained.

Her "family", which she said were not blood relatives but more like a small pack that lived together, rejoiced at her return and wept bitterly at the loss of Mahlia. Inquiring of Drey if there was any way to avenge her.

"It would mean war with Belial." Drey told them honestly.

"Do not worry about that now! Not to speak of it again! We must see this man safely to his home." Nadya commanded them.

SO THEY SENT HIM, well provisioned on horses, with Nadya and two more family members, to the nearest port town, only a short day's ride. She paid a small fortune to buy his comfortable passage directly to Atlantis on a cargo ship. When he thanked her, Nadya waved it off.

"Pah! Money is nothing to us! We live so long it is work to *not* accumulate wealth."

It was harder than they imagined, saying goodbye. "Tragedy binds the heart." Nadya reminded.

"Please come to visit me soon, dear one." Drey begged, hugging her hard lithe form. "I cannot help but think, despite the evil circumstances, that all of this has a greater meaning. Perhaps you are destined to come to Atlantis."

"I will not forget your kindness... Are you safe there? Will they come to finish you?" She searched his eyes for the truth of his worry.

"Right now Balek most likely thinks we're dead, so that gives me an advantage. I will find a way to protect myself and my family. If nothing else, we can move to High City and live under their protection. Though, what I have to tell them may start a war...the blood penalties are high between Atlantis and Belial."

Nadya sighed the sigh of an old woman. "War is a terrible price to pay. Perhaps you should come live here! If ever you need me, or my people, we will help. Go now. Go to your family and be grateful for them every day."

18

TAYA

9,982 BCE HIGH CITY, ATLANTIS

"The whole of science is nothing more than a refinement of everyday thoughts".

— ALBERT EINSTEIN

TAYA

*A*t last it was done. The three crystal's entire eighty-foot lengths were covered in patterns. She'd even changed their colors using a simple device that reconfigured molecular patterns, resulting in various colors.

The platinum offered sacred geometry. A ring of Life Flowers wrapped its very center, their many-layered design representing the twelve strand DNA from which original Human Bodies were structured. Spreading up and down from there were symmetrical rings of the creation process expressed in geometric shapes in descending stages, until the very base and the very tiptop were ringed with single points, the originating point of the consciousness of Source. The "In the beginning..."

The blue crystal mapped this universe with astrology symbols marking the location of galaxies, their planets and suns—even moons and star groups. She'd had to borrow actual maps from the Oracles and the

Temple of Dreams, aghast at her own ignorance. At first glance, the Crystal looked to be mostly blank, reflecting, accurately as possible, the vast empty spaces.

The emerald one told a story of Earth's creations with images crowded tightly together, contrasting the scattered bareness of the Universe Crystal. Symbols of air, water, earth, and fire ringed the base, with plant life, bacteria, sea-life, reptiles, birds, and mammals ascending up in an explosion of verdant life forces. A woman stood near the top with her arms halfway wrapping the crystal, cherishing all this life. On the opposite site, a man matched her posture, their hands linked as if both embraced the earth itself.

"I depicted it in a linear story."

"Very clever! Ziel beamed approval. "I believe your designs will be their names; the Creation Crystal, the Universe Crystal and the Earth Crystal."

TWO DAYS before she returned home, Taya and Ziel gathered the twelve Programmers he'd carefully handpicked over the last moon. Each of them must be someone Ziel could trust with such a secret—plus skilled enough for the type of programming specific to such oversized Crystals.

He hadn't chosen the most powerful or gifted. Instead, these were the quiet ones, those content to remain in the background. One by one they'd met with Ziel privately to discuss the nature of what was being asked of them.

He gave each the same enigmatic speech. "If you agree to this task, you will be administered a drug. No trace will remain in your memory once it's finished. This protects you. I cannot tell you any more, except that you will be serving Atlantis."

And so it was that shortly after dawn, twelve Programmers were injected by Ziel and Taya. Packed into tiny maze trolleys, they rolled like a train through the endless tunnels.

Taya realized this was the first time she'd used the main entrance, guarded day and night. No one gained entry unless accompanied by Ruler Ziel or one of his small council.

Arrived and assembled in the Crystal Cathedral, Ziel commenced with instructions. These twelve were well versed in the programming of crystals but still they gasped when they saw the size.

Ziel checked the drug levels in their blood, while Taya handed out copies of diagrams showing how the molecular structure of each Crystal was to be arranged. This would be accomplished by combining and magnifying the mind power of these twelve. All of their highly developed minds focused on the same thing, directed through a machine which magnified energy a thousand times over. It would literally rearrange the physical structure of that which was focused on.

The machine was set up. About four feet tall and two feet wide, the focusing machine looked like an oval made of glass with a triquetra drawn in the middle. Cords attached to twelve points of the symbol on the glass panel, their other ends held to the third eye of each participant with a crystal studded band encircling the head. The band's crystals were placed at key energy points on the skull, but the cone-shaped crystal directly over their pineal glands were what gathered and focused the intentions of their thoughts.

The work began. One hundred percent of the mind power of these twelve people stayed focused, unwavering on the first part of the process; the destabilization of each crystal's molecules. This took a full hour. Once they reported that the breakdown was complete, Taya called for a rest before phase two. They drank water and ate, shaking out muscles, letting the mind recharge.

Crystals used by Atlanteans in day to day life could be re-coded by one Programmer in just minutes to an hour depending on the complexity of the function needed. The list was long of what crystals were used for. Communication. Storing information, audio, visual or thoughtform. Cleansing or raising energetic frequency for everything from plants and animals to humans, earth and water. Many methods of healing. City, country, planet or universal navigation. Lighting. Powering a myriad of machines.

Returning to the process, they held focus on the new structure of the molecules in graduated complexity ending with programs that would receive information from whomever "played" a certain sequence of the surface designs. Once connected to the grid spanning all of Atlantis, the Crystals would upgrade basic energy collection and utility usages auto-matically, as needed. They would require specific sound and touch sequence frequencies for more sensitive functions such as high-energy outputs and accessing information from the grid. It would take a complex combination before their destructive capacity could be accessed.

The entire day was spent setting and stabilizing the new molecular designs, and finally, connecting the Crystals to the grid.

The programmers slumped in spacey exhaustion on the long trundle back to the surface. Ziel had arranged a dormitory in the palace where he could monitor them. Each of them ate a large meal dense with revitalizing nutrients and fell into bed where sleep could replenish as well as purge the drugs from their systems.

The next morning Ziel ran simple tests to ensure no trace remained in their conscious memory of the work they had completed.

ON HER LAST day in High City, Taya travelled early to check on the newly programmed Crystals. She tested them, pleased with the responses, results surpassing her expectations. "Oh you beautiful things!" She murmured. "I shall miss you as if you were my children."

That night, Ziel had a special feast prepared of all the things Taya especially liked. They tarried at his pretty rosewood table, celebrating this completed task, this monumental step that could change Atlantis' future.

By their second bottle of exotic wine, Ziel grew melancholy. They discussed the things she would miss about High City—and those she was glad to leave behind. They agreed she would return at least once a year to retrain herself as "Keeper of the Crystals", and adjust or upgrade them if needed.

Tongue loosed by the wine, Ziel admitted another hidden fear. "It's been called Black Matter, also known as Anti-Matter. There are events not recorded in any official history, things my predecessor told me. Best I can understand, they saw it as a way to create time travel, portals, so they could change history and shape events any way they liked. But they didn't realize how very very destructive it can be."

Taya was round-eyed, asking questions. She'd never heard of antimatter.

"Explained very basically," Ziel expounded, "it is a reversal of the creation process. Atoms are given a negative polarity which create an energy or matter-eating black hole. The experiments began affecting the very grid our universe is created on. I suspect it contributed heavily to the destruction of that epoch, wiping out knowledge of antimatter, resetting humanity to a much earlier age, far far away from such danger. It was like handing charged laser weapons to toddlers and setting them loose. They neither understood the power, nor considered the outcome."

Draining his wine cup, Ziel peered into the bottle with one eye, grunting disappointment at its void. "We approach that fatal knowledge again. Our own scientists have discovered the existence of what they're calling 'unelement' and they have very good ideas of how it could be used. Of course, the Rulers and I have stopped it in its tracks but we cannot monitor all of Atlantis—much less the rest of the world. And if *we're* on the brink of it, who else might be? I worry too much, I know. It's just irritating to repeat the same mistakes over and over. Irritating and wasteful!"

19

BARGAIN OF A LIFE

9,982 BCE CHIFFON, ATLANTIS

"Existence is a strange bargain."

— WILLIAM COWPER

DREY

*H*e arrived home before Taya was back from High City. No one had even missed him. No one knew of his dramatic and nasty brush with death.

He spoke with Sage half the night, while the twins slept, pouring out the story in all its ugliness. "I guess we should pack—take the girls and leave for High City at first light..." Drey paused to inhale the clementine steam of a new batch of tea, pushing down the panic rising within. They'd gone through numerous pots. "...so I can tell Ziel, and whoever else needs to hear my story, of the atrocities Mardu and his son are committing."

"Mm. Perhaps..." Sage sipped from her mug "but for what purpose?"

"What purpose?! They must be punished! What they did to Nadya. The inhumane testing on those animals. Stealing me! There must be atonement, and confiscation of these nodes we made for them. No one should have such a thing, there is no positive use for them."

"Yes, but you are speaking of the *leader* of the Belial nation, not some random outlier. This man commands an army Drey. Do you think he will submit quietly to directions from people he despises? And what would their atonement be for what they've done? We do not punish, we reform. Do you really think for a moment that Mardu would allow his *son* to be kept at our Aades of Sacrifice? We hold no authority over them."

"We have the blood code…"

"Yes and it applies when a Belial takes the life of an Atlantean. From what you told me, no Atlantean died at their hand." Sage spoke with compassion even as she reasoned against his outrage.

"So, their kidnapping of me, their intent to kill me will not matter?"

"Of course it will! If you take this to Ziel he will involve our military and demand retribution from Mardu. *Because* it is you, it will be personal to Ziel and he'll most likely overreact. Mardu will retaliate. I have no doubt at all that this incident, once reported, will lead to war. It's been brewing for centuries and the Belials need only the tiniest trigger to vent generations of rage against Atlantis. They'll need absolute victory or be forced to leave our continent—abandon everything—if they lose. The stakes are too high. They will go for our throats."

Drey nodded and slumped back. A look of bitter defeat settling on his face. "I understand what you're saying, the stakes are disproportionate to the wrong done me. Perhaps disproportionate to even the loss of my life."

"Oh sweet son." Sage stood, moving to his side, "You, Taya, the girls are my heart. I cannot bear the thought of losing any one of you. I'm only giving you all the facts so you can make a decision you won't regret." She held his bowed shoulders, tears in her eyes as Drey finally broke, sobbing in her arms like a small child stuck in the futile space between two impossible choices.

THEY ROUSED QUIETLY the next morning, waiting until the twins were at their classes to resume the conversation.

Drey had wanted to keep Ahna and Aiela home, paranoia convincing him that Mardu could come for them at any moment. But Sage gently overruled him. "They'll be as safe in town as they will be here. And we need time to find a solution."

Ahna, as usual, didn't miss a thing. "Look! I lotht a tooth… Papa *whath wrong*? Why are you upthet?"

"I have to decide between two terrible things." Drey refused to lie to her. She knew when he did anyway.

Ahna kissed his cheek then poked him in the ribs. "Tho make up a new choith thilly, thomthing not terrible."

"How come you're so much smarter than me?" Drey wiggled his eyebrows and tweaked her freckled nose, her absolute certainty in him a comfort.

Her twiggy shoulders lifted to her ears as she flashed him a gap-toothed smile, reassured by his teasing. "I don't know. ELAAAA!" She hollered unceremoniously, "TIME TO GO. C'mon Papa," tugging at his hand, "today we thould thkip all the way to thchool. You haven't forgotten how to thkip have you?"

Sage was waiting when Drey returned, her face a study of morphing emotions, like clouds re-arranging images in cross-air currents. "We'll have to move to High City for your protection."

Drey was shaking his head even before she finished. "Taya would *hate* living there! I would too. There has to be another way. What if I went to Mardu, made a vow to him that I will protect and keep my knowledge of his nodes from the Rulers in exchange for leaving me and my family alone? That technology must be important to him with all the trouble they went to. Maybe I could make him believe that I will not seek retribution, will not tell Ziel of Balek's atrocities, will not start a war against him. All that I ask is the lives, the safety of me and mine." His words spilled out, piling atop one another, reaching for some hanging hope, a return of security to his shattered world.

Sage sat staring at him for many moments. "It's the risk of a lifetime. The biggest game you'll ever play—trusting the man who hopes his son killed you."

"No matter what I do, I risk losing". Drey ran frustrated hands through unkempt sand-colored hair. "He'll find out soon enough that I'm alive. I can't do nothing. That's certain death for us."

"I don't know Drey...let's meditate on it today, sleep on it tonight. We have one day left before Taya gets home."

They sat in silence, each sinking in the rising maelstrom of worry, fear, and choices to be made.

MARDU CAME, on Drey's terms, to a busy Atlantean town at the Belial border, stuffed with Atlantis guards.

Once the two of them stood alone, facing each other in the town's

Healing Temple, the Belial leader pushed a concealing hood off his great, cruelly handsome head. Drey waited for him to speak first.

"So. You are Drey whom my son swore to me was dead!" Each word he made ominous, bit off with savage, cold disdain.

Drey struggled to stand his ground. "What Balek did to me—to others there—will be seen as a crime between our nations. You know the blood price! And you can scant afford it!" Though his insides quaked, he refused to cower as Mardu pressed his menacing face closer, growling a taunt.

"Then either die quietly or it is war! Tell me, will you give your life to save your precious Atlantis? To keep your country intact? We are a power you no longer understand. If we go to war, I *will* become the Ruler of your people."

Drey didn't blink. "You forget, I hold the key to your new nodes. *This,* this knowledge is what I am prepared to bargain. To prevent war between our people, I vow to you, I will not reveal what your son did, or what I know of your nodes, not even to my closest ones. *BUT,* it is all written— the entire account, sworn by me, already placed in the hands of people you will never find. If I am harmed, if anyone I love is harmed by you, that knowledge will release directly to the Rulers and to our military leaders. You know as well as I, if they learn of this, there will be a reckoning." Somehow, Drey held Mardu's gaze without wavering, looking into an abyss of unknown threats. He had no faith in this man. Could only hope that it would be enough, this threat of war, this pawn of knowledge, for which they had risked stealing him away in the first place.

Mardu

Mardu held his silence long, staring down at this smaller man who bargained so boldly for his life—felt scraps of respect niggle into his considerations. Drey could have taken his family and disappeared. Could've let their nations go to war and used his knowledge to cripple the Belials. Could have simply assumed that Mardu would never find out he had escaped the fire and lived still. Instead, here he stood, toe to toe with his greatest adversary, asking that they trust the word of each other.

Atlanteans held their vows sacred, Mardu had been trained in the same ways. He knew that Drey considered the vows he proposed soul-binding. Those of the Law of One lived as if each lifetime was only a chapter in the bigger story. Every action was chosen in respect of the law of karma.

Karma can kiss my flatulent ass! Mardu thought it all hypothesis

134

anyway. No one had ever proven Karma existed, or any other "laws" they held to dear. *I make my own story. I know the law of free will better than they do and I shall use it well. Freely. Still, it is not yet time to take Atlantis. Better I stick to my plan.*

He rearranged his features into a condescending smile, "You can keep your pitiful life Drey—and your pathetic knowledge. Doubtful we will use the nodes anyway, but hold tight to your wee drop of delusional security, and never stop being wary. One day, I may decide to break your vow..." He yanked the hood back up and turned to leave, relieved that the muta key would not be revealed, that his hand would not be forced. A war against Atlantis now could ruin everything.

Drey called after him, "I vow to you Mardu..."

He paused at the door, keeping his back to Drey.

"...if you come against Atlantis in any way, my knowledge will be released."

Mardu snorted. "If I come against Atlantis your life will be forfeit anyway you look at it. You'll be dead long before as well as any..."

Drey

Mardu's boredom-infused words faded out as the door closed behind him. Drey tried to still his breathing.

Had he made the right decision?

Was it folly to believe he could bargain with one of such dark power?

Would it be enough?

20

THE HAMMOCK

9,980 BCE CHIFFON, ATLANTIS

"Nothing in life is to be feared, it is only to be understood. Now is the time to understand more, so that we may fear less."

— MARIE CURIE

AHNA

*A*hna curled like a young leaf in a storm. Her hammock swayed in the considerate fragrant breeze that her twisty old rubber tree filtered through fat glossy leaves the color of dark olives. It was sometime after midday meal and she missed her father intensely. She'd escaped from the usual hubbub of eating and play to come out here. To examine, and perhaps undo her fears with the stillness and freedom of the forest.

Aiela missed her presence immediately. Even as Ahna was ghosting into the forest edges, her sister had sent a big question mark wrapped in concern. Translation, "Where are you going? Is everything alright? Do you need me?" All contained in the barest graze of one tiny thought.

Ahna sent back a picture of Papa reading to them in the hammock that she was fixing to climb into, along with a mist of sad calm. Translation, "I miss Papa too much. Wanna be in my hammock."

They both knew Aiela would make certain no one else sought her.

When you are ten, one moon cycle without your father feels endless.

Ahna thought about explaining this carefully to Papa when he got back. Maybe he'd forgotten what it was like to be a child. Maybe he would stay home more often if he knew that his absence felt like a hollow in her chest stuffed with stale air, tinged now with a new unwelcome fear that he might not come back.

Loud mewls announced the arrival of Yowl, her cat. He was a panther really, but most people mistook him for a female lion because of his tawny color. She didn't remember when she started calling him Yowl. Mama said it was because he "talked" as much as a person, in mews, purrs, growls and most of all, yowling. Papa brought him back from a trip, abandoned—probably for being the runt of the litter—and dying. Aiela had nursed him back to life but somewhere along the way he became Ahna's pet.

Perching on the limb just above, he licked his paws as if unconcerned, long tail flicking back and forth just within reach.

"Thank you for coming. You always know when I'm sad." She wrapped her hand around the silken rope of a tail, sliding it down to the tip.

Reaching for the journal tucked inside the largest pillow, she started writing.

"Awful awful vision this morning right in the middle of meditation. If I write it, I will remember it all for Aiela—not that I'd forget. Wish I could!

Aiela and me were somewhere else, gone, I don't know where. Papa and Mama were having fun and so so happy because they were playing. In a place that was real bright. Lots of sand? Not sure. It was just mostly light. There were big big men there watching them but Papa didn't know they were watching him and Mama. Then the ground started shaking and it was loud. Everywhere was LOUD. The earth was loud and moving and there were mountains. Anyway they were scared then and they wanted to run only they couldn't and then something hit them, whatever the noise was hit them and they were buried in it and it just kept coming and burying them for a long long time and then they couldn't breathe anymore. The big men watched all of it and didn't do a thing. When Papa and Mama couldn't breathe I felt their sadness. They were just pure sad and they wanted Aiela and me. That's all there was and then I went out of class and cried because it felt worse than it sounds, now that I say it write it. It was scary and I'm trying to stop seeing it and I hope it's not real. What if it's real?? It can't be. I won't let it be and neither will Aiela."

SHE AND AIELA would talk about it, whispering in bed tonight, deciding together if they should tell Mama. Sometimes they worried that telling anyone might make things real.

Ahna dozed, releasing the disturbance of these thoughts into the fern green canvas hammock that Papa had hung for her on their seventh birth day. Mama had made it sturdy, strong enough that all four of them could pile in together. It was a rectangular shape with shallow boxy sides. Woven into the bed was a picture of a mighty rooted tree filled with birds, taking up the entire length of the hammock. The birds were very bright colors—every size and shape imaginable. There were firm little pillows and a flap that buttoned over for a blanket. It was the most beautiful and precious thing that she owned, filled with memories of love and family.

Even before the hammock, she used to run with Yowl to this tree. Its sprawling dark branches comforted her when she needed space or had a particularly difficult problem. Following Yowl, climbing like a wiry monkey, she'd go high enough to escape whatever plagued her. Papa said it was her sacred spot and it must be honored, so he'd blessed it for harboring his daughter and then adorned it with the glorious hammock. They came here often for picnics and tag games and reading.

A long time ago, when Papa stayed home with them because Mama needed to be gone, they came every single day to read a story together. It was one of many books that Papa and Mama took turns reading aloud.

AHNA WOKE WITH A JOLT. Yowl's tail tickled her cheek and Aiela shouted inside her head. "Ahna! COME BACK!"

She sent a picture of herself running, to let Aiela know she was coming, surprised that she'd heard words. They couldn't usually send each other words very well. Pictures, yes—feelings were easiest. Words were hard to get across.

"Bye!" She shouted to Yowl's form still stretched on his limb. Already on the ground and running she heard a faint chiming sound.

Teacher was stirring the singing bowl to alert everyone it was time to come in for last studies. Today was Fourthday and Ahna's almost favorite teacher instructed them on Fourthday. Each teacher had their own unique calling of the students, except Firstday teacher, who just waited until everyone assembled of their own accord. He was Ahna's very favorite and most always the students came early to hear his jokes and help him feed his odd collection of sea creatures, so he didn't really need to call them anyway.

Fourthday Teacher Mia instructed in Meditation, Music and Writing. She played the singing bowls often and was known as a Maester of the Bowls, even in High City. Ahna felt the growing sound in her heart chakra. Whimsical ringing strummed the center of her breastbone before the rich notes reached her ears. Soon, she was within sight of the village center, running through Chiffon's fruit orchards and sprawling vegetable gardens that the forest abruptly butted against.

A grouping of tall, white buildings clustered serenely beyond a quartz wall. The wall—not even as tall as Ahna was now—shone purest white in the sunshine, surrounding the entire village. Inside it, the buildings massed, reaching up like ordered mountain ranges in unplanned peaks. There were lovely courtyards of manicured grass or baked white bricks. Pathways, pebbled with small round pea gravel, also white, guided her through this small grotto that nestled along Atlantis' northwestern edge. Ranging from one to five stories high, the buildings that clung onto and held each other were clearly built in stages with many generations of additions and renovations. The only unifying aspect to the motley of architecture was that all the materials used were white. White bricks, white adobe—sometimes ornamented and textured with white seashells, white stonework, and in a few places, silvery-white, peeled logs.

Flowers grew everywhere during spring, summer and autumn moons. Riotous colors filled trellises, climbing buildings and courtyard walls. Hanging bouquets and pots of exotic shapes shocked the eye with their boldness against all that aged white—a visual beauty rivaled only by the scents.

At least five-hundred people lived in the village itself, with many more spread into the countryside around it.

Teacher Mia sat calmly in the alcove entrance to her suite, swirling her crystal wand outside the bowl one last time, when Ahna arrived, breathless. Pausing to bow respectfully and remove her sandals, she panted, "I'm sorry I'm late."

Glancing at the words curved over the doorway and touching a hand to her heart, she quoted them dutifully, "Beauty in mind, body and soul" before crossing the threshold.

Teacher Mia's suite had four rooms. The inner two were her private residence and the outer two were for student instruction. Known in the village as the Meditation Room, the first and largest space was favored by adults too. A handful of villagers used it before sunrise on any given morning, practicing introspective peace here in this unusual space.

The Meditation Room was quite an artistic tribute. Its pure white flagstone floor was glazed to a sparkling shine. It held cool in the summer and warmth in the winter due to a system of small tubing that circulated water beneath the flagstones, water of whatever temperature the heater/cooler was set to. During a technology project long ago, when Firstday teacher Nate began here with his initial class of students, a particularly bright student had proposed this system. Now its use had spread all over Atlantis.

The room's ceiling was very high, domed and inset with sunlight panels which had to be cleaned often because of the birds that perched and nested all over the taller neighboring roofs, making a splattered shitmess of them. Firstday teacher Nate said perhaps that's why the original planners made all the buildings white, to camouflage the gallons of bird doo.

Ahna passed quickly through this septagon-shaped room where each of the seven walls was molded with images the color of the seven "earth" chakras. Hanging from its domed ceiling were five tapestries in pale watercolors depicting the five "heaven" chakras. But Ahna loved the earth chakra walls because that is what she understood, what she could see and touch.

It began to the left with the root chakra wall; things nature had colored any shade of red. A tiny, pale pink fetus grew inside a dark womb, purpley-red umbilical cord connecting the two. Perfectly molded red roses bloomed in three stages of flower. There were red sea bass, strawberries and passion. Raw crusted rubies split open to reveal their sharp crystalline centers. Smiling lips contrasted hot anger. There were hearts pumping blood and predatory swooping redhawks, a scarlet sunrise, sweet red wine and nipples. Maple leaves turned the brick red of autumn. Fire beetles sparkled. A cardinal carried its pale pink earthworm. Cranberry sprays, long pointy hot peppers, and ladybugs faded into the background.

Ahna liked the green heart chakra wall best. A bridge between the yellow solar plexus and the blue throat chakra, the heart chakra transforms simple, physical experience into higher meaning. Or simplifies things too abstract to grasp into the lower senses of earth. The green wall was framed on two sides by vibrant trees. Each branch had varying shapes of leaves reaching across the apex of the wall. Blended onto one branch was a thick, straw-green boa constrictor. Tiny neon frogs were suspended mid-hop. A praying mantis bowed and a pair of parrots perched, while long-bodied grasshoppers and a fat luscious caterpillar crawled among the leaves. Feathery fronds of emerald ferns spiked across the bottom of the wall, as if they indeed grew from the white stone floor. Collaged into the center were limes in shades of yellow green, a vine of snow peas going from flower to pod, sprigs of bright shamrocks and sunrosened pears. Depicted in every possible shade of green were cacti, asparagus, envy, ivy, lettuce, juicy kiwi slices, pistachio nuts, seaweed, artichokes, fresh, raw and unripened things, emeralds, hope, jade and spring. Traditionally, green was the color of success. Cleverly woven in, were malachite, olives, immortality and staring green cat-eyes.

Aiela's favorite, of course, was the inner-eye chakra wall with its queenly purple royalty. Dark plump grapes dreamt of transforming someday into a pleasing red wine, cycling back again to the base chakra, where all earth life begins. Rosy purple mountain ranges reached to the heavens across the top of the wall, footed with fields of irises, phlox and heather. There were odd shapes and hues of bruises, clusters of amethyst and sea serpents that flowered and morphed into dragons. Purple is the color of dreams and wisdom, royalty, lilacs, plums and cabbage. Featured prominently, were the luminous violet pearls that black sea clams spun inside their mystical, midnight shells.

The last student to arrive, Ahna bowed a sort of apology to the class, already humming and singing this afternoon's lesson. Early in the day was Meditation and then Writing, with Music following afternoon rest. Today, music class was vocals—not easy for Ahna with her soft breathy voice, but Teacher Mia made it interesting and fun at least.

She found Aiela sitting cross-legged on floor cushions, surrounded by her usual adoring friends. A girl knelt behind Aiela, fingers flying, twining her long, shiny hair into braids. She must have been working on it during most of rest-time because there were about twenty braids, some very thin and others thicker. It made her look alot like Mama. Aiela's hair had always been a magnet for exotic hair stylists, unlike Ahna's, thin and straw-blonde, managing to always look choppy. Settling in next to her sister, Ahna touched Aiela's hand in greeting and a silent "I'm better now".

She began to hum along with the harmony. Back in her center, feeling balance restored, she let herself go into the music of the moment.

MARDU'S MUTAZIO

9,979 BCE SOUTH AMERICA MUTAZIO CAMP

"...the objective was to fully experience earth life. Tho' unpredictable and treacherous. Tho' monotonously grueling. To glean the sweetness, to treasure the subtle beauties, to find the love and expand it. To choose what will shape you."

— ATLANTIS BOOK OF DEATH

MARDU

"*D*ominus Mardu." General Rogan bowed. "Sorry about the flies. We've had a dozen deaths in this camp alone. Virus outbreak. The bodies are being burned...You're here sooner than I expected." General Rogan hefted Mardu's bags, leading him towards a gaping cave entrance.

"Yes, I find out more when I deviate from plans. Hot as a cunt here! Is it always like this?" Mardu eyed his favorite General, swabbing sweat from his forehead then jerked a thumb back at the aero, "I've brought you several barrels of beer, best batch I could find. A small payment for your loyalty and service. I know it hasn't been easy running this miserable lot of animals. I'd hoped to relieve you sooner, give you some time off at home....or whatever recreation you'd like, but there are too few I trust. If you can hang on for a while longer we'll finish this business. We're getting close. I want to plan the Greece invasion while I'm here—with your help.

It's time. I believe we are ready. I'll want you to take the lead of course and I need to know who else you want beside you."

Mardu took in the expansive dim inside headquarters, relieved by abrupt, deep-earth-cooled air. This cave was one of many in a landscape of choppy ridges and valleys, mazed with naturally carved pockets in the earth. Extensively expanded, it served as quarters for the muta handlers. A table was laid with freshly roasted meats. Farther back Mardu espied beds separated by thatched screens, crude but serviceable.

General Rogan nodded once, gestured at the waiting food and deposited Mardu's bags behind a screen creating a small room of its own. "Please sit Dominus, you must be hungry."

Mardu poked at it. All manner of living things served as food in these camps.

"It's lamb and veal. Three-three-oh-two-six, there are barrels in the aero. Bring them here." Rogan spoke to a muta, smaller than normal, standing in the shadows.

Mardu hadn't seen it, so still it had been and he startled when it stepped into the light, on its way to obey. Sparse black hair was bound into stringy braids partially exposing its scalp. No nose—save two nostril holes—topped thick lips. Its bone structure was lopsided, mismatched, creating an effect of different people cobbled into one. Only a few inches taller than Mardu, it had breast points under its short, sleeveless tunic. Crudely tattooed numbers 33026, adorned its neck, with a matching tattoo on its right forearm.

Mardu grimaced, "You let those things in here? Its grotesque! I thought we put down the deformed ones."

Rogan nodded. "We do—if their deformities prevent service. This one's just ugly. No lack of ability though and smarter than the others. She's useful as a cook and household servant so I kept her. She understands more than most, but is mute since birth. I'm told her mother hid her from us until the child could show how useful it could be."

"I see. She's not a breeder...?"

Rogan shook his head. "Inside's as deformed as her face. No uterus."

Onus Belial, right up to the moment he died, had never ceased striving to realize his duel dreams: to rule Atlantis and to discover a way to immortality. All manner of atrocities had been committed by the Sons of Belial in the ensuing experiments. Mutating and cloning humans was among the first. When the Belials figured out how to custom-make humans that lived to adulthood and could function, they set about cloning as many as they could.

These current mutas were closer to an animal in intelligence, but also easily trained, a great improvement on earlier generations—though occasionally with unexpected, or hideous, side effects.

These warrior Mutazio were bred solely for enormous size, mixing human DNA with particular genes from giant apes. Standing between seven and twelve-feet tall, they ranged from bone-thin, to elephantine-ponderous, to apelike-muscular.

A ratio of five males to every female were bred.

The side effects from cloning were as varied and odd as mixed fruit in an orchard created by children. A full third were partially or fully bald. When they had hair, it was black and wild as an orangutang's. Some had extra large skulls, all had unusually dense bones, and many had double rows of teeth or extra digits on their hands and feet. Their features were blunted, overt, animalistic. Many of them could not talk at all and communicated with their hands or by grunts, howls and shrieks. Those that did talk were the ones who had the most contact with their handlers. They had no names, only the identification number assigned in the lab where they were created. This was tattooed onto their neck, left of the esophagus, where everyone could see it, and onto their forearms where they could see it.

Prior generations had an amputated thumb to clearly distinguish them as a muta, and prevent them from ever claiming to be a "real" human. Their thumbless handprints marked many a cave wall in this deserted country, flashes of mutilation in sooty desperate lives. But not these current generations of giant warriors—a missing digit inhibited their fighting ability, ceasing that practice.

Living in camps, they raised food, trained, and fought. Their Sons-of-Belial handlers were there for one purpose, turning thousands of engineered human giants into weapons of war.

Occasionally, there would be one too soft to survive the camps, perhaps too small to be a fighter. These were taken as house slaves for the Belials or sold in markets across the globe. More often, there were mutas born too deformed for use. Blindness was common. So was missing limbs, and fused joints. All of these were put down as children or even babies, as soon as their lack was discovered, their small carcasses used as meat for the others.

The muta women were used for birthing. Embryos, created in the labs, were implanted into female wombs, two or three fetuses at a time. The turnaround time was roughly eight months, so the women were constantly pregnant. Their bodies wore out fifty percent faster than males. "Real" fetuses, conceived, birthed and grown, lived three times as long as lab grown Mutazio, so traditional conception was also used, inserting the females with frozen sperm taken from young males. Traditional pregnancies weren't popular because of lower production, but necessary to maintain a stronger DNA structure.

The men were castrated after reaching manhood. This cut down their sex drive, creating apter pupils and finer performance in daily drills. It also eliminated the problem of unplanned births, giving the scientists complete control. Synthetic testosterone gave back the aggression required for fighting.

By now, some twenty generations after Onus Belial's time, the Sons of Belial had amassed close to a quarter million Mutazio. Although an imperfect science, it was fairly regulated. The Mutazio hunted, eating mostly meat, supplemented with grains, squashes and cabbage they grew and harvested.

"Tell me about these deaths. A dozen is too many, what's the problem?" Mardu pulled a platter of meat close, and began eating.

"According to the scientists, mixing DNA made the Mutazio vulnerable to all the bacterias and viruses of both species. Viruses that cross the barrier separating animals and humans are becoming something else altogether. I'm told they're evolving too fast to keep up. I've increased our vigilance in the camps, quarantining any that become ill. A graver concern is that humans are susceptible to these new strains. It could conceivably breed an epidemic that wipes us out completely." Rogan explained all this in his clipped efficient way.

Mardu appreciated that his number one General did not waste words, movements or time. "I will give you a dozen scientists. Where do you want them?"

Rogan swatted a fly away, thinking. "They'd work better at more advanced labs, better equipped than the field. I could have samples delivered anywhere...let's set them up at base." He was referring to their main muta research and development laboratory hidden in Temple City. "I'll send samples home with you to get them started. Give me a few days to round up my top people on this and I'll send them to base to work with your group. Our losses are still relatively low. I don't want to reach the point of being unable to keep up. I don't have the manpower to focus on this, with our high populations in the camps."

"Well, I'm not happy to pull my scientists off of projects either. They're close to creating any human behavior we want." He tried the beer he'd brought. Quite inferior to what he had at home but Rogan wouldn't notice. Not out here in the wilds with nothing to compare it to. "Machines and chemicals are the future of controllable humans. Imagine; we become the world power, we control populations, create an entirely new culture paradigm. Virtually wipe out the imperfections that exist in the self-centered Belials *and* the self-righteous Atlanteans. We can balance personalities, perfect appearances, and eliminate unnecessary emotions. It'll be paradise my friend, and they'll look to us as their gods. My trans-mutators are coming up with enhanced animals, suitable as servants. We will recreate the world as it should be." Mardu felt like a god with the endless possibilities, open as the women who gladly spread their legs for him.

Rogan bowed slightly. "Yes… well I appreciate your assistance. It should help us get ahead of a potential outbreak that could delay our plan."

"I've a minor matter before we settle to strategizing." Mardu paused, helping himself to more food. "I will be sending my sons to learn your ways here. Some of them, I hope, will one day serve as Generals. I'd value your opinion on how they conduct themselves, which of them shows promise. You've full authority to discipline them while under your care."

"Tell me of them." Rogan hadn't seen Mardu's boys since they were small.

"Balek, the eldest, is vicious… stupid—but I've no need of his brains." Mardu began. "The willingness—the *pleasure*—he takes in intimidating and killing is useful enough. There's the peculiar talents of silver-tongued Ramon. He manipulates and lies so well, he gets grown men attacking each other on nothing else but his say-so. He thrives on chaos and has discovered how easy it is to propagate. Sarim is physically tough and eager to please. He runs endless errands without question or need for power like the older boys. Norse is the humorous one, always looking for ways to upstage his brothers. Very useful."

Mardu didn't mention the youngest, Carver, the runt off a slave woman. The boy was an embarrassment. Too sensitive, unpredictable, artsy, not to mention, a goddamned cripple. Of all his sons, Carver physically resembled him the most, yet acted the least like him.

Rogan nodded thoughtfully. "It will be good for them to learn the operation and handling of the Mutazio." Chewing in silence then, he paused only to direct the deformed muta in clearing away the food and refilling his mug.

While Rogan savored the inferior brew, Mardu crossed the worn cave floor to fetch Grecian maps from his bags, feeling the boyish joy of plotting adventures. The camaraderie of Rogan's quiet company took him back to when they were young men sleeping rough during Atlantis' endless summers, strategizing games or imagining the dragons they would battle and the heroes they would become. Now, they would create a real war—and win it—together. They would be heroes and much more too. It was close enough he could almost touch it, this lifelong dream, this apex of all that he'd worked so hard for.

22

AIELA'S ROCKS

9,974 BCE CHIFFON, ATLANTIS

"Turning my face to the sunrise, I created a wonder for you. I made the islands of Paradise come here to you, with all their fragrant flowers, to beg your peace and breathe your air."

— STELE OF AMON

AIELA

She ran, chased by shadows of panic and a dark unknown. The steady slap-slap-slap of leather soles against hard-packed earth, rose into the towering tree canopy she fled beneath. Aiela's single goal at this moment was to make it to her rock before the sun broke the horizon. She raced the wild swirl of sunrise pinks and purples with the surety of winning and they spread in all directions around her, washing the leafy ceiling she passed under with silvers, blues and glittering promises of green coming with daybreak.

Behind her sounded the panting of Charl. Aged now, the brindled dog was still determined to follow her to the ends of earth.

Panic gripped, shoved its way into her chest on labored breath just as her dreams did last night. She pushed back, propelling herself even faster. Ebony hair streamed behind her, as wild and unkempt as she felt. She'd done this before, outrun the dream, scrubbed it away with the shadow-demolishing power of the sun. But it came back with the inevitability of sleep, and this time she had drowned. There was no curly haired, dark-eyed man pulling her to safety. And so she ran faster than ever, heart pounding in her ears, eyes desperately seeking her rock, her safety, her sunrise.

She broke free from the trees just as the vast sky melted into a canvas of gold. There it was, her sentinel of stone just twenty paces ahead up the yellow grass hillside. With a final burst of adrenaline, she crested the hill and rounded the silent stones into the security of their cold, solid arms.

Gasping for air, she flopped onto the woven hemp and lemongrass pallet within her cave-like enclosure between three towering stones. As a child she'd felt like a mouse under the giant's chair. Oddly comforted. Protected.

Watching early morning blue fill with innocent light, Charl crowded closer, nosing, then licking her fear-chilled cheek before settling on his haunches, tongue lolling at the rising sun.

The sisters had spent many hours here. It was their palace, fortress, ship, cave, temple, and anything else their imaginations could dream. It was unclear exactly when it had become hers, but somewhere along the way, this was unofficially and silently declared "Aiela's", just as the ancient Eiller tree was claimed by Ahna with her hammock and the great naming ceremony. It wasn't that they didn't spend time in the others 'place'. They were together more than not, but everyone needs a sacred space some-times. With silent understanding, they knew what the other needed.

Approaching their sixteenth birthday, it seemed they sought solitude often, especially Ahna of late. Aiela could feel the changing in her twin just as in herself. But it wasn't like the transitions of younger years. They were growing into individuals more with each passing year and part of her mourned the inseparability of childhood.

Settling lanky limbs into a cross-legged pose, Aiela dug the old ratty cotton blanket from under its rainproof tarp and wrapped it around her, tucking long fingers into soft corners against the morning chill.

Charl whined and leaned into her again. *I'm here. Cheer up.*

She inhaled deep, bringing the salt-tanged morning air up through her body, up her spine to the top of her head and held it, one, two, three, four, five before letting it out in a long whoosh. Twice more, in and out, eyes unfocused on the spectacular morning sea before her. Papa's low melodic voice echoed in the back of her mind... "Send your tailbone cord deep into the earth. Down through mother Gaia's warm layers, brown, black, gold, into her secret blue/green reservoir of life energy. Float around in her essence, let it wash away all the darkness that clings to you."

Stillness at last. Fleeting maybe, but she took it with thanks. Ahna joked that Aiela got all the energy and she got all the brains and Aiela smiled, considering the partial truth of it. It pained her to sit still. Their meditation teacher was sorely tried with her fidgeting and restlessness over the years—which was why she had Zan every third day afternoon. "The still-life tutor", she called him, hoping to get a rise out of him. Instead he bowed deeply and said thank you for the gift of naming bestowed upon him. Hopeless! He was one of the few adults she couldn't ruffle no matter what she tried. (And she had secretly devoted her undying allegiance to him for it.)

Ahna also pointed out the power Aiela had, attracting others with her blazing light and wit. Her adventures *were* legendary. Classmates fluttered like moths to her flame.

She ran a hand over the cold stone walls, needing the familiar grounding force. Today she didn't feel like a flame—more like a soggy cloth flapping in the gales of change.

The panic disappeared, replaced by calmer brooding as she carefully, one step at a time, revisited last night's dream. This particular dream had replayed again and again throughout her childhood. But this time, it had ended different.

Starting, as always, in a boat, a small one made from a yellow wood she couldn't name. They were fleeing—she knew not what, nor where they were going. Nighttime hid a storm's treachery beyond the borders of the tiny boat and the agitated sea lifted and enclosed them in turn. Low clouds pressed down like a smothering gray cloak overhead, reflecting flashes of light that wasn't lightening. Ahna was with her, and a few others and Aiela gripped an oar in her hands, desperately trying, with the help of a man using the other oar, to keep the boat from capsizing. Irregular waves bristled and loomed and she fought them, muscular arms straining. A pale blue linen tunic clung to her body, soaked with frigid ocean spray. Dripping hair slapped against her face in a cyclone unleashed from her long braid. On and on it went, battling the madcap waves. Ahna sat across from her on a plank, small hands anchoring her knees. Aiela knew Ahna was connected with Source, co-creating safe passage for them through the storm. Desperate urgency gripped them all as an impossibly giant wave towered up from the lee side. All in the boat braced except for Aiela. Anger took her and she stood, brandishing her oar overhead, shouting at the flashing sky, "Come on you bastard, do your best—we'll survive! We always survive!" She felt Ahna's hands grip her legs through rough wool pants, trying to yank her down. Then the wave crashed over them, plucking her like a wayward feather from the tiny boat. She crashed against something fixed, sucked down into a swift and shocking black.

That was when she had woke this morning, heart pounding, panic rising.

Always before, the dream ended with hands pulling her to the surface before she crashed or sank. Usually she felt her body stretched on a narrow wood bench and opened her eyes to meet the oddly familiar gaze of a stranger. But not this time.

What did it all mean? Was it just a change in her psyche? Some new fear triggered by the trip they were leaving on today? Or had something happened to change her course in time? Always changes. Always questions.

Everyone said she asked too many questions—as if she could help it that her mind rarely stopped. Letting her thoughts out seemed the only way to sanity.

She thought of her quiet sister, reached towards her. Ahna never judged the crazy wanderings of her mind. Really, Ahna was her rock and she saw in her twin all the beauties of nature that she loved and sought out. Even this thought calmed her.

She felt the gentle nudging of Ahna's mind on hers, visions of eggs and warm bread—so real their scents touched her tongue. Time to go and launch this long anticipated day.

Aiela stretched and bowed to the morning's majestic entrance.

Stowing the blanket back under its oilcloth, she made her way, more slowly this time, back to their simple home. Charl panted along beside her.

AHNA'S JOURNAL

9,974 BCE CHIFFON, ATLANTIS

"Life unfolds itself in mysterious ways."

— KHALIL GIBRAN

AHNA

I will begin at the end and work backwards. Then you will understand what it is like. I am sometimes prophetic, which everyone insists is a gift. Everyone that hasn't experienced it, because anyone who has, knows the truth; It's more of a curse.

Vision:

I stand beside Aiela on a high, stone balcony. The balcony is huge but deserted. Far below us we watch the sea angrily charge at sheer, black coca cliffs that drop from our feet down down down. The cliffs just stoically stand there, ignoring each wave which ends spitting sprays of frustration high in the air. Small prelude of what's coming. The sky is foaming with tarnished silver clouds which toss lightening back and forth across great expanses, the sound of it like a crushing from one horizon to the other. Soon, it will be fully dark. Soon we will no longer be able to see what's coming toward us.

We are beautiful, my sister and I. She's taller than me by almost a hand, with hair so black, it's purple and eyes the color of sapphires. Just like our mother. They look more like twins than El and I. The gown she's wearing has only thin strands crisscrossing her back, exhibiting muscles better defined than most boy's. Her shoulders speak of the stunning power she can wield. Seeing her like this, framed by nature's raw emotions, I understand that she intimidates people. Why have I not noticed that before?

I am very much her opposite. Pale hair, like millet after it's bleached in the field all season. Emerald eyes flinting gold specks and sort of spooky or unsettling I'm told. Built like a bird. Small, light, which gives the impression (incorrectly) that I'm fragile. Less trusting, I feel like I've lived a thousand ages already. We share the same angular structure of our faces with long, proud noses and sensitive mouths. We function as a team without even thinking. Often, I'm the wisdom, she's the power. Although sometimes we switch.

Soaked wind slams into us as lightning reaches greedy fingers closer. We grab hands like we've always done, leaning together into this assault that tastes of seawater and change. Looking at each other with wild smiles, we raise couraged faces towards the storm and begin a cacophony of long mournful howls, half challenge, half approval, mostly just celebrating our naked joy in this moment.

It's something Papa taught us.

End of Vision

I'm sixteen today and no matter how hard I cling to reality, desperately claw onto each present moment, I get bits and pieces of other moments. Other places. Other events. Usually, the visions are about me. Less often, I see someone else's times. Which is probably because I'm very entwined in their energy—like family or close friends. Sometimes, I suspect it's more that I'm picking up on the visions they'd be having if they had the awareness—like I'm tuned in to their frequency. Rarely and randomly, I get visions about strangers. I can't seem to predict what sort of connection will bring visions about people and I don't share these bits of information. People already think I'm odd and sort of keep their distance.

I have few close friends because I can't stand too many. Papa says he worries that I've learned to blend in and be nearly invisible. But it's so people won't be interested in me. It's just that I get so much more from them than I want.

Aiela's abilities are actually useful. She can see the colors of energy and know what someone is experiencing in their body when she touches them. She is already an excellent healer and works with Auntie Sage, who is like that too, but less intense or clear. Aiela has rescued and fixed injured animals as long as I can remember. She'll see the colors surrounding different parts of their body and she'll know where the pain is, or hunger or whatever. Say a healthy leg has a yellowish aura. When it's broken, the color turns murky. If there's infection, grey or brown might creep in. Aura's change depending on lots of things like mood and overall health, but Aiela can tell if a color is off. It can hurt her when she touches someone in pain. It's a quick way to know exactly where the problem is though. She helped birth a baby dolphin recently, in the pod that are all her pets. She limped for almost an entire day just from the memory of it and said it was hell and that she's never ever having babies—possibly never having sex just to make sure.

We're sixteen. Not the time to be making decisions like that.

Today we are headed to High City—for fourteen days!!! We'll have time to see a lot. Papa says there are a few people we must meet and once we've been there and know what it's like then we will make a decision about apprenticing there. It's been expected that we will both apprentice there since we were little. Papa and Mama say it should be our decision though, and the time to make it is finally here. They don't want us to be forced into anything and they didn't want us to pick our life-long work too early when we were still childish and dazzled by things foreign.

I'm very excited. So is Aiela. We've packed and repacked several times. Papa gave us each a crystal to capture the images and sights that we want to remember.

HIGH CITY TRIP

9,974 BCE. HIGH CITY, ATLANTIS

There is magic in names and the mightiest among these words is Atlantis...as if this vision of a lost culture touched the most hidden thought of our soul.

— H.G. WELLS

AIELA

She had anticipated this day for what felt like eons and it didn't yet seem real that it was finally here. Already, she could envision walking through massive gilded doors into Poseidon's Palace, seeing first the immense statue of Poseidon driving his six, winged horses, surrounded by leaping golden dolphins with sea nymphs riding on their backs.

"The base alone," Mama always exclaimed, "is bigger than our entire home!".

As the ground flew by beneath them, Papa and Mama both enthused about the wonders they would see. It was four hours by Aero from their little northern seaside village to High City, which spread inland from the east coast of Atlantis.

The Aero they used was triangle-shaped, painted as brightly as a tropical bird, and seated up to six passengers. It was permitted to fly low for seeing Atlantis' countryside, provided they went slow.

Aiela studied valleys, ornamented with lakes, some ancient, blue and deep, others milky-white and newly-formed as if to cache all the sorrowful grief from Earth's last great upheaval. From this high up, the great continent looked a web of rivers. Natural ones tumbled shallow and fast down from high mountain springs. Man-made canals wide and full-bodied like fat, muddy slugs watered vineyards, orchards, fields and pastures as they lazed past. Dotting all these waterways, boats and barges distributed food and goods across the land.

Villages looked like bouquets of architecture, blending layered eons of past trends with modern ideas that slowly replaced or refaced. "Look there, you can see Honeycomb City." Mama pointed north but it was too far to see well.

There still survived touches of occasional rainforest in the deeper valleys, ever moist with dense canopies of brilliant greens.

Gem, mineral and orichalcum mines, not yet completely healed by overgrowth, still scarred and defaced certain places from an earlier age.

"I can't imagine how any sort of mining was ever tolerated here." Papa frowned at the scars. "Atlantis has always been unstable, irritable as a sea lion in labor, without us poking and pounding into it."

A colorful canyon with mysterious winding patterns and a ragged, naked beauty, lent a sacred diversity to the land sliding past under the Aero.

Papa could hardly keep up, pointing out sites from Atlantean legends and myths, telling them what caused the Earth to take a certain form in this place or that, narrating the scenic glory as they drank it in with appropriate awe and wonder.

"Look! A giant eagle!" Aiela spotted it first, heard her own voice announce it overly loud in her excitement—a childish habit she cringed at now. She had sensed it before she could see it—useful when searching for animals, lost or injured.

"Would you look at that! It's a Horis." Papa said with wonder. "Big enough to carry you away. They nest on cliffs and plague the mountain towns, carrying off their livestock. There's not many left."

Aiela's eyes followed the eagle's spectral glide as he disappeared between the trees below, while her body leaned and swayed, mimicking his path. "He's hunting." She pulled her awareness back. She'd been five, and too connected when monkey died. Auntie Sage had worked with her extensively, teaching ways to ground and block their pain responses when she tuned in to help them.

Still powered by saltwater, even though the crystal grid was mostly used, this outdated Aero was easy to fly and Papa let them take turns. Aeros were used only for travelling long distance. Ground transportation consumed much less energy and was safer. Atlantis had learned costly lessons from pollution, wasteful energy consumption, and the folly of too many aeros in the sky at once.

HOURS LATER, they came in sight of High City's immense outer wall, twenty stories high and blindingly white. Papa turned the aero to circumnavigate their curve towards Old Forest, where they would be staying.

Mama pointed out the outer sprawl of city that flowed beyond the walls in beautiful homes and neat wide roads. Farther out still, were farms dotted with sheep and goats, camels, horses, fowl, deer and elephants. Fields of summer crops in alternating waves of green and gold created a painter's landscape of pattern and movement, a gentle contrast to the colorful spires inside ancient walls that announced one had arrived at the fabled High City of Atlantis. Even from this distance, they could see the outline of Poseidon's Palace ringing Holy Mountain. Papa took the aero a little higher so they could see the beautiful geometry formed by the canals and land rings.

"Ooh," they breathed in unison, eyes drinking in sights below. As she'd expected, no amount of stories prepared Aiela for actually seeing these wonders. The towering wall, grown up from the outermost canal ring, was sleek, flawless. Aeros parked atop it, with people coming and going about their business bringing goods in or taking them home from the city. Two young boys raced towards a staircase that zigzagged down the wall. Another group of people boarded a larger silver aero as they flew over and a few squinted up and waved.

Aiela waved back marveling, "So much going on!" She'd longed for this bustle and rush without ever realizing or being able to name what was missing in their quiet, friendly village on the coast.

"Mama what's your cousin's name again? The lady we're staying with?" Ahna abruptly withdrew from the window. Sinking back in her seat, she stared off in the direction the Aero was headed, at that immense, dark forest in the distance. A worried frown creased between her eyebrows.

"Charis—why? Is everything alright?" Mama moved nearer. Aiela sensed the worry Ahna felt.

Ahna shook her head as if to clear it. "I saw...I saw her I think. She's dark? Short and thick?"

Mama nodded, "Yes, I guess she could be thicker now... She has a narrow jaw, brown eyes, and her nose is longer than mine. What did you see?"

Ahna blew out before she spoke. "Well I don't know if she's well or not. I saw her sitting on a wooden deck and some heavy dark things crawling around her, sort of trying to envelope her. It's hard to explain..." she trailed off and Mama suggested, "Let's wrap her with love-light, shall we?" She took Ahna's hand and they sent their love in a stream of light to surround Charis, wherever she was.

Aiela's attention had already strayed, eyes glued below, "You HAVE to come see this!"

Ahna joined her sister at the window. "The Temple of Healing." Mama smiled from behind. "Wait till you see it up close!"

Oversized and glorious, the Temple of Healing was a sphere, fitted inside the frame of a four-sided pyramid. Melded shades of blue and green stone formed its perfectly square foundation and from it, thick platinum beams slanted upwards until they met, forming the pyramid. Inside this frame, polished blue pectolite formed the bowl of the sphere and clear quartz crystal completed it like a bubble that reflected light in all the colors of the rainbow. From the center of the dome rose a gold, spiral pedestal, supporting a long silver staff that extended to meet the pyramid pinnacle. A snake made of brilliant lapis lazuli wrapped around the silver staff, with its giant head stretched towards the heavens. In its wide-open mouth was a crescent moon carved from moonstone.

Papa took them lower. "That pedestal enables the whole staff to rotate in any direction so it can follow both sunrise and moonrise. See there, the building has 'arms', curving out from the main sphere. Their arc represents perpetual motion, eternally cycling through evolution and devolution. Just like the entire Cosmos."

"What's in them?" Aiela studied the curved buildings.

"One houses the expanding of healing practices, another the learning of them. The remaining two have rooms for those that need to stay for a duration of care."

Aiela felt a deep pull to that wonderland of healing. How much she could learn with an endless supply of patients! Living and practicing alongside other passionate and gifted healers.

Ahna teased. "And then, a *miracle* happened...her words dried up." But she knew the yearning Aiela felt.

Mama pointed. "See the twelve gardens? All of their trees, shrubs, flowers and herbs are made into medicines. Your father brought back some of these plants from his travels." The gardens spread out from the Temple, mandalas drawn with plants, and colored in blooms.

"We'll tour it day after tomorrow. You're all set to test there El." Papa navigated the Aero onwards. "And look, there's the sacred Temple of Beauty. Talk about a marvel!"

An enormous complex of white marble, the Temple of Beauty glowed in sunlight, its architectural design as magnetic as a hypnotist swinging a golden disk. The mandorla-shaped main building was capped with a dome of rose quartz, bulging like a giant pink eye watching the heavens.

"You can't see it from up here," Papa said, "but the lower sections of its walls are decorated with oversized murals carved in stone. Images of beauty; trees, flowers, sunsets, dolphins, waterfalls, turtles and more. You could spend days poring over their details."

The dome was topped by the giant double spiral—symbol of the Divine Feminine—made from silver and gold, reflecting the bright afternoon sun in sharp spiking rays.

Mama pointed out the far off spires of the Temple of the Sun and its counterpart Temple of the Moon. "That oval with columns is the Hall of Records and beside it, the World Library. That really tall one way off is for the Houses of Education, Justice and Agriculture. That's where Charis works." And then they were past the city, nearing a vast sprawl of enormous trees.

They would stay with Charis in Old Forest to the west of High City. A packed itinerary included touring four Temples, seven Houses, and the Hall of Records. At the very end would be Poseidon's Palace and Ruler Ziel.

After High City's colorful fullness, it was oddly deserted below as they lowered to Old Forest's landing pad and Ahna wondered aloud where all the people were.

"Tree people keep to themselves." Mama explained as Papa guided their Aero to a gentle stop. "I hope I remember the way to Charis' home. You girls are going to love it here." She gave Aiela's long braids a little tug as she reached past to collect bags. "The biggest trees that ever there has been!"

CHARIS

9,974 BCE OLD FOREST, ATLANTIS

"What hurts you, blesses you. Darkness too is your candle."

— RUMI

CHARIS

*C*haris walked onto the knotty pine veranda for surely the tenth time today, staring over dense, leafy treetops to the west. Why did this anticipation feel heavy? The blazing midday sun met the darkness of forest in geometric shapes with no names, filtered through powerful branches. Few rays made it to the scattered flowers poking above moss-covered ground far below.

Despite happy chirps and trilling tweeted songs from the birds sharing her home, she could not shake this sinking swirl of bright-dark feeling stuck stubbornly in her chest. Even her morning meditation with tea and toast, usually a balancing balm, was no respite from the strange thoughts and feelings that had taken up residence inside her. *Maybe another cup of tea*, she decided, pulling a deep brown and gold robe closer around her thickening middle. But the chill was only inside of her—certainly not in the warmth of the summer noontime sun. Up here a pleasant breeze flowed most of the time, whispering ancient anthems among the vast sea of massive leaves that made up both canopy and roofs for this neighborhood of tree homes. Today's whispers she felt more as, what... excitement? Dread? Perhaps a little of both.

Walking inside to slide the teakettle back on the heating spot, her thoughts turned to Taya and their last conversation face to face. It must have been nearly ten years ago—still unpleasant to recall. She shared her cousin's direct approach to conversation, as well as strong-willed opinions. They had differed greatly in how they saw the issue at hand.

Taya had come for regular visits while working in High City during that time. She wouldn't say what she had been doing—which irked Charis, offended her even. Growing up together in the small town of Chiffon, they were inseparable as teenagers, even though Charis was three years older and in her opinion, wiser by far. They had told each other everything back in those days, and she had covered for Taya, saving her from well-earned consequences in more situations than she could count. When Charis moved to High City to apprentice in the House of Agriculture, things shifted. But even as the years distanced them further they had managed to stay connected, sharing memories and kinship.

Their disagreement happened the year after Charis lost Bren, the year she nearly lost her mind. Hers was a blessed mating, built firmly on commitment. They'd moved into this treehouse so long ago, with big plans and aspirations, but Charis didn't want to think of that now. Her orderly mind wanted only one difficult memory at a time. Yet they persisted in piling up around her, taunting her with that old familiar darkness-edging-towards-madness.

It was all connected, linked in a long highway of failure and loss.

She went to her herb cupboard and pulled out bags of kava kava root and chamomile. *Best put gaba in too.* She grabbed that vial of powder. *It won't do to be dark and gloomy when the girls arrive.* Settling on the faded green cushion that covered her chair at the polished, round table, she clucked at a finch who perched on her shoulder to escape a rowdy pursuer. As her hardened, knobby fingers began their memorized ritual of pounding and crumbling herbs into the oversized mug, she tried to recall what it was that had caused her to feel so angry with Taya during that conversation.

She remembered feeling so right, so *justified* in her opinion! Something about the way Taya was raising the girls, and she just wouldn't listen to Charis. Taya retorted something to the effect of "Don't give me advice in an area you know nothing about." Which led to resentment on Charis' part because she had badly wanted children—had miscarried three before Bren died so unexpectedly. Looking back now, Charis could see she had poured out years of grief, misery, anger, and despair on Taya, then added shame to the pile like a stone on top. She couldn't forget the look in Taya's big dark eyes. Hurt, disbelief, and possibly pity, cutting like a knife, before Taya walked out without another word.

Oh sure, she hadn't exactly cut her off. Taya was good about sending news of the girls as they grew, making sure Charis knew she was loved and always welcome to visit. As the years passed, Charis eventually tried to apologize for her tirade and Taya had replied "No need, I understand." But Charis couldn't quite forgive herself, hadn't allowed the broken relationship to fully mend. Hence, both anticipation and apprehension.

Letting the tea brew, she walked through the open rooms of the tree-house yet again to make sure every pillow was in place, every corner clean of deadfall, dirt and dust.

Old Forest was the first known suburb of High City, dating back thousands of years. These cypress, alerce, sequoia and beech giants were young when the first Atlanteans inhabited them. Connecting and communing, shaping the ever-growing branches into homes intertwined the consciousness of man and tree, evolving together in harmony. Over time, the outer city sprawled right up to treeline where once there had been nothing but a plain of wild grasses.

Homes weren't the only gift of the forest. Oxygen-rich air, herbs and mushrooms, wild tubers and tiny sweet strawberries grew in abundance. Chokeberry bushes, rose hips and ample varieties of moss were used for all manner of things. Chamomile, wild mint, beechnuts, shagbark, all this and more were offered copiously and freely. Generation after generation cultivated Old Forest, grateful and well-versed in the bounty it provided.

Dwellers in Old Forest, commonly referred to as the "Tree People", were known for keeping to themselves. A close-knit community, they operated quite independently from the rest of the cosmopolitan capital, although not shut out by any means. Many of them worked in High City, as did Charis.

Even after living in this community for twenty years, she felt an outsider because she hadn't grown up here. After Bren had perished at sea, she'd made no effort, almost severed her connection to this community that birthed and raised him. No matter how much they reached out, tried to make her a part of them, she only withdrew inside herself further, refusing their shy offerings of aid, until finally, they left her as she wished. Alone.

Her job at the Department of Agriculture was a lonely affair after Bren passed over. Everywhere he went, he'd been the star and she'd flourished in the light that surrounded him.

She sighed and sat again, sipping the cooled tea. *What a miserable old woman I've become,* she grimaced, examining a snag in the thick braided pad under her hot pot. Loneliness had given her too much time, and she hadn't used it wisely.

But she was determined to change, to open herself—which was why she had practically begged Taya to bring the girls and stay with her during their momentous trip to the City. The two of them had been so close once. If she couldn't find a way to reconnect with Taya, then she felt doomed to live out her days alone and lonely in this silent, wooden entity she called home.

Picking up the heavy mug, Charis returned to her sun-warm veranda, settling on the bench where her book waited. It wouldn't be long now, and these bitter thoughts were better off left in the dark than strewn about here on such a beautiful day, watching with her for the first guests she would welcome into her home in ten long years.

Before the sun had passed the giant mossy burl on the south-west side of the deck marking mid-afternoon, she heard voices and laughter wafting among leaves. The whispering forest seemed to still as they passed, enhancing their human noises even more.

"... and Charis was unable to stop laughing!" Tayas voice ended on a high note of warmth. "Ah here we are. Charis cousin! Are you up there?"

Charis stood and took a deep breath yanking her robes into what was hopefully order, and scurried to the edge of the balcony to peer down at her guests. "Taya! Drey! Welcome welcome, please come up! And the girls!" Her voice was rushed and a tinge too sharp. "Welcome Ahna and Aiela! I must have a look at you."

Aiela

She followed Mama 'round the massive, red-brown trunk. "It's the grandest tree I've ever seen!

"I didn't even know they grew this big!" Ahna ran a hand along deeply ridged bark, stopping to press both hands and face against the odd, soft wood, inhaling deeply.

Aiela too trailed a palm along the tree. It thrummed a primal, startling energy into her. "Oh!...do you feel th—?" She looked over at her sister and stopped. Ahna's eyes were closed and reverence played across her face as she melded with the tree energy. Aiela could see the colors of it, knew it was a memory of worlds before this one, ages before humans.

"Let's see...it's the second knot over from the darkest ridge...halfway up, aha! Yes I still remember, here we are, Drey mind the door." Mama's words stopped when she realized no one was behind her. "Drey? Girls? where did you, oh..." As she walked back around the tree trunk she smiled at all three pressed against the primitive entity. "Quite something, isn't it?"

Her voice brought them back and they reluctantly broke contact to retrieve bags that had somehow made their way to the ground.

"It never gets old," Mama said as they followed her this time, to the door that stood open. Wide, worn-to-a-polish steps spiraled up into darkness. They climbed and stone globes, positioned every few feet, began to glow, activated by motion. The base of the tree was close to thirty feet in diameter and narrowed only slightly as they made their way to an opening streaming light from above.

When they surfaced into the main level of the tree house, Charis and Mama exclaimed at the same time "Cousin!" and Mama dropped her bags to envelop Charis in a great warm hug.

The girls gasped in delight, grinning at each other in the interior of this twined branch house. Much bigger than their own home, its balconies flowed outside in all directions. There was a kitchen with all the modern comforts, a sitting area with couchbeds offering brightly colored cushions and blankets. A stout wooden table had wide chairs around it, and more stairs in the far corner led higher. The roof was a combination of giant leaves and thatched branches.

Charis finally let go of Mama, happiness moistening her eyes as she came to meet them.

With effort, Aiela tore her gaze from this astonishing, cozy splendor to meet their host.

Charis squeezed them tight one after the other. "Look at you! All grown and lovely. You've no idea what comfort it is to have you here in my home. I have been in great...anticipation." She spoke rapidly as if trying to get it all out at once. "Come, I will show you your rooms and do help yourself to anything. My home is yours now!" She grasped some bags and led them towards the stairs in the corner. "The water closet is in the corner behind the table and there is another upstairs. I will show you how they work. It's been so long since I've had guests, forgive me if I forget anything and just ask if you've a need. Here we are." She topped the stairs, turned into a room on the left that was small and airy, with a wide, low bed, a chest of drawers, and a little balcony that let a soft stream of sunlight in to warm the room. "Drey and Taya I've put you in here since it has the larger bed, and—"

"No," Mama protested, "you can't give us your room, we'll sleep downstairs!"

"Nonsense. My house my rules." Charis replied briskly and plunked down the bags. "Now, onto you girls' room." She walked out before Mama could say anything else. The girls grinned at their mother and followed. Nobody else got their way with Mama that quickly!

Their room was set apart by a short walkway carved into a branch that rose slightly and to the right, taking them onto a circular platform surrounded by gauzy cloth walls in front of layers and layers of leaves. The light trickling through created an effect of being the tree yourself, with leaves brushing sound while they danced in tranquil, nonsensical patterns.

Aiela dropped her bags to the floor and began to dance and sway with the moving mosaic, while Ahna slowly turned in the middle of the room to take it all in. "It's magical!" she said softly.

"Like being a fairy."

"Exactly what I was hoping for." Charis smiled, watching them. "And the reason I gave you this space. Memories of better days...countless hours I spent with Bren up here, loving, laughing. I don't...I barely come up here anymore." Her eyes shone an old and brittle pain and it tugged at Aiela's healer heart. Charis stepped to a creamy fabric wall. "I left these down so I can show you how to put them up when you want to."

They watched as Charis unhooked a wooden dowel securing the fabric panel to the floor, and began to roll it upward to another hook hanging from the eave of the roof.

"Its perfect Aunt Charis thank you. I think we may never want to leave this room." Aiela could feel how badly this woman wanted—*needed* affirmation and love.

"Well, I'll let you two settle in. When you're ready, there will be tea, muffins and fruit downstairs, you're probably hungry."

"Muffins? We'll be right down!" She turned to Ahna, suddenly all business. "Which bed do you want?"

They stowed their bags beside the two low couches which would serve as beds, arranged end to end on one side of the room, and flopped down to try them out.

"Already the best trip imaginable!" Aiela rolled up on one side to grin at her twin.

"It's so much to take in—"

"Let's get food I'm starving."

HIGH CITY II

9,974 BCE HIGH CITY, ATLANTIS

"The world is a book and those who do not travel read only one page."

— AUGUSTINE OF HIPPO

AIELA

*I*tinerary
        Day 1- Temple of Beauty
Day 2 - Temple of Healing
Day 3- Aades of Sacrifice
Day 4- Temple of Dreams and Markets
Day 5- Poseidon's Jubilee Holi Day
Day 6- Hall of Records and Old World Library
Day 7- Rest and explore The Forest.
Day 8- Houses: Healing Arts, Education
Day 9- Houses: Justice, Foreign Relations
Day 10- Houses: Technology/Science, Economics
Day 11- House of Agriculture, Gardens with Papa
Day 12- Poseidon's Palace, meet with Ziel
Day 13- any unfinished business
Day 14- return home

.   .   .

AIELA WOKE TO RICH AROMAS; coffee, spiced fruit compote, almond sweet-bread, and Mama's rolling laughter wafting up from below. She yawned and stretched loudly when she noticed her sister already in lotus position for morning meditation. With a groan, she begrudgingly mimicked it. Leave it to Ahna to still meditate even when she could barely contain her excitement for the big day ahead.

Five never-ending minutes later, she gave up and went downstairs to break the night's fast.

Bellies full, they set out. Ruler Ziel was sending a guide with a trolley to the sun gate to meet them. Today was the Temple of Beauty, and Aiela could hardly wait.

She barely noticed the trees as they walked towards the city wall. Ahna, on the other hand, was in her element, whispering to the giant sentinels as she passed, pausing to trail a delicate hand along their trunks. "I'll be back," she murmured.

The day was already warm, with lazy morning clouds visible through occasional gaps in the shadowy green canopy. As promised, a trolley waited at the gate, really a wide, arched opening that tunneled through the enormous wall. A man with reddish brown hair, wearing a royal blue tunic, stood very erect as they approached.

"Ms. Taya, Mr. Drey?" He queried in a clipped, booming voice. At their nod he clicked the worn heels of walking boots together, bowed low and said "Yorn at your service! Sent from Ruler Ziel and instructed to take very good care of you. I have much knowledge of this city and am honored to be your guide."

Papa smiled, reaching out to clasp forearms with him. "Thank you Yorn. We are grateful to have your assistance and expertise. These are our daughters, Aiela," placing a hand on her back, "and Ahna," motioning her forward.

The girls bowed and Yorn smiled. "Pleasure to serve you. Are we ready to begin?" He motioned to the trolley and once they were all squashed into the tiny space, they set off.

Just inside the wall tunnel, a high bridge arced across the wide, outer-most canal and brought them into the first ring of land. Immediately surrounded by city buzz, they joined the morning flow.

"Workdays are busiest at this time." Yorn explained, maneuvering through all manner of people. "Everyone's heading to laboratories, class-rooms or markets."

Aiela studied the vastly varied attire befitting specific professions or activities for the day. Most people walked, some rode in trolleys like theirs. Even with all the morning traffic, the streets were clean.

Yorn took them to high vantage points. "We haven't far to go for your first tour so there is time for an overview. Here you can see the four rivers flowing out from the central canal which rings Holy Mountain below Poseidon's Palace. These rivers were built for irrigation in ancient times, doubling as easy trade routes, a much faster way to move goods than the elephants and camels used back then."

"Also you can see the Golden Gates—did you know they called this the 'City of the Golden Gates' at one time when the canal gates were the only entrances?"

"Yes." Ahna answered politely because she was sitting right next to him.

"We learned basic history when we were seven." Aiela just wanted to get to the good stuff.

"Each gate is ornamented with our sacred symbols. You know their meaning?" Yorn launched into the meanings without waiting for an answer. "At the east canal is the Spiral Gate—still the symbol of Atlantis throughout the world, signifying our knowing that all are One yet each must walk the ascending path of soul lessons. Also it is the coiled serpent which represents knowledge. We entered through the southern Sun Gate and you already know why we revere the sun. West is the Swastika Gate, the perpetual motion of energies, the four cosmic forces hinged at the center, serving the greater good. Did you know," he directed the question to Mama, "that the swastika has a largely forgotten meaning, starting out as the cross, which was the meeting of time and space, evolving with bent arms denoting other dimensions?"

"I did not." Mama replied, but Yorn was already forging ahead.

"Finally, to the north is the Bull Gate—often simplified as honoring Poseidon's home constellation. Equally important is our gift of fertility which it's said Poseidon enhanced with his DNA. Certainly, he gave humanity the gift of twins." He sighed. "Knowledge of the old ways is disappearing rapidly. But," his face brightened, "progress is more important than nostalgia is it not?"

Noticing the slight boredom of his youngest charges, Yorn rushed his description of how the enormous gates were forged of steel but decorated with Atlantis' most beautiful metals; gold, silver, illumin and orichalcum. "In times of old, the canals were the only way in. Our recent generations have installed many land and bridge passages as the world became safer and quieter." He boomed with patriotic pride.

Mama asked, "Are the gates closed ever? They're certainly well-maintained."

Yorn was pleased by her observance. "Yes M'dame, they are maintained by the City Order Committee as is everything here in High City. Beauty and order are divine gifts from the One and it is our duty to work together for the benefit of all. The gates are closed and reopened for ceremonies such as when a new Ruler is instated, and for various holi-days such as Poseidon's Jubilee, Winter Solstice and First Day, or Festival of the Sun. The opening of the gates is merely a formality of honor. And how fortuitous that you will be here during Poseidon's Jubilee to celebrate with us!"

Aiela did have many questions about this. Yorn explained to her in great detail the best places to observe the races and games of Jubilee in High City.

Near the Temple of Beauty, the oversized double spiral atop its main dome caught gleaming morning sunshine, coming alive with metallic flow. "As Children of the Law of One, we know wholeness is an essence of the One... " Yorn turned fervent. "... and this magnificent Temple holds Beauty sacred, because it unites us with wholeness."

He steered the trolley into a tree-lined lane leading towards the soaring Temple center. "You know the double spiral—the Divine Feminine—significance?"

"Sure." Aiela replied. "It was Mama's first tattoo. It connects the path of male and female energies. Having found perfect balance and integration of both, the feminine becomes divine because she can create new life, begin a new cycle for another soul."

"A most excellent interpretation!" Yorn boomed. "More succinct than my own."

They passed manicured lawns, tame and fragrant green pauses separating High City's most prized gardens. Painters crouched or stood in front of easels, sketching, mixing or dabbing with elaborate concentration. Groups of children moved through intricate dance steps. Further on the haunting sounds of the hang drums drifted from a trio of teenage boys settled on the grass, creating odes to the flawless precision of nature.

Yorn stopped the trolley by a wide path flanked with tall marble columns. Leaping from their tops, crystal dolphins in graduating shades of blue, from the lightest translucence of water to an inky deep cobalt, touched noses.

The girls scrambled from the trolley pointing wordlessly at each new wonder. Mama arranged for a time that Yorn would pick them up after their tour. Together, they headed down the long, dolphin-lined tunnel towards massive doors.

The main temple doors rose twenty feet and spread twelve, each curiously carved with a shimmering golden dolphin, its tail split into legs. These enormous golden dolphins swept up from the bottom as if leaping to catch a cascade of crystal stars just above graceful, elongated snouts. At the top of each door, a small winged angel floated, showering stars from a hand. Above this vision, spanning both doors was a dedication in curling script:

All that I create is service to the Light.

"It's almost too much to take in." Aiela breathed, turning in circles.

"It's too much." Ahna massaged her temples.

An expansive space just inside, housed a rainbow of light. Colored window panes pigmented the air itself, and the glowing rose quartz dome overhead was even prettier from within.

"Welcome to the Temple of Beauty. May you be well in the love light of the One." A young girl wearing a fitted white robe, adorned with a pink sash had appeared in front of them. Palms touched in front of her heart when she bowed the traditional Atlantean greeting.

They returned the bow and responded as expected; "Greetings in the love light of our Oneness."

The girl spoke shyly, "I am Kura, here to serve you. What is your desire today?"

"We've an appointment with OldMother for a tour." Papa replied.

The girl looked startled. "Are you sure? She does not conduct tours—I mean, I believe you… it's just… well… " She stopped, flustered and unsure what to do.

Papa smiled, "Kura is it?"

She nodded, confusion pinked her face.

"I tell you what Kura, go tell OldMother that Drey and his family have arrived for their appointment and I promise you won't be reprimanded."

The girl's blush faded, her posture relaxing as she realized he really must know OldMother—if he knew she would be in trouble for disturbing the ancient Temple Priestess unnecessarily. "Yes, right away!" She bobbed low again, fleeing towards the back of the gigantic light-filled room.

Mama cast a curious look at Papa.

He shrugged. "I spent quite a lot of time here during my first period of apprentice. OldMother, formally known as Silena, High Priestess of the Temple of Beauty, took a liking to me—rare I was told. When I requested a tour and introduction for the girls she insisted on doing it herself. Apparently, she forgot to mention it to her staff." He chuckled. "She's a real character —perhaps an understatement. It'll be an interesting tour—to say the least!"

Aiela and Ahna wandered to a large wave sculpture of blown glass, carrying rare shells and families of seahorses inside. It looked so realistic Ahna had to touch it. Aiela's attention had already moved to the next sculpture, a life-sized smilodon, carved from flawless, smooth obsidian, ivory saber teeth curving longer than her forearm.

"Drey darling you've arrived!" A clear, vigorous voice rang across the space—unmatched to the tiny woman moving with the unseen force of a gale. Kura fluttered in her wake. Ancient, like a flower past its prime, OldMother seemed to grow smaller the closer she came, but the hug she enveloped Papa in was outside all proper greetings in Atlantean custom.

He laughed and swung her around as Kura looked on in astonishment.

Aiela saw the havoc of time on OldMother's face, yet her movements and voice belied it. Warm energy and power exuded from her, at total odds with her drab brown and gray robes and short, spiky white hair. Even her eyes smiled. Mama went to hug her—though she was normally less affectionate than Papa.

"I figured I'd adore you." OldMother murmured, pushing Mama out with small strong arms. "Let me look at you child, ah yes, a real firecracker beauty we have here." She scrutinized Mama with sharp eyes. Mama just stared right back. "Thank you OldMother—er should I call you High Priestess?"

Kura still stood back, her look of disbelief increasing.

"I don't think people usually talk to High Priestess Silena like this." Aiela whispered.

"I get the feeling they either revere or fear her." Ahna whispered back.

OldMother tinkled a laugh, patting Mama's cheek with an age-spotted hand, "Child, you call me what you want to. Now, where are your girls? Let's get moving. Day's waning!" Spying them, she held out both hands. "Come here so I can see you properly." Holding a hand of each, she studied them head to toe. "You may call me OldMother and what shall I call you?"

"I am Ahna, OldMother."

"And I am Aiela."

"So fresh and pretty! Both of you. But do you know the value of

Beauty? I think not! Look at me, allowing my body to age without enhancement or treatments to maintain a perfect facade. Do you know why? I don't yet! I am waiting for the teacher to appear. Ah but I speak riddles and it is boring to you! Come on, we've wonders in my Temple like you've never seen before!" And off they went.

Their tour began with the Galleries—which served also as classrooms —surrounding the Great Hall.

OldMother explained very simply the temple philosophy, the spirituality tying all things of beauty together. "Why is beauty held sacred? I will use art as an example. All art should point toward higher ideals and possess a spiritual quality of the Oneness or Wholeness of all that is. When our creations are powerful and true, their physical presence aligns with the artist's soul. Four pillars connect us to our Wholeness and reflect the essence of the One: Beauty, Truth, Love, and Light. Our mission and sacred duty here at the Temple of Beauty is to teach, honor and expand every form these pillars take."

She talked of the framework of self-discipline and self-restraint that all Atlantean artists worked within, showing examples of this in each area they entered. "Beauty in poetry is more than just words and form, it is a beauty of thought and emotion. Ugliness is a dull and heavy vibration. So all forms of it such as violence, despair, cruelty, or anger, must be avoided."

Aiela whispered behind her hand, "What she's wearing should be avoided!"

"Shh!" Ahna giggled back.

Every room held creations in progress, "If it can be imagined, it can become." OldMother repeated, pointing out how the works carried the high idealism of their Law of One principals.

They slid silently into expansive dance studios, watching pairs and groups practice their art, forms weaving knowledge of joy through sacred body expression. OldMother pointed, "They're dancing the Dance of Creation." A tightly melded dot of dancers gracefully morphed out into a circle, then two, and three circles intertwined, drawing the sequence of sacred geometry from the beginning of all that is, mapping every stage from awareness, to thought, to sound and then manifest creation. What began as a simple dot of Divine consciousness, ended with the intricate flower of life.

Papa's face held wonder as the muscular dancers finished and bowed to each other. "It's magnificent! Imagine, one dance containing the structure of every molecule and DNA strand in this Universe, the story of how it all begins again and again—a circle without end."

OldMother looked proud. "Indeed. Atlanteans have danced this story since our history began in the first epoch. The only difference is that humanity no longer flies. Originally, it was performed in three dimensions with dancers levitating above the ground. Imagine what it would have looked like then!"

Painting studios were half-filled with artists who pondered groupings of ordinary objects, or far-off views, or each other. Their canvases shimmered vivid and dramatic, or pale and translucent, like mosaics made from shards of light. "Crystals are ground into the paints which causes them to glow." OldMother explained. "Their favored technique uses spiral strokes from tiny to large, lifting the image off of the canvas and into one's senses." Most of the paintings did look incredibly three dimensional.

Small music rooms were lined with instruments, their workings made of crystal and glass spun so fragile it had to be cased in wood. Even the jarring starts and stops of the practicing musicians seemed capable of evoking the entire array of human emotions.

"It opens us, opens our very muscles, our heart, our brain. Music can heal things nothing else touches." OldMother whispered as a trio of flute players paused to make notes on their music sheets. "These rooms—like every concert space and hall in the City—are acoustically exact, to amplify the timbre and tones." One entire music room was devoted to instruments, mostly carved wood and bone, that mimicked the sounds of nature and animals.

Mama was entranced by the sculptures. Spacious rooms, more utilitarian than the others, held artisans spinning hypnotic potter's wheels. Others bent and squinted through magnifying lenses to sculpt miniscule details of life, and still more soared overhead on ladders, using strange looking tools to articulate movement on figures breathtaking in sheer size. There were sculpture studios for glass, metal, stone, wood and even paper.

"Do you see how their sculptures evoke flight?" OldMother waved a hand at two artists working side by side. "And those express subtle emotions like gratitude, trust and whimsy?" She directed their attention to the far side of the studio.

"It's all so amazing! And overwhelming." Mama put words to what they each were feeling.

When the tireless OldMother announced it was time for noonday meal to be served outside on the lawns, the whole family sighed in relief.

. . .

Ahna

Ahna flopped onto the verdant carpet of grass, pressing her palms against soft blades, fingers searching out earth underneath.

Aiela stretched out on her back while their parents helped OldMother unpack a meal basket, containers of salads with chilled citrus water in delicate blue glass containers. "There's too much to learn—I'll never know as much as I want to." She rolled over on her belly to watch a group of children playing tag across the immense lawn. "You should see the concentrated energy here, do you feel it?"

Ahna studied the ground, not admitting how hard she was trying not to. Unsure why this unequalled grandeur so completely overwhelmed her.

Perceptive as ever to her mood, Aiela rolled closer. "Is it too much?" Do you want me to take some?"

Ahna reached out gratefully, joining hands in the grass. She felt the healing strength flow into her and the buzzing inside her head lessened instantly. This exchange had become second nature to them.

Their restful lunch seemed too brief when Oldmother bounded to her doll-sized feet, announcing it was time to finish the tour. She led them through a mahogany backdoor, inlaid with a lake scene in contrasting woods. "We go to the sanctuary of reflection now my children." OldMother's voice lowered in timbres of reverence, gliding down a gleaming, columned hall. "Here we come to take refuge in silence. This, I consider the culmination of all the Beauty." With that she slid open the soundless door and motioned for them to enter.

Aiela stepped through first, stopping abruptly—causing Ahna to run into the back of her. Papa bumped into her from behind and then they stood and gaped.

Placed directly in the center, towering high in the otherwise bare room, was a statue of such immense size and grotesque perfection it seemed alive. Staring down at them, its hooded, bestial eyes glowed in the divine countenance of a human. Cloven hooves were planted in a miniature cityscape, unmistakably High City. From them rose the legs and hindquarters of a muskox, transforming just above its waist to the flawless chest and muscular arms of a man, heartbreakingly beautiful. He lofted a black pyramid on upraised palms, as if intending to smash it on the city below. His face reflected resentment and a manic joy in his action. Giant wings of exquisite detail rose from his back, opened as if beating the air into motion and chaos.

It was Darkness. Drawn in smokey quartz perfection. They fanned around it, their soundlessness interrupted by OldMother's sharp gasp of horror.

Ahna was confused. Foreign energies surrounded the strangely beautiful sculpture...and a storm of emotions exploded from OldMother as she took it in.

Papa began to examine every angle of the sculpture, muttering "No signs of tools...excellent artistry...so many materials used."

Mama seemed on the verge of laughter, looking to OldMother instead. "Surely there is some mistake. THIS is the culmination of all beauty?"

Silena, High Priestess of this temple for the better part of a century, was struck mute. Outrage built quickly, coming out a rabid growl—turned shriek—erupting from her like a volcano finally spilling its long-held magma.

All four of them jumped at the defiled sound reverberating off mahogany walls, magnified into something chilling down their backs.

OldMother faced off with the monstrosity, the morning's flow shattered at the hooves of this beautifully idealized darkness. Her face was caustic yet still she had no words.

Mama cleared her throat. "Well it certainly is a work of art!" She spoke neutrally, stepping closer to the statue, reaching out to touch it.

"Don't!" The OldMother's command stopped her hand mid-motion and Mama froze. "It is an abomination, an *insult* to all this Temple stands for. Do Not Touch It." Clearly, OldMother was accustomed to unquestioning obedience.

Mama shifted her stance only slightly and they all recognized her feisty rebellion rising. Papa moved to her, sliding his arm around her waist, a silent peace-keeping.

She got his message, lowered her hand replying, "Clearly this is unexpected and unwelcome Silena, but you cannot deny the artistry of the work—however it came to be. Beauty lies in things light *and* dark, do you not agree?" She looked to the girls, still rooted in place, absorbing this scene with their acute senses. "The 'Oneness and Wholeness of All that Is' you said. There is balance even in shadow—is there not?"

OldMother's eyes flicked from the statue to the girls, then met Mama's with a flat look.

"I am aware of the totality of Oneness Taya. What *you* fail to understand is the meaning of this appearing—in my *sanctuary*. It is an ugly act. Pure anarchy, mocking my authority and all that this Temple holds sacred. So please, you will leave the regulation of this temple's renditions of Beauty to the one charged with that duty these past ninety-five years."

With that she whirled, drab robes a spinning tornado, and headed out the door. "You will kindly follow me," floated curtly on her wake.

Ahna and Aiela went first, relieved to leave the tension-filled room.

Mama and Papa followed more reluctantly, whispering that they'd like to examine the statue more thoroughly.

OldMother deposited them at the front door where their day had started, muttering formal apologies for the "monstrous incident" and snapping instructions at Kura to call their driver. Distracted farewells led to a swift departure. A smirched, abrupt end to their first day.

Riding out towards Old Forest, Yorn's chatter about what they passed and what the next day held, was soothing. Mama and Papa talked quietly behind them, discussing, Ahna knew, the odd statue and OldMother's even odder reaction to it.

Following supper and fellowship with Charis, exhaustion from the day's excitement sent them to an early bed and the next day Yorn arrived promptly.

Today was the Temple of Healing.

HIGH CITY III

9,974 BCE HIGH CITY, ATLANTIS

"Effective healing equals the wounding in complexity and strength, thereby restoring balance. Compassion, intention and knowledge are the healers."

— ATLANTIS TEXTBOOK

AIELA

"Will you get a journal for Auntie Charis? I think red." Aiela thought of it while trying not to fall asleep last night in the gently swaying boughs of Aunt Charis' treehouse. "I want to give her a gift for taking care of us. *And* it will be therapeutic for her to hand-write her thoughts and feelings. They're stuck. I doubt she'd speak them, but they need to come out."

"I'll find a nice one for her." Ahna agreed. "Maybe I'll get her a new mug. The one she uses is chipped."

Aiela waved farewell to her family from the ornate, arched doorway of the Healing Temple. Yorn was showing them to the nearest market while Aiela tested to apprentice.

They'd spent half the morning touring it, starting at the soaring central dome where many came once a moon to rebalance their chakras— a sort of maintenance to prevent dis-ease. Sleek tan pods resembling the sycamore seed, cradled one's body in a cloud of faint, white sound. The pod's great fan rose like an elongated, oversize fin along the top. Translucent and dainty as a butterfly wing, it spliced vibration and light through the body's energy centers.

"Enhancements" was the busiest section. An entire division teemed with people come to smooth out blotchy skin or wrinkles, remove excess fat deposits, reshape crooked teeth, even reduce or enlarge body parts or facial features that displeased them.

"Atlanteans are vibrant because of the harmonious environment we live in," their apprentice Guide explained, "but unparalleled in beauty because of the work we do here. Something you may not know; most will return again and again for the same alteration. See, our Ka shines forth its physical expression as our body, much like a crystal projects a hologram. So what is not changed in the Ka cannot be changed permanently in the body. It is like the dying of the hair. Though its color is changed for a time, the true color will continue to grow out of the head unless the genomes are altered. Genomes are altered by the Ka.

Really," he whispered to the twins, "this should be called the Center of Utmost Vanity."

Aiela had smiled at him, felt the surge of attraction. Not more than five years her elder, he was so sophisticated, so wise. Tall, with red-blonde hair cropped short and bright blue eyes, he focused intently on her. *Because I'm interested in healing? Or is it more?* Mostly, she was drawn to his apparent passion for this work.

There were of course, the altogether gorgeous birthing spas where everything was controlled, from the barometric pressure, temperature, humidity and oxygen saturation, to the scents, sounds and colors. Methods of birthing were surprisingly numerous. Mama had harrumphed at it all. "Having babies here is like a vacation—quite the opposite of how you were born!" Ahna and Aiela shrugged at each other. They were not yet concerned with such things. But the Guide asked to hear the story. He'd been incredulous at the circumstances Mama described and Aiela felt pride at being different—at Mama's fierce stamina and the way she waved off the pain. "I'm stronger for it. I've had an experience few Atlantean mothers have."

The "Transition Beyond" was a collection of spaces dedicated to the end, the last chapter of life. "It is the graceful close of a human lifetime, the journey home to continue one's soul path." Their Guide spoke reverently. "Our transition healers go to abodes of the dying, to comfort, ease and inform. As counselors, they narrate and guide the passing of a beloved family member to those who must now release them." He showed them small, peaceful rooms, resting empty. "There are some who come here to cross over. Perhaps they have no family near or perhaps they are not yet old—just done with this life, desiring to return home. These ones are guided through the spiritual Way, how to leave their physical body behind and enter the thoroughfare of Beyond. This is the area I apprentice in." He beamed at them, clearly enamored with his daily work.

Their tour ended with the advanced wing of inner sanctums where the most skilled Healers worked on long-term patients. Here, lost or destroyed parts of the body were restored. Accidents were frequent across Atlantis where experimentation and exploration were prized above all else—including safety. The primary goal was a continual push beyond current limits. Dismemberment and death held no fear. Indeed, the healers here could cause limbs to regenerate and bodies to mend themselves. Pain was trivial, momentary, the brain easily tricked to shut out these protective sensations.

Gathered inside a surgical room, Aiela studied the equipment. Terminators of crystals made patterns around a platform where the injured person would lie.

"Sit on it." The Guide instructed the girls. "See, it is very comfortable. It travels underneath the colors in the right sequence." He gestured towards various colors of flame-shaped generators hanging above. "In the wrong sequence it could cause ill health. Even death. The beam strengths are adjustable so they can be used to cut or to regenerate. Each of these lamps contain all colors of light but represent a different body to heal. White; Etheric and Astral body. Green; Physical body. Blue; Emotional body. Red: Causal body. All of our bodies are interconnected, all must be healed of residual or mirrored damage."

Back inside the blue-glowing sphere of the central dome, Papa asked a parting question. "Doesn't all this require tremendous amounts of power?"

"More than any other three structures in the City combined!" The Guide pointed upward. "We've our own power source. Our silver staff, around which the serpent of knowledge entwines, is more than decorative. It is a storage cell, the newest science in gathering not only solar energy, but moon and star light as well."

"And why's that the symbol of healing?" Ahna asked..

Aiela wanted to answer—anything to do with healing she'd actually retained from primary school. But it would be rude to answer a question asked of someone else. She wanted to appear mature and polite just now.

"Why the snake on a tree? Well, both represent many things. The tree symbolizes totality of a human life. Roots, trunk, branches; soul, mind, body. The snake is our symbol of knowledge of course but remember, it's reborn again and again, shedding its skins—as we do a cell at a time. Its form resembles the twining helix of DNA strands when wrapped 'round the tree of life. Also, the serpent is a symbol of human sexuality..." His eyes landed on Aiela.

She held his gaze, curving her lips slightly.

"Legend tells of a time when humans were immortal, but unable to procreate. It is said we were given the choice; sexuality—with which we could control our own re-creation—in exchange for mortality. There had to be some means of death if we were granted reproduction ability, see? The sum of it is, this symbol carries the power of life and death given into our own hands. We became creators, like God, in exchange for our physical aging and death."

"Did you know our spiral represents, in part, a coiled snake?" Papa added, stepping between Aiela and the Guide. "Making the serpent the oldest Atlantean symbol of them all."

Now, much later in the day, Aiela stood shifting rapidly side to side, drumming her fingers against the cool quartz wall under the entrance arch where everyone had left her. Was she good enough for acceptance here? What sorts of things might they test? Probably basic knowledge of bodies, perhaps what healing modalities she had studied or practiced.

She'd been hoping their handsome Guide would return. He was called away and her hopes of being alone with him waned, as nervousness set in.

What if I fail? There's nothing else I am good at! Please Great Divine, do not let me fail... Moments stretched her worries brittle until a girl, younger than herself, came to escort her to the Temple teacher who would test her.

They passed through the wing of Advancement—the only place they hadn't toured. "It is just laboratories and offices. Everything you've seen before." Their Guide had said. But Aiela loved the frenetic busyness here. Friends worked together in labs to study bacteria, systems of the human body, the energetic changes of tissue cells caused by combinations of plants, light or sound. Their discussion was a low, pleasant hum. She lingered, observing three apprentices, rapt as their teacher explained the treatment they would assist her with today and why she'd chosen it.

"Rizele is waiting..." the young girl chided to get Aiela moving.

A higher concentration of females worked in this vocation and Aiela wondered at it.

"I am Rizele. Welcome! I'm here to understand why you wish to apprentice with us." Rizele's voice was melodic, simple and smiling, accurately reflecting the very tall, comfortably padded person beckoning Aiela forward.

Aiela bowed, "I'm Aiela. Honored to be considered."

"Sit here. I'm having tea, would you like some?"

"Yes please." She sat obediently on long, low cushions the startling color of poppies.

Rizele brewed tea, chatting without pause as if they'd been friends for some time. "What a day, what a day! I'm so glad you're here—it gives me a much-needed break. Firstly, we received five crewmen off a seacruiser which exploded in half right down there in the inner harbor! Accident during the installation of a new engine. They will be with us for awhile. Two missing limbs—just *gone* I tell you—burns all over, and a blown off face! Gruesome. That was what I woke to this morning. I specialized for a number of years in burns, you understand, speaking of which, don't burn your lips, haha."

Without pausing, she handed Aiela a mug of steaming brew, rather the color of blood but smelling of fresh rose and fruit. "Next came the mate of someone everyone in our City knows—but whom I shall not name—livid with my staff and speaking very ugly to them, because her rump is large....again. She expects to eat sticky buns, custard puffs and sweets all day long and still be lean! Demanding we fix it. I told her we certainly could...by sealing her mouth shut! *That* wasn't received well at all.

But the absolute topper was an entire batch of Conrectus brought to us in excruciating pain. Some strange new sickness we've not seen before. They'd just been delivered from Belial—those cow-like creatures meant to be taken south to the fruit orchards you know—but they were writhing and bawling and miserable, poor things! And us not understanding much about hybrids because it has been forbidden to make them here for so long. They are becoming patients in our Temples across the country more and more as Belial practices grow out of control.

Of course there's the usual influx of patients who become mentally *unhinged* around full moons. Then three births. Three! In one morning I tell you! Two went as if automated, but the other was terribly premature. The mother had drank the wrong herbs in her tea and didn't realize she was in labor until it was too late. The baby will be fine of course, we're helping him finish developing his lungs..." She stopped to draw breath and sip tea, looking Aiela over from crown to sole. "So. Tell me why you want to be a healer."

Aiela squirmed at this abrupt scrutiny. She'd been enjoying the tale of daily happenings. "Well, be-because I already am a healer and I find everything about it interesting...compelling. It is my gift."

"You are gifted? Tell me of that."

"I see the energy colors of the physical body and when I touch a body, I feel the pain they are experiencing."

"Hmm, twice gifted then. I see." She waited in silence, so Aiela continued.

"I, um, have used herbs and plant extracts to heal a number of animals and less serious conditions for my friends and neighbors. Aunt Sage taught me what to use...and some energy healing, I'm getting better at that."

"Mm-hmm, what is easiest for you in your healing work?"

"Animals. Definitely. Because they can't explain what they're feeling, so it's simple to examine and then treat them. Whereas people misdiagnose their symptoms or their pain refers and then you're searching in the wrong direction making it difficult to locate the real cause. Human beliefs get in the way of everything—usually contributing to the condition, often blocking the healing—and they all have strong opinion on what you should do, how you should heal them!"

Rizele chortled, sipping her tea, eyeing Aiela over the rim of her cup. "You've summed it up quite nicely. Clearly, you're more than a dabbler, how long have you been practicing?"

Aiela stifled her shrug. "Since I can remember. My Mother says I've doctored animals since I could walk. I don't remember a time before I was fixing them."

"Impressive. You are a true natural it seems. Most welcome—*needed* here! We gratefully accept all the help we can get."

"So, next I will test then?"

Rizele smiled, making notes in a small book before looking up again. "You passed dear. We turn no one away if they desire to apprentice here. No matter the skill level or gifts, we can train anyone for a role—whatever best suits their ability. It takes more than just healers to fill the myriad of positions at Healing Temples. But I will be honest with you, we lose a number early on. It's plain hard work. Confusing. Heartbreaking at times. It takes a strong *and* soft heart, empathy, perseverance and flexible intellect to excel in this profession. The inevitable mistakes and failures have a much higher cost for us and some can simply not forgive themselves a mistake that costs a life. People like you rarely come along; gifted, along with the drive to develop and use those gifts. What questions do you have for me?"

"Why is the majority here women?"

Rizele's eyes glittered approval at Aiela's observation. "Because the energy of healing is compassion, nurturing. You know that both yin and yang energies have positive and negative charge. Yin positive, the same energy that creates life, is required to heal it. Every human possesses both yin and yang energy, the goal being to balance them and the point of balance being unique to each person. We have men here who are excellent healers because they can access their yin energy easily. Of course more women carry and use, or express, that energy...oh just one moment."

A comm on her writing desk was vibrating and Rizele spoke rapidly to the voice that Aiela couldn't make out on the other end.

"I am needed in the surgery wing to oversee some new horror. Sorry to leave so soon. I will make the necessary arrangements for you to apprentice here... if that is what you want?"

"Oh yes!" Aiela pressed her hands together. "More than anything!"

HIGH CITY REVELATIONS

9,974 BCE HIGH CITY, ATLANTIS

"In the path to self-realization and mastery there are many ways, many paths and many choices. Neither is better than the other. It is simply that each choice brings with it consequences."

— MARY MAGDALEN

AHNA

"*How* often do they have to clean it?" Ahna studied the Aades of Sacrifice, really an extension of the Healing Temple, separated by lawns and gardens. A four-sided pyramid, it was sheeted with manufactured crystal that caught and reflected light in a shimmer of pastels. Workers were using high-powered water spray from an aero to wash the massive sides.

"Once a moon at least". Yorn stopped the trolley and they all got out.

"The Aades sits upon a layer of underground chambers that resemble rather cozy earth-lined caves—but we won't tour past the reception area." Today he wore a robe of softened linen the color of chocolate, with stylized tiger scenes embroidered heavily in shades of gold. "Those who live here don't appreciate their home being invaded by strangers anymore than we would. The Aades' tends those who cannot take care of themselves. Those indulging criminal behavior are rehabilitated here—and those who will not contribute to society as is our custom. Workers in this place are dedicated—they believe they are called—to helping these confused souls. Residents are given every opportunity to learn and grow, or to rest and be cared for, as their needs dictate. With healing care, many are rehabilitated and go on to live productive lives. Now, what questions have you before we go on?"

"What are the caves used for?" Mama asked.

"They are furnished as normal living spaces. The energy of the earth and the dimness are simply more comfortable to certain residents, whereas others need air and sky around them. Some crave water, others sunlight. It's a matter of providing the most comfortable and supportive environment to the individual."

"Why, in your opinion, do some tend toward criminal behavior and not the rest of us?" Papa was more interested than Aiela. She was still exhilarated at being accepted to the Temple of Healing, daydreaming of working with that handsome Guide—giving him a chance to follow up on the promises he made with his eyes...

Yorn's voice interrupted these pleasant thoughts. "...previous lifetimes. Those who were terribly traumatized, hurt, or perhaps learned to like the feeling of power from hurting others in past lives. Then too, some of these souls are of a lower vibration or have simply chosen to experience living in those frequencies. Ultimately, it is those who have not the self-control our society requires of them. The Aades becomes an outer control for them—a few being restrained even—until they are healed enough to manage themselves. Picture very young children who are taught they cannot hit others or destroy things, and must treat all with respect and kindness."

Ahna

"I don't like the messages I get through my dreams." Aiela grumped the next day.

"Maybe you're misunderstanding them." Ahna suggested.

The two of them were finishing a tour through the Temple of Sacred Mysteries, called simply "Dream Temple" by most. But more than just the interpretation and manipulation of dreams was explored here. From communication with higher Spiritual Beings, to reviewing past lives, the mysteries of the Universe were studied.

"This temple works closely with the House of Oracles." Yorn told them. He seemed almost a part of the family now, spending day after day telling stories through this lavish masterpiece of a City that he clearly cherished.

Today, Mama met privately with Ruler Ziel for some business or other. Papa was asked to be an advisor at a convention, way out in the House of Agriculture, so Yorn was conducting tours with just them.

"Are they doing math?" Ahna peeked into a room where apprentices worked together chalking endless mathematical calculations across slate walls.

"They study parallel dimensions, alternate lives and worlds that extend into infinity. How they all impact each other. How we might visit them. They theorize why and where other dimensions exist. It's an underexplored area many seek to understand."

Ahna listened as the apprentices discussed the correctness of each addition to the equations before writing them in. A vision formed, here and gone in an instant. She saw dimensional possibilities as a multiverse spreading around her, above and below, north, south, east, west and within—going inside itself to infinity.

She studied again those intrinsic mathematical computations on the classroom walls, hoping they were some kind of key. But they remained illogical as static, an unintelligible babble that her brain rejected.

"Aren't there other ways to explore dimensions?" She asked Yorn.

"Oh sure! The astral Oracles travel the planes. With actual experiences, we can theorize why dimensions exist. Knowledge is only the intellectual understanding of *how*, which in this case is expressed through mathematics. Wisdom, therefore the ability to go further, comes from experience. Both are necessary."

Aiela yawned. "I wonder if we might find that salad cart again for our midday meal. Remember the rosemary beets? The spiced honey nuts they roasted? Mmmm." She fixed a beady eye on her small, golden sister. "Are you thinking of apprenticing here?"

Ahna shrugged. "I'd hoped for the House of Oracles, but Charis said those with lesser abilities are placed here. I mean, *look* at these people! If these are *lesser* gifted, there's no way I'm smart enough to be an Oracle. There are things here that might be fun to learn..."

Aiela had stopped walking to frown. "Gifted enough? Smart enough? Do you even *know* anybody else who can do the things you can?"

Ahna rolled her eyes. "My abilities don't exactly help anyone."

But Aiela had a hand on her hip, tone growing adamant behind an accusing finger. "You see everybody else, but you can't see your own self —what you really are. I've no idea where all this 'not good enough' came from, but it's not true! What if it's a choice you make, whether or not you're 'enough'. What if it's really your choice all along, not anybody else's?"

The words echoed like an impromptu tap dance. *Choice you make, choice you make. Enough, enough, enough.*

"Don't give up on what you want because of an assumption. When will you be enough for *yourself?*" Aiela smiled, triumphant in her accuracy—and to dull the sharp edges of truth. "Yorn, I think we're done here. Can we go to the same place for midday meal, where you took us yesterday?"

"Certainly." Yorn glanced uncertainly between them at the abrupt change of subject. "But there's many new foods to sample too..."

THE DAYS FLEW BY, stuffed full enough that Ahna dropped into bed each night, spinning from overstimulation. She'd come to love the serenity of Charis' cozy tree home, but she missed home.

Between Yorn's formal introductions at the Temples and Houses and markets and galleries, and several old friends from when Papa apprenticed here, the names and faces mingled and merged until she couldn't recall any of them with certainty. Except OldMother. There'd be no forgetting her!

Poseidon's Jubilee was held on Midsummer's Day. Papa and Mama turned them loose to roam at will, doing as they pleased, now that they knew the way home. The City rang with music to announce competitions of great variety, as muscular, lithe athletes from the breadth and corners of Atlantis, lined up to outdo each other. Foot races 'round the top of the radiant city wall, glutted its great span with roaring, applauding fans. Rowing races engorged the canals and their shady, tree-lined banks. Ahna and Aiela cheered on swimmers and acrobats and even pilots performing pageantry overhead with agile little aeros. Competition was the most ferocious between teams who'd trained all year for the games. Spectators grew feverish, wild, and border-line unscrupulous in their ferocious support.

She and Aiela made as much noise as possible in this city released from its usual spiritless inhibitions, eating too much, pushing their way to the forefront, and gawking at the endless supply of boys—boys of all colors, shapes and sizes. Boys burgeoning into men.

"We're going to *love* living here!" Aiela enthused.

"It's a lot of energy to deal with." Ahna wished fervently, for the thousandth time, to turn off her sensitivity.

ON THE LAST FULL DAY, Mama led them through Poseidon's Palace to explore the House of Oracles and enjoy a private supper with Ruler Ziel.

"Look at them all!" Aiela and Ahna both gaped, heads craned back, at the feet of immense sculptures adorning the Palace exterior. "Who are they?"

Papa was enthralled too. "Rulers or significant people from the epochs of history. See the knowledge stone beneath? It tells their story—what's known of it. Some of these statues have been destroyed or damaged from epoch to epoch, now restored. Few have been added from our own times. I imagine Ruler Ziel will one day have one in his honor."

Indeed, the statues began at the summit of the Palace with Poseidon, his wife and ten sons. Continuous golden figures posed between snow-white columns, winding around the palace rings, with blank niches still on the bottom.

"Come girls. Drey. Much more to see inside!" Mama promised.

The learning centers, meditation chambers, kitchens and concert halls, along with art, artifacts and historical scenes that decorated it all were dizzying. Mama showed them her favorite places to explore, read or meditate from the time she'd spent here.

They were resting in Ziel's small apartment when he returned.

"My family! Oh how I've looked forward to this time with you!" He hugged them all, kissing their cheeks with deep affection. Quite a small man, his energy felt like power distilled, deep and strong—yet calming too.

"Do you remember the times I visited you?" He asked her and Aiela.

"Some of them." Ahna replied.

He slipped out of an ornate mantle that officiated his robes. "Well, I see you're as glorious all grown up as you were at two, and three and five!" He studied them as if searching for something, then removed his diadema, a beautiful band of illumin with a large, deep-blue stone inset against his forehead. The stone matched the blue of his satin robes, intricately cut and embroidered with gold.

They stared at the finery.

"I'm expected to don this getup for official business. Mostly it's heavy and hot! This though," He held out the diadema for them to inspect, "is very useful. You understand why the Rulers, Priests and Oracles wear diademas?"

"So we know who's important?" Aiela ventured.

"Something to do with the stones?" Ahna guessed.

"The stones, yes!" Ziel beamed. "Wearing a gem or crystal with certain attributes can balance and enhance us. For this aged brain it makes quite a difference in thinking clearly. Makes for better decisions. The metal holding it plays a part too. Even motivations are affected, keeping us above the ego level. We, with the greatest responsibilities, grasp for all the help and wisdom we can get!" He looked at Aiela, still beaming. "You're correct too—but in the future. I've seen a time when people think Rulers wear diadems for those reasons. They'll call them crowns. I'd best change before eating—else the launderette chides me and spreads nasty rumors about my clumsy eating habits!"

"I make a mess when eating too." Ahna blurted, inwardly cringing at her awkwardness. Why was she so eager to please him?

He winked. "We shall be great friends then!"

A knock at the door heralded supper. Three apprentices carried in dishes, platters and pots that smelled tangy, buttery and spiced. Ahna hovered close while they laid Ziel's little table, putting what didn't fit on the tea counter. With shy smiles and bows, they retreated, closing the door behind them.

Returning in plain cotton tunic and pants, Ziel joined them at table and blessed the food. "What do you think of our City? Tell me of all that you've done here!"

Papa and Mama explained where Yorn had taken them. Aiela filled in her dramatic impressions, regaling him with the story of High Priestess Silena's illegal statue. Ziel's eyes relaxed and his laughter sparkled at her animation. He asked questions all during supper, which Ahna recognized as well-disguised testing inquiries about both of their gifts, their under-standing of metaphysics, their maturity and wisdom and aptitudes.

As they grew quiet, enjoying after-supper tea, Ziel quite naturally broached the subject they were here to discuss. "Ahna, do you have a specific interest? Any ideas of where you might wish to apprentice?"

"I liked several things. The Hall of Records with the Old World Library, and the Temple of Dreams... either record-keeping or perhaps dream-interpretation seems interesting."

"What would you think of apprenticing with the Oracles?"

"I don't know if my abilities are good..." Aiela kicked her under the table "er... at that level."

Ziel smiled, "What nature has given you is beyond what many Oracles began with."

She raised her eyebrows. Felt the tingle of hope. "Really? But I thought they're all very gifted—more than me."

Ziel shook his head, unbound silver hair spread across his shoulders. "We start with a sensitivity, or inclination, perhaps just the interest, which usually indicates a *capacity* to learn. We recognize the seeds of abilities, create the right environment, fertilize, nurture and teach. Believe me, you're far ahead of where the majority of apprentices begin." His pale eyes twinkled at her and one finger smoothed his bushy silver eyebrow over and over. "You don't have to make the decision yet. I do hope you'll consider it though."

He looked to Aiela. "And you my dear? Where does your passion lie?"

"Definitely the Healing Temple! It is marvelous beyond anything I'd imagined. Even when we were passing over—the very first time I saw it—I knew, that is where I'm meant to be. I've committed to them already and been accepted. Priestess Rizele is making arrangements."

He nodded, eyes wide at her certainty. He didn't yet know that Aiela was always certain of what she wanted. Ahna envied her that.

"Your er, enthusiasm is refreshing. It's good to know without question what your calling is, yes?"

"Oh yes! I've known from the beginning. I can't *wait* to get started! There's *huge* amounts to learn. The outer edges of medicine keep growing and growing. Rizele says—"

"Yes well," Ziel interrupted gently, "in addition to your healing abilities, you've the gift of leadership, so consider also the Rulers. I'm not saying—" Ziel spoke over Aiela's frown and beginning protest, "—you must. I'm only giving you my humble opinion to broaden your considerations."

"Alright. Yes, thank you but I won't change my mind." Aiela spoke from the depths of her iron will.

PART II

1

GOODBYES

9,972 BCE ARMANTH, NORTH COAST OF ATLANTIS

"How lucky I am to have something that makes saying goodbye so hard."

— WINNIE THE POOH

AHNA

She fidgeted beside Aiela, as they stood with Papa and Mama, watching the departures docks below. Their larger luggage was already gone. Taken off in carts for Armanth workers to load. A few people mingled around them, while others pushed past, hurrying to and fro in the late morning warmth, bright with the calling of gulls, voices, well-tuned engines and waves.

Seventy-two souls would board their Sea Cruiser bound for Ireland; forty-nine students, a teacher from each of the seven Governing Houses, a trip leader who had coordinated the whole thing, and fifteen assorted crew members. The crew would return with the ship, once their passengers were safely delivered.

Most Atlantean students between seventeen and twenty years of age took a sea voyage to explore some part of the world. This rite-of-passage was both a celebration of the end of primary schooling, and a gateway from the freedom and immaturity of childhood, into the larger complex world of their elders.

The teachers would function as evaluators in their field of expertise. Each student was to be assessed on their understanding of Ireland's systems.

The voyage from Atlantis' northernmost point to Ireland's southwest shore would take only two days on a Sea Cruiser. Light, fast-moving vessels that were hydro-powered and moved at speeds up to sixty knots. Built of a tough, lightweight magnesium alloy, finished with sleek bamboo, the vessel was wide, shallow, and nearly indestructible. Tiny rooms with hammock-style bunks surrounded the cargo hold, just under the deck. An enclosed eating area squatted on center of the deck.

Most educational trips sailed, for the increased opportunity to teach sea life, weather patterns, and travel-by-sea methods. It added to the adventure and provided time for the group to bond, being confined in such a limited space.

Ahna had seen snippets about this trip during the last moon cycle, confusing, wild and nonsensical things. She'd never been so excited. It wasn't just the travel or the strange lands and natives and foods she'd explore, it was also meeting other young people from far-flung parts of Atlantis. There were twenty-four boys and twenty-five girls, most of them traveling with pods of three to five friends.

"Look how organized they are!" Papa watched the busyness flow around them as they made their way down to the boarding dock. He grinned at Mama. "See? I told you they'd be fine. Better than fine!" He'd been trying to ease Mama's worries for at least a week now. She hadn't travelled outside Atlantis except as a baby and worried the twins might get lost, or their luggage would, or they'd be stranded somewhere primitive and terrible.

Atlantis ports were clean and orderly to an extreme. This one, Armanth, a main hub for northern Atlantis, had a constant supply of ships coming and going, bearing worldwide goods and people, yet you would never know that so much business passed through here.

Ships were routed to their appropriate docks according to the nature of their business. Foreign cargo offloaded the many imports brought to Atlanteans from around the globe. In a different space, brawny dock-hands, often with the help of elephants, transferred cargo to boats, used for distribution via the network of rivers. Passengers arrived and departed. Fishing boats and pleasure craft came and went. All had assigned docks, and plenty of workers to direct and assist. Adequate space was key. To the Armanth townspeople, chaos was an enemy, and confusion bred nothing but trouble; bothersome things like disease, dishonesties such as robbery, and aggression. But order—well that brought peace.

They stopped beside the glossy, pink balsa ramp and Mama pulled them both into an embrace, delaying the inevitable parting. "I know we've been giving you reminders and warnings for moons and I know that anything else I say won't penetrate now. So I shall just hold my precious ones tight." Taking a deep, shaky breath in, all three let it out as they squeezed together one last time.

"When exactly, did they grow up?" She asked Papa over their shoulders.

But Papa was watching the other students boarding the sea vessel.

"Just look at them." Eyes shining, he turned back to his family. "It's quite wondrous really. You've studied the world's cultures and people groups, the anthropology, climates and animals, the socio-economics, politics and religions. Now, you get to experience it firsthand. Walk in other worlds, breathe their beliefs and taste their customs." These passions of his life, fueled his words with palpable energy. "Listen to the hearts of the people." He reminded one more time. "And invite their wisdom. They may appear simpler but they've much to teach you."

A pair of seagulls squabbled loudly around them as Drey dug inside the worn leather pouch that went with him everywhere, handing each of his daughters a small package wrapped in creamy fabric, tied with purple and green hemp ribbon. It was no bigger than his hand. "A gift I made for you. I hope you find them useful. The wrapping is a handkerchief, from your Mother of course."

Ahna and Aiela turned the packages over curiously.

"Best put them in your bags and open later." Mama murmured, watching the last of the students trickle onboard.

Papa looked seriously and long into their eyes. "Remember, you have everything you will ever need, right here." He tapped his heart center.

Seeing his brave face crumple and tears rise to tip out the corners of his creased blonde eyes, she, Aiela and Mama moved as one into Papa, tight as a ball of the llama yarn that Mama crocheted with. Arms wrapped this way and that, Papa's tears fertilized the rich love blooming, twining their hearts together. A peaceful moment later, they straightened and drew apart.

"And so we part like we began, in sweetness and tears." Mama smiled brightly for the first time since they'd arrived. Her tattoos glowed from sun-browned skin.

Papa bent to pick up their overflowing packs, finishing Mama's thought, "Let this be another beginning." He handed them their bags. "Go on. It's time I get your Ma all to myself, *finally*. We've our own fun planned you know…"

Mama raised an eyebrow, puckering her lips at him.

"Oh gag." Aiela was backing away towards the Sea Cruiser clutching her pack, "You're leaving us with *that?*"

"Eww." Ahna agreed, grinning. "Probably won't even miss us!" She made her voice light-hearted to hide the churning from these emotional goodbyes.. Shouldering her own pack, she turned towards all the unknowns that lay ahead, and ran with her sister up the ramp.

Finding their way to the Sea Cruiser's railing, already lined with wildly waving and yelling students, the girls cupped their hands around their mouths calling out, along with the rest of them, "Goodbye!"

"I love you Papa."

"I love you Mama."

"See you next moon!"

As the Sea Cruiser floated serenely away, everyone waved madly, shouting words completely lost in the din of a hundred people, filled to capacity with the breathtaking joy of travel.

2

VOYAGE

9,972 BCE ATLANTIS OCEAN AND SOUTH SHORE, IRELAND

"There is one kiss we want with our whole life."

— RUMI

AIELA

*R*elaxed in the middle of a pale orange couch the color of unripened squash, Aiela surveyed the room. She'd stretched out long legs, crossed at the ankles, on a weathered plank floor, dark head resting on the uncomfortably straight back. Around her posed a knot of self-conscious girls engaged mostly in the ancient art of boy-watching.

They were in the gala, a cabin on deck that the ship used interchangeably, becoming a dining, cargo or meeting space depending on who their passengers were. For the students, it had six narrow tables flanked with benches, eight matching—rather bland—couches lining the room, groupings of high-back chairs, and stacks of games. Crew members offered a variety of exotic beverages. The boys arm-wrestled on long, bamboo tables, laughing loudly at rude things, or slurped drinks in gangly silence, stealing glances at the females. The girls were strewn like sweet-smelling garments across sofas, hanging onto the sides or backs of bolted down chairs. They whispered and chattered to each other, bonding quickly as females do, giggling at everything.

Aiela watched the colored excitement of future affairs and drama paint the air as if infusing hope, full and fresh with possibilities. Adventure was seducing them, romance was tempting them and every boy and girl in the room was bursting with the wonder of it all in a magnificent explosion of hues. She could feel her own aura responding to the array.

"Does someone know who that blond boy is?" Nanat hissed, fingering strawberry blonde curls. She rolled intricately lined eyes towards a golden-haired boy with a practiced smile, staring down his adversary as they arm-wrestled. Biceps humped and strained.

"I believe he likes me. He spoke to me when we boarded and he keeps looking at me. I think he's HANDSOME. And quite strong, isn't he?"

Nanat probably imagined all boys were taken with her, Aiela decided. She seemed the type to think she was the main attraction. Trying hard not to roll her eyes, Aiela suggested, "Why don't you go talk to him? If he likes you and you like him, it's best to get going with it soon as possible. We only have one moon together you know." To her, mating should be simple. She tired quickly of coy games, saw no point to the endless chase.

"Yes... yes I believe you're right! Only one moon and twenty-five boys to meet! Or maybe just the one... " Nanat sighed dreamily, watching blond boy raise both arms to the sky with a shout of victory.

"SO!" Aiela was bored of this. "What else do you all do? What's your favorite thing? I'm a healer. I love animals, rock hunting and climbing—preferably at night when the moon's bright."

"Is that why your arms are so muscular? Because you climb?" Mouse-plain Felicia, here with Nanat, was clearly in awe.

"I also sail, ride horses, and play sports, so it's hard to say. They're just... natural I guess." Aiela shrugged, accustomed to admiration. "But come, I truly want to know what you all do. Felicia, what are you best at?"

"Is that your sister?" Felicia asked instead, eyeing the slight, golden-haired figure weaving towards them through the crowd.

Both male and female heads turned to watch as Ahna slid past carrying a game box, but she seemed oblivious to the interested looks, and comments trailing in her wake.

"Twins actually." Aiela spoke with pride, and relief, as she spotted Ahna.

"She's so pretty! You do look a lot alike, just with different hair." Said the girl on Aiela's right.

"There's something... regal about her, like she knows more." Felicia spoke with open admiration. "I would have guessed she was older."

"*I* think she acts stuck up!" Nanat sniffed, her tone ringing jealous as she turned to Aiela. "You poor sweet thing—tied to a condescending sister!" Her voice turned conspiratorial. "Don't worry, you have all of *us* now, and we just LOVE you, don't we girls?"

Aiela raised both eyebrows and cocked her head, flushed with sudden fury. Her voice bristled, turning cold and dry like the gravelled bottom of a quarry. "You're mistaken. I am neither poor nor sweet and Ahna is *shy*, not stuck up. Although if you knew her, you'd wonder why she *doesn't* condescend to the rest of us—considering we don't understand ourselves or our world even half as well as she does!"

Ahna reached them just then. "What are we talking about?" She glanced around the circle, registering the tension.

"Just discussing what Mama always says," Aiela stared pointedly at Nanat, who shifted and looked away, "your words are either constructive or destructive, and the person they'll affect most is you."

"Oh, well that's appropriate" Ahna settled onto the gently rocking floor. "I brought us a word game, but I've never played it before so I'm hoping some of you have..."

Ahna

Outside on deck, spaced between a few other students, Ahna sat wrapped in a wool blanket to fend against the chilly spray peppering up, watching the sky and sea turn mysterious and haunting as night approached. Loud laughter and boisterous conversation from the students in the gala, arranged in little pods of newly-minted friends, vied with the wind roaring in her ears as the seacruiser skimmed over the waves.

She watched several pairs hang shyly at the fringes, as loners pretended to read while sizing up their trip companions, building hopes about who might notice or accept them.

When night had blotted away everything beyond the vessel's edges, with no moon risen yet, she drifted slowly back inside. Faint music began twinkling through the gaps between torsos, arms and legs of the nearest student-cluster and Ahna's eyes tracked the whimsical notes back to a dulcimer. Sporadically visible through the tangle of bodies, it looked battered and ancient, but its music was like melancholy set to rhythm.

That's how she first saw those hands, through a mosaic of gangly male bodies surrounding the seated player, performing half mocking, half skillful dance steps—movements that spoke of conquest, like roosters strutting flamboyant and stiff desires.

Her first impression of him was the contours of those hands. They were large, sculptured with bold detail, and as riveting as the melody they created. Intrigued, she couldn't recall ever particularly noticing or even liking hands—until she met Carver's.

It wasn't so much what they were doing, not even who they were attached to, since she couldn't see the rest of him. It was their sensuous proportions, their rich whispers of expression. They hungrily stroked and roamed and danced, nonchalant with revelled freedom. She knew him first and best, by his hands. Perhaps because they betrayed who Carver really was behind the layered masks that fate and sorrow had custom made and contracted to him.

Carver would come to her in bits and pieces. But this, the first bit, was haunting and foreign. The image of his hands flowing gracefully across a damaged dulcimer would commandeer her dreams later, unknowable, unreachable, incomparably enticing.

Finding a place to sit, she listened to his music, both dauntless and soothing, until the evening grew tired and teachers began sifting through the room, gently reminding it was bedtime.

That's when she caught a second memorable glimpse, this time passing by, jostled slowly through the roomful of flirty eighteen-year-olds all trying to leave simultaneously.

He leaned against the bamboo wall cradling the dulcimer, long fingers absentmindedly tapping out some rhythm until suddenly, they went very still. Ahna was too close. Their sudden calm and a sense of sharp energy being focused on her made her look up.

Straight black strands fell across a closed face. His eyes were deep-set and probed at her with defensive curiosity. She looked away fast, pretending his intensity didn't shock her. Pretending she hadn't just got caught obsessively watching those hands that moved with blunt and restless eloquence.

THE REMAINDER of the two-day boat ride was a flurry of social discovery and planning.

Unstructured mealtimes filled the air with festive food smells. Gathering with their teams to discuss travel itineraries and expectations, adjustments were made when certain personalities weren't clicking. New friendships and bonds happened magically with the callow speed of youth.

Several significant things occurred;

-Aiela had examined all the boys aboard and was disappointed. "Too weak. Too immature. Too fragile. Too dumb. Too egotistical. Too smelly. Too serious. Too tall." She ticked them off one by one to Ahna and sighed. "I was really hoping to meet someone interesting."

-Ahna discovered a Teacher was watching her and Aiela. It was one of their team's adult leaders, acting overly friendly, too interested, even favoring them at times. Her name was Jaydee and she was like honey-coated poison. She seemed intent on knowing all about them. Studying them almost.

"She's a threat. I don't know why yet." Ahna whispered to Aiela.

"Yes well she has little masses of darkness that cling to her." Aiela whispered

back.

-Aiela became student leader of the entire group. In small group meetings, each team was encouraged to choose a team leader, and nominate a leader for the whole body. It was meant for practice in governing, learning to settle their own disputes, and make decisions as a team or entire group. "We want you as self-sufficient as possible" The teacher assigned to each small group explained. "It builds wisdom and maturity, and also gives us reprieve to enjoy the trip."

This came about in late afternoon of the second day. Ahna arrived breathless in their quarters where Aiela was playing cards on the floor, gambling their face powders and mostly losing it. Already out most of their jewelry.

"Aiela, a word please. *Now.*" Ahna was insistent.

Aiela shrugged at the other girls and dumped her cards following Ahna out.

"We need to sit at the front table for supper. It's important. I will tell you what to do and when. We need some clout, some power, and everybody likes you already so we're going to make you student leader. You'll have to look strong and we should get there soon to get that table, so go change. Make your eyes dark and put a diadema on, the one with the ruby. It makes you look older, more mature...sanctioned..." Ahna trailed off at the expression on Aiela's face. "What?'

"I think I lost that one in the game."

Ahna narrowed her eyes at her twin. "That was *special!* A gift from Papa!"

"Oh stop looking at me like that. I'll get it back. I was just playing them up to put in better things before I start winning. You know that."

"You sure you want to do that? There's a little known word that no one likes much. It starts with a ch and ends with an ing and it can make people very angry."

"I don't cheat! I just....use my talents." Aiela smirked at her sister.

"Uh-huh. Tell the girls that when they're all bitter at you for 'playing them up'. Just be careful El. Be wise. There's much that matters about this trip. Bigger things at stake. I wish I knew what, and why....but I don't, yet."

"Don't make this trip boring!" Aiela frowned. "I'm here to have fun."

"Don't make this trip all about you!" Ahna retorted. "You can have fun without being irresponsible."

Aiela rolled her eyes but gave in. "Fine. Just give me a few more minutes. I'll get them to give me a chance to win everything back in one hand. I'll have to stake the rest of our body art, I could lose it all....you go save the table, just to be sure? "

Ahna grinned at her. "At least you're a good bluff. With your luck you'll get a shit hand now, only because it matters. Don't forget about the fancy party at the end, we might need some nice things to wear for that."

"Well, I'm betting we can borrow stuff...if the worst happens." Aiela became serious for a moment, "You're not angry, are you?"

Ahna squeezed her sister's forearm with affectionate pride. "No. Just don't go losing our clothes, I don't mind unadorned, I *do* mind naked." They both laughed at the thought. "You don't need to cheat you know. You're already better than them."

They went separate directions, Ahna calculating their slightly diabolical plan.

Later, during dessert tea, the trip coordinator Helena, asked for each small team's leader to please stand. Ahna stood for their team. Earlier that day, her small group had selected her for being "balanced", liking her quiet pleasant way. "It is time now," Helena told them "to choose a leader. The team heads will adjourn to a back table and select the student to represent the whole group. Ahna tapped her sister's chair. *Now. Go up now and take it.*

Aiela rose and walked the few steps to stand beside Helena. "I am." She announced to the entire room with a confident charm. "I will be your student group leader."

Helena looked bewildered a moment but then asked fifty rapt faces. "Well, it's usually more of an election, but if this is who you want...? If there are no objections...?" She waited while discussion floated back and forth across the tables.

Ahna called out first, "Yes, for my team." And then the other leaders began calling out one by one.

"We choose Aiela."

"Fine for us."

"Sure, she's good as any."

Until every team except one had agreed. The blond boy, Nirka, was the only dissident. "I disagree. We should follow procedure and the elected leaders should decide privately amongst themselves." Probably, he'd planned to be the leader, Ahna figured. He sat down sour-faced and fuming.

Helena raised her eyebrows but she was smiling while she nodded. "We have a majority decision then. That certainly saved some time! Thank you Aiela." She bowed slightly to dismiss her, but Aiela wasn't done.

She addressed the students. "From what I understand, I'm to settle disagreements, decide courses of action that affect the group, and make rules... " She paused, and then winked "... but I'd rather abolish them. How about this? We're all here to have fun and learn. If we don't take things personally, if we're generous with each other, we'll be fine. I request you bring your team leader along to discuss any issue with me. We're adults now. I trust we will act responsibly. I'm also to treat with our teachers in matters that concern our trip at large and believe me, I'm a skilled negotiator and I will work on your behalf." She smiled, dark eyes resting on each student as if they shared a secret, connecting her energy to theirs. The thin orichalcum diadema encircled her piles of blackberry hair, its single crimson ruby dangling between her eyebrows, reflecting rays of endless vitality. Everyone in the room was caught up in her charisma. Ahna could feel it. The boys looked besotted and the girls who had already befriended her were smug. Teachers raised eyebrows and murmured to each other "This one shows promise." and "Such leadership in one so young!" Even Nirka looked impressed. But Nanat's eyes narrowed when she noticed his admiring gaze.

Aiela sat down amid applause, and Ahna gave her hand a hard, victorious squeeze under the table. *Well done!*

Jaydee leaned between the girls, her cloistering perfume invading, a smile stretched wide, "Your parents would be terribly proud of you! You must tell me all about them! So I can regale them when we return home, with stories of their bright, shiny daughters who impressed us all!"

After Helena's closing instructions, Ahna hurried her twin along, through a hail of student's congratulating, buddying-up and wanting-to-get-in-good, to fetch their luggage. The ship had begun its slow nudging way up to the dock. They would bed down in Ireland tonight!

"And THAT my dear, is how we do it!" Aiela smiled triumphantly, repacking their body adornments and a good many new things that Ahna didn't recognize.

"You were perfect and now we know, leadership *is* something you can take. The goal being to put it in the hands of somebody good. It was either going to be crazy Nanat or her 'boyfriend' who thinks he should be a god. Either of them would've made things miserable, possibly even dangerous for us."

"Really? You saw all that?"

"Yes, I actually saw enough to figure out what was happening. For once."

One thing that didn't happen: Ahna and Carver didn't speak even though they walked off the Seacruiser side by side. He was tall and less gangly than the others. Solid and manly. Acutely aware of his presence and the glances he kept slanting her way, she felt embarrassed still by the hand-staring incident. Aiela was the beauty and the charmer. Ahna thought herself rather plain—which had never bothered her until this moment. Her quiet personality certainly wasn't the alluring magnet her sister's was. She wouldn't know what to say to him.

And then there were rumors—vicious rounds of them, each juicier than the last: Why had students from the Sons of Belial joined their trip? Why had he been restricted to his room since last night? The stories were varied and colorful. But all of them agreed, he was dangerous. Volatile.

Ahna sensed another truth but it was buried and inaccessible. So she concentrated hard on pretending she didn't see him, suddenly talkative to Aiela on her other side, or the girls behind them. Besides, she found it hard to breathe this close to him. It panicked her a little that she couldn't explain why. Or what the disconnected fluttery feeling in her stomach was. As if she was about to do something risky.

3

CARVER

9,972 BCE ATLANTIC OCEAN

"A human being is part of a whole, called by us 'Universe'. A part limited in time and space. He experiences himself, his thoughts and feelings as something separated from the rest—a kind of optical delusion of consciousness."

— ALBERT EINSTEIN

CARVER

*C*arver replayed the bird-like blonde girl staring at his hands as if entranced, again and again. Her eyes were the colors of an ancient forest in sunlight, mixed greens with tiny gold specks of mischief peeking out. What would it feel like if she gazed with those eyes into him?

But it hadn't happened, not even close, and he felt foolish for wanting it. He knew better than to want. The more you want something, the more it hurts when you don't get it.

He carried so many secrets he could barely open his mouth without lying. Everything had to be an act—during this Ireland trip especially. The weight of his deceptions, the burden of his tasks, the dread of what could happen if he failed, turned him edgy and sour.

He hadn't much experience with social settings. He'd spent little time with people his own age—even less with girls. They liked him enough back home, flocked to him lately as he'd grown into a broad and muscular height, but he lacked the confidence, and mainly the trust, to take any of them up on uninhibited offers. Mardu had brought him a girl recently as a gift, but Carver had quietly returned her. He didn't want anything purchased or forced. For certain, he didn't want anything that came from Mardu.

All he really knew was what he didn't want. He'd yet to discover a girl that felt right. There had not been such luxuries as purity or love in Carver's life. These were foreign,

uncomfortable things to him.

The fifth son of Mardu, Carver had been abandoned early. Mardu clothed, housed and fed him, only because Carver's foreign-slave mother left him behind to return home. All that Carver remembered about his mother was a sense of safety, and music. He liked to imagine that she'd played the dulcimer for him to fall asleep to every night. That same dulcimer he'd learned as a child to play, and the only bit of her that he had. Mardu told him that she'd never loved him. That she'd gone home to her land across the water, too embarrassed of her child to keep him. A mild example of Mardu's lies, and his capacity for cruelty. Orja had told him a different story—which was even harder to hear than Mardu's lies.

Carver was never allowed to shed the shame of being unwanted. His half brothers liked to knock him around when he was little and Mardu encouraged them, loudly and repeatedly, favoring his "pure" flesh and blood over this mixed-blood child foisted on him because "the whore claimed it was mine".

Around twelve, Carver began to resemble Mardu. More so, the older he got. He despised this even more than his father did—had grown a turbid hate for his father long before then. It added a new sort of hopelessness to have confirmation, every time he looked in the mirror, that he actually was Mardu's offspring.

If possible, Mardu became crueler, enraged by the fact that this embarrassing child looked so much like all the parts of himself he was most proud of. They shared a sun-bronzed complexion and thick black hair, as if birthed at the center of a god's smoldering fire. Their icy blue eyes gleamed cold and hard like the steel blades they carried. Where Mardu's features were raw and blunt, Carver's were finer, as if shaped by an artisan. His brothers mocked his "prettiness", smacking his chest where "someday your tits will grow in." By fifteen, Carver was as tall as Mardu and continued to grow, outranging every one of his brothers— who suddenly found less time and reason to abuse him.

He determined to let the hard upbringing make him different, and began to forge an inner strength, instead of the bitterness that drove his brothers. Watching and listening, he decided to be smart instead of violent. Ultimately, he vowed to be nothing like the callously cruel family that both abandoned and controlled him.

His father's business associates began looking to Carver for advice. Long years of learning to read people—because a smorgasbord of pain might depend on knowing where danger lay—had shaped habits of keen hyper-vigilance. He knew instinctively when someone was lying, and he read moods or emotions fluently. He knew whether someone was a bully, shrewd, or had any sort of compassion. And the exact caliber of their courage.

Mardu had recently shifted from outright contempt, to using Carver for his purposes. At first he'd ignored those who praised Carver. Then he decided Carver held power over people and started exploiting it, giving Carver small tasks, delivering messages, and fetching things or information of value. Then he asked Carver to convince certain reluctant merchants to do business with the Sons of Belial.

Carver was unusually successful. He found that the more he participated in his father's schemes, the more he could be gone from home. He found he enjoyed travel, seeing new places and odd customs. He also discovered a gift for languages.

This trip to Ireland seemed to be an important mission for his father. Secretly, Carver hoped it might bring something to fill the hollowness inside of him. He couldn't name what he was looking for exactly, maybe a noble meaning for his life, or some sort of healing. What he needed was a permanent escape.

The hard part was traveling over water. It scared Carver in a way he would never admit to anyone. Fear didn't plague him much anymore. He'd lived a life that required him to either overcome his fears or live huddled in a corner. He'd learned that fear is only as real as you make it. Still, being in the midst of endlessly deep water held a sort of dark terror that reached in to gut him.

During the second morning, a sea serpent was sighted following their ship. Sea serpents were rare, having been hunted almost to extinction for their colorful hides. Its colors were muted far beneath the surface waves, but the enormous length and shape was unmistakable. Carver felt blood drain from his face when his excited bunkmates told him about it. Then he vomited, claiming he was seasick. The other boys never suspected he was reacting to the proximity of a sea serpent and not the monotonous movement of the water.

. . .

WHEN CARVER WAS EIGHT, he went on a three-day hunting trip with his brothers and their friends. He was the youngest and only got to go because no one cared one way or the other whether he went or stayed. They were a group of rowdy boys, free of adult supervision, ranging from twelve to twenty years old—except for eight-year-old Carver.

They'd gone to an island where the beasts were so wild and plentiful, no humans wanted to live there. Back when the Sons of Belial first started crossbreeding and mixing DNA, this island was their lab. Eventually, they'd been forced to move their experiments, and the island had continued to breed grotesque monsters and predators and oversized man-eating mammals. The Belials used it both for training their boys into fearless killers, and for sport hunting.

It was on the return trip that tragedy struck. They'd dropped anchor to swim. Summers in the south of Atlantis were relentless with sweltering heat and the boys were grimy from camping and wrestling, and stank of blood from the kill and butchering of two giant razorback creatures. High on the thrill of dangers past, and heading into exhaustion, the older boys were floating or treading water in a calm sea. Telling tall tales to each other of their adventures, while Carver was diving a little ways off, out of cuffing and ridicule range.

Uneasy even then in deep water, he didn't like not seeing the bottom. It made him feel dizzy to think of all that dark space beneath him.

A long bright shape circled up from the murky depths beneath him, taking him completely by surprise. Sea Serpents were a rarity but they tended to like the Belial territory because food was more plentiful there. Carcasses, more human than animal, found their way into Belial waters— not often live ones though.

Carver caught movement on his periphery, a blur of vivid orange, just in time to lunge, panicked, towards the boat.

The serpent was lined up to swallow him whole, shooting out of the water, gaping maw streaming bloody seawater and ragged with teeth. It screamed a high-pitched wail. A haunting sound of terror and tragedy that none would ever forget. But it had gotten only a trailing leg.

Carver made it to the boat at the same time as most the other boys, who went scrambling for their weapons.

Somebody pulled him in. It was then they noticed his right leg was missing below the knee. They tied it off and bandaged the stump as best they could, speeding home instead of fighting the beautiful, deadly creature circling them.

That Carver lived was a miracle, losing so much blood, being that exposed to infection. The venom of a sea serpent is like fire to human flesh. It seared just enough to save Carver's life, while a single drop had landed on his right eyelid, eating right through the cornea.

Through the interventions of Orja, he spent close to a year at an Atlantean Healing Temple. Despite the traumatic episode, the nightmares, the pain of regenerating an eyeball and both tibia and fibula bones, it was the best year of his life. He fell in love with the caring, gentle Atlanteans who healed him.

By the time he turned ten, he had an eye that was practically new and a whole leg. But the foot was prosthetic. They'd gotten his leg to regenerate, but not the foot. He was crippled—which brought shame to Mardu like nothing else before. A member of his own household, weakened, imperfect. Less than whole. Just another reason for Mardu to write the boy off as the family blight. The other boys did what they saw done, treating Carver as less than nothing as well.

His best days were when everyone simply ignored him.

It was during his healing year, under Atlantean encouragement, that he started making music. The Healers noted how desperately he was drawn to instruments, and brought in instructors for both the dulcimer and harp. It soothed and distracted Carver from the pain, and challenged him. He kept at it. Even after returning home, he sought out the servants and few Belials who could help him learn music. He began to write melody at the age of twelve and though few knew of it, he grew into quite a remarkable musician. This only sharpened the ridicule at home. There would be no acceptance or forgiveness for these betrayals of Mardu. For becoming a Cripple and a Musician, in a family of hardened warrior-kings.

MARDU HAD SENT two other boys on this trip to Ireland. Sons of Mardu's trusted men, they were told to blend in, watch over, protect and assist Carver. To report back on everything done or said.

Drommen was overly average. Average height and build, average intelligence, even his hair color was ashy brown under a long, average face. He sort of faded and left no impression whatsoever. Most people forgot he was even there.

Lister, on the other hand, stuck out like a crooked door. With bright hair the color of rusted pipes, and pale freckled skin that burned easily, he was soft all over. He was also clumsier than a camel with three legs. If there was a hole, Lister would fall into it. Not find it, just fall in—and probably break something too.

They both lacked confidence or imagination, but at least they were nice. Revering Carver, they stayed with him unless specifically ordered not to, appearing to be the best of friends—which struck Carver as funny and a bit sad. If anything, they were his hired friends.

Neither Drommen or Lister understood a bit of Irish and they were puzzled when Carver tried to teach them basic Irish words.

"What for? They'll know Atlantean, surely. Don't ever'body have to speak Atlantean? It's the only real language anyway."

Carver was patient with them. "Alright Lister, I'll try to explain this. Dromm, you listening? The Atlanteans don't think like we do. Their Law of One teaches that everyone's equal no matter who they are. That everything and everybody is part of the same Whole—even if they're not Atlantean. So you can't say bad things about the Irish, their language, their country, or anything else being inferior. Do you understand? It'll mark us as different, and remember, it's important we blend in."

"I don't know what inferior means." Lister's voice was soft, like the rest of him.

"Not as good as. Less than. At home the Belials believe our half-animals are inferior to humans, that children are inferior to adults and that women are inferior to men."

Drommen and Lister nodded in understanding. "Well yeah. Of course they are."

"No!" Carver said, "They're not. See, that's what I mean. You have to think and act differently on this trip or you're going to offend everyone! You have to treat all of them as your equal. Especially the girls! They will pick up on it quicker than anybody else. I saw you looking at that tall red-haired girl when we boarded Dromm. If you want her, you have to be kind and do things for her, listen to her, show her a great lot of respect."

The boys were unbelieving. "But why? You can just tell 'em. Back home the girls just need to be tole' what to do and what a man wants."

"What does respect mean?" Lister again.

Carver groaned, rubbing his eyes. This could take all night. The gap between Atlanteans and Belials had grown wide indeed.

He finally ordered them to just stay away from the girls. "Watch and listen to how the Atlantean boys act. I don't want you having as much as a conversation with any of the girls until you learn how the Atlanteans treat them."

Then he threateningly forbade them to tell anyone that he was Mardu's son. The boys were aghast, "But you're a *prince*! You could be the next Belial leader and that makes you more better than any of these Atlanteans!"

Carver grew fierce. "NO! You will NOT tell them. I will literally cut out your tongues or 'lose' you somewhere along the way. Lots of ocean we'll be crossing, lots of wilds in Ireland..." He glared ominously from one to the other. "Swear to me you will play your parts. We are all normal and equal and here to learn about the Irish. Joining the Atlanteans because we want to know more of their ways..."

Drommen and Lister made blood pacts, eager for Carver to trust them, and believing every threat he made. He was, after all, a son of the great and terrible Dominus Mardu.

Still, when it came down to it, his hired friends failed in their most basic duties.

Nirka, a bull-headed boy who might've been alright if you could get around his giant, empty head, took an instant dislike to Carver and by proxy, Drommen and Lister. It took Nirka exactly four hours into the voyage to form a gang around himself, instinctively grabbing power and loyalties to wrap up in, as if he could shore up the emptiness of his pretenses. In the world of young men, Carver knew, pretense is all it takes, empty or not, to gain a following.

Carver had been playing his dulcimer after evening meal in the large common room on the sea cruiser, out of the windy sea spray. Drommen and Lister, deprived of music in the Belial culture, were enjoying Carver's private concert, until Nirka and his boys started making comments about inferior Belial music. Then the bumping and shoving. Carver ignored Nirka's taunts, simply moving to another side of the room.

Later that night, Nirka and two of his new buddies had come strolling into Carver's room, swaggering and boasting and irritating because Carver was desperate to fall asleep, hoping to escape his anxiety from being in the middle of the deep ocean. He told them to leave and Nirka made the mistake of handling the dulcimer. Picking it up, he pretended to play it, banging the strings roughly.

"Get your hands off my things." Carver had growled.

"Sure." Nirka sneered and drop-kicked the instrument into a bunk, bouncing it off the ceiling first. Carver shoved Nirka in the tiny space and Nirka hit his head on the wall about the same time that Carver hit him full-on in the face. He was bleeding from two places, whimpering while Carver fought off the two buddies.

When the teachers arrived and pulled them apart, they sentenced Carver to his room until they docked. He didn't bother to tell the teachers that golden boy had tried to smash his dulcimer, for no reason except to challenge him. The teachers had already decided to be disappointed in him. Decided to believe that he was just another violent Sons-of-Belial cliche. "He seemed different at first", they whispered to each other in disapproving tones.

Drommen and Lister had stayed out of the way in their bunks, watching wide-eyed, ducking or frozen the whole time while Carver battled Nirka and his two followers. It didn't occur to them to refute the story Nirka told the teachers.

Carver patiently waited until the next morning to give them instructions about how exactly he would like to be protected.

THAT FIRST NIGHT he dreamt of a half-size angel. She hovered just behind him and was pouring something warm and fresh, viscous as honey onto his crown, where a hole opened up and funneled the golden substance into the space where his heart should be. The echoing hollow confirmed all his worst fears and he was crying and strangling on horror, realizing that he indeed was missing a heart. Pleading for help, but unable to form words, he finally caught a glimpse of the angel before she disappeared into the depths, disappointed at his heartlessness.

She was sunlit green with flashing delicate gold wings, humming a familiar tune and oblivious to his despair. She had kissed his hands with sweet feathery lips, then flew straight down into a clear sea with no bottom. He wanted to follow but instead awoke, terrified of the monsters that lived in that deep.

4

JAYDEE

9,972 BCE ATLANTIC OCEAN

"We penetrated deeper and deeper into the heart of darkness"

— JOSEPH CONRAD, "HEART OF DARKNESS"

JAYDEE

*H*is presence looming over her in the darkness, and her vagina flooded at the same time as her eyes. Lust, sharpened with fear, pushed up and out of her towards the dark shape pressing her into a moving bed. Burying her fingers in his hair, she kissed him roughly, just as he liked. Sexual charges crackled through her as she spoke softly. "My lover, you've come! I've missed you, it's been so long, I—"

"I hate it when you talk." He interrupted. "I am not yours—but you are mine to use...aren't you."

She shuddered at his tender tone. Always the sound of his voice seemed as one cherishing his beloved, even as his words stabbed her most vulnerable places, opening her against her will. "Forgive me Dominus. I, I've been th-thinking about you so often and missing your touch. I feel so alone, it's..." Her words drifted away as she felt his hand move to her hips and a pressure between her legs. Would he feel the wetness? she wondered. Her desire for him, her devotion? Mardu had never really understood the love she had for him.

She moved, pushing against the pressure, seeking some sort of relief from

215

pent-up emotions scouring her body like rough sand. The sensations began to build and Mardu whispered "Is this what you've been missing, is this what you want?"

She moaned softly, arching higher and he kept on, his stroking and voice a hypnotic combination turning her need frantic, demanding she open fully to his wicked quenching. She reached the cusp of orgasm and abruptly the pressure ceased.

"I've a job for you. Perhaps later I'll give what you're so desperate for."

Frustrated, she hastened to answer. "Of course. What is it? Anything you ask..."

"There's a student trip headed to Ireland next moon. Investigate two of the students—I've history with their father that's becoming relevant now. Get close to them, find out what they know of me and the dealings their father had with Belial."

"But...I'd have to find a way to replace one of the teachers. You know I'm awkward with youth. Are you sure this is important? What's the significance...?" Her words stopped short as iron hands closed around her throat and the weight on her increased.

"You worthless whore! You'd question me?" The words grated and twisted around her like serrated steel. Choking, freezing, she lay paralyzed with fear, unable to breathe, unsafe to resist in any way.

"I give you this opportunity to be of service and you question me?"

Lacking oxygen, she began to shake and tears streamed down the sharp angles of her pale face. All desire forgotten, fear overwhelmed her. His iron hands squeezed tighter. "Do not fail me Jaydee, you don't want to see what happens then."

Abruptly the pressure released and her breath came back in a ragged gasp of terror.

"Jaydee? Jaydee are you alright?" A hand reached to touch her forehead and she reacted violently batting it away.

"NO, I—leave me alone!" She sat up, eyes adjusting to predawn darkness in the cabin of the sea cruiser bound for Ireland. It was only Lira the Healer, standing next to her bed concerned for her. Gulping in the cool night air she tried to calm herself before speaking again. "I'm sorry Lira, I'm...fine. It was only a bad dream. Go back to bed, sorry to wake you."

"Well if you're sure you're alright—" Lira brushed her shoulder lightly in acknowledgment. "You're ice-cold! Let me get you another blanket!"

Lira was the group healer, Jaydee knew it would be best to let her do something, assure herself Jaydee really was alright. So she lay back and

216

accepted the blanket being tucked over her, hoping Lira would leave her be. "Thank you." She said softly, turning over to close her eyes.

Jaydee had never been good with people, felt undeserving when someone did her a kindness. Even as a child her intellect outweighed her social skills, leaving her isolated and unbalanced. She struggled through classes, trying and failing to fit in and make friends.

Her parents were no help. Her mother died giving birth to her, and her father was distant, spending most of his time at his office in the Foreign Relations department, or in his study at home. Jaydee was raised by teachers and the endless syndicate of books that she read in a lonely home.

She followed in her father's footsteps to work in Foreign Relations. The only way she merited his attention was showing interest in his field. He was a cold, intellectual man, incapable of connection. She learned to equate any attention from him with some twisted form of the love she'd never had. So she poured herself into learning everything she could about that house of government. Finishing top of her class, she had a position in the foreign trade department before she was even done with her apprenticeship.

This was where she'd met Mardu all those years ago. She was young and naive in the ways of men. He was a senior advisor in the Military department, brilliant, charismatic and powerful. He flaunted his sexual energy to her. Even understanding that women came easy to him, knowing he did this with many girls, she fell instantly in love. The first night he took her was the night he got passed over for the seat on the High Council—losing to a woman.

Still an intern, she'd been working late to finish father's reports. He always left things for her to organize. She overheard Mardu raging. Heavily drunk and cursing, he vowed to take down the whole department, the whole Council, the whole world! When he finally left, he passed her father's office and saw her. Lust took over. Not understanding all that had transpired that night, Jaydee thought he was finally confessing his love for her and gave him every bit of herself willingly, eagerly. That was the last time she saw him for several years, the last time anyone saw him. That night he left High City, and began his climb to lead the Sons of Belial.

Jaydee curled tighter under the blankets, remembering the golden days when Mardu reappeared in her life and they'd begun their affair. He had wooed her, bound her to him.

He'd asked that she meet him at the Belial border so they could spend the moon getting to know one another better, saying he'd been intoxicated with her and could not get her off his mind ever since his last night in High City. They'd stolen away together many times after that, and she didn't mind his moods that swung abruptly from grandiose plans to black sullen rages. Or the sex that could be romantic and adventurous when he was pleased, or brutal and insatiable when he wasn't. She'd never had attention from men, and his was a drug she'd give anything for. He was a powerful man, and she determined to be valuable, remain important to him. Mistaking fear-laced excitement for love, she was desperate for more. It didn't matter that he became threatening and was rough with her. This was simply his way and she was his to do with as he pleased. No one suspected her connection with the Sons of Belial, or the man who made himself their leader.

After that terrifying meeting that kept reappearing as nightmares, she'd told Mardu which teacher from the House of Foreign Relations was going on the trip. When the teacher had fallen very ill, she'd requested to replace him. It required forged documents (a fictional former teaching position), and more than a little convincing to get assigned to the trip. She didn't understand young people at all but it was necessary to pretend she did, for Mardu.

So here she was, even though she'd been told little of why she was watching them or the plans behind it. How many times had she learned she must not question. She must simply obey. That was how she would keep his attention, total compliance.

Her thoughts drifted, envisioning ways to befriend the girls while on this journey she already despised. Sea travel didn't agree with her—but she must put that aside too. Mardu was trusting her with this important task. Surely she would be rewarded greatly. He'd only been cruel lately because she'd given him nothing to love her for. Once she'd proven how loyal and smart she was, she would earn his love again, his devotion. A chill shuddered at the thought of failure. Fear lurked, prowling the edges of her double life, waiting to devour her.

5

TURNER

9,972 BCE SOUTH SHORE, IRELAND

"...and the vessel was not full, his intellect was not satisfied, his soul was not at peace, his heart was not still."

— HERMANN HESSE, "SIDDHARTHA"

TURNER

He sat on a rough stone wall overlooking the crowded harbor, watching a pair of seagulls squabble over a half-eaten fish skeleton in the dead blue sky. Their shrill of squawks and screams echoed his inner state, although you would never know it from his focused gaze, or the way he seemed to fit into his surroundings like a well-worn bench.

Restless; in a word that was Turner. Not in a fidgety, uneasy sort of way—in fact, he could remain still longer than anyone. Restless as in, his insatiable mind never stopped questing, yearning for new and exhilarating experiences. Restless as in, he felt he might just shrivel up inside, dry up like the cracked mud bogs in summer, if he didn't escape soon.

He wasn't supposed to be stuck still, in this bleak and banal place. His normally sunny face creased into a scowl at the thought. Born and raised in this dreary backwater, he'd become impatient to start the next part of his life, chafing to be halfway across the continent. Desperate even.

His mother's family was Grecian and he'd spent three moons there every year. During the rainy season, his father moored the ships in those sunny, protected coves, to keep them and the crew safe from the pounding storms that could ravage, or swallow them whole. The revenue Da lost from not merchanting for this period, was still less than the repairs and replacements of running the storms. Not to mention, the loss of good men.

Turner had long anticipated the day when he would leave home and make his own life. He'd started learned sailing and the merchant trade since before he could remember, and so of course, wanted nothing to do with it now. He was his father's only son. But he had his own dreams, and the drive to make them happen. Yet instead of basking in the hot sun of Greece, getting settled into an apprenticeship with his uncles, he was here still—caretaking a group of Atlantean students.

He spat in disgust. That's what he thought of Atlantis with their high and mighty, holier-than-you attitudes. Their fancy clothes and flamboyant cities. Their technology and crystals and riches. The almighty power they believed they held over the rest of the world.

One of Da's men was supposed to have been the expedition leader, but there'd been an accident, resulting in a broken leg, four days before the group's arrival. Da had told Turner—not even asking—but told him like it was a *privilege*, that he would be entrusted with this 'important role'.

The group of fifty, including all their entourage, would be here for a full moon. Their itinerary was set. All Turner had to do was keep them on schedule and see to their safety. Make sure they had everything they needed. Their expedition would take them all the way north, along the coast for the most part, and across the land bridge into Scotland, where they'd sail home from Scottish shores.

Da's connection with Atlantis went way back. He was deeply successful for one reason; he'd invested several years, and the small fortune he'd inherited, into learning Atlantean sailing. Eventually, he'd replaced the entire fleet with Atlantean designed vessels, and was the most dependable and trusted merchant-trader outside of Atlantis. When there were costly goods, or time-sensitive cargo that needed transported 'round the world, it was Da's vessels that carried them.

Turner took a long pull from his waterskin and stood, splashing water in his hands to run through his unruly mop of curls. It wouldn't create order for long, but it would cool him for a bit before he worked up a sweat getting his charges situated for the long trip ahead.

He paced the neat line of empty wagons waiting for his pampered guests to arrive. He'd sent the Drivers down to where the Seacruiser was docking, with handcarts to fetch up the luggage. It was the busiest time of the day at the harbour. High tide always brought a rush of ships that needed to offload goods, the last frenzied loading of those wanting to depart, and foreign vessels stopping in to re-stock fresh water and foodstuff.

Seems more congested than usual, Turner thought, eyeing stray ruffians and poor people mingling with the crowd. Sure an' they'd be pickpocketing the unwary. All society's castaways ended up here. Deserters from ships—or those criminal enough to be forcefully removed, and the usual dregs who couldn't or wouldn't work, found ways to survive at this salt-brimmed and thriving port town.

The first few Atlanteans came sifting towards the wagons, wearing elegant clothing as impractical as a rain cloak made of lace. One by one, the Drivers were returning, pushing carts laden high with luggage. Turner put on a charming smile and bowed—Atlantean style—greeting a trio of teachers in Atlantean. "Welcome! Ya must be the leaders of this em, esteemed group. An' I'll be Turner, yer guide." He gestured to the harbor scene below, " We're no' as unruly as all this. Figured we'd start wi' the worst ta make ever'thing else look nicer." Directing, answering questions, assuring them of the pleasure to be had in this perennially green land, he forced an ease and cheer that he didn't feel.

They were arriving slower than he'd anticipated, what with the mass of people, and dusk falling. It would certainly be easy to get lost in this muck. He was counting, keeping a running tally in his head, and starting to fret. What would his plan be if there were missing students? He'd send the wagons ahead and keep as many adults as possible to help search. Maybe pay a few coins to the savvier street kids who were always out en force on evenings such as this. This was a thief's paradise with lots of foreigners moving through the growing darkness and confusion. But they'd know instinctively—even in full dark—the 'rich' Atlanteans. Yes. He'd offer them a whole penny for every one they brought back safe, and unrobbed.

A commotion in the crowd drew his eye. A tall black-haired lad about his own age dashed towards him, toting a wee girl in his arms. A child, Turner thought. His attention averted like an off-course magnet, to the most stunning girl he'd ever laid eyes on. Exotic, muscular, wild—even dangerous looking, she followed Black-hair, urging him faster. Turner's pulse quickened. Black-hair was shouting as they neared him, and Turner's nose flared at the sharp tang of blood running from a long gash down the face of the girl he carried, jolting him out of his trance. Guilt stung him at the thought of the plans he'd just been making, 'in case'. Another student it was, not a child.

Black-hair barked at the adults staring dumbly at him. "Find the healer and an Irish driver!" The exotic girl, hefted a large pack in front of her, despite another strapped on her back, throwing it into a wagon. Together, they maneuvered the unconscious girl aboard.

"Round up the rest o' the group, there'd be ferty-foor o' them yet, an' drive em' ta the lodging fer tonight. We'll meet ya there. MAKE SURE ya count!" Turner spoke tersely to his nearest Driver, waiting only for a nod of understanding, before vaulting lightly into the driver's seat of the wagon. Black-hair and the exotic girl were still settling, their healer climbing in, as Turner directed the aurochs away towards the east. Headed for Vargo's.

"Hang on. Will be bumpy." Turner looked back and spoke directly to Black-hair, still holding the bleeding girl. Meeting Turner's eyes coolly, Black-hair nodded, returning his attention to the girl sitting next to him. It took effort for Turner to force his eyes back on the road. She was fierce up close, as fierce as she was exotic, as she stroked the blonde-hair of the bleeding girl and murmured comfort.

It occured to Turner that he'd spoken in his own Celtic language, yet Black-hair seemed to understand perfectly. Odd. Atlanteans weren't known for bothering with other languages, always expecting, assuming, that everyone would know theirs. And usually that was the case, being that Atlantis was the world power. Had been for ages and ages.

Turner pushed the aurochs faster—which seemed a snail's pace, guilty thoughts crowding his head. He should've thought to have the Driver's escort them all safely through the crowds. He'd assumed their teachers would have a plan for staying together and staying safe. But then he remembered the occasions he'd visited Atlantis with Da. They didn't have unruly mobs like here. And they certainly didn't have street thieves and beggars. Of course they wouldn't have been expecting danger, or getting separated. Da would be furious with him once he found out. If he found out. Great almighty gods, let the girl be alright. Whatever became of her would be on his head.

He urged the beasts even faster as they left the city, his mind a riot of prayers and plans. Not much further now. Please let Vargo be home and not out with someone having a baby or helping someone die, or in some dank drinking hole... Best plot a plan B just in case. They had their Atlantean healer with them. Surely she'd know as much as Vargo. They could use his surgery with or without him and patch the girl up.

Turner's boots hit the ground before the wagon stopped rolling. Not thinking to knock on the rough door, thick as a young tree, he shoved it open. "Vargo, we need help here. They're Atlanteans. She's bleeding from the face...."

Short and stout as a pug, Vargo didn't even blink at the intrusion, just got up with a grunt from his chair at the plain table where he was eating eel and roots stew by candlelight. Without comment, he grabbed the wide, thin plank wrapped in sheep's wool that stood next to the door, and charged towards the wagon.

"There there lass, ye'll be fine now. We'll take care o' ya, we will." Vargo's rough voice crooned soothing words in Celtic, as the black-haired lad laid the unconscious girl onto the stretcher. Together they picked up the plank and carried it into Vargo's surgery, the fierce and exotic girl glued alongside.

The Atlantean Healer followed close behind, rattling a slew of words at Vargo. Words that Vargo understood not a one of, until Black-hair starting translating. "This is Healer Lira. She asks if you've any sort of laser. Or at least some Eiller root compound to seal the gash."

Vargo shook his head. "I've needles an' verra fine thread. That'll have ta do 'er."

Healer Lira's look of alarm at the translation made Vargo chuckle. "Tell 'er I'm skilled in the auld ways e'en if she's not. Twill be fine. I'll fix the lass up."

Unable to do any more for them, Turner sighed and wandered back to the eating room that adjoined the surgery. Fine start this was. Was it his fault, all this madness, since he hadn't wanted this responsibility? He sank into a corner, letting the guilt and fear eat away his confidence. Da could easily say that he couldn't go to Greece after all. That he needed to become more responsible before apprenticing—or some such nonsense.

6

THE ARRIVAL

9,972 BCE SOUTH SHORE PORT, IRELAND

"That first night, when all was loud chaos and the muddied ones tried to take her, I came for her. That night I vowed I would always come for her."

— A SONG OF IRELAND

AHNA

*I*reland was a cacophony of humanity tonight, as they docked at the busy harbour on the southeast tip of the almost-island. Other ships moored nearby, had recently arrived, and several more huge vessels laden with cargo were preparing to depart. It was impossible for their group to stay together, as they disembarked into the tangle of people hurrying in cross-directions to each other.

Ahna and Aiela linked hands, letting the jostle of the crowd carry them as they stared in wonder at their first foreign town.

The village grew out from the harbour in a misshapen half-circle. Cleaving to hillsides that rose at sharp angles from the sea, brightly colored shops, homes and a multitude of tiny buildings leaned on each other in haphazard patterns like mismatched puzzle pieces. Some structures seemed brand new and vibrant. Others washed out to a bleak grey after centuries of salted air stinging around them. The streets were uneven, paved with crushed shells that had hardened in sunbaked sand.

Sharp and gritty, it could've been pretty in a faded way, if it weren't for all the filth. Trash and dung were trampled underfoot. They tried to avoid it but soon gave up, sensing the futility. Dull animal stink and the sharp reek of long-dead fish assaulted their senses and instinctively they held the edge of their travel cloaks over their noses. It didn't help.

"Welcome to the rest of the world." Aiela yelled, making them both smile into the din of brassy foreign sounds as they pushed through.

The voices spoke dialects unrecognizable. Mangy, burdened donkeys were led, carts pulled by man and beasts, smaller handcarts, balanced on one wheel, full of crates, bags and boxes were pushed by many colors of people. There seemed to be no order at all. Even the busiest of harbours back home had neatly defined sectors, lines and signs, rules and space—always lots of space so that nothing ever felt crowded or jumbled. Not like this mess of sweaty, strangely garbed humans brushing against each other. As if mimicking the noise below, huge washes of seagulls wailed and squawked overhead. Calling to each other constantly as they brazenly crowded the evening-greyed sky.

Ahna gazed upward at them, letting Aiela pull her through the bumping bodies. Thinking how all of nature likes to reflect itself over and over, like two opposing mirrors that—

"Look out!" Aiela stopped abruptly to let a cart pass and Ahna bumped into her, distracted and overwhelmed by all that was moving around her. A sudden strong vision buzzed within. *Her pack clinging to her back, secured with the strap across her chest, being cut off, stolen by someone oozing desperation.* She felt it happen, and then the jolt of coming back to real time, where her eyes were drawn to a boy about her own size but younger, sliding through the press of bodies straight for her.

He didn't see her watching him, so focused he was on intercepting them, on disentangling a small blade from his pocket.

Ahna knew his heart was pounding with anticipation. A hard, awful desperation eeked out of him. She took in his matted hair, skinny legs ending in bare feet, black with grime. His gaunt, weather-reddened face peaked in an oversized, crooked beak of a nose under eyes that simply broke her heart. Why did his eyes look like that? She didn't understand the hopelessness or helplessness bleeding out of this boy through his eyes.

In less than a blink Ahna made a decision. Her pack contained everything most precious to her, every convenience and connection to her life at home.

It all happened at once. Aiela turned to see why she'd stopped. Ahna was taking the pack off, saying "El, it's alright. He must need it..." The boy reached her, his blade coming up in a smooth arc aimed towards the strap that had been across her chest. Removing the pack to give to the boy, knocked his hand higher as Ahna leaned in. His blade tip sliced her from chin to temple, barely missing the outside of her left eye.

Ahna gasped.

Aiela yelled "Stop! No!"

The boy froze, face round with horror.

"Go!" Ahna pushed the pack at him as the sting intensified. Swiping at the sting, she felt queasy at the sight of slick red washing her hand. Wet warmth spread over her cheek, her chin.

Aiela was between them then, furious and grabbing for the boy but he ducked, fading into the knotted crowds of people, clutching the pack.

One glance at Ahna's face and Aiela began pushing people aside, pulling her along, trying to see anyone familiar. "Hurry." She snapped. "We need Healer Lira. You're bleeding too much. Does it...." Her words faded into the imbroglio around them as Ahna drifted along behind, head starting to lighten and spin slowly. Warmth running down her arm, dripping— somewhere.

Aiela

Aiela was getting frantic, trapped in this endless crowd, seeing no one they knew, with no idea where they were headed. Unsure how badly Ahna was hurt, she felt remnants of everything Ahna was feeling. The light-headed spinning was not at all helpful. "Hang on to me tight. Just keep walking." She barked, trying to drag her sister faster. "Where the hell are they? Why can't I see ANYONE from our group?" She turned wildly around, suddenly disoriented. Pushing and shoving. Pulling Ahna behind her. "Excuse us. Let us through. My sister's hurt."

"El, I'm—I can't...." Ahna swayed against Aiela and melted slowly and gracefully towards the dirt-encrusted shells.

"Shit, shit, shit!" Aiela grabbed her sister under her arms as she fell, and began to entreat anyone close. "Can you help us? My sister was cut and robbed. She's fainting and we need our people!" The people around them stared. But they only backed away from this pair, one bleeding and slumping, the other roaring and bawling with an edge of hysteria in a foreign tongue.

"Hold onto me, I've got you." She forced surety into her tone. Ahna was still conscious. Barely. Fighting a dark tunnel closing tighter and tighter. Aiela knew exactly what she was feeling. It was like being two people in one body when she was connected to a patient.

"What is WRONG with you people?? Somebody help us!" Aiela was shouting now that the blood, no longer staunched by Ahna's limp hand, was dripping steadily onto her own forearms wrapped tightly around her sister's sagging body. Back home, people would have dropped everything to help, the instant tragedy happened. But these people turned away or simply ignored and avoided them.

"Take my pack. Give her to me." A firm male voice loomed suddenly over them. Dropping his bag, Carver picked Ahna up all in one motion.

"Drommen, Lister, clear me a path! You," he glanced at Aiela, "stay close. We're almost out."

Ahna completely lost to the tunnel now. Head lolling back, arms flopping, she didn't register the finely wrought hands that now held her. Carver ran with her, single-minded in his focus to get her to help. His friends obeyed instantly, bodily shoving people aside, clearing a path before him.

Aiela kept pace easily, despite the heavy extra pack she carried in her blood-streaked arms. "Can you see where we're supposed to go? How do you know this is the right direction?" And then they were there. Out of the madness of the wharf, at a road where large carts harnessed to giant black and auburn beasts were surrounded by the rest of the students and teachers. The group's luggage was being neatly loaded onto the back wagon.

"Teachers! We need help. Over here!" Carver's urgent voice carried command not request. Heads turned, staring dumbly at them. Teachers came running.

"What happened? Who is it? Why is there blood! Carver, what did you do?"

Ignoring their commentary, Carver laid Ahna carefully onto the narrow bench of a wagon, with Aiela supporting her head and shoulders, staying as close to her sister as possible.

"My bag. Where's my bag?" Pulling the top open, he grabbed the first cloth he touched, pressing it against Ahna's wound. Aiela immediately covered it with her hand, applying pressure to staunch the still-flowing blood.

The teachers were pushing in closer to see, all talking at once.

"Where is their healing temple?"

"Someone find Lira."

"Is it deep? What happened?"

Carver was climbing in the wagon, and pulling Ahna's dead weight into his arms once again. "Help me hold her." Aiela crammed in next to him, holding her sister's head. He barked at the useless, anxious teachers, "Stop gawking and get us a driver. Now! Somebody Irish. Where is our healer? Bring our healer", perfectly comfortable snapping a steady stream of commands at them.

Then a Driver was there, vaulting into the seat, and they were bouncing through the shell-paved streets. The passing town with its hordes of sea travelers became a blur to Aiela. She sucked in deep breaths, trying to calm herself, telling her mind over and over " All is well, We are fine. All is well." Going a little mad at the insistent, raw, deep sting, shooting along the side of her face, and the metallic blood smell that eclipsed all others.

Carver cradled Ahna like a small child against his chest and Aiela kept her sister's head tucked against the thin fabric of Carver's shirt. "Your tunic is getting soaked." Sticky warmth escaped from the cloth that she struggled to hold on Ahna's face.

Carver glanced down at his shirt that was black as an escort of ravens. "At least it won't be ruined by bloodstain."

The wagon bucked and jounced and her hand flew up smacking his taut, squared-off jaw, leaving a swipe of fresh red. "Sorry." She muttered, but he didn't seem to notice. Looking at Carver, really seeing him for the first time, she wondered about this man who had never spoken to them or even acknowledged their existence on the trip. And yet had come to their rescue. As he held her sister in the thoughtful embrace of a lover, she could see his green heart energy feeding into Ahna. Doubtful he even knew he was doing it.

Carver spoke tightly to their healer, "Can't you stop the bleeding? She might be losing too much."

Healer Lira was pawing through her pack, squinting in the evening dusk, to read the labels on boxes, tubes and bottles. She sat backwards on the front bench, next to the Driver. All three pairs of their legs and knees crowded together.

Carver lowered Ahna onto their shared laps until her head rested on Aiela and that's when Ahna opened her eyes.

"El? What's.....happening? My face *hurts!*" She struggled to sit up, sending fresh blood out of the gash.

Aiela wanted to cry out too at the stabs of fresh pain. "Shhh, you have to lay still! We're taking you to their temple. You're going to be fine. I know your face hurts. That boy cut you—"

"Ahna, I'm putting something on your cut to stop the bleeding." Healer Lira interrupted. "Carver, Aiela, hold her still. This will sting." Lira removed the blood-soaked cloth from Ahna's face and poured something thin from a small bottle along the seeping gap that ran from Ahna's high cheekbone down to her jaw. It barely missed the corner of her mouth.

Ahna and Aiela both wailed as it hit the opened flesh and Ahna fainted again, dropped into the black comfort of oblivion. Aiela was crying a little, clutching her sister's limp head. "Shhh. We're going to be fine. I'm sorry, so sorry...I should've stopped him. Please be fine. Please—"

"She will be." Carver's voice offered soft certainty, as he helped Healer Lira place a poultice over the wound and bind it around Ahna's head with thin strips of gauze. "Head wounds bleed a lot. But she's not going to die. Alright?" Scrutinizing her, Carver frowned. "Are you hurt too?"

Aiela realized she was clutching her face as if it might soothe the pain. "No. I just—I can feel what Ahna's feeling. We're very connected. Being twins."

"Really? That's terrible. How bad is it? Is there anything that can stop you from feeling it? Should we numb it or something?"

Aiela paused at his surprise and concern. It felt good to tell somebody about the pain she'd endured since Ahna got cut, though she wasn't expecting Carver to care. He was supposedly a rather bad Belial.

"You'll feel less if you stop touching her." Lira interjected. You need to stay as far away from your sister as possible while we're cleansing and closing the cut. The closer you are, the more of it you'll experience."

"I'm not leaving her! I don't care if it hurts. I'm *staying* with her!"

"Aiela, listen to me. As soon as we get there I'll dose Ahna to stay asleep but it may not numb *your* pain. You're not thinking straight because you're feeling too much." Lira placed a hand gently on Aiela's face and turned it towards her, waiting for Aiela's eyes to focus on her. "Just follow my voice. I want you to breathe in very deeply. Feel your breath. Hold it for as long as you can. Now breathe all the way out...and again."

Carver

Carver concentrated on balancing Ahna's small body while Lira talked Aiela into breathing. He'd never known that was possible, a bond so strong they shared sensation. What would that be like? To be so connected to another human. To be so loved by someone. He felt himself calming too, the adrenaline subsiding as he automatically began breathing along with Lira's instructions.

It was near full-dark now and they were well away from the harbour town. The wagon banged along at a gallop, passing a thatch roofed home every now and then, but mostly they were alone on the pitted, hard-packed road. He leaned to put his ear closer to Ahna's face, listening for her breath, relieved by the shallow waves of sound. Her body felt small and light on his lap. The outline of her reminded him of a little broken doll he'd once seen a child carrying around the streets of Temple City. Her thin legs and sandaled feet banged against him as the wagon swayed. He arranged her arms to a more comfortable looking position, careful with the delicate wrists and hands, keeping ahold of them to warm them up a bit. That's what he told himself anyway. Later, he'd think about the irony of how badly he'd wanted to touch her since the first time he saw her, saying goodbye to her parents before boarding the seacruiser in Atlantis.

The Irish "Healing Temple" turned out to be a simple amoeba-like building close to the road. It was also clearly a home, and—judging by the smells and sounds of sheep—surrounded by a farm. Carver gathered Ahna's prone form to his chest, scooting slowly to the lip of the wagon. Their young Irish driver was already returning from the building, leading a stocky man, who helped Carver lay Ahna onto a wool-bundled board. Together, they carried her inside, while Lira tried to tell the white-bearded Irishman what had happened and what she needed from him. None of which he understood, until Carver took over and translated, glad that he'd studied the Irish language once Mardu assigned this errand.

The surgery was a small room, with a padded table down the middle, and whitewashed walls of baked clay. Rather modern for Ireland. But since sea travel had become common, the coastal towns were known for modernizing due to a transient population from all over the world visiting, and sometimes settling. The Driver had hurried ahead to light four giant oil lamps that made the small room glow with a pearly and comforting light.

Aiela was still clutching Ahna's bloody hand, stubbornly in everyone's way.

Lira took her shoulders. "Aiela, *please* go into the other room and give us space to work. Your sister will be fine, I promise. You must trust me. Carver, I need you to stay and translate so I can communicate with this good healer."

Aiela

Aiela wanted to argue, wanted to fight for her right to watch over her sister. But she knew Lira was not going to let her stay. She'd just be delaying Ahna's healing. So she let Lira guide her to the door, and then it shut and bolted behind her.

She walked woodenly down a dark hallway towards a back room with flickering light. It appeared to be an eating area. A small table and stools along the far wall held carved wooden bowls of something fragrant and hearty. Half a loaf of round bread heavily flecked with dark green bits sat beside a wedge of cheese. Candles dripped and ran as their light blazed, jumping off the walls in tall shadows. She suddenly felt exhausted, and very hungry.

Going to the table for a small bit of bread and cheese, she realized her hands and arms were still sticky with blood. "Ugh." She muttered softly to herself. "Water.....there's gotta be a place to wash around here somewhere..."

"Oot back. I'll bring the light fer ya."

Aiela jumped visibly as a thick male shape rose from the shadowed corner, and stepped towards her.

"Gods, you startled me! I thought I was alone...."

"Ya aren't. Girls bonny as yerself should niver be aloon."

She stared harder, trying to see his face in the dim light. "I just need to wash up."

"Sorry. Dinna mean ta startle ya." He lit an oil lamp that sat on a wooden shelf by the back door. "Water's oot here....what's yer name?"

Aiela realized he was speaking fluent Atlantean with a charming Irish lilt. The lamplight showed her a solid outline of muscled shoulder and arm, which accounted for a general impression of thickness. He was about a hand length taller than her. As he turned the lamp up and she saw his face, she startled again. This time audibly. "Oh! You're ... I know you!...Who are you?"

He only raised an eyebrow at her. "Most dazzlin' girl I've seen...an daft. Joost my luck!" But his eyes held humor and she realized he was trying to be charming.

He looked roughly her age, with a round face ending in a slightly jutting jaw, and topped with light brown curls winding and springing every which way. Aiela tried to explain, "You must think I'm crazy. I've dreamt of you—uh, nevermind. It's been a long, strange day. Can you just show me where to wash?" She was in no mood to flirt.

He nodded, interest deepening his rather cherubic face. "Ya've dreamt of me have ya? Fer sure the first time an attractive female—let's be honest, *any* female—has said *that* ta me." He led her out the back door to a long metal trough attached to the back wall of the house. A pail full of water and a ladle with a long handle sat next to it. Turner dipped the ladle into the water, waiting to pour it over her hands. "Surely yer wonderin' who's this, em, specimen of a man what can't keep his mouth shut?" He handed her a small ball of fatty soap that smelled of lemon balm and yarrow and then bowed. "I'm Turner. Meant ta be head guide fer yer trip. I drove ya here." His tone softened. "No' that ya'd notice wi' yer sister bleedin' oot." Working together, Aiela scrubbing and Turner rinsing, the blood was finally washed gone.

"Thank you. I'm Aiela." She liked that he had managed to distract her from the throbbing of her sister's wound. She liked that he was quiet and helpful just now, seeming to understand her worry. She liked that he stood a little taller than her, his solid forearm nudging hers lightly when he trickled water over her soapy hands.

He held out a rough towel and caught her eyes as she reached for it. But instead of relinquishing it, he stepped closer to gently catch and dry her hands. This first focused awareness, wrapped as it was in Turner's strong attraction, felt like a pleasant punch of invasion into her center.

"If yer hungry, Vargo'd want'ya ta eat." He was still holding onto her hands inside the towel.

"I am hungry, if you think it'd be alright..." And that was the first time she saw him smile. Even in the dim light of the star-turned night, it was rather spectacular. Like when the sun emerges after a snowfall and turns the whole world sparkly. That smile, the accent and the way he was caring for her, captivated her. She actually felt herself start the fall. An exquisite intensity, tilted at first, dumping her headlong into a freefall of new and unspeakable sensations.

"Ya comin' then?" Turner poked his head back out from the doorway. She became aware then that she was just standing there holding the towel, and he'd already gone inside.

"Yes. Definitely. I'm coming and I'm hungry and I should check on my sister."

He fixed her a bowl of the stew, dark and brothy with chunks of things that smelled strange but tasted fantastic. "What is this?" She asked, spooning up more, feeling it renew her.

"Em," he studied it. "Appears ta be slippery black-eel meat, most likely smoked. Parsnips, beets, turnips a'course..." His accent struck her as erotic.

The bread was sea-flavored, sort of salty.

"Lavar." He pronounced it lay-ver. "Bread wi' kelp. It's all the nutrients we're needin', apparently, available year-round. We tend ta use kelp fer everythin', food, medicine, even fertilizer in fields that are too sandy or too thick wi' clay. We eat mostly sea-meat an' grains in the winter season. Now, in the summer, we've plenty o' vegetables an' berries an' wet grains as well. Vera different from Atlantis I know. Sure an' I've been there a few times..." Turner continued to talk while she ate, telling her small stories of where he'd visited in Atlantis and what his impressions had been. It gave her a reason to stare at him and feel the surreality of meeting this man who'd so often visited her dreams.

He'd made regular appearances in her sleeping-world, even the nightmares, for as long as she could remember, always connected to her in some mysterious way. Familiar by now, she'd come to accept him as some imagined friend that her heart needed. He was with her during her boring dreams, sometimes even her romantic dreams.

"Aaurgh!" Aiela dropped the bread, a spoonful of soup splattering as she clutched her face. Jumping up and knocking the chair over, eyes wild, breath coming in painful gasps, she cursed, "shit shit shit!", turning this way and that as if there might be an escape.

Turner was on his feet too. "What?! What's happenin'? For love of the Holy, Aiela, tell us what's wrong! Shall I be gettin' Vargo?"

"Nooo." Aiela sank to her knees on the floor, both hands holding her face together as if it wanted to come apart under her fingers.

Turner followed her down trying to catch her.

"Cold. Cloth." Aiela gasped.

Turner leapt at the door, returning in a heartbeat with a cloth dripping cold water from the pail out back.

Aiela took it, pressing it against her cheek. "Ahhh. 'S better." She was nodding gently. Looking at Turner through pain-glazed eyes, heavy tears started to roll down her cheeks but she barely noticed. She sat clutching the cloth to her face and rocking slightly, willing the pain to lessen.

Turner watched her for a moment, then reached slowly and wiped a tear from each side of her nose with a fingertip. It was enough to distract her.

Then his eyes widened. "Yer sister! Sure an' they're stitching yer sister right now an' ya feel it!" Without thinking or asking, he scooted beside her and wrapped both arms around her rocking body. Holding her against him, he moved with her, like a parent cradles a child for comfort.

She felt instantly better. Not that the pinching searing pain lessened, more that he was lending her his strength. His energy created space to hold, and then release the pain.

"How's it possible?" He murmured into her hair.

It seemed forever but was probably only minutes until the stabbing sensations faded to a dull throb. She became too aware of his heat, the solid bulk of his arms. Atlantean men were tall, but slender—sylphlike even—compared to him.

She cleared her throat. "One day I'm running carefree along the beach at home. The next I'm a thousand miles away in Ireland, sitting on a floor in the arms of some man that talks funny. Crying."

He let go and drew back to look at her. "Is it ow'er then? How's it now?"

"Achy. Better."

She held out the cloth and he took it along with her hand. Reaching with the other, he touched her face in a tender gesture of concern. "I don't understand Aiela."

He pronounced it "Aay-ela" and it sounded like a sonnet from his lips. His hip pressed along the side of hers, a connection both charged and comforting.

"We're twins. One soul, two bodies, our Mother likes to say. When Ahna's awake, she can block things so they don't pass to me. But not when she's unconscious apparently. If I'd seen that coming, I would've had Lira dope me up too!" Aiela was rallying now, self-conscious that Turner had seen her vulnerable and crying.

"What's 'dope'?"

She smiled at him. The way he said dope with his accent.

"You know, anesthetize. Drugs. Uhhh, numb, take away feeling…"

"I get it, I get it." He grinned at her—again with the heart-stopping smile. Then they heard the door down the hall open and the moment was over. She was off, running to see her sister.

TURNER

He sat down again at the table staring at the wet washcloth still dripping in his hands. This was all a bit surreal. Like his world had just tilted upside down or sideways—or maybe, for the first time ever, right side up.

7

WELCOME FEAST

"He liked her; it was as simple as that."

— NICHOLAS SPARKS

AHNA

*A*hna came awake with a start. It must've been the wind. A shivery moaning faded in and out as if the storm outside had sleep apnea. It took a moment to remember where she was, and then the rest came crashing in around her.

She tentatively touched fingers to her face in the dark. A scab crusted along the tender gash and it was throbbing. Was she going to look hideous for the rest of the trip? For the rest of her life? Lira had been putting a bouquet of oils on it so it was no longer swollen. Other than the throbbing, there wasn't much pain.

"Whatsamatter? Why are you awake?" Aiela reached across the space between their grass woven sleeping mats, groping for Ahna's arm.

"I don't know. Maybe the wind. Probably I slept too much yesterday. I'm well enough." She felt the warm pressure of Aiela's fingers wrap around her forearm, then go slack. She knew her sister was gauging the truth of her wound. Then a sleep slurred whisper.

"I think….Turner's a possibility. His hair is maybe the most glorious thing I've seen yet in Ireland, so twisty and strange... I just want to touch it."

Ahna smiled, then winced as it pulled sharply on the muscles of her cheek and jaw, still too sore to move that way. Turning towards her sister in the night even though she couldn't see her, Ahna had to whisper loudly over the wind's ghosting voice. "Is that really Aiela speaking? That no-boy-is-worthy-or-half-attractive-enough sister of mine?!"

"I know. It's weird. It's the accent, I could lose myself in the way he talks. By that I mean I'd *like* to lose myself in the way he talks. It's….tingly. Like bubble rain during a gentle storm."

They both lay quiet a moment contemplating the wonders of a foreign accent on a cute boy.

"He'll probably end up being violent or addicted to something terrible. I bet you he's already mated... I might as well face it now, he's going to be gay, or just into any other type of girl except Atlantean." Aiela was always pessimistic when it came to possible love interests. "There's something very interesting about him though..."

"Well, we've most of the trip left for you to explore him, along with all his complications and wickedness. I can't wait to meet him. Any boy who has intrigued my sister-the-finicky has to be *something* special." So far unconscious or resting, Ahna had yet to even see him.

"You know, it's nice that we've both found boys we like, at the same time."

"I don't know if I *like* Carver yet," Ahna protested, lying to them both. "I've barely seen him. Haven't really met him. He's so...a Belial, and I'm not sure I want those complications. What would Papa say?"

Aiela snorted softly, "Papa wouldn't give a damn that Carver's Belial and you know it. It's everyone else *but* Papa that would judge him for it. Besides, it's not like Carver was exactly given a choice who to be born and raised with. He was gentle, and I'd say *overly* concerned for you. He pretty much *rescued* you."

"Mm I guess so. He was concerned? How? What did he say?"

"Well for one, the way he scooped you up and ran with you, then didn't leave your side. He held you the entire wagon ride and I'm pretty sure he liked it—the holding you part. He was gloriously bossy and made people do what he wanted them to so you wouldn't bleed anymore, and, Jove Ahna! I was such a mess! I was so afraid for you and then feeling your pain….I'm eternally glad Carver was there. I owe him. We both do. The least we can do is not condemn him like everyone else has. I think it's right, the two of you..." Aiela was winding down, sounding sleepy again.

Ahna squeezed her hand. "Go back to sleep El, my face hurts when I talk."

The wind continued its moaning dance, composing a ballad of love and loss that Ahna's thoughts wrote words for. Tall, shadowy, beguiling Carver. She wished she could remember him holding her. Had he really touched her with those intriguing hands? The thought of it made her warm all over.

She drifted away into a dream where he was in love with her, but would not let her see his face. He kept saying "I will always be with you", but his back was continually turned to her until she became angry, demanding he look at her. Finally giving up, she wept bitterly at the profound loss, of his gaze being upon anything and everything but her.

THE MOANING WIND ushered in a grey drizzle sometime before dawn. They'd spent the night in a circle of yurts; round huts built from sticks and mud, and roofed with thatch woven from tall wild grasses that grew lush enough for a grown man to disappear in. The yurts had mats of woven sweetgrass laid side by side across their hard-packed, clay floors. The students slept wrapped in the bedrolls they'd been instructed to bring from home. Ireland was poor and coarse and they'd come prepared to meet their own needs, outside of food and water.

Ahna woke with Aiela leaning over her, already dressed.

"I'll bring your breakfast back, just stay put."

"Stop bossing me." She replied and closed her eyes again. Then remembered. "Where's our mirror?"

Aiela rummaged in her large bag. "It looks good actually—for its depth and how much it bled. I'm surprised. Lira said it might scar pretty good, but she can fix it when we get home."

Ahna stared at the mirror in the dim gray light, touching her face lightly where the brown line puckered into jagged crusts from her high cheekbone down to her chin, crossing too close to the corner of her mouth. Great. Along with her tangled strings of hair she looked like some heathen back-woods girl who'd lost a fight or three. She put down the mirror and laid back with a defeated sigh. "All the body art in Ireland won't fix this mess."

"You won't believe me, but I'll still say it. It would take a lot more than one rather impressive looking scar to make you not pretty. Please stop worrying, it makes me worry too. Want me to bring Lira back?"

Ahna nodded. "Hurts a little to talk."

The girls around them whispered restlessly, casting curious glances at Ahna.

"Come on girls," Aiela led the way, "let's go eat and I'll tell you about our little trip to the 'healing temple' here. I use that term quite loosely, but still, that *is* where I met our heroic leader Turner, and had black eel stew by candlelight with him…" Their voices faded as they trooped out into the misty morning.

Ahna breathed deep with relief. She wasn't quite ready to have them all staring at her ruined face and asking questions. Waves of aching homesickness washed over her and tears welled. She'd been looking forward to this trip for so long, and look how it'd started. She'd been entranced with Carver on the boat but now she dreaded having to see him—or anybody else. Maybe she could just wrap a silk scarf around her face like the women of Lemuria in the history books. For the first time it occurred to her that perfection was a standard in Atlantis. Women, especially, were not content with mere beauty. They sought perfection. Nobody had to live with scars or malformed features; every-thing was redeemable there. What would it be like if her face looked like this for the rest of her life? Misery clenched her chest, and she tried, but couldn't seem to push it away. It might as well be the rest of her life. This trip was the only time she'd ever have to get to know these people. To get to know Carver, and it seemed unlikely he'd be drawn to her ragged face. A cold dark pool of self-pity beckoned her in. As she waded deeper, Lira appeared at the door, hands full of jars and bottles.

She knelt beside Ahna's mat and meticulously lined them up in the order to be used. "Sweet Ahna, is it hurting so bad? You could've sent for me sooner, I was hoping you'd sleep late." Lira's soft efficient hands moved over her face, gently dabbing oils onto the cut and around it. "Are you hungry?"

Welcoming the disruption of her pity party, Ahna shook her head slightly. "Hurts when I move my jaw. Can't feel my cheek though, up high."

"Yes, I'm sure. This will soothe the pain. It actually looks better than I expected this morning. We'll keep putting oils on it and getting tea into you. At this rate, it'll be close to healed by tomorrow. The nerves and muscles will take a bit longer to feel normal again, but your skin is mending fast. Aiela says she's been doing healing work on you too. She must be quite skilled, it's made a big difference."

Ahna nodded, letting Healer Lira's assurances penetrate and sink in. Maybe she wouldn't feel or look hideous the whole trip.

"When you feel well enough, I'd like you to journal the entire incident. Write every detail you can remember. We'll talk about it when you are ready, and release the trauma your body is holding. This psychological release will speed the physical healing."

Ahna made a noise of assent, inhaling the concentrated fragrance of essential oils emanating from her face. Marvelous. Add "super smelly" to the reasons everyone would want to keep distance from her now. "Why is it always the worst smelling ones that do the healing." She grouched, but Lira only smiled.

"I want you to drink as much as you can today and sleep. Stay quiet one more day before joining the group, and don't touch it—we mustn't risk infection. Aiela said she's bringing you breakfast. It's porridge so you won't need to chew much. I will send tea in now and I'll come back every couple hours or so."

"Thank you Lira." The tears of disappointment were threatening.

"I'm sorry your trip began this way Ahna. Truly, you're fine though, and you'll even be able to enjoy most of it. Let's be thankful it wasn't a broken bone and that it missed your eye and mouth. Remember to journal." And she was gone, leaving Ahna to her healing.

Rising to relieve her bladder, Ahna lingered under the wide, dripping eaves of the yurt. Bedroll draped around her, she sat on a log and inspected the sodden camp crouched amidst a lush green landscape, intense in its hue.

Thin wisps of cedar-scented smoke trailed up from a separate yurt for cooking and eating, to meet and blend with a heavy fog hanging low overhead. Rain so light it misted without even the slightest sensation, dampened the students as they walked between the sleeping and eating yurts. Rising when they got hungry, some of the earlier breakfasters returned to their pallets to journal or sleep longer, after a helping of thick porridge, chewy from a blend of locally grown grains and crunchy with toasted seeds.

The same steaming porridge Aiela delivered. "Oh good, you're up. Want me to stay with you awhile?"

Ahna shook her head. "I'm sure you're needed, as the fearless leader. And I'd rather eat in peace."

A handful of girls, as delicate and pretty as hot-house flowers, floated around the unadorned beauty of her twin, exuding devotion and talking nonstop. Oddly reassured, Ahna sighed. Some things never change. You could swap out the people, the weather, the circumstances, and apparently even the continent, but Aiela would always be magnetic.

The porridge was good, served with tiny tangy forest berries and fresh cream from the aurochs that accompanied the group.

Aurochs were impressive beasts. Standing six foot tall at the shoulder, with lyre shaped horns pointing forward, they carried a large bony hump just behind their heads. The male aurochs were black with a pale gray stripe down their back and were usually castrated to curb their famed aggression. Still, the group had been warned to keep their distance from the animals—except for two milking females who were quite friendly. The females were a reddish auburn color, also with horns and a pale stripe down their backs. Every auroch had a large metal ring through its nose, which struck the Atlanteans as barbaric, but Turner explained it was the only way to control them when they got angry. Their noses were the only part sensitive enough that when a grown man yanked on the ring, it would cause enough pain to deter the auroch attack.

Wild aurochs still roamed Ireland's middle grasslands and the students had been warned to steer clear if they happened upon one. The wild ones were territorial and cranky about it, especially if they were with a female. These aurochs, born in domestication and raised with humans feeding and caring for them, peacefully grazed every chance they got, dutifully pulling the heavy laden wagons when harnessed. Turner was careful to keep them fed and watered. As a backup, he had a large barrel of hemp as well, which could calm them.

Across camp, Nanat huddled inside her own group of friends, pretending not to see Aiela as she passed and called out a cheery morning greeting. Ahna could feel the venom rolling from Nanat's lovely, overdressed form.

She shook her head. "It's pointless," she wanted to advise the poor jealous girl. "Nobody can resist her for long."

Aiela

By afternoon, the group rallied to visit the great Dark Woods.

Luscious and ever-green forests covered much of Ireland. A hundred different species of trees dangled lichens like disorderly lace from massive, moss-draped branches, or crowded together in a muddle of limbs, with leaves feathered and soft, or needles hard and thin. Ferns grew tall and broad enough for a family of humans to nest in.

Atlantis had forests, but they were tamed and orderly after eons of cultivation. Not redolent and riotous as only untouched nature with her sense of majestic disorder, can design.

The yurt camp crouched within a pebble toss of the edge of a dark woods. Aiela couldn't see inside the dense border of trees. Today's clouded sky turned it a shade of ominous as the group ventured into the rain sodden tangle. The Irish drivers used machetes to hack a way through where the little-used path had grown over.

Turner led them, explaining as they walked. "We Irish believe small folk, called faeries an' gnomes, live here in the woods. Gnomes would be aboot a foot er two tall, rather portly—sure an' uncommonly grouchy. They've lived here much longer than we humans, an' function as a more advanced...em... society. Faeries range in size according ta species, some almos' too tiny ta see, others a hands length er more. They are vera shy, have magical powers, an' like ta be...em...mischievous—a few even dangerously so."

There were many questions. Turner answered them all patiently if not honestly, twinkling eyes lingering on Aiela often until she smiled at his tales.

The girls were full of chatter, hoping to glimpse some of the mystical smallfolk.

The boys wanted to chance upon Ireland's wildlife.

"Sure an' we've native giant elk weighing upwards o' two thousand pounds, wi' racks like six-fingered hands. They'll span up ta twelve feet across. Their antler sheds can be found all ow'er the peat-bogs inland. We use them fer everything; grinding inta medicinals, ta make small frames that can be covered wi' animal skins er thick...em...cloth fer transitory homes."

"Do you eat them?" Nirka called out.

"I do! Aye! Evera chance I get." Turner replied, smiling.

"We've packs o' brown wolves roamin' an' foragin' as well, causin' problems when the packs grow large. Tho, neither the wolves nor the giant elk are this far south durin' summer moons. They much prefer the colder climates o' the upper Mainland until winter chases them doon from the vast north, across the land bridge that connects Ireland ta its Motherland. They hunt an' forage in the grasslands, forests, an' bogs o' central Ireland—which never freeze during the cold season—places where humans are few an' game is plentiful. An' we don't eat those!" He added for Nirka's benefit.

Aiela glanced around the group, noting the other girls' rapt attention, listening to Turner's monologue as they walked slowly under the cleansing drips of the trees.

"Hedgehogs, rabbits, otters, fox an' badger are common year-round, as well as swan, duck, tern an' o' course, our ever-present hoards o' gulls. In the winter, migrations of geese come south, feedin' many an Irish household ta...em...augment our bland winter grains, stored roots an' seafood. Sure an' they provide goose down and feathers fer household goods, grease fer cookin' an' lamp oil or keepin' leather goods supple. Even the bones we put ta use. They're hollow, in case ya didna know, an' fashioned inta flutes an' toys, or carved an' dipped in melted copper fer huntin' wi'. Many a Irish spear, knife, arrowhead and hand tool began as naught but carved bones," Turner held up a hip knife with a smooth carved handle and a blade longer than his hand to illustrate, "because bones weigh little. Coated wi' metal, vera strong as well."

They grew hushed, trekking deeper into the darkness of trees that dripped muted greens from roots to the heavy branches visible above their heads, and reaching around them to the ground like a silent earth embrace. Speaking in whispers and stepping lightly, their eyes darted this way and that, tracking any movement of leaf or grass. Alert to see tiny people.

But it did not happen.

By late afternoon, they straggled back to camp, soaked and chilled, but refreshed too. Bonfires were built and the group slowly warmed up despite the persistent mist.

Aiela checked on Ahna often and lingered round the fires the rest of the time, talking to new friends. Her eyes automatically tracked Turners whereabouts like some force of gravity. He seemed so much older than her, leading the band of men who served as wagon drivers. Earlier, talking them through the Dark Woods, she'd seen his confidence wrap around him like a comfortably formal cloak.

Supper that night was to be a special feast at Turner's family home to welcome the group. Aiela felt neglectful, leaving Ahna behind with Lira, but couldn't deny her excitement to see what Turner's home was like.

He'd been so busy all day, sweat and all the wet in the forest had plastered his hair to his head in tight, careless curls that turned dark as mahogany when wet. His usually loose, woven shirt clung soggy to his body. Aiela wasn't the only one who took note of the hewn muscles that turned his torso into a pleasant sculpture of ripples and bumps in all the right places.

The bonfires were in full roar when Turner came to stand beside her. "How's Ahna feelin'? I o'werheard one o' yer girls saying she was grouchy as a pregnant camel—whatever that means. Is she needin' anythin'?"

Aiela laughed. "Less people fawning over her. She finds most people... tiresome. But it's good for her. You don't know what a camel is?"

"O' course I know what a camel is! I saw one once in yer land."

"Silly me. Of course you did. Well they get uncommonly mean when they're carrying."

"I also heard yer the leader o' this expedition. Ya didna mention it b'fore."

"I'm the *people* leader." She amended. "The expedition is under *your* command I believe."

His eyes twinkled at her. "So I ha' the right ta tell ya what ta do then?"

"You can certainly try." Aiela lifted her chin. "I didn't really believe you, you know, when you said you were our head guide."

"What?" Turner gave an expression of mock outrage. "But ya've *dreamt* o' me!"

She felt her color rising. She'd hoped he'd forgotten. But her retort was lost as the other girls edged in and began to bombard him with questions and flirtations, until he made an excuse to slip away.

"I want this Irishman!" Nanat simpered loudly when Turner was almost out of earshot. "SO stout! I think he likes me."

Aiela rolled her eyes muttering under her breath. "Could you *be* any more stupid? Gods!"

"What?" Nanat said sharply.

"I *said*, I'm going to check on my sister." Aiela stalked away.

They all washed with the icy water from rain barrels—to a chorus of shivering complaints—and dressed up before the welcome feast. Moods improved as they braided and adorned one another's hair. Everyone was in high spirits despite a drizzly first day.

Ahna put the finishing touches on Aiela's face paint. "You look like a storm princess. Turner won't be able to resist you. Make like a tornado and suck him in."

"Shh!" Aiela glanced around but no one else was listening. "Nanat laid 'claims' on him earlier. I wanted to hit her in her perfectly irritating face. Now she'll be at him all the time. I feel terrible leaving you tonight. Maybe I should just stay with you, then I won't have to beat the snot out of Nanat."

Ahna giggled, and then winced as it contorted her fragile face. "No no. I want you to go. Especially if there's a chance of you fighting—deep down you've always wanted to. Really, please go. Lira is bringing me a book to read and will be here doctoring me and it'll all just be terribly boring for you. Besides, you're their leader. You can't be absent from our first big event. There'll be more feasts El, just have a doubly good time, for me, yes? You look entirely gorgeous tonight."

Ahna handed Aiela their mirror and Aiela raised her eyebrows at her own reflection. "Wow! I'm like a work of art."

"Don't be ridiculous, you're more than that! Your face and my skills...like whipped cream on the berries."

The Drivers had hung coated tarps over the wagons, to keep the rain from soaking everybody. It was only a quarter hour's ride and Turner hopped in from the side, next to Aiela, just after they'd set off. He looked at her for a moment, crammed tight and unexpected against her. When he flashed that smile, she forgot all the pithy witticisms she was going to charm him with.

"Ya look pretty." He said simply. "Like a night lily in bloom."

She frowned. "You're calling me a...*flower?*"

"I did. Aye, a lily flower—the prettiest thing I could think of."

"Pah! Flowers are perfumed and delicate, neither of which apply to me. But... pretty? I'll take that. Thank you."

"Right... I must do better!" He studied her for what seemed an eternity, until she began to glower at him. "I know what ya remind me of—since ya so meanly reject my flower." He switched on a deep dramatic voice, "Yer Aiela, the Moon Goddess, come down ta tempt us all with yer untouchable beauty. I joost didna recognize ya at first."

Something shot through her system like a strong wine. Boys were rarely this audacious with her, never this confidant. Impulsively, she kissed him on the cheek, breathing into his ear, "Not always untouchable. Not to everyone."

His sharp intake of breath made her smile with satisfaction. He looked more serious now. "Will ya dance wi' me?"

She glanced around. "And you called me daft? We're in a wagon."

"Tonight. After we eat, there'll be dancin', I'd like ta reserve ya now, in case I don't get the chance later."

Aiela nodded, holding his gaze, stomach doing funny little flips. For once she was serious. "Thank you Turner. I'd be honored to dance with you. Is Irish dancing difficult?"

"It's not. A little different, sure. It's fast, but something tells me that when it comes ta you, the faster the better, you'll be learnin' it quick an' probably teachin' me new things by the end o' the night. If I've any luck at all." The slow wicked grin spread across his face and then he turned and jumped off the side.

She twisted to watch him run back to the wagon in the rear which seemed to be having trouble keeping up, the aurochs trundling slow, resistant. Aiela pressed a hand to her chest, marveling at the strong thu-thumps, heart already dancing.

The girls around her whispered and giggled behind hands, eyes flicking her way, but she knew the rain on the tarps had masked most of their conversation, just as it was drowning out the words being spoken around her now. She sat higher and watched the dripping fields and forest move slowly by until they turned down a long roadway graveled with crushed pink shells.

Knobbed trees lined both sides of the drive, twining with each other overhead, forming a long, wide tunnel. Intense green moss and fringed lichen hung from lower branches here and there. At the end, they emerged into a clearing where the drive looped in a huge circle in front of a grey stone manor.

Aiela gasped. *This* was Turner's home? Stone turrets bookended the front corners, with various shapes of spires in between, like a tatting with no pattern. Both elegant and wild, it looked like nature had decided to build itself a mansion as a whimsical work of art. Rain soak had turned the stones a shiny, soft black and two oversized oaken doors stood open, bidding the group to enter.

If the exterior was an ode to the rambunctious beauty of nature, the inside was a vibrant melody that borrowed notes from every human culture and country in the world. A true merchant's home, it was clear many generations had collected the valuable, the fancy, the strange and the exquisite.

Aiela stood gaping, until most of the group had left her, They gathered in a room at the back of the house, where long tables were set in front of a hearth large enough to roast an aurochs.

"Ya comin?" Turner was beside her again, smelling damp, his deep-ocean, blue shirt ornate with muscle.

She struggled to say something suitable, highly inappropriate thoughts streaming through her mind. "I really wasn't expecting this." She gestured at their surroundings. "It's...fantastic."

"It is, I guess... what were ya expectin'?"

She shrugged, "I don't know." *Hovels and caves, in truth.* "Your father, he's a merchant?"

"He is. An' my grandfather and his father's father. As far back as humans have sailed ta transport goods, my family has too. Which is why I'm aimin' ta start anew. Break the assumed tradition." His voice held a wistful resolve.

She followed him towards the large back hall where a stout, middle-aged man with neatly trimmed red hair and a jovial smile, welcomed each guest in a booming voice, as they entered. Two cocoa-skinned women directed a host of similarly exotic looking teenagers and children, as they carried steaming platters and bowls of food to the long wooden trestle tables.

"Is that your father?" Aiela whispered to Turner.

He nodded, and gestured towards the wall dominated by the massive stone fireplace. "He is, an' ower there's my Mam, my Auntie, my siblings an' cousins. I'm the eldest, an' smartest an' best looking o' course."

Aiela rolled her eyes and elbowed him. "They look nice. How fun for you to have so much family and this huge gorgeous house!"

"Right. Fun." He dramatically mimicked her eye roll. " C'mon, let's eat."

The tables were laden with spit-roasted, deep-sea fish big as a bear, with hot, tender white flesh bursting from crisp silver skin. Bowls heaped with assorted shellfish, swimming in garlic butter broth. Mashed root vegetables swirled orange with yellow and white. Platters of black and golden rolls were served with maple honey. Unidentified mounds of assorted green vegetables steamed tantalizing scents of fresh herbs. And for dessert, tart forest berries were piled in a sweet golden custard. It was a rainbow of a meal, and left everyone groaning with appreciation when the plates were finally cleared away. Turner's family helped four Irish musicians set up in a corner, and then instructed the students in pushing the heavy tables against the walls. A clear square was left in the center, where the teenagers and children began to demonstrate steps to an Irish dance. Bodhrans struck up a beat. A mandolin, flute and fiddle joined in. The music rollicked, daring anyone to resist moving their body.

Turner and Aiela had talked more than they ate. Teasing and flirting, they learned of each other, lost in a world of their own. His mother's appearance behind them jolted her back to forgotten responsibilities.

"Greetings and welcome to my home. I am Diaedra, Turner's mother. You, who have spell-bound our eldest, are...?"

Diaedra's tawny skin, and deep caramel eyes seemed at odds with her light brown, curly hair, like she had been pieced together from the best of several races. She spoke slow, formal Atlantean, with a thick accent very different than Turner's.

Aiela turned on her bench and dipped a deep and respectful bow as best she could while sitting. "Oh! Your house is like nothing I've seen before. Incredible! And thank you for supper, it was delicious." She spoke with deep sincerity, and then remembered Diaedra's question. "Oh yes, I'm Aiela. It's wonderful to meet you. Turner has been invaluable. When my sister got hurt, Turner helped us—"

"Your sister is hurt? Where is she? What happened?" Diaedra turned her piercing caramel gaze to Turner.

He froze, looking every bit the proverbial deer caught unaware, and Aiela, realizing she'd accidentally opened an awkward moment, mouthed "sorry" too late.

"Mam, she's goin' ta be fine. She got cut at the harbour while bein'," he paused, cringing, "robbed o' her pack. I wasn't wi' them because the crowds were too thick ta keep them all together. I took them ta Vargo an' they've their own healer...Lira says the cut is healin' fast an' Ahna is no' here because Lira wanted her ta rest an' stay quiet until we travel tomorrow." His words became rushed as he tried to explain.

Diaedra listened without changing expression. "Does your father know?"

Turner shifted and looked away. "No, I havena had the chance ta tell him..."

Turner's mother launched into a rapid tirade in Irish then and Aiela couldn't follow. She didn't sound pleased.

"Yes Mam" was all that Turner responded, and Diaedra turned once more to Aiela.

"Pardon our private conversation. Are you sure your sister does not need anything? Perhaps we should bring her here until she heals. We can at least replace some of her things that were stolen...?"

"Truly, she is healing well. Lira is with her tonight. I'm sorry you found out like this, I—I didn't mean to...and really, I just want you to know how thankful we are for Turner and your wagons and Drivers. He's been looking out for our every need."

Diaedra smiled at this and rested her hand briefly on Turner's shoulder. "Yes, he is quite the man. We are very proud. I welcome you to our Green Isle, Aiela. We are always honored to have Atlanteans visit here and I'm sorry we did not protect you and your sister adequately. Every effort will be made to ensure nothing like this happens again. I'm afraid we're a bit rougher here than Atlantis."

They exchanged a few more pleasantries before Diaedra was called away and Turner gazed with narrowed eyes at Aiela. "Joost toss me inta the mouth o' a dragon next time!"

"I'm sorry! I didn't think at all before I spoke, and your 'Mam' is a little intimidating you know? Take that into account!"

He laughed and nodded, relaxing the slight tension that had built. "Ya've no idea! That's her bein' mild. Sure an' it's better she found out with you here. At least she treated me as the man ya think I am, instead of the child she thinks I am." Unwinding his legs to stand, he extended his hand palm up, in formal request. "C'mere Moon Goddess, it's time fer our first dance."

8

AHNA AND CARVER

If all the tenderness in the world could reflect from my eyes, would you accept that love?

— ST. FRANCIS OF ASSISI

AHNA

*P*ropped against a pillow-sized lump in the earthen wall of the yurt, Ahna read an Atlantis storybook that Lira had brought. Being a rare treasure in most of the world, this book and others would be gifted to those they encountered along the way, along with essential oils, jewelry and tools. This one was a volume of short stories, part fact and part embellishment—as all history eventually becomes. It told ancient stories of Lemuria and its fall, interspersed with the planting and rise of Atlantis. Ahna had grown up with these stories, but there was nothing else to do just now, and this at least distracted her from the regret of missing the party.

Lira came often, delivering soft foods or tea, dotting more oil blends on Ahna's face. She alternated warm poultices with pine sap salve from Vargo, clucking about "taking Atlantis Healing Temples for granted" and "practicing medicine out here in the wilds with nothing but the very basics..."

Ahna was in the middle of "The Great Gods," wherein Poseidon and his tribe of super humans had come to earth, landing in Atlantis, when someone knocked at the door. Lira didn't knock, and everyone else was at the feast. "Hello?" Ahna called.

A tall shadow opened the door, then hesitated a beat before ducking inside the low entrance. "Ahna?" He stood there waiting for her to say something.

"Oh! I wasn't expecting...*you*. I thought everyone went to the welcome feast." She suddenly felt breathless. *Holy great ones! It was Carver!*

Stepped carefully over all the sleeping pallets, he came within the light circle of the oil lamp. "Nah, didn't feel like a party tonight. Is this alright, coming to visit you? I'll go if you don't want...if it's not. I just thought we could, talk maybe...we haven't actually spoken yet."

"No—I mean yes! It's good, thank you for coming. To visit me." *Why couldn't she be smooth and clever just now? Why could she not think of one single thing to say to the one man she'd been hoping to talk to this whole trip?*

"I brought you something. Sorry it's not much." He held out a bushy bouquet of multi-shaded green leaves. There were giant five-cornered ones, and smaller almond shaped ones with reeds and fern fronds and curly twigs spiking out between them. One pale flower drooped from the front. Some sort of woodrose she guessed. Ahna took it, automatically inhaling the scent of the little flower. It smelled sweet with faint musk.

"Since you didn't get to see the Dark Woods I brought a little of it to you." He sat down on Aiela's pallet, his long legs awkward and fitting nowhere. The bouquet of forest was bound at the stems with grass strands tied into a simple, rustic knot.

Ahna smiled too big of a smile, wincing as the sharp pinch reminded her what her face looked like. "Yargh" She gasped, hand flying up to hide her cheek.

"I'm sorry. I shouldn't be here, don't know what I was thinking..." Carver mumbled. Suddenly unsure of himself, he moved to rise, but froze in the act as she spoke his name.

"Carver?"

He looked straight into her eyes then, and she stifled another gasp. For the first time, she saw him. Saw *into* him. Intensity, vulnerability, hope, a host of things flooded her awareness at the contact with those deep-set, ice-frosted windows into his guarded depths. "This is the most welcome thing you could have done. Please stay. Tell me about the Dark Woods. I'm excruciatingly bored and I'll even turn the lamp down so you don't have to look at this grotesque thing." Ahna gestured at her face.

He almost smiled then. A slow relaxing of a face already perfect, into something that made her think of warm summer storms. "It's not grotesque. Nothing about your face could ever be *that*. It looks good—compared to when I first saw it. Lira's a great healer huh?" He'd resettled onto Aiela's pallet in a more comfortable cross-legged position, leaning closer to peer at her cheek. He smelled of fresh-dug earth and woodsmoke.

"Well she's in here putting something on it every five minutes, so yes, she has done a thorough job." She settled back, relieved that he would stay. "It doesn't hurt much anymore—except if I laugh, so you mustn't be funny. We can only speak of sad, dull or frightening things."

Another half-smile as he bowed. "My usual genres actually, sad, dull and sinister. I thought the Dark Woods were....spectacular. Bigger than I expected and so thick they had to cut a way through in parts. For some reason I always assume we have the biggest and best of everything back home. Once again, I am wrong. These trees all blend together at the tops so there's not much sunlight that gets through and it's just layer upon layer of shadows. That's how the little forest people live too, in layers. Starting with the smallest, the leaf faeries, who live in the very tip-tops of the highest trees where it's warm and nobody can mess with them because the highest branches won't support anything but a leaf faerie's weight. Then there's the gnomes who live in the hollow tree trunks of the auldest trees." His tone unconsciously mimicked Turner's accent as he relayed their lessons on the forest walk. "There was this one tree, twisted, like it couldn't decide which direction to grow in, that Drommen and Lister and I all three together couldn't wrap our arms around finger to finger. We tried, and while we were there, all hugging it like lunatics, I heard the tree gnomes talking inside—"

"You did not!"

He held her eye until she said something else.

"I don't believe you... what were they saying?"

He grinned at her then, one eyebrow crooking. "I speak only truth...Interruptor."

Careful to keep a straight face, she bumped his leg with a loose fist. "Oh *pardone* tall-tale-teller. Do continue."

Leaning back and closing her eyes, she could hear the wind in the leaves, and smell the rich loam of the earth through Carver's quiet words. The little people he described in fanciful detail, danced inside her eyelids. He couldn't just be heroic or gorgeous, he had to be kind and fun too. With delectable hands.

Lira came in midway through his story, and listened quietly while dropping a cocktail of oils on Ahna's face, refreshing the bouquet of ruthless smells. She made no comment on Carver being there, just smiled, handed Ahna the jug of water to finish, and left.

"You know, you're going to owe me a whole lot of talking when you're healed." Carver commented.

"About what? I'm not gifted in story like you."

"I have questions. You can tell me all about you—the details—for a start. You're only exempt now because you're wounded."

Ahna raised her eyebrows. "I probably owe you a little more than that. Aiela told me how you helped us. Helped me..."

His straight black hair fell to hide his face, as he stared down at his hands and shrugged. "Anybody would've done the same—"

"Except they didn't." Ahna pointed out, puzzled at his sudden shyness. "You did."

An awkward silence filled the space. Carver rose suddenly from the pallet. "Stay here. I'll be right back."

She grabbed for the mirror as soon as the door shut behind him, combing her fingers through sleep-tangled hair. Wishing she didn't look like a ill-kempt rat's nest and smell of twenty pungent oils. She'd just met a paragon of male specimens *and* he was choosing to be with her *and* seemed to be having a good time. She stared with chagrin at her carved-up face, then turned down the lamp. Maybe shadows and dimness would hide the worst of it. She couldn't wait to tell Aiela, Carver had come to visit her!!

He returned shortly, an oblong leather bag slightly larger on one end, slung over his shoulder, and a cup of tea balanced in one hand. "Lira says you must drink this all because it will help you sleep."

"What's that?" Ahna pointed to the bag, ignoring the tea and instructions.

"Patience wee one, patience." He teased, in an accurate Scottish brogue. Putting the black case on Aiela's pallet, he knelt to hand her the tea with both hands. When she took the warm pottery, his fingers slid over hers. She jerked as a searing wave of vibration passed through that grazing contact, layering on top of the intensity of being this close to him.

"What? Too hot?" He supported the mug with her for a heartbeat.

His hands felt huge and hard covering hers, like sun-warmed leather. Heart racing, she shook her head slowly, trying desperately to think of a believable lie, finally settling on diversion. "S-so what is that you brought?"

Withdrawing from the contact, he mimicked a girl falsetto. "Thank you Carver for the tea. And for saving me from being drowned in more oils by that prodding healer Lira."

She pressed her lips together but a giggle still escaped. Hiding behind the steaming mug, she watched him open the case and settle onto the pallet with his dulcimer. Of course. It was the battered black dulcimer.

He picked at the strings, tuning for a moment and then began to play, strumming a simple melody that began softly and then built like waves before a coming storm. Ahna sat, openly staring at the pure sensation that flowed from his hands, disguised as notes. When the song ended as quietly as it had begun, he looked up at her. A shy smile escaped one side of his mouth when he saw her naked admiration. He squirmed with discomfort. "Drink your tea Ahna."

"That, that's...wondrous! How are you so talented? I could listen to you for the rest of my life and not get enough of it. Do you perform at home? In your city?" Ahna knew she was gushing, but couldn't make herself stop.

Carver shrugged her words off, embarrassed. "Nah. It's not *that* special. I spent too much alone-time as a child" another shrug, "and this was the only part of my Mother I had." He absently caressed the softly-shaped instrument dulled by age and use, as he talked. "So, I just... play a lot."

Strumming again, he launched into another tune while Ahna obediently sipped her tea. Reveling in the pleasure of this rare and talented male sitting so near and playing music just for her. Getting to watch those hands up close was intoxicating....

The tea worked quickly and Ahna fought drowsiness. *Not fair Lira! The best night of my life and you're stealing it away...*

Carver had begun to hum and then sing softly when Ahna lost the battle to keep her eyes open. Masculine tones flowed around her, smooth and thick like the chocolate Auntie Sage made sometimes. Round, sad words that she couldn't quite catch, before sinking too far away to know what was happening anymore.

9

CARVER'S BARGAIN

"I'm different. I will give you my treasure chest of darkness first. If you can handle that, then I'll bring out my shining moons. If one cannot handle the darkness, then one should not deserve the light."

— C. JOYBELL C.

CARVER

$\mathcal{H}$e ended his lullaby to the soft and provocative rhythm of Ahna's chest rising and falling, feeling guilt twinge that his eyes were on her chest.

Healer Lira had warned him the tea would work quickly. That Ahna needed to sleep long and deep tonight before their travel day tomorrow.

Even with the jagged line curving down her face, she looked innocent. Enthralling and desirable—far more so than the painted, crass and cynical charlatans of Belial. Was it wrong to lust for a girl while she was sleeping? This was the second time he'd watched her, relaxed in unconsciousness. He felt more comfortable around her when she wasn't watching him with those gently piercing green eyes that looked deeper into him than he allowed anyone to.

He stopped playing and put the dulcimer away, feeling giddy with the glow of her delight in his music, her acceptance of him. It felt foreign, and he certainly would not have basked like this, had she been awake. Turning back to Ahna he pulled the bedroll cover up to her chin. An excuse to breathe in her warm scents. She smelled sweet and safe, under Lira's layers of potions. He sat close, for long moments.

Blonde strands fell across her face when she turned to snuggle deeper and he couldn't resist tucking them back. It felt like silk across his fingertips and her skin looked something altogether heavenly. Why did she entice him so? It bothered him, the vulnerability of feeling... this for someone. It seemed an out-of-control knowing, like he might not be able to turn off if he needed to. Right now he just wanted to spend the next several thousand nights like this, talking to her, playing for her, touching her....

He grabbed his dulcimer and fled the yurt before he did anything else. Hoping that someday, maybe he'd be this close, touch her this tenderly, while she was awake.

Stopping to hide the dulcimer in his bedroll and grab a large pouch made of gilded satin from his pack, Carver started to run. Turner's house wasn't far and running off all those feelings in the fresh night air was just what he needed. Self-flagellating thoughts eased his pulsing ache as much as the exercise and cool night. *How could I want someone like her? People as crooked and broken as me don't get pure, sweet girls. I'd probably ruin her. More likely, she'll find out what I really am and be disgusted. End up despising me.* His thoughts spiraled, dismal as deep pond murk, until he arrived at the feast.

It was too dark to fully see the house, but its shape was enormous. It looked as big as his father's—except Mardu's was gaudy and monstrous, not like the natural elegance this one held. He let himself in the heavy wooden door, slipping through a house full of curiosities he would very much like to see in the daytime, and into the background of the dancing.

Scanning the room, he picked at a few platters of food still left on tables against the walls, ravenous after his unexpectedly sweet evening and the punishing run.

Most of the students were dancing a lively hopping combination of steps that seemed to get faster and faster until the song wound down. Then, two dark-skinned women stepped out to explain a new dance involving linking hands and performing spins and twirls together. The music started again, this time slower and full of drama.

Turner's father watched the dancing and Carver made his way across the room to stand before the powerfully built, red-haired man. Bowing deeply he said, "Meihal, I am Carver from Belial. Sent with a message for you from Mardu. Will you speak with me?"

Meihal's eyes widened. He rose and led Carver away from the revelry and up the stairs to a room filled with books and charts, and a large collection of ancient nautical instruments.

When the door was shut and the lamps lit, Meihal stared at Carver, guarded but curious. "Well this is a surprise, a messenger from Belial travelling with Atlantean students?" He framed it as a question, and Carver replied smoothly.

"Come to acquire your services, I hope. Mardu has need of your three best ships for a simple errand. I bring some payment in advance and the promise of Mardu's—therefore all of Belial's—goodwill to you and yours."

Meihal sat back contemplating this dark young man and what all his surprising offer entailed. "Why? Mardu has fleets that outnumber mine thrice over." They had been a plague to Meihal. Overtaking one or two cargos a year, costing him lives and goods and sometimes the ship itself, either stolen, damaged or burnt. His best defense was simply to evade them, not cross their path. Belial's didn't really seek to pirate, they merely took what came to them, every chance they got. Tending to be strong and nearly unbeatable in battle, they were still pleasure-mongers and lazy.

Carver leaned forward so that his face was in the brightest circle of light. "We have made some contracts with Atlantis, to merchant certain goods to them, but they require that we use vessels and crews not Belial. The Atlanteans do not trust Belial ships that close to High City and neither do we trust Atlantean vessels in our secret places. The Atlantean people have not been told of Mardu's direct involvement. He would rather stay invisible, be simply the deal-maker. But the cargo is precious."

"What is the cargo?"

Carver hesitated, hoping this small show of secrecy would enhance the lure. He drew out the silence but Meihal sat patiently, waiting. Carver exhaled roundly as if letting go of his reluctance. "Crystals. Unusually powerful ones. Mardu would not want me to share too much but I can see you are a man to be trusted. We discovered a mine, the largest quartz-mine in the world, much closer than any of Atlantis's previous sources with unheard of quality and strength. We've been fully operational for some time now and High City would rather buy up our excellent stock than see it sold to other continents. They will receive three shipments from us via your vessels. They will have all the top-grade crystals they could ever need, Mardu will profit handsomely and you will be paid ten times your normal price for the use of your ships, fully crewed of course. Everybody wins. He sends these as surety." Setting the silken pouch between them, Carver slid its contents onto Meihal's scarred wood desk.

First an ornate box, gilded in orichalcum and intricately molded with Atlantis' sacred symbol, the Spiral of Life. Carver ceremoniously opened it to display its treasures. "These are some of the rarest and most potent healing oils known in Atlantis and this scroll contains sources, properties and uses for each."

Meihal's eyes widened. Atlantis did not share such information. It was their power.

Next came a cluster of crystals the size of two large fists, its pointed spires, clear and blue as water, grew every which way in a beautiful formation. "This is a sample from our mines. More importantly, this book outlines for you the powers of all crystals and basics of how to activate and program them for any purpose you could intend."

Meihal took the book from Carver carefully. Growing reverent at the tooled leather cover, he opened it, staring at the pages of detailed drawings and writings.

"I'm sorry it's in Atlantean. There was not time to have it translated."

"No no, this is...priceless, as it is. I can read Atlantean well enough. With this I can do much for my people." Meihal laid the book on his desk.

"So it is agreed then? You will send your three finest vessels to Belial before the stormy season?" Relief had crept into Carver's tone.

Meihal's eyes burned into Carver, narrowed in thought. "If Mardu is paying me ten times my normal price, then he is profiting one hundred times that in his scheme. Here are *my* terms. I want a shipment of precious oils and two—no three—Atlantean healers to teach my people the arts of healing. And I want a full shipment of crystals from your mines. It's high time Atlantis *and* Belial stop hoarding all their knowledge and technology and start developing the rest of humanity. Ireland is the perfect place to start."

Carver thought rapidly, deeply surprised at this outrageously high price. Still, Mardu's exact words had been; "Agree to anything he asks— even if it's the moon, the sun and the stars. This is the easiest deal you'll ever make boy, but do not mistake easy with unimportant. I'm sending you and not your stupid, useless brothers or my conniving business partners because this is the most important deal entrusted to anyone other than myself. If you fail me, do not think I will spare the lives of anyone you care about."

Carver pretended to sputter a bit, finally saying, "You don't know what you're asking! Even for Mardu, that is a fortune! If I return to him with this price he'll punish me every day for a moon." Possibly an understatement.

"Take it or leave." Meihal said stubbornly.

Carver exhaled in resignation, nodding once. "Here is the final gift then, to seal our deal."

It was a monstrosity. A huge ring crafted from gold in the shape of a man's head. Its eyes were two glowing rubies. Goat horns made of pointed black diamonds protruded from the top of its forehead, and fangs of white diamond from its screaming mouth. The famed ring of Belial, identical to the ones worn by Mardu and his closest few.

"This will ensure your protection and that of anyone you speak for. Show this ring to whomever threatens or seeks to harm you and you will have whatever you ask of them. This ring carries the full power of the Dominus. Mardu bids you use it wisely."

Meihal hesitated at the sight of it. "Why do I feel like I'm making a deal with the devil?" But he took it, placing it heavily onto the desk next to the other offerings, then clasped Carver's forearm in a gesture of sealing.

"Because you are, Meihal." Carver said with sadness in his voice. "Never say I didn't warn you."

AUTONOMOUS

HIGH CITY, ATLANTIS

"Avert the danger which has not yet come."

— YOGA SUTRA

TAYA

"You can't imagine how much easier it is to rebalance Belial's energies using all three Crystals. I don't know why I insisted we only needed the one for so long." Ziel lifted his tiny teacup in a toast to Taya. "I guess what I'm really saying is thank-you, for pushing me to listen to my own people."

The Comm's round eye glowed yellow as it transmitted its sight hundreds of miles through the air, from where Taya sat at her own cherry-wood table, lifting her large, pottery mug of tea back to him with a wide smile.

"Good. You're welcome! What else is happening over there? You know the girls are gone now so I'm having 'alone time' until Drey gets back in a couple days. Then we leave on our own little adventure. I'm so bored I'm actually cleaning the house! Sage is beside herself with joy at all the gleaming surfaces, pleasant smelling water closets and cobwebless corners. I'm making her stay with me so I don't go completely mad at all the peace and quiet."

Ziel chuckled, "Give her my greetings will you? Maybe you should have visited High City instead of waiting to come with the girls this autumn. But listen, for all their convenient uses, the Crystals have been acting….different lately. It's why I needed to talk to you so urgently."

Taya's brow furrowed, scrutinizing the holographic image being projected from her Comm crystal, docked in its flat disc base. Unported, it transmitted audio only, but when both comms were docked they could transmit a hologram of the person whose body matrix was programmed to the Comm. Ziel was seated at his little breakfast table. "What do you mean they're acting different? I wasn't aware they were 'acting' at all."

Ziel leaned forward, setting down the teacup.

"They've started performing certain functions on their own. Just small things, basic, like ramping up their output to the grid when needed without us turning it up—which has been rather nice because we don't have to monitor it closely anymore, they just handle it."

Taya frowned deeper. "What else are they doing?"

"Well, other than the grid and the Belial converters, we aren't using them for much, but every morning and evening we have to adjust polarities to compensate for the power Belial is using. We've been programming the Crystals to magnify the negative ions throughout the grid and increase the positive charge of the earth's subtle body—at least as much of it as we can access. Last week, the Crystals made these adjustments on their own before the technician got to it. Not all of it, the techs still monitor and fine tune, but it's like the Crystals are learning. I think the Crystals are developing some sort of ability to learn from patterns of their usage." He paused to let that sink in. "So I was wondering what you think of that possibility?"

Taya sat stunned, her brows frozen in wrinkles of perplexion. "So...so you're saying they have some sort of automatic function? They're predicting what to do?"

"Yes, that's it exactly. What do you make of it?"

"I never considered it... we didn't program them to be autonomous. Have you sent any programmers down to check on them?"

"No. You know we cannot allow anyone there except you, me and the others of the High Seven—who haven't been interested since the very beginning."

Taya spoke slowly and thoughtfully, "Maybe you should Ziel. If the Crystals are 'learning', that suggests intelligence. They do see and hear so much that goes on in the entire country via the grid, and we know they have more latent power than we understand. I'm not a programmer, I think you should consider taking some experts in. Drug them like before if you have to, but we should at least see if the Crystal's matrix has changed, and exactly how much." She absently tapped the table as she thought out loud. " It's...odd."

"It is. That's what I thought too. I will make arrangements to take two of the programmers in to check on them if that's what you think is best." Ziel bowed his head in acknowledgement, pouring another cup of tea.

Taya sighed, picking up her own mug and taking a long draw. "Let me know what you find. If I need to come there sooner, I will. If the Crystals are going to go evolving on us, I may need more than one re-training a year to keep up with them."

"Once a year isn't nearly enough anyway my dear. I miss you." Ziel said with a sad, kind smile, and she returned it.

"When the girls start their apprentices, you'll see me so much you'll probably regret saying that! Drey will find excuses to be there even more —mark my words. He's having breakdowns on a regular basis just thinking about them living so far away. Speaking of which, when do you plan to tell them of the prophe—"

"We can discuss that in person once you are all here. Ears everywhere my dear, and many things that aren't meant for those ears."

Taya raised her eyebrows. "I hadn't thought of the ears... what else is everyone up to there? Tell me all the latest discoveries..."

He talked until she started yawning and stretching, delighted in his broad interests, irreverent criticisms, and quirky mind. Then, as was his pattern, he became serious. "Everything's becoming more and more unsettled in the House of Oracles. We seem to be preparing for something that our conscious minds won't acknowledge. It's a restless, edgy energy. Ramping up—but to what peak, not even we Oracles can divine. Perhaps it's only the changing of the seasons." Ziel reasoned, somewhat to himself. "I've lived long enough to see the larger cycles. The broader planetary ebb and flow which brings about more intense seasonal patterns of change every few decades, centuries and millenniums." He paused, studying her heavy eyes. "Sleep well dear Taya and don't forget to give my greetings to your Aunt."

"And you Ziel. Are you sure that's all you want me to give Aunt Sage?" She winked and smiled, making him scowl.

"I've no idea what you mean. I'll be in touch when I have news." A corner of his mouth quirked up though, as he leaned to switch off his Comm.

JAYDEE STRIKES

"There were many beautiful vipers in those days and she was one of them."

— MARY ELIZABETH BRADDON

AHNA

They breakfasted early. Again the stout porridge, heavily beaded with tart forest berries that ambushed and shocked the taste buds, amid the dense, chewy bland. Ahna sat by Carver while they ate, and he mimicked Turner's rolling speech of yesterday—which she had missed. "Sure an' we'll be travelin' north, up Ireland's coast all the way ta the land bridge, crossin' ta Scotland's shore, and frim there yer ta board a Sea Cruiser ta return home."

"Not bad." She appraised him out of the corner of her eye. "I've never been able to do voices—"

A loud snort sounded behind her. "No' bad?! Sure an' it was pitiful! My brayin' *ass* could roll better r's." Turner pointed at a low-moving V in the grey sky. "These geese flyin' ow'erhead have more music to their honkin', than this bungling o' my sacred and spectral brogue." He was rolling every r with prolonged aplomb, his eyes twinkling in challenge.

Carver deadpanned to the Irish guide, "Tell us *more* about yer brayin' ass. Let me guess, ya have long, intimate conversations wi' him and he's the best friend ya have?" He was affecting the Irish accent more than ever.

Ignoring Carver, Turner bowed. "And you must be Ahna. I'm the blackheart who failed ta protect ya, and fer that, I sincerely apologize."

Ahna shook her head. "I don't understand it. You only had fifty people to look after, in a sea of thousands. Why were you not at my side?"

Turner grinned and Ahna saw why her sister was smitten.

"What's that ya said? Ya've already forgiven me froom the bottom o' yer bonny wee heart?"

"No." Ahna told him. "You misheard. I said I can do my own protecting —and there's nothing to forgive."

Aiela slid in beside her, with a steaming bowl of porridge. "All the boys trying to impress you again sister? Tsk tsk." She smiled at Turner and Carver with angelic sweetness. "She may be small, but she's tough. You'll see."

Two drivers summoned Turner and he hurried off with a parting "Loovely ta finally meet ya!" and another heartbreaking smile. This one aimed at Aiela.

Carver left too, saying nothing, to intercept Drommen and Lister, headed this way.

"Well that's just dandy." Ahna elbowed her sister. "For once I was the one surrounded by handsome men, and then you came and scared them all away."

Aiela spooned up porridge, wincing when it burned. "Well. What do you think?"

"He'll do. Your babies will have unruly hair and be nothing but a bulging, shapely muscle."

Aiela elbowed her this time.

The mist hung heavy this morning. A veiled melancholy perfumed with peat smoke, it crept along the ground as they piled into wagons. Everyone moved as if half asleep, tired and subdued after last night's feasting and revelry.

As she settled into the wagon next to her sister, Ahna observed the cliques and couples that had formed over the last two days she'd been healing in the yurt. More than half of the students kept their bedrolls around them for warmth, leaning and lying against, around and through each other, rather like litters of puppies. Some dozed off again, lulled by the sway of the wagons. The bonding energy around her was a sort of comfort and loneliness together.

Even the teachers were in their own pairs and groupings, chatting sporadically, enjoying the dewy soft air so fresh with last night's rain. The earth cast a friendly, romance-tinged spell over them and Ahna wished Carver was beside her again.

For two hours they rode at a fair clip, bumping and jostling along, before the sun drank up the low-lying vapors and began to warm and dry its sodden land. Long called the "Green Isle", Ireland's countryside shimmered as all its vibrant shades of green came awake in the sunshine. Fingers pointed at a spectacularly huge fern or a moss-covered pile of stone shaped like a crouching wolf, or the ancient trees with knotted faces that seemed to watch and whisper amongst themselves, as these loud younglings passed by.

Bedrolls peeled away, stretching commenced, and soon they began jumping off the wagons, eager to use their legs and touch the world they were passing. Gingerly patting the docile and smelly aurochs, the boys challenged each other to races along the road. The girls found plenty of wildflowers to sniff, plucking them to braid into colorful chains, or tuck behind an ear. Ahna joined in, glad to walk, feeling almost normal again.

Around noon, Turner called a halt to rest the faithful aurochs and feed everyone. Crunchy herbed vegetables were wrapped inside of a tough, flat, kelp bread. Dried fish, fresh melon and cheese curds completed the meal. Everyone washed the remnants of food from their hands in a tiny loch not far from the road. The two boys who'd fallen wrestling, into a steaming pile of Auroch shit, had a good scrub in the cold clear water, and change of clothes before being let back into a wagon. The aurochs had been watered and allowed to graze during the break. By the time everyone loaded up and settled in, they grew drowsy in the afternoon warmth.

Jaydee's long brown hair gleamed in the sun and her viciously shaped mouth curved a smile when she squeezed in next to Ahna, cooing and clucking over her. "Oh *little Ahna*, are you feeling alright? You know I can get you anything that you want. Tell me how you're doing."

Ahna was respectful but distant. "I feel well, thank you for asking and I don't want anything. At all." She shifted away ever so slightly, repelled by the manipulative energy slithering about her, but Jaydee scooted closer, wrapping an arm around Ahna's shoulders, hissing loudly in her ear.

"I saw Carver talking to you earlier. If he bothers you, you come to me. That boy's no good and I won't let him ruin your trip just because he wants a sweet little thing like you to prey on." She rocked back to look at Ahna, giggling in a high pitched voice as if they'd just shared an intimate secret.

Ahna squirmed and leaned out of Jaydee's embrace, her stomach queasy. "I *like* Carver actually. He sa—"

Jaydee cut in, frowning. "No. No you don't. But you know who is perfect for you? That handsome boy back there, Nirka." She sighed wistfully, "Even his name is perfect! You two would make the most bee-u-tiful pair."

Ahna wrinkled her nose, still trying to lean and then scoot away from the overpowering flowery perfume. "Nanat is interested in Nirka. They'd be well-matched."

Jaydee snorted. "No, that's all wrong. He'd tire of Nanat soon. She's too stupid. In fact, I could pull some strings to make it even sooner!" The squealing giggle again, as if she found herself very clever.

Her arm clamped down like a vice then, her too shiny eyes bored into Ahna's and that's when Ahna felt the psychic bombardment. An overwhelming force rammed into her consciousness, wrapping around it like the arm around her shoulders, determined to penetrate her mind. Going very still, she trapped Jaydee's gaze with the steel of her own. "I don't like what you're saying or what you're doing. Stay away from me, stay away from my sister and get your slimy arm off me!

Forcefully pushing out of the hold, Ahna jumped down off the side of the wagon, mentally pushing with all her strength at the psychic force. It broke off quite easily as she jogged towards the front wagon where Aiela sat beside Turner.

"Aiela, can we walk for awhile?"

"Everything alright? Ya needin' anythin'?" Turner was instantly concerned.

"No I'm fine, I just need to talk to El."

Aiela was already beside her. "Catch up with you later." She called to Turner, as they slowed to a walk and the wagon kept on moving.

"That woman, Jaydee, just attacked...or...tried to get into my *mind!*" Ahna recounted their short conversation, then broke off as the wagon she'd been in passed them by. Standing shoulder to shoulder, both girls put their hands on their hips and glared at Jaydee. She saw them as they came abreast, and looked away quickly, pretending not to notice their pointed stares. Falling back to walk behind the last wagon, Ahna finished telling Aiela all that was said, as well as what wasn't said. "We need to find out who she is and what she wants from us. Why would she go inside our minds?" They puzzled in stillness for a bit.

"Maybe we should talk to Healer Lira. Tell her. She might know something. It's not normal. And not good!"

Aiela nodded, swatting a bug from her hair. "We should confront her. Just ask outright what she wants from us."

"I suppose we could." Ahna disliked confrontation. Too many strong energies in play all at once. But Aiela preferred it.

The road had become little more than matching ruts, as they passed through fields of rough grass that grew tall, stretching out to the horizon on all sides. Gentle hills interrupted the general flatness occasionally and they could still smell the sea, even though they couldn't see it anymore. Every so often, the procession startled a family of ground-dwelling fowl who squawked and fluttered their indignance at their territory being invaded.

"It's so pretty here! Don't you think it's uncommonly lovely? It even smells better than at home. Everything at home smells planned, sort of designed, nothing new or strange. I like strange. We definitely need more *odd* and *unintended* at home." Aiela was chatty and whimsical, bursting with happiness.

"Planning has a smell?" Ahna teased, letting her sister's infectious cheer chase away all baleful worries. "No. It's actually sort of average right here. I mean look around, it's just….prairie, and it *smells* like miles and miles of grass and then… sea. And it's too wet—dank even. I think something is *enhancing* your experience." She tapped a finger against her lip. "Hmmm, what could that *be*?"

Aiela laughed, bowing a deep agreement at Ahna, which turned into a bit of the dance she had learned the night before. "He can sail! He's been sailing since he was three and he races horses and once in another country he raced *ostriches.* He's been so many places and done so many things. I'm surprised, I mean, I was expecting all the Irish to be backwards, a lot less sophisticated than us but here he is with eight times the world experiences that I have. He's *interesting*—c'mon now, have you ever heard me say that about a boy? He asks me odd questions like what's the most horrible and best thing I've eaten and if I could be an animal, what would I be? It's like starting a new book. One that is riveting and infinite. One I can't put down."

Ahna raised her hands, palms open to the sky in mock plea. "Heaven help us! My fierce, warrior sister's become *bubbly*! It appears she's lost her mind over an Irishman!"

"Not my mind." Aiela shot back. "Just my heart. And maybe you should try it sometime, letting someone steal your heart."

EVENING WAS CLOSE, by the time they came to a small village. More of a settlement, it was like nothing they had seen before. Atlantis advanced far beyond this primitive setting ages before any of them had been born.

A handful of children came running to the roadside as Turner called the caravan to a halt. Skinny, barefoot and wearing well-mended rags or animal skins, they clustered around him with hopeful faces and bright eyes as he walked to the food wagon and began rooting through the bags of supplies.

Digging out a large package, he said something in Irish that sent two of the children racing towards a large, grass-covered mound of earth. The rest remained around him jabbering and vying for his attention.

"Could ya mabbe help me here?" He called to Aiela and Ahna. Handing a cloth bag filled with hard honey and maple candies over the flock of little heads, he gestured at the children pressing around them. "Right. Give each a handful. That'll draw 'em off so I can unload. These people are vera poor an' vera proud. Da sends cloth, medicine an' foodstuff they've no access ta." He handed another bag across to them. "That'll be apples froom the mainland. Eight or nine families live here. Sure an' we'll exchange these gifts fer fresh water an' a place ta sleep. Irish pride is iron pride, easily injured by charity. Two days we'll spend here before continuin' north, ta give ya a true picture of how most irish live."

A few adults, as ragged and skinny as the children, came smiling to Turner. As they made arrangements, negotiating in their rolling cadence of Irish speak, Aiela and Ahna offered sweets to the children. Thin, dirty little faces lit up, they held out both hands before scampering off to crouch in the tall grass and suck on the sticky treats.

The rest of the group began unloading as Turner called instructions to the drivers, where to park wagons and stake aurochs for water and grazing. Gathering the group, he explained that the girls would be housed in the largest earth home and the boys in another. "Sure an' it'll be a bit tight, wi' eatin' meals outside. The families will enjoy havin' such exotic visitors an' vera much want ta know ya all." He finished.

By now, more had come out to greet their uncommon guests, shyly smiling and nodding, which seemed the traditional Irish greeting. There were three men, all older, missing varying amounts of teeth and hair. Five women, one of them severely pregnant, two with babes in their arms, and two elderly with prune-like faces and bent backs. They were somehow so gracious, Ahna thought, even without words, even with little to offer these privileged youths. Welcoming this unexpected company from the great wide world, they held out hands, offering to carry packs and bedrolls into the homes they were so willing to share.

A prehistoric-looking woman was led over by two children, who accepted sweets and scampered off, once she'd been delivered. She had long, thin strands of sky-grey hair falling in a rent curtain, around the most wrinkled face Ahna had ever seen. Bent almost in half, she walked with the aid of a peeled stick that resembled an ashy, knotted snake. She gestured and garbled at them hopefully and toothlessly for a bit, but they couldn't recognize any of her words. She shouted to Turner and he hurried over to translate.

"She wants ya ta follow her. Her family home is where ya'll be sleepin'."

Obediently, they traipsed behind the ancient lady's slow, rocking gait as she leaned on Turner's arm, to a thick, curtain-like door of woven grasses that led down inside a grass-covered mound.

Dim light streamed from a hole above the indoor fire pit. A tiny window of sorts lit the opposite side. "Look at that." Ahna whispered. A beehive ceiling made by stacking flat rocks in concentric circles, interlocked and balanced each ascending layer as they climbed tighter and tighter to the center.

Turner was translating again. "Here I was born. Here I have lived my life and it is here I will leave this life fer another. I am honored that royalty has come ta visit an' sleep in this home that I cherish. I did never think ta meet a queen and now I have met two! Welcome ta my home. May you find comfort an' rest innit."

Ahna looked to Turner, "What is her name?"

Her whole ancient face smiled at the simple question. "Caoimhe." (kwee-va) She beamed at the girls, as if they had asked her to tell the story of her beloved.

Aiela was full of questions. "Why do you call us queens? We're far from it..."

"Sure an' I see yer souls. If no' in this life, the ones before or after, I do no' know. Ya shine the light o' greater wisdom, the valor o' sacrifice, humility that allows much power ta be placed in yer hands."

Caoimhe squinted in silence then, back and forth between the three of them, smacking her gums together, bird-like eyes flicking rapidly, unblinking, from face to face.

Then she pushed Turner and Aiela closer to each other. "Ahhh yes, they fit well t'gether, these two hearts. T'gether yer stronger." Turner had hesitated, looking at Aiela shyly before translating, but Caoimhe poked her crooked finger sharply into his chest until he repeated what she'd said.

Then the other girls started trickling in with their bedrolls and bags, exclaiming at the intricate dome of interlocking stones, just as Ahna had.

"Tell her thank you." Ahna smiled into the little woman's eyes. "Thank you and your words will not be forgotten."

By the time they set about cooking a simple supper of fish and boiled vegetables, the rest of the village families were back from their day's work of fishing, hunting, or working in their fields. The bigger children had simple jobs like hauling fire fuel, harvesting from their gardens, or gathering edible roots and berries in a forest some distance away.

Food preparation was assigned to a different team each meal and tonight was Ahna's team. They started with strings of salt-packed fish and baskets of mixed vegetables, pungent earth clods still clinging to them. The village supplied pails of water and bone knives for washing, scraping and chopping. Spits stretched along both sides of the fire rings. Gourds were stacked, ready to serve as cooking pots. Kelp and leaves were wetted, and wrapped around the more delicate or smaller fish, to be laid at the edges of the coals to roast.

Long low tables of rough-split logs held the heaping piles of steaming food as the cooks turned it out in batches. Small, woven grass mats served as plates of sorts and everyone sat on the ground, eating with their hands. Though rough and simple, it seemed a novelty to these who were used to dining on artisan-made pottery.

The villagers joined in the plentiful meal and everyone gathered around two large central cook fires, Irish and Atlantean, mingling and trying valiantly to communicate.

Done with cooking, Ahna spotted Carver talking with a local man near his own age. For once, Drommen and Lister seemed to be elsewhere, so Ahna settled cross-legged on the softly trampled weeds next to him, hoping to ask the questions piling up since last night. She was curious why he'd joined this trip. What was it like where he lived and what area would he apprentice in? Really, she just wanted to be with him. All day he had been in the middle of a group of boys, sometimes helping Turner and the Drivers with something, or napping in a wagon between his two ever-present companions.

As she listened, it was clear Carver struggled to understand the dialect spoken here and even more in trying to speak it. He glanced at her and one side of his mouth lifted. It set something buzzing inside her.

"Ahna, this is Eran. I *think* he's saying he's a good fisherman and wants to teach me something. Or, he could be saying the fish we ate tonight was good and could I teach him..." Carver turned back to Eran and spoke in a thick, slow tongue, gesturing to Ahna and saying her name. Eran smiled at her and nodded, saying something in return. The two of them conversed like this with some laughter before one of the older women, his mother perhaps? called to Eran and he went off with her.

Carver arced an amused glance at her. "He asked if I was your man...if you had 'claimed' me. When I told him no, he asked if you might want to claim him. He said to tell you good things about him in case you want a strong Irishman."

Ahna raised an eyebrow. "That's how it's done here? A woman 'claims' the man she chooses? And what if he doesn't want to be claimed?"

"I don't think you would have that problem."

They stared into the fire, adjusting to the awkward compliment.

"How was your travels today? Did you see that nest of baby birds we passed? Quail maybe? I was on alert, see, because I knew you would say there had been wee grass people. Here, you want this? I'm full." Ahna passed her remaining smoked fish to him. He accepted it, answering between bites.

"Yes, but did you look *up*? There was a swarm of what appeared to be gnats. I just happened to be laying on my back in the wagon, otherwise, I would have missed them. They were not in fact gnats, but rather a mass of the smallest variety of faery. Tiny air faeries that live among flowers during the summer and make empty nutshells into palaces for the winter. They tame insects to ride or work and it's said they are the keepers of the seeds, deciding when and where seeds germinate, nourishing them until they take root and start to grow. They must have been travelling, the mass was moving fast overhead. I can't think what they might travel for. Where do you think they were going...?"

Ahna listened wide-eyed, inserting just enough questions to keep him talking.

First the Drivers retired to their wagons where they would sleep close to the aurochs.

Then the village families, having rearranged their customary sleeping arrangements to accommodate their guests, bedded down, weary after a day's hard work. Saying "rest well" in Atlantean, they shyly returned the bows given them before disappearing into grass-covered mounds. They would sleep closer than usual tonight, happy to share their homes with these exotic youngsters.

The Atlantean students sat up late enjoying the fires, the softly scented darkness breeding a deeper form of companionship. Ahna and Carver bantered back and forth, mixing light-hearted imaginings about this strange and pretty country, with questions they wanted to know about the other. She noticed he avoided answering most of hers.

"How's your face feel? I can barely see the cut when it's dark." Carver leaned closer to peer at her cheek. His dark hair fell into his eyes and she wanted terribly much to touch it, to feel his face, to make physical contact. The urge was so overwhelming, she forgot to answer him.

"All right then. Next subject." He said lightly, stretching wide towards starry horizons.

Ahna came back to the moment. "It's better, feels almost normal most of the—" She broke off abruptly when he accidentally put his hand down on top of hers. The sudden contact shot through her.

"...time." She finished at the same instant he said "Sorry." Jerking his large, gloriously warm hand from on top of hers.

Gods, what is my problem? It's not like this is the first time I've touched a boy. What is it about him?

She decided to be bravely honest. "Carver." She said his name softly, waiting until he looked at her. "It's alright." She reached across the few inches between them and slid her hand inside his, heart pounding, craving this connection with him. *Please let him want this too. Why does this feel so risky? And yet so good.*

He dropped her hand as if it were a hot coal, standing abruptly as Drommen and Lister appeared beside him. Without so much as a glance in her direction he walked away, talking with them.

She sat, feeling stunned and foolish and then a little angry. Why would he be so friendly and then react like this? Maybe she had him all wrong. Maybe he was in love with another girl at home and he was just being nice to her, just wanted a friend on this trip. Clearly, he wasn't attracted to her in the way she was to him. She tried not to feel too embarrassed at her error in judgement. It's just that this had never happened before. She usually read other's energy like a book.

Finding Aiela, she joined the migration towards their homes for the night, letting the silky murmur of girl talk surround and soothe her heart while they all bedded down in the hollow hill that smelled of damp earth. Which reminded her of Carver all over again.

THE OPENING

"My heart's been torn wide open, just like I feared it would be,and I have no willpower to close it back up."

— MARIE LU,

AHNA

By afternoon the next day, the skies hung low, trailing an underbelly of shaggy bulges in shades of smoky gray and white.

Ahna wandered out to find the ocean, weary of being surrounded by the girls with their relentless chattering, which began the moment they awoke.

She craved solace, empty space.

She'd spent the morning grinding grains, nuts and seeds. Blisters dotted her palms from the unfamiliar work.

After breaking their fast with the routine porridge, they'd been split up and sent off by Aiela. Each small group engaging in some task to learn the ways of this austere and friendly culture, and offering help as a gesture of goodwill and caring. They more than quadrupled the workforce and the families were grateful. Especially the children who would get the luxury of some playtime, now that so much work was being done by the guests.

Ahna knew she'd been deliberately placed in a group with less physically demanding tasks. There were five other girls and one boy in her group, including Nanat and several of her adherents. They gossiped happily around Ahna all morning. She did try to join in the talk that rolled seamlessly from one subject to the next, but everything she said came out awkward and stilted. Each topic or person was dissected— discussed to death sometimes. It was all highly animated and desperately dramatic. The boy's name was Jai. Willowy, effeminate and really very pretty, he fit in better with the girls than with the boys. He came from Atlantis' farthest southern tip and his skin was creamy brown, like cacao milk. Disappointed to find no other boys with his sexual orientation on the trip, he'd had no trouble making friends. His outrageously flamboyant personality rivaled Nanat's, except without the snottiness.

Jai worked beside Ahna all morning, and she was grateful for the distraction from Nanat's constant yammer. He was full of questions, intrigued by the fact that she was a twin. "Your sister and Turner are ogling each other huh? That one is dreamy! Of all the boys here, if I could have my choice, mmm yes, he'd be it. Those *muscles....*" Jai feigned a dramatic fainting motion that made Ahna laugh.

"He's handsome I guess..."

"Oh honey, he's far beyond handsome, have you heard him *speak?* That accent, mm-mm-mm. Maybe he's got some brothers or cousins who would love to love a gorgeous Atlantean boy. We should ask him. I can massage your hands after we're done with this. I'm going to High City this autumn to apprentice a Masseuse. I've studied bodywork for the last two seasons and I'm top of my class but that's only in my little forgotten town, which won't count for beans in the Big Time! I'm trying to get as much experience as possible before I get there. Worried that everybody else will somehow be ahead of me I guess." Jai's voice took on a wheedling tone, "Really Ahna, all this crushing and grinding is going to make you stiff and sore, but I can help with that...?"

Ahna stopped to rest, stretching. Her forearms and hands already starting to cramp a little. "No convincing needed. I'll gladly take you up on that! The other girls will want you to work on them too, once they know what you do." She popped a round cobnut in her mouth from the basket they were working through. "Aiela and I are moving to High City this fall too. We won't know anybody but a few adults. Let's plan to meet...."

Following a lunch of traditional lavar bread, alongside cheese and vegetables, Ahna helped sort and wash baskets of berries brought back by a group who were out foraging and picking all morning.

Two hours later, Caoimhe hobbled to where Ahna was stooped over racks made of green bush reeds, spreading berries out to dry in the sun. The ancient lady carried an empty sack, woven from tough grass rope. It clearly had once held kelp. She pointed at a long strand of lingering seaweed and then in the direction of the ocean, thrusting the sack into Ahna's hands, making a shooing motion. The message was clear. Go to the ocean. Bring back more kelp.

Ahna smiled gratefully, wanting to throw her arms around the tiny, leathered woman for giving her an escape. Instead, she bowed respect-fully, one hand touching her heart, before running off. Finally she would have some alone time to recharge.

She walked perhaps a mile along a narrow dirt track, worn into a waving field of tall, sharp grass. It led from the sparse settlement of domed earth homes to a rocky seashore, and the place they used as a dock for narrow, tar-coated fishing boats. The grass ended abruptly in a little rise and then rocks, jagged and black with age, piled in great expanses down to where the waves rolled up to drown them at high tide. The tide was out, exposing a smooth stretch of coarse sand the color of raw cane sugar, and heavily littered with mixed varieties of kelp, shells and all sizes of pebbles, multi-colored and rounded by the endless roll of the waves.

The crashing of the sea, and the breeze it stirred up, caressed her senses, soothing and clearing out the overfilled spaces in her psyche. She meditated some few minutes, finding the calm center of balance she was craving, while the ocean performed its song of blessed solitude

Eventually, she began roaming along the wet sand. Picking up slimy strands and tangles of the tired kelp discarded by the shallows, she rinsed and lay them out along the black rocks to drain. Spotting a tiny, perfect, starfish bleached to a sandy pink, she tucked it into a pocket. So many intricate shells and rocks that she wanted to keep. Instead, she built tiny cairns of them. Painstakingly, she constructed perfectly balanced, minia-ture shrines, from the bounty of a sea that broke and swallowed entire land masses in its power, yet protected and carried its smallest, most deli-cate treasures, depositing them whole onto its shores. Even knowing they would be washed away by midnight, the cairn-building brought Ahna deep pleasure. Leaving a trail of draining kelp strewn like lost hairs of a sea giant along the rocks behind her, she wandered down shore, thinking myriads of things and sometimes nothing, until she heard her name.

He was jogging towards her along the sand, in a graceful lope that favored one side. She stood still, watching his abundant black hair, usually falling into his eyes, now flying back from an angled forehead, square jaw tipped down slightly. Had he always limped? He carried something but she didn't recognize what, until he was beside her, inhaling deeply to catch his breath. Half grown, prone, and most peculiarly, black, a baby seagull sprawled inside his hands.

"Is it dead?" Ahna touched it gently on its little chest. It moved very slightly.

"Almost. I thought you might know what to do."

They squatted together on the dry part of the grainy sand and Carver spread his hands wide so Ahna could examine the baby bird.

"We should take it back to Aiela. She's the healer." Ahna stroked the little black pile of feathers with a fingertip, gauging its lifeforce. She could barely feel it. "My sister had as much to do with my face healing as Lira and the oils. She has a gift for working with broken things, helping them know how to mend. How did you find me?"

Carver's lips curved with crafty knowing. "We got back from fishing and I saw your little cairns. I knew it was you." He shrugged, "We like the same things. That's something I do at our beach back home, make sculptures of stuff interesting or pretty, or just overly common. Do you think we can help him?"

She wanted to freeze time just then, with this carefree smile relaxing Carver's face, and his open trust that she'd help him save a life. This close, his icy eyes were flecked with a dark spice. For once, he looked at her with naked interest instead of hiding or wary. She realized she was staring again, entranced by the exquisite artistry of those large well-formed hands spread wide, cradling the helpless baby bird, hanging onto life by only a thread. *I wonder what he'd do if I just kissed him on those mysterious looking lips. Right here, right now....only a foot away.*

But she couldn't bring herself to risk it. Not after last night.

"We should go back. Poor little thing, doesn't feel like it'll last much longer. I have to take all this kelp too...maybe you should go on ahead." Ahna stood to start piling the damp, drained seaweed into the bag, working her way back along the shore.

Carver didn't leave. Following her, he used his free hand to help with the seaweed, while cradling the bird against his chest.

"Try holding it slightly upside down. Reverse its gravity a little and very gently massage its heart. Think about giving it some of your energy, send it out from your heart space. Aiela will find what its problem is."

Carver angled his hand to slant the baby bird's head down, using the other hand to draw tiny light circles around the heart area, walking slow to keep pace with Ahna's hurried kelp gathering. "I think it's breathing a little stronger."

She could feel the eensy pick up in its small energy. Like a tide turning, its life was ebbing back now, instead of away. "You have strong healing energy. Keep doing it just like that. How was fishing?"

He shrugged. "Alright. I didn't want to go, but Eran kept asking until I said yes. He's nice—real tired of being here. He's not been anywhere else and he dreams of seeing the world. Reminds me how privileged we are. We talked as if we're regular friends. Surprises me to connect like that with somebody way out here. Between all of us, we caught enough fish to fill up all three of their boats. I imagine that's what we'll be eating tonight and they'll fillet and dry the rest. We didn't go out deep enough to catch the real big ones, thanks be. Their boats aren't made for deep sea."

She'd felt his relief and his anxiety in turns as he spoke. "Why didn't you want to go fishing? And what's the story with you and deep water?"

He stood very still. Ahna could feel his indecision whether to open to her or not. She felt his edges, his uncertainty with her probing, her noticing and interest in the neglected places he'd buried. She kept moving, stuffing her bag, letting him confront his inner torments in peace.

"Here, you take the bird, I'll carry that bag." Carver said.

It had grown heavy, sagging long. She'd started dragging it. "Thanks."

He transferred the little black gull with such gentleness, their hands brushing each other during the exchange, their bodies almost touching. Then Carver looked into her eyes for an instant and she saw. She felt it. He was every bit as aware of her as she was of him. Every bit as caught up in this alchemical attraction. *Why does he deny it? Why is he resisting so?*

He picked up the plump, squishing kelp bag and continued filling, while Ahna tended to the tiny black pile in her hands, brushing circles around its heart chakra as Carver had been doing. It felt boneless and delicate. So very vulnerable. She thought about how vulnerable she must had been when Carver had come along and carried her away.

He rescues. He reshapes life by stepping in. Yet some fear rules him —but what?

Carver

Carver liked the wet satin feel of the kelp. Concentrating on that, he ignored Ahna's questions. He was opening to her too much already, seeking her out like this. Every time they were together was such deep pleasure—and such a threat.

Today he felt like everybody else, safe, happy and accepted. Eran had offered friendship so freely—not out of fear or greed like people back home. Out on the water, without nausea or terror the whole time, he'd actually begun to enjoy it. Being here, alone with Ahna who hummed with everything he yearned for, radiating life into him like a sunlit rainbow invades the gray shadowed world, it became too much.

Last night he'd reacted to the danger when she slipped her hand so unexpectedly into his, just as Drommen and Lister found him. He'd felt terrible, dropping it, leaving without explanation. But how could he explain? If he told her the whole truth of why he couldn't be seen to care about her, then she sure as hell no longer would. She'd know who and what he was.

When he was twelve, he'd found a puppy in the streets. Abandoned, mangy, so hungry its stomach bulged, he took it home and fed it. Every day, he spent hours holding and loving her until she was strong, accidentally bonding with her. She followed him everywhere, obeyed any command and slept in his bed at night. He named her Hunter because she liked to chase small rodents, birds, fish in the water or even bugs, sniffing them out, stalking and growling like a mighty hunter.

Carver's brothers made fun of him at first, caring that much for an animal. Then they graduated to taunting him by threatening the pup. He tried to keep Hunter with him so no harm would come to her but there were certain chores and errands that she had to sit out.

One day he came home to find her very sick. They had fed her rotten meat just to spite him. They took special pleasure in hurting Hunter worse and worse, because it was an agony to Carver to see her suffer, and they could get him to do just about anything to avoid his dog being tortured. In his twelve-year-old mind, he couldn't decide whether to give her to some traveling merchant who might care for her, or take her far away and abandon her in a nice forest somewhere, hoping she was big enough to make it on her own. He even considered taking her life as a mercy. The thought of any of those made him cry. It was the first time he'd loved anything like this.

The day he came home to find Hunter bleeding and blinded in one eye, he snapped. His two eldest brothers were the worst tormentors, cruel and amused by driving Carver to anger or tears. He waited until they were asleep and then tied Balek to his bed, striking him again and again with a stick until he screamed loud enough to wake Mardu. Mardu had

come, snatched the stick and hit Carver so hard it knocked him unconscious. When Carver woke sometime before morning, still on the floor of
his brother's room, he staggered back to his own room clutching his
swollen, split face. Hunter had been hanged from the rafter above his bed.
He cut her down and sat crying with her limp little body until dawn,
hopeless and defeated.

That was the day he understood. Anything he loved would become a
tool, a twisted power over him in the hands of his family.

It had crossed his mind to run away again—this time, so far that no
Belial would ever find him. Surely the Atlanteans would take him in,
maybe protect him. But he remembered all too well, bore scars from the
retribution his father had taken the other times he'd tried to run. Mardu
wouldn't just hurt Carver, he'd maim or kill anyone he imagined had
helped or even known. He knew his father cared little whether he left or
stayed, it was about control. Mardu would not let Carver leave unless it
was Mardu's will. He'd told Carver the next time he ran away, he'd be
buried alive—describing in ghastly detail exactly what that would be like.
Carver believed him. He'd had nightmares for a long long time.

Drommen and Lister would report everything from this trip to Mardu
—for sure, a tiny golden-haired Atlantean girl that Carver helped,
befriended and became romantic with. To Mardu, that would be especially valuable information. Carver was religious in avoiding the appearance of caring for anyone in particular at home.

Though he was grown now, and overt abuse was mostly in the past, he
knew beyond a doubt that Mardu and his brothers would still use
anything or anyone to maintain absolute control over him. He also knew
a day was fast coming when there would be a limit to what he was willing
to do for them. Or with them.

"I...can't answer all the questions you ask Ahna. I want to. You're the...
the greatest girl I've known. You're warm and...beautiful and I need you
not to care for me. I can't explain that either...." He was mumbling as they
came in sight of the fishing boats, swishing in and out with the tides to
the end of their taut ropes. He stopped where the path met the beach
rocks, leading back to the village of earth mounds.

She'd been quietly stroking and murmuring to the baby bird. Patient
in letting him continue to speak to her. Or not.

Under the ashen sky, with the beach playing urgent love songs in the
waves, he wanted so badly to connect. To love her, even if this were the
only time he'd ever get to. But his painful prison of shame, timbered and
roofed in fear, seemed an eternal sentence of isolation and he didn't know

how to escape it. He stood by the sea, watching its blue-grey dance of the divine, unsure what to do or say next, simply waiting for her to walk away from him, abandon him back to the quasi-human existence he'd come from.

He startled when she laid her hand lightly on his arm. Stepping around in front of him, she slid it to his chest, a bold pressure blazing into his heart. Her caress dismantled him. He wanted to run away and he wanted to cry and he wanted to put his arms around her. She reached to touch his cheek then, looking up into his eyes, his name rising from her lips like a prayer.

"Carver, I don't need to know...whatever you can't tell me. I'd just like to know *you*. If we must hide our friendship from Drommen and Lister—and anyone else—fine. We'll be a secret." Her conspiratorial smile held compassion too. "Here's what I know; you've a heroic heart. I know the truth of it even though you cover and hide it. That's what you are to me, a hero. Always. Even if we never speak again." She touched a fingertip lightly to his lips to seal the promise and then turned to the path, trailing words behind her. "But we won't be a secret long if we don't get back. Thank you for carrying the bag."

He slung the long bag, soggy with seaweed, onto his back and followed her, too confused to sort out what just happened. Her stories of today with the girls and Jai washed over him, lightening his burdens. He reciprocated with a story of sea faeries that he may or may not have seen, making her laugh and grill him with doubtful questions until they arrived back to the smoky cookfires, already burning midst a weary crowd, waiting for supper to be ready.

Ahna

She fell asleep that night cradling the memory of his heartbeat under her palm, the smooth heat of his lips on her fingertip.

Oh Carver, who are you and what are you so afraid of?

13

THE KILLING

"You're lucky to have a friend who will kill for you. So. I once had a friend who died for me, and now one who killed for me. Why didn't I feel lucky?"

— CARRIE VAUGHN

AHNA

She woke feeling droopy. Like an overwatered plant in desperate need of some energizing sunshine. Perhaps these late nights talking around the fires were getting to her, or was it the overbearing clouds, lingering again this morning? At least it wasn't raining, keeping them damp and chilled. This land seemed more often steeped in mist than anything else.

They breakfasted on bread pudding made with quail eggs, auroch cream, and dense bread from the finest of their milled flours, gifted from Turner's father. Spiced with ground nutmeg and a topping of toasted seeds and burnt honey, it was a rare treat, made specially for them by these grateful Irish families. Its autumnal taste was like coming home.

Overall, it was a difficult goodbye. Ahna noticed that Eran never left Carver's side while they packed and loaded the wagons. She still stared too much. Something within her was compelled to learn all that she could of him. He caught her more than once, their eyes colliding before turning away in the private agony of hidden yearning.

She and Aiela ate with Caoimhe, and though they couldn't communicate in words, the love and wisdom that flowed between them was enough. Right before climbing into a wagon, Ahna made her a gift of their diadem with the ruby. It seemed right, a gesture of giving their best as Caoimhe had done for them. When they enfolded her gently in a double-sided farewell hug, the tiny primitive lady shed two small tears, but it was clear they were joyful. She nodded and garbled at them rapidly, her face squinched into wrinkles of smiles that showed off her pale, dusty-rose gums, then sent them on their way with little pats upon the cheek.

The road was lined with people, waving and calling in their complex Irish tongue, "Thankee fer comin' ta us", "Blessed be", and "Until we meet again...". Barefoot children ran alongside the wagons for a fair bit before falling back to return to their mounded cave-like homes.

Aiela and Ahna burrowed between barrels, crates and folded tarps in the rear wagon, opting to be alone for awhile. Still early morning when the caravan rolled out, students in the other wagons soon fell back asleep, nestled in bedrolls under pewter clouds.

"Well, that was nice, making heart friends and then leaving them. Forever. Carver was in my seat next to Turner..." Aiela sounded as brackish as the occasional swamps they'd passed.

"We just weren't expecting to bond with these people. Our own group maybe but not random natives." Ahna was wriggling down inside her own fleecy bedroll, hoping to sleep away the fatigue, wanting to slough away the great clouds of sadness she felt.

She'd just closed her eyes when voices sounded and Carver and Turner swung into the wagon from either side. Much shuffling ensued as they settled into small leftover spaces unoccupied by supplies.

Ahna stared at Carver, eyebrows raised in silent question.

"Dromm and Lister fell asleep." He shrugged, "And... I told them last night that I want to make more friends in this group—to give me some space."

Turner interrupted, "Carver and I went lookin' fer the two o' ya. 'Where', we asked each other, 'are those two bonny girls?' We searched every wagon. I was startin' ta believe we'd left ya behind. Gave me a scare, mind ya!" He tried to glare at them but couldn't quite manage it. "Anyway, now we've found ya, conveniently together, and here we all are."

"And what would you have done," Aiela asked, "if we had been left behind?"

"We'd ha' gone ta the ends o' the earth ta find ya!" Turner said grandly. "Then we'd ha' stolen ya both away ta a beautiful tropical isle where ya'd be our ladies foorever while we roamed the high seas searchin' fer jewels and pomegranates ta please ya, silk gowns, auld wine and anything else ya commanded o' us."

A smile played at Aiela's lips but she hid it well. "We have a word for men like you Turner of Ireland. You're a Rogue."

Turner squinted at Carver's snicker, mock whispering, "Help me oot mate, is't a grand thing oor a black thing ta be a rogue?"

"For most girls, it's a black thing." Carver replied slowly. "But for these, I believe it might be grand."

Ahna couldn't hide her grin.

Aiela snorted. "Nope. It's a black thing."

But Turner only scooted closer. "Weel, lucky fer me, yer a moon goddess, an' ya light the blackest o' the black."

Both boys seemed in a jubilant mood.

Carver's awkwardness was conspicuously missing. He held up a small grass bag, clearly woven by someone they'd just left. Inside was the baby bird, curled in a nest of fern leaves. "This one was asking for you."

"Aww. How's he doing? Better?" Ahna reached in to stroke the little black feathers with a finger, making it wriggle as the tiny head poked up, beady eyes slitting open. "He's certainly more alert. Aiela, can you check him again?"

Aiela had been talking with Turner during Ahna and Carver's exchange. Now, Turner took Aiela's hand and lifted it to his lips, announcing, "Moon goddess is grouchy, but allowin' me ta stay at her side." Then speaking to Carver, "Our evil plan has worked!" He and Carver shared a grin.

It was fun, the four of them being together. They talked and joked, getting more acquainted, finding and settling into commonalities, discovering the places of personality overlaps, while the wagons trundled along at a fair pace, passing through endless grasslands. An occasional Loch offered up petite silver waves hurrying back and forth between its shores, as the breeze dictated from just above.

Carver and Turner seemed very much to like each other, bantering endlessly. A magnetic camaraderie springing to life between them. Their deep guffaws and besting of each other's stories rolled back and forth in a sweet rumble. Turner often reverted to Irish until he caught himself, or the girls asked him to repeat something, but Carver understood it all, even trying out a bit of his own Irish, making Turner hoot with laughter and correct him.

Ahna and Aiela passed silent looks of pleasure, secret smiles and nudges, jumping in to challenge the boys with their own tales, or tease one or the other of them.

"What's this? I haven't seen you wearing it before." Ahna reached to touch the miniature pouch strung on a cord around Carver's neck. Two perfect circles made of very thin leather had been stitched together forming a tiny round pouch, with the Atlantis Spiral of Life crudely embossed, or perhaps burned, onto both sides. Concealing whatever the contents were, the leather was the same shade as the raw sugary sand at their beach yesterday. It almost blended into the bronzed skin of his throat.

"Caoimhe gave it to me. She tied it around my neck and...see? Permanent knot. I couldn't understand much of what she said except when she chanted...something about bringing balance and removing barriers to love."

Ahna felt a tingle of warmth pass through her when she touched it. "What's inside?"

Carver shrugged. "I don't know. It's sewn shut so I'm assuming it's not for me to know."

"It suits you." Ahna said.

Turner looked at the three of them, puzzled. "Ya don' have talismans in Atlantis? Huh. We've somethin' that ya don't?" He pulled from beneath his shirt, his own tiny pouch, slate grey and a little larger. It featured the gordian knot. "Talismans are made by wise women who can see yer soul an' its overarchin' lack. They're made as a...emm, attractant—or as protection. Ta attract what ya need so ya can fulfill the soul's purpose, or ta deflect what might harm or...em, deter ya. What's inside is a mystery, symbolizing yer willingness ta follow yer path—even though it's unknown. I've no' actually had one before..." His mouth curved upside down as he gazed the awkward angle, trying to see the charm so close to his own throat.

Aiela leaned in to examine the talisman too and with their faces almost touching, Ahna could feel the intense attraction sizzling between them. Their combined energy was as powerful as a stormtide, and probably just as unstoppable. For sure this was a first. Aiela had liked a lot of boys—but in the way a child likes a toy for awhile, until something else claims their attention. This with Turner, was something else. Ahna couldn't quite describe what was happening between them. Just that it was new.

The wind had picked up, carrying a chilly humidity. The bronzed, hairless skin along Carvers forearms began prickling. Ahna began to unwrap from her bedroll. "You're cold. I suppose it's like the Arctics here, to you hot-blooded, southern-born people." She crawled around, tucking it over them both. "Whereas I'm from the north. We're made of *much* tougher stuff."

"Yeah, long as you've got a bedroll wrapped around you." He teased back.

He stiffened as she resettled against him, their shoulders pressed together. Slowly, he relaxed into her warmth, adjusting with concentrated effort, to her nearness. His energy spoke of inner trepidation, no longer the rejection or coldness that it seemed at first. Ahna was beginning to suspect any human touch might be strange to him. Or somehow dangerous.

When their hands bumped against each other under the cover, she didn't move away and it wasn't long before he slowly wrapped his fingers around her wrist, touching it, feeling her small softer hand in tentative gentle movements before twining his fingers loosely through hers. Those hands felt every bit as sensual as they looked. Touching him, this prolonged connection, brought a barrage of his energy. Rather than try to decode it, she just let it wash over her. Like listening to someone talk when the words aren't meant for you. She felt like she might burst with this secret joy, to be near him, having her bewildering and overwhelming desire fed.

Turner and Aiela were also snuggling up together. Talking sporadically, they quieted slowly, soon drowsing with his arms wrapped around her.

"Are you tired?..." Carver eyed her uncertainly, as if she was an unknown species, or maybe expected something from him and he had no idea what.

She nodded. "I am sleepy but...I drool—I'm giving you fair warning." He relaxed into a smile and they scooched down to half sit-half lay against the side of the wagon. She rested her forehead against his shoulder, nestling lightly along the length of his body, instinctively seeking his warmth. Tentatively, she touched his chest, fingertips absorbing his heartbeat, fast and strong. Boldening, she caressed a few small circles around it, learning this bit of muscled curves and ridges, determined not to fall asleep and miss one second of this magic.

"TURNER! WE'VE TROUBLE."

Kinny, their wagon driver's, shout brought all four of them upright, struggling out of their napping fog to a driving wind full of sea-humid scents.

The wagon train had stopped. A band of ragged and rough looking men stood blocking the road. Dressed in skins, brandishing crude weapons, they were shouting at the drivers of the front wagons.

Heads popped up en masse from the wagons and a low buzz of mutters began.

Turner was already on his feet. "Islanders! Let's go. I may need all o' ya ta deal wi' this." He spoke rapidly in Irish to Kinny, and all five jumped down to stride towards the splayed band of threatening men blockading the road.

Turner spoke the same words to each wagon driver they passed.

"He's telling them to bring weapons." Carver translated.

Beside him, Aiela gave terse instructions to the Atlantean passengers. "Stay in the wagon. Be ready to come if needed." A couple of the teachers tried to argue but Aiela overrode them. "We are strangers here. Turner knows better than us."

They had to lean into the wind gusts at times to keep their balance, passing by the oversize aurochs who were snorting and shuffling with pooled edginess from the intense people energy, and the storming wind. Turner watched their movements, muttering, "What's better? The drivers at our back or controlling the aurochs?" But there wasn't time to consider.

A vision flashed through Ahna's mind;

Turner, talking to the raiders, trying to mollify, offering them whatever they needed from their supplies, but that's not what they are interested in. They're eyeing the aurochs, the wagons and mostly, the girls. These are men without homes, men that have been turned out from the settled places. Men that are no longer welcome because of the brutality they take pleasure in. It happens so fast, the huge blade drawn and flashing as it cuts Turner almost in half. Aiela screams seeing Turner's intestines spill from his stomach. There's not much blood, just a lot of pale, ropelike tissue bursting out, fluid glistening all over. Carver and Kinny crumple slowly to the ground beside her but she didn't see from what. The other drivers and male teachers are being stabbed through with long ragged pikes and blades. And then two men grab Aiela by the hair, forcing her to the ground as she fights them...

"Turner stop! Wait, I have to tell you...." Ahna grappled with the rising hysteria. She touched her sister's arm, the quickest way to share with Aiela what she was feeling.

Aiela grabbed Turner's shoulder in a death grip, physically stopping his determined charge. "You'll want to listen to her Turner." Then turning to her horrified sister, "What did you see?"

Ahna spoke fast describing what exactly they must do. "These men will take what they want and many of us will d-die." She hated that her teeth were chattering. From nerves—not the chill. "They won't bargain. You—we have to strike first and....fatally. The leaders—we must stop the leaders. They won't be expecting it—it might be enough to deter them." Ahna's thoughts were disjointed, but her words came out clear.

"But, we've more people, better weapons by far! I can bargain wi' them. We've enough supplies, we can spare whatever they want. If I tell them who I am, they won't risk angerin' my father. He is known...."

Turner argued, Ahna knew, because he was unsure whether to believe her. Whether to make such a weighty decision based on her supposed vision. "No Turner you can't." She spoke calmly now, as if to a confused child. "They kill you and your Drivers in seconds. Then they take it all, every wagon, everything we have, and all of us girls..."

Turner hesitated, looking at each of them in turn.

Aiela's eyes bored into him and she lifted her chin. "What Ahna sees is truth. It *will* happen—unless we change it. We must fight."

Ahna appreciated that Turner was looking to all of them instead of making the decision on his own.

Carver was rolling his shoulders. "Let's ready then. What weapons do we have?" He already held a dagger the length of a man's forearm, its blue steel blade flashed a wicked thin comfort.

Turner nodded with quick acceptance, pressing tiny, sheathed, triangular blades into each of their hands, blades so small, they were concealed behind a palm. "Whatever ya do, don' touch the naked tips. Stab the neck front, either side o' the windpipe, then slice out ta the side. Move out o' the way, they'll bleed an drop fast. Pick a target an' watch me. If I strike, you strike. Immediately. An' stay oot o' the way o' their blades. They're no' sharp but they carry a wallup."

The remaining drivers were at their back now and there was no more time.

Face to face with the mayhem, turned now to outright violence, Turner squared his shoulders, pushed his chest out and broke into the circle, interrupting the islanders who'd surrounded the front wagon drivers. Mistaking these unfortunate men as the caravan leaders, some of the islanders were holding them, others hitting them hard in the face every time they insisted they could not give over the wagon train.

Turner bellowed with surprising force over the hurling wind and the shouting of these vicious men. Ahna didn't understand what was said and Carver was too focused to translate.

Their leader turned immediately to face Turner. By far the largest of the men, he was both tall and thick with more hair than Ahna had ever seen. He stepped up close to Turner, a menacing move meant to intimidate, growling down at him, but Turner didn't flinch when he answered.

Aiela, Ahna, Carver and Kinny stayed close at Turner's back, watching the other men to see who else might step out as a leader. But the other men merely paused, watching with some amusement, as these young ones challenged their hulking Chief.

Ahna sensed the hairy giant watching Turner's body language too closely, judging Turner an easy first target. Fast as a scorpion striking, the Chief's right hand grabbed, wrapping easily around Turner's throat, lifting him, while the left hand lifted a huge knife.

Ahna stepped up beside Turner, hips swaying. Twirling her golden hair around a finger and smiling, she spoke to the big man in Atlantean. "You're not going to win this one." It was enough to distract him.

Turner slammed the small triangular blades, concealed in both palms, into the man's windpipe, slicing out both sides of his neck.

Simultaneously and perfectly timed, Kinny, Carver and Aiela did the same to the men standing closest, distracted by what they were witnessing.

Hot blood sprayed, spurting in time to their heartbeats. Too stunned to react, they swayed and stumbled. The hairy chief, neck opened on both sides, lay wide-eyed and lifeless by the time the last victim fell.

The Drivers, spread in a half circle behind her, held weapons ready. As the big chief, then three more men crumpled, gasping noisily, the four students and Kinny already had their tiny lethal blades on the throats of five more men.

Carver was doublehanded, the right at his man's throat, and his own pretty blade in the left hand, pressing sharply into the man's crotch. He stared without blinking into the man's eyes, who held very very still, suddenly sneerless.

"They're poisoned." Turner shouted in Irish. "One scrape will kill you slow."

Carver muttered a translation for Ahna and Aiela's benefit.

The other islanders, the ones not being held at poisoned points, were stumbling backwards, trying to escape the bloody carnage. The Drivers pressed forward with steel in their hands and resolve in their eyes.

Confused, unsure what to do with no one giving orders, the islanders turned and fled, wild-eyed at this unexpected savage killing. Men they'd thought invincible lay dead at the feet of mere youthlings.

Turner ordered the remaining men to be bound. Leather straps, meant for repairing auroch harnesses were brought, and he and Carver questioned the sullen prisoners.

Ahna knew their answers as truth or lies, even though she didn't understand the words. Turner was wary every time she cut in, telling him when a hostage lied. Carver's face was unreadable but she felt belief warring inside him too. Her whole life she'd been keeping such knowledge to herself. But there'd never been anything this important at stake. Atlanteans didn't steal from each other and they certainly didn't die at each other's hands.

No matter how she justified it, she still felt sick at the cost of speaking out. A life for a life. Was it right? The reality of violence made her lightheaded and biliously nauseous.

Aiela and Lira bandaged minor nicks, a few deeper cuts and split, bruised faces on the Drivers who'd been beaten.

The others dug shallow graves and gathered rocks, to bury the dead Chief and his unfortunate cohorts.

Deeply afraid, the Atlantean students were quiet and somber in tight clumps by the wagons, following Aiela's instructions as if in a daze.

Finally, Turner announced to the group. "These men were islanders from the north, foragin' far south in hopes o' robbin' merchanting caravans—common durin' our summer moons. We'll go ta Semias (Seh-MY-us) tonight. Load up. We've a fair way ta cover before dark." Then to the Atlantean teachers who were quietly demanding answers for the slaughter—this unexpected violence witnessed by their entire student group, "I will explain better, later. Right now, we need someplace safe. I canna assure ya the others will'nt return in...em, vengeance."

The Drivers pushed the aurochs, stopping only for water. There was no midday meal, but shock kept the group subdued. Only low pitched murmurs sounded as they headed due northeast.

Aiela sat staring at her hands and arms, at the blood dried into crusty sprays that began flaking off. Carver noticed and took his water jug out, trickling it over her hands as she scrubbed, then his own. Ahna had only a few spatters on her face which Aiela dabbed at. Turner had cleaned his hands already, not bothering with the huge dark stains making his shirt into a stiffened, grisly map.

The four of them were settled together on a bench just behind the Driver in the middle wagon—where they could keep an eye on the entire caravan.

You alright? Ahna asked her sister without speaking aloud. Aiela nodded but her eyes were straining to hold in the trauma. Taking a human life was an unspeakable tragedy to these raised in the Law of One, condoned only in defense of one's own life. Innocent and peaceable, killing went against all that they held sacred.

Carver was examining the small triangular blades. Their handle was a circle with a hole cut to fit on the middle finger. One by one he and Turner rinsed them of human gore. "They really poisoned?" he asked.

Turner nodded. "The scabbard tips are a...emm, reservoir. Every time ya sheath the blade it's retipped in a poison my father keeps. Shipped from far south of our continent and yers. Harvested from jungle frogs, we mix it in a solid fat so it won' spill or...em, evaporate. Sure an' it paralyzes gradually on skin, instantly in the bloodstream. Ya want ta be careful. We call them 'Amharu' (am-HA-ree) because they're meant fer one thing. I...I jus' didna think we'd actually have ta use them."

His bravado slipped entirely away then. "Never did I think somethin' like this'd happen. These outland bands wouldna dare ta cross my fami-ly...these may'nt have known who we are. Mabbe they meant fer word ta never get back on who attacked us. Those last ones I let go so they can tell the rest. They know Da's vengeance'll come. I don't think we'll have anymoor trouble, but I don't want ta be oot in the open tonight jus' in case. I'll send fer guards fer protection. We can wait in Semias until they arrive."

Aiela took his hand and they rode in silence awhile.

But Ahna felt increasingly trapped. Discomforted. Itchy. Like a space packed tight with spiders—everything moving—not quite pain but suffo-cating and oppressive just the same. Looking around desperately for an escape, she realized there was nowhere to go. The entire group had been traumatized and were off-gassing thick, slow-moving energies like the steam from animal dung in winter.

"We need to talk about the killing." She finally blurted. Anything would be better than this agonized stuckness. "We're in various stages of shock and," she eyed Turner, "you're still wondering if I was wrong. If it couldn't have been settled without killing them."

"Ya read minds now too?"

"Of course not! I feel energy...emotions...what you're all feeling...I just can't..." She took a deep breath, trying to level her voice, pinning Turner with her eyes. "You think there was a better way? Because that's my biggest fear right now too. You think I wanted those men to die? Do you have any idea how permanently disappointed my parents are going to be that my own sister took a life on my say so?? You didn't see what was going to happen to us. You were going to DIE Turner. Carver, Kinny, these teachers, boys, all the drivers too, and the things they would have done to the girls, to Aiela and me—it wasn't just your decision. I would've found a way to fight, with or without you...it's not your fault." She stopped, swiping furiously at the tears spilling from her eyes.

Then in a quieter voice, "This—what you had to do—was unthinkable. Especially to your own people. But it was *nothing* compared to what would've happened. We saved fifty lives, for the price of four."

Aiela's eyes filled too as she rubbed soothing circles on her sister's back, trying to comfort them both. "She's right. We've just killed humans —people more like us than not. I—I'd never imagined..." She let the haunting terror and revulsion flood out, one shuddering deep breath at a time.

Carver placed a hand of wordless support on both Aiela and Ahna's shoulders, still vigilantly watching the trees they were passing, but with compassionate eyes, connected to these, his first true friends.

Turner's face grew heavier as he looked at each of them, seeing how deeply traumatic the violence had been for these more sensitive ones. "I'm sorry. It is my fault. I should've added more protection, should've thought oot the dangers more..." He rested his head in his hands, letting his own tears wash away the adrenaline, the clinging regrets. Together and unashamedly, the four of them cleansed this gruesome shock from their systems.

It was some time before silent tears slowed and Aiela proposed "I've a simple healing technique that will help. It physically releases the shock from our bodies and minds. Demonstrating, she led them through an algorithm of tapping on certain energy points while replaying the trauma in their memory.

Turner expressed deep surprise. "It's like it melted away! The regrets an' the... the *wretchedness*. Sure an' that's some trick ya got."

"It's not a trick." Aiela smiled, "It's science. Carver? Any better?"

He shrugged. "Doesn't seem as intense as it was."

Another long silence wrapped around, comforting, while they adjusted to this new intimacy.

Turner touched Ahna's arm. "I do believe ya. Thank ya fer savin' my life an' these lives I'm meant ta be protectin'."

Aiela agreed. "That took courage—bearing the weight of our lives, and deaths... "

Which wetted Ahna's eyes again, the relief of these ones trusting in her.

As Aiela asked Turner about the town of Semias and altering travel plans for the next few days, Carver gently took Ahna by the waist and shifted her, until she was sitting in front of him. Wrapping his arms around her from behind, he pulled her against his chest in his own quiet support. He no longer seemed to care who saw them together. Long, black-clad legs outlined her hips and thighs.

They listened to Turner tell the story of Semias, bodies settling to this new fitting together, souls marveling at the simple joy of molding themselves around each other.

Ahna inhaled his unique scent of summer-warmed earth, each cell registering the velvet invitation of his arms curled loosely around her, the gallant strength of his chest at her back. His heart thumped enticing messages into her own. Relaxing her head back against his shoulder, his jaw brushed her temple. So this was infatuation, this perfect storm of aliveness, the awakening of sensation in untouched places.

And then she felt him hardening against her. Holy Goddess. She hadn't considered that. The bumping and jostling of the wagon kept her moving subtly against him.

She felt him panic when he realized this natural response of his body. Ahna reached to touch his cheek, looking at him with a rueful smile, letting him know it was alright. Perhaps not the time or setting she'd have chosen, but that couldn't be helped. If only he knew how her own body was swelling, opening, responding to him, he'd forget all about his misplaced embarrassment.

Aiela

Daylight had faded to early night when they arrived at the outskirts of Semias. This harbor town was smaller than where they'd arrived in this fertile and violent country. Shabbier, dirtier, poorer, it looked ill-equipped to handle the crews of sailors that stopped through for provisions, and it took some time for Turner and his Drivers to find them all room to sleep for the night, and a hot supper.

They were hungry enough to be truly grateful for the salty fish gruel and tired enough that sharing hard wooden or earthen floors, wrapped in their bedrolls, felt almost as good as the soft mattresses they were accustomed to.

When Turner gathered the somber group together, his ineffable handsomeness wore humility, his geniality downcast and serious. He began to explain the fiasco—leaving out the part where Ahna foresaw what their fates would have been. "I heard tell o' this band o' dangerous men." He said simply. "An' I felt the only way ta save the lives o' my Drivers, myself, an' every one o' you, was ta attack first… an' hard. Already I've dispatched a rider ta inform my father. Sure an' Da'll send a dozen armed guards ta travel wi' us the rest o' the trip. It won't happen again. I can promise, ya need no' fear it." He was openly and sincerely apologetic. Reassuring. Understanding of the questions they asked.

Jaydee's face was a fury when she spoke. "First Ahna was attacked and now this? Four men dead? And you armed three of our *students*, involved them in the killing! I don't think we should continue this… this travesty! Too much has gone wrong already. Turner, you will have your father come get us from here and take us home!"

"It's not up to you!" Aiela stood up next to Turner, blazing indignance. "This is *our* trip and you don't get to decide for us to end it early! We all knew there were dangers. We've heard stories of what goes on outside our protected little bubble at home, and now we've witnessed it first hand. It's part of what we signed up for. Of course we never thought we'd have to do these…things…to protect ourselves, but it's the chance we took." She paused to search faces, noting the intensity of colors swirling around heads and hearts. "If anyone else thinks we should go home early, please stand. We will go with the majority." Aiela took Turner's hand hoping that she hadn't wagered wrong.

Only three Atlanteans stood, all of them teachers.

Aiela aimed a smile of triumph at Turner, abundantly making her point. "Thank you for your protection and making painful decisions that saved us."

Ahna appeared at her side. Carver quickly took Ahna's other side, Dromm and Lister tailing Carver and before long the entire student body were on their feet. Linking hands, they surrounded Turner in dramatic approval and determination to stand with him and for him.

Aiela let out the breath she hadn't realized she'd been holding. "We're staying to finish the trip." She loved seeing the relief in his eyes.

MUCH LATER, despite a bone-deep weariness, Carver, Ahna, Turner and Aiela sat together in front of a small peat cookfire.

Healer Lira had mixed them a potion to help them sleep, advising they take it in honey wine to mask its bitterness. The room was dark and close with a low ceiling. Splintery walls had yawning, irregular gaps letting in tiny drafts of sea air. The room was hazy with smoke as the fire wound down and Aiela held up her crookedly chipped pottery cup with the last bit of laced honey wine. "A toast I think."

They raised their cups, waiting.

"To our future adventures together. May they be a bit more fun and a lot less bloody."

"More fun, less blood" they echoed, laughing a little with the effects of the wine and the relief of being alive and well and together.

14

BEACH FIRES

"...somewhere after midnight, in my wildest fantasy, somewhere just beyond my reach there's someone reaching back for me. Racing on the thunder, rising with the heat. It's gonna take a Superman to sweep me off my feet."

— ELLA MAE BOWEN

TURNER

*A*s if determined to dispel any lingering gloom, the sun shone from bright, early dawn to soft, colored dusk the next day.

After a hearty breakfast of fresh mutton, stewed with purple cabbage, Turner stood in front of the still-subdued Atlantean travelers, Aiela at his side. He announced, "If I can arrange a ferry, there's an island here, wi' history as colorful an' deep as the rock caves that riddle an entire side o' it. We'll head over next morning an' explore, after which we'll bed down inside the caves overnight before headin' back ta the mainland."

The students rustled and chattered excitedly at this unusual adventure.

Aiela gave them leave to roam the humble town and beaches, as long as they stayed in multiples and had an Irish Driver with them.

He was deviating from the original plan, figuring it much safer to let things die down inland for a day or even two. Give Da's guards time to catch up, before heading farther north. The land got wilder, as did the people and beasts. He wasn't about to take any more chances with their lives. That's the perfectly logical reason he gave to his Drivers anyway.

Turner had other, more surreptitious reasons—primarily romance. Unwillingly tasked with leading this trip, it was turning out quite different than imagined. He'd been bull-headedly resistant, wanting to refuse Da's orders outright—except it wouldn't have done any good. But that was all before he met Aiela, this alluring girl who was as mysterious and colorful as a full moon rising. He racked his brain to think of places of dramatic beauty, just so he could show them to her. He wanted to sweep her off her feet. He wanted to make her feel this helpless desire and overwhelming attraction, just like he felt every time he was with her. Or saw her across the way. Or thought of her.

By late afternoon he'd arranged two boats to ferry them the next morning. The aurochs were tended to, the next three days planned and provided for. So Turner turned his full attention to the further wooing of Aiela.

He found Carver and enlisted his help. Aiela would be more comfortable with her sister included in his scheme. Also, he still felt guilty for the grimness of yesterday, wanting to make it up to both sisters. And he'd seen the way Ahna watched Carver.

He and Carver wandered the shoreline, plotting happily until they found a perfect spot, then set about foraging driftwood and gathering food.

By the time everyone was milling, awaiting supper in the town's largest Inn, he was ready.

"Aiela, Ahna, come. I've a surprise fer ya..." Turner had come up behind them, catching both their hands, tugging them insistently free of the crowded room. Once outside, he presented Ahna's hand with a bow to Carver, who was seated on a stone wall, patiently waiting beside two baskets, smiling mysteriously, offering no explanations.

Ahna

Ahna hadn't seen much of Carver today. She, Aiela, Jai, Felicia, Healer Lira and four other students had wandered the town's cramped market, stopping to play with tiny Irish children, toddling about while their mothers were busy with wash. She'd enjoyed entertaining the shrieking, giggling children with animated rhymes and games from her own childhood. Once the frayed but clean garments were flapping in the wind, grateful mothers whisked their babies away for naptime.

Jai wanted to explore the wharves.

A ship came in, the kind Atlantis didn't let inside the inner harbors. Creaking and rickety, its sailors were slaves whose stench hung thicker than the rags that served as clothing. Perhaps twenty men eyed them from carefully blank faces until Lira and the Irish Driver moved them along.

"Is *everyone* else in the world like this then?" Ahna asked. It seemed to be so.

"We're taught history and general cultures of other lands—the good bits—not the current plight apparently." Aiela agreed thoughtfully.

Still, it had been a glorious, rare day with the sun shining hot enough that they splashed in shallow tides to cool down. Ahna's mind returned often to the long wagon ride with Carver holding her against him. Last night, the erotic knowledge of his erection had spilled over into her dreams. Tangled bodies, doing things that she'd not yet experienced, pushed her to the edge of a desire she'd resisted even in dreaming, afraid of falling with no safety net. She'd awoken restless, wet between her legs and blushing, wondering if Carver had experienced girls bodies. Belials were known for their pleasures of the flesh so he must have—but he also seemed shy about touch, so that was confusing.

It was a nice break today from the intensity of the attraction energy that flared between them.

Yet when Turner placed her hand precisely into Carver's and when Carver held onto it all the way down to the beach, she wondered how she had ever thought it was nice to be apart from him. His black hair swept back from his face in the coastal breeze. She sensed his gaze on her, wavering between intensity and insecurity. His hand surrounded hers completely, fingers moving sensuously between hers and back out, again and again as they walked beside Turner and Aiela towards water sparkling with sun reflections. A spectacular sunset was just beginning to color the sky behind them.

Two piles of peat, ready to light once sunlight ran out, sat next to tarps held down by driftwood. Spaced apart for privacy, they were close enough for comfort. Ahna felt her breathing shallow and her heartbeat lose its rhythm. She was going to be alone, mostly, with Carver for an entire evening.

"I hope you're not too hungry. I've still got to cook our supper but the thing is—I don't know how to cook." He dumped the contents of the basket onto their tarp. A large, brownish-gray crab waved its pincers weakly beside a gourd full of oysters, mussels, and clams of many colors. There was a hard wedge of cheese, a stoppered jug, half a loaf of lavar and four small, slightly shriveled peaches. Carver shrugged at it. "It's what Turner and I could scare up on short notice."

"All my favorites." Ahna bit into one of the peaches, juice dribbling down her chin as she gestured at the gourd, "You get water and I'll light the fire."

He smiled in relief, the slight tension between them melting as he ran to the noisy surf to fill the gourd with salty water for boiling their shellfish.

When he returned she was still trying to get the peat to light. "Damn this peat..."

Carver gave it a try but it fizzled out every time in the wind. They ended up racing to the upper beachline to bring back armfuls of the scraggly grasses that rimmed it. Kneeling close so their bodies blocked the air currents, they waited until their kindling was burning strong enough to set the peat finally ablaze. Gathering rocks to stack, they finally got the pot balanced over the hot little fire.

"Cooking's hard." He eyed the precarious setup. "Seems like it might take awhile."

"Not like pushing a button on our cook boxes at home. It's kind of fun though, figuring out how to fix food without technology."

"It's fun with you." Carver pulled the dulcimer out of his pack. Strumming softly he tuned it, then played for them. Melodies that felt like forbidden desire, lost dreams, and new hope, blended with the music of waves and wind and birds. Ahna heard the tacit messages in his music, realized this was perhaps the truest way he could express himself. She drank him in with eyes and ears and heart, letting each moment cradle her.

Then he sang, his voice like dark honey, thick and smooth, dramatically adding just a little grit at the bottom.

"It took two to light the fire.
Then her green eyes made it grow.
Burning higher and hotter,
while the crab pot simmered slow.

Well I've never met a girl before
who could light up the whole night.

Until I came to bonny Ireland,
where she got me in a fight.

So now I've found the Beauty
I never knew I missed.
The sweetest one I've ever met
who someday I'd like to kiss..."

His gaze landed on her, flicking away, still strumming the short, catchy tune. She knew the deep risk he was taking, the asking, his heart starting to break as he forced it to open to her.

Moving to kneel beside him, she took his face between her hands, placing her lips against his. It was a gentle force, like air pushing between the driftwood spaces to spin the flames hotter, while his lips felt cool and firm.

Carver set aside his dulcimer, taking Ahna by the hips, pulling her with exquisite tenderness onto his lap, straddling him, but loosely, holding a careful space between their bodies. It already felt too hurried, knowing they had such a short time,and not knowing if there would be anything for them beyond this night.

"Carver". She whispered his name, touching the angles of his face, memorizing exactly how his hair felt. "Do you know that you are by far the most attractive man I've ever seen?"

"Huh, then you were raised in a place without males?" He kissed her this time. A little bolder.

She leaned back shaking her head. "No—there were tons of boys. Hundreds. Counting the trips to High City and other towns, probably even thousands. Accept your beauty. Don't fight it." She giggled at him, dodging as he tried to silence her with a kiss. She turned away to check the boiling pot. "It's done, let's eat."

Carver pulled his knife from its sheath in his boot, glancing at her as they both remembered the last time he'd used it.

"It's well cleaned. Sorry I didn't bring something else."

They ate side by side while the sun sank into shadows, passing the knife back and forth, sucking the small bits of sea meat from their shells, burning fingers and tongues in the process.

"Can I ask you a question?" Ahna was curious, even if it wasn't any of her business. "Have you had a lot of girls...special, er loved anyone? Because you seem like you have and that's good, you know, I mean how

could you not have a hundred girls after you all the time, *look* at you..."
She couldn't seem to stop the word rush, her tongue tangling with itself.

He had a queer expression on his face. Then she realized he didn't
know if she was serious or teasing him. "It's not my concern. You don't
have to talk about it." She smiled to show she meant it and took a swig of
the cold, slightly bitter beverage in the jug. He spoke slowly, haltingly.

"You would be the first girl...special...ever. My family, they're not nice.
I don't have a mother, so we're not girl-friendly... Do you want to hear the
story of how I lost my foot?" She held her breath, surprised at this shift,
afraid to break the spell. Afraid that any tiny move might stopper his
words once again.

He kept talking, spilling the whole gut-wrenching tale of the sea
serpent and his long recovery. They had finished eating by the end of the
story and he showed her how his leg morphed just above the ankle into a
prosthetic foot. "It's Atlantean-made of course." He finished lightly.

Her heart ached for that neglected little boy and she scooted close
behind him, wrapping her arms around his chest as if she could somehow
reach back in time to comfort old wounds, to hold that frightened, lost
child. "That's a very sad story," she said as he picked up the dulcimer and
began strumming again, "but I loved hearing it."

So they sat like that, alternately speaking of what they each held dear,
while Carver spun notes into catchy seaside rhythms and ballads about
enamored nights in faraway places.

Ahna told Carver about Papa who travelled the world discovering and
studying plants. How much she had missed him when she was little, how
he brought Aiela odd, broken animals and spent every minute playing
with them while he was home.

Carver composed more songs, outrageously silly and sweetly serious,
mostly about her and the things she was telling him.

Somewhere along the way Turner and Aiela moved over to join them.
Wrapped up together in their tarp, they lay back, quietly watching the
stars, and listening to the ballads flowing out of the dulcimer, until the
moon was high overhead and he had run out of music. Ahna almost fell
asleep against his back, while the fire turned to coals.

Carver

Carver had never felt this accepted, this safe.

Maybe his mother's shabby black dulcimer had finally sung him home.

15

THE COLORED CAVES

OFF THE COAST OF SEMIAS, IRELAND

"I don't know why people are afraid of lust. Then I can imagine that they are very afraid of me, for I have a great lust for everything. A lust for life, a lust for how the summer-heated street feels beneath my feet, a lust for the touch of another's skin on my skin...a lust for everything. I even lust after cake. Yes, I am very lusty and very scary."

— C. JOYBELL C.

AIELA

*H*igh noon next day found the travelers inside the largest cavern of the cave system Turner had promised, working together to set up camp, prepare food, and boil drinking water.

Breakfast had been a hurried affair, a few bites punctuating the urgency. Aiela struggled to get everyone up in time, with their essentials loaded into ferry boats before the tide turned. Nanat had held them up.

"She's still just laying there." Felicia reported to Aiela. "I can't get her to get up."

"Nanat!" Aiela said loudly to the unmoving lump on the floor. "We are literally leaving right now. Come on. I'll help you pack your things."

"I don't want to go." Nanat muttered, eyes slitted at Aiela from a mass of golden hair that looked like Mama's balls of yarn after Yowl got done with them. "I'm too tired and I don't want to sleep in dirty old *caves*. This is bad enough!"

Aiela began shoving Nanat's clothing and toiletries into the too-small pack. "You can't stay here. If I have to pick you up and load you on the boat like a sack of rotten Irish turnips, I will."

"I don't like you." Nanat declared. But she was already rolling upright, reaching for her clothing. "Everybody else might, but I don't! You're mean and, and *bossy* and—"

"I don't like you much either." Aiela cut in, yanking Nanat's bedroll from under her so she could roll it up. "But you know who does?" She waited, letting the bait dangle.

It was at least two full minutes while Nanat finished dressing. "Who?" She finally asked, jerking her pack onto her back as Aiela shouldered the bedroll.

"Nirka." Aiela left, knowing Nanat would follow close to hear the rest. "He was asking about you. Was the first to notice you were missing... " It worked, as Aiela knew it would. She needed to find common ground with this spoiled, insecure girl, or end up battling her the entire trip.

The sky had returned to its usual massive-gray-spitting-moisture by the time they'd reached the island. Little more than a series of ascending hills and cliffs, Aiela loved its bold wildness. Dividing supplies, food and water between everyone's packs, they trekked two long, steep miles from the boats, clambering up battered basalt crags to an opening that didn't look particularly grand. A cleft between two rocks, it was weathered jagged and narrow.

Entering one at a time, they followed Turner single file, crouching through awkward tunnels, dodging low-hanging clumps of rock, skidding down a smoothly curved bank to a hidden passage.

It was slow going with everyone heavily laden and less than a dozen lanterns to light the way. But in the end—more than worth it. As colorful and strange as Turner predicted, the passageways, tiny water-carved rooms and this largest cathedral-like cavern, were ringed in ancient layers of ocher, gold, rust and even purple. Not jewel colors, but muted earthy tones, like root vegetables freshly pulled from fertile dirt. Around this enormous room ran ledges, some high up and dripping stalactites from their undersides. Offshoot tunnels stretched away into the darkness from crooked gaps and cracks. An opening high in the roof on one side let in enough daylight to break the utter darkness they'd travelled through getting here. Later, that opening would pull the smoke from their fire up and away into the sky.

The hollow complex funneled sounds of ocean surf, dueted with the calling of gulls, off the cave system's myriad of angles, amplifying it in places, muting it in others until they became something altogether different.

"Like a city full of invisible people," Jai marveled, fascinated by the mutations of pitch. At first, it was disquieting to the group, making them jumpy. The rise and fall of roaring, whispering, moaning, whistling and raucous gull keowing sometimes sounded like laughter. The cave shaped the notes into its own unique symphony.

Ahna and Aiela worked side by side chopping tiny green apples. "Nanat doesn't like me." Aiela finally had enough privacy to discuss the exchange from this morning. "I lied to get her going faster. Told her Nirka had been looking for her."

Ahna smiled. "First of all, she's just jealous because of you and Turner. Secondly, I know you're used to being everyone's favorite person in the world, but try to get used to having *one* person dislike you. And next time, just carry her out in her bedroll. It'll be much more entertaining for the rest of us."

Aiela sighed. "I don't want to have to fight her every step of the way."

"Then we'll take extra steps to distract her from her woes. Plant a few seeds in the tiny mind of Nirka. They have a lot in common. It'll be a match made in... the land of the shallow and the golden."

"It'll take more than a few seeds to get his attention! He's so focused on himself."

"Plant a full-grown tree then. Whatever. Just use small words and repeat them every little bit until he gets the message."

"I shouldn't tell lies. I should be a better leader than that."

"Not me. I was born to be a liar. Jai will help me. We'll find ways to shove them together, devise clever little strategies and whisper in their ears the sweet yearnings they each have for the other."

"You're not supposed to be the devious one." Aiela nudged her twin. "Did you forget? You're supposed to be the innocent, wise one."

"Things change." Ahna shrugged, nudging her back. "And I learned from the best."

They helped shred boiled mutton, shell nuts, slice vegetables, and crush grains. Another team was clearing spaces to lay out bedrolls for later tonight, piling rocks into makeshift walls bordering the edge of a trickle of water along the cave floor. Seepage, Turner explained, from the openings above and condensation from uncharted spaces hidden deep inside the island. Aiela imagined being high on one of the ledges looking down at the bustle. They must look like ants moving around in this large space.

Every noise echoed grandly. Loud cracks of rock stacking and sweeping, crunchy thumping from the grain crushers, ringing strikes from shovels digging a fire pit.

Jai stood at a large tunnel calling out animal sounds, then singing complex melodies, exploring the phenomena of these morphing echoes. Those nearest him began laughing at the sounds returned and he urged them one by one to take a turn creating something interesting, beautiful or funny. Soon it was a contest, a showcase of acoustics. The energy was high and the mood light as they played together, settling into this strange underground realm.

Finally, after travelling back and forth through the mouth of the cave, the other teams had foraged and stacked enough peat, brush and driftwood to last for the two nights they planned to spend here. It made them proud, Aiela noticed, the self-sufficiency.

Sharing a leisurely, simple meal, they ventured back out to explore the closest bits of this island that seemed built for mountain goats and gulls. Behind slate clouds the light began to fade.

"Time ta settle in!" Turner urged, a sly smile sparkling under his magnificent curls. "I've verra special plans...sure an' we've saved the best o' this place for t'night."

They ate an early supper, then Kinny the Driver and protector of their supply wagon, born and raised in this area, set about telling stories. Regaling them, he recited from memory the legends of ancient Ireland with its gods and goddesses who lived here first. Turner translated Kinny's thick, lisping words, as the Atlanteans listened to his tale made magical in this holy underground;

"....then, after the great ice age ended and Ireland thawed enough to allow habitation, Danu, the 'Mother of Ireland' came out of the sea where her kind had always lived. Tall and slim with very pale skin and hair of flaming coral red, she was almost killed at first by the small dark-skinned wolf people who lived here in Ireland, because of her strange appearance. They thought her to be some demon come up from the underworld. But entranced by her beauty and gentleness, they reasoned that she could be no demon, so instead they taught her to walk and speak. In exchange, she brought them fish to eat and pearls to wear and showed them how to make boats that would not leak or sink. Danu was the first to teach our kind that it is better to make peace than to live always in warring or fear.

Saddened by the short life spans of the wolf people, Danu did not seem to age and soon became the revered leader of new generations of Irish people. With their help, she built a castle of stones decorated with seashells, just north of us on the mainland. But it was here, on this very island that she met her first love.

Ithe was a sailor from the far south of Spain where the people were fierce explorers and conquerors. Sent out by his nephew Milesius, the young King of Spain, Ithe was to find a new homeland for their people who were suffering from a twenty-six year famine. A prophecy had foretold that the peoples of Spain would settle on a new isle which was lush and fertile, whose green would never fade away.

Ithe and his men shipwrecked on this very island, its lower parts being hidden beneath the sea level at that time. It was during that same time, the high tides were still carving out this very floor we sit on now.

Unable to swim so far to the mainland, Ithe and his sailors survived for some time on birds they snared and fish, finding fresh water and shelter in the higher caves around us.

Danu heard of these Spanish invaders from her sea friends and sailed out to save them—thinking her benevolent act might forge a friendship with their nation.

Being conquerors and men, Ithe's crew saw them coming, hid and attacked Danu's wolf people as they came ashore—even though the wolf people were small, and taught by Danu to be gentle and peaceful. The Spaniard men saw only the stature of these simple people and knew they could kill them easily and steal their ship, using it to complete their mission.

Because she was a woman, the Spaniards did not kill Danu and she wept bitterly at the loss of her men. The soldiers brought her to Ithe who, as royalty, was to be protected from battle and was waiting in these caves.

When Ithe saw the tall, fair-skinned woman with the flaming red hair, he fell instantly in love. Sending his men away with instructions they were not to enter the cave except once a day to bring food and firewood, Ithe set about learning to communicate with Danu and woo her.

This was difficult because of her grief, but Ithe cared for her gently and patiently. Bathing her tears away, keeping her warm with fires, bringing her food and even flowers.

Danu could not help but respond to his great love for her, and she grew quite attracted to this man with the smooth dark skin who sat trying to understand her all day, and held her tenderly all night. Most of all, she saw a way to forge a bond and prevent this powerful nation from wiping out her beloved people.

When Ithe saw that Danu was returning his love, he took her deep into the caves where the hot pools are" (at this a great buzzing of speculations broke out among the Atlantean students but died down quickly so as not to miss Kinny's continuing story).

"...and they made passion many times" (a good many giggles and whispers all around)

"....and pledged their love to each other for eternity. Next they set about making plans to preserve the Irish land from Spanish invasion. Ithe was willing to renounce his mission and even his heritage for his love of Danu.

A full moon after Danu had been brought to Ithe, the couple emerged from the caves, where Ithe slew his entire crew as retribution to Danu for her men's deaths, dressing one of the dead Spaniards in his own clothing so that if they were ever found, his Spanish family would think Ithe too was killed. Then Ithe and Danu sailed back to her castle planning to raise many children.

Ithe taught the wolf people, who now called themselves 'Tuatha de Danan' which means 'people of Danu', to defend themselves and their lands against the coming invasions, setting up Danann 'kings' along the coasts with soldiers who built fortresses and towns.

Danu birthed a son exactly nine months after their first mating in the hot pools, but the baby looked more like a monster than a human. He had an extra eye and anything the baby looked upon with his third eye withered or burst into flames. Danu knew that she and Ithe were being punished for their deliberate killing. He, of her Wolf People and she, indirectly, of his Spaniard crew. She gave their firstborn child to her sea family to raise, for it was only they who might keep him from destroying the earth with his wicked eye. They named him Balor.

Years passed in which Ithe and Danu had many children and loved each other with a devotion that inspired their people.

The famine had ended when Milesius sent another ship to investigate the fate of Ithe and why he had never returned. Ithe's spanish son, Lughaide, found what he believed was his father's body and took it back to Spain, declaring that the terrible people of Ireland, the Tuatha de Danan, had killed everyone aboard the ship.

In vengeance, Milesius sent his eight sons with a fleet to conquer the lush green land. Along the way a vicious storm claimed the lives of five of the sons including Ir, the eldest whom this land was eventually named for. Finally landing, the remaining three sons and fleets slew or drove out the

Danann kings, dividing the land between themselves and Lughaide and ruling for many years.

Ithe and Danu escaped without their identity ever being known. And eventually Balor returned from the sea to wreak havoc on the foreign kings of Ireland.... but that is another story for another time. Perhaps when we visit Balor's island."

Kinny ended his story, then looked to Turner for the revealing of the great surprise.

"Fetch yer bathing towels," Turner instructed, "an' follow me." Eyes wide, curiosity as thick as the cave dark around them, they kept close behind the lantern-wielding Drivers through a maze of tunnels. Voices grew loud with excitement when they first saw the steam swirling up in the light of the lanterns.

The hot pools were shallow and wide, in a cavern barely large enough to hold them all at once. No one cared about the close quarters. Splashing, all talking at once, they debated Kinny's story—whether it was true. "Oh how romantic this would be", more than one girl sighed to another.

"There's a spot by Nirka." Aiela whispered as she passed Nanat. But Nanat only stuck her perfectly shaped nose up and pointedly turned away. Aiela sighed and moved over to Nirka. "Nanat very much wants to talk to you, but she's too shy. Just thought you might want to know."

"Why is that your business? And who made you matchmaker? Oh that's right, you make yourself whatever you want to." Nirka hadn't yet forgiven her for being the Group Leader.

"It's not much fun you know." Aiela replied. "No matter what choices you make as a leader, there's someone who's not happy about it. And someone who thinks they can do better."

"Or maybe you're just not good at it."

"Possibly." Aiela agreed. "But I'm getting a lot of practice." She stayed beside him just long enough to bother Nanat, maybe impel her to do more than flirt from a distance.

Not seeing Turner, she floated in the middle of the pool, letting her body and mind relax. Barely able to see one another through the soupy steam, they played and soaked until everyone grew sated and sleepy. Wrapped in towels, the drivers led them back, to burrow in bedrolls and conjure up dreams of dark foreign sailors and the mesmerizing sea-born women they wooed.

AIELA WOKE to a tickly whisper in her ear. The air was thin blackness outside a slight fire glow. Turner was above her, lightly shaking her shoulder.

"Aiela," he whispered, "Come wi' me".

Her heart swelled, rhythm quickening as she slipped silently from her just-warmed bedroll. Heated anticipation blazed across her chest into her arms and legs, immunizing her to the chill of the night air.

Turner was already a silent moving shadow, headed in the direction they had taken earlier to the hot pools. She followed, concentrating to see —and not step on—haphazard rows of slumbering bodies. Her heart thudded so loud in her ears she was certain if someone was awake they would hear it.

Her eyes adjusted to the dark, aided by a full moon tinting the main cavern with a faint silver glow that turned corners into statues. Love of the night served her well as she entered a tunnel of inky darkness, and felt a steady hand pulling her into warmth and a heart beating as wildly as hers.

Those generous Irish lips she had watched for days as they gave orders and told jokes, were suddenly on the first thing they found—her right eyebrow. Pressing with hungry softness.

She captured his jaw in her hands and guided his lips to hers, as he clasped her body hard against his own. Nerve endings and blood vessels flared in recognition and a jolt of passion. Clay-scented and displaced, the moment they lingered in was rich with cave music, heightened by too many days of anticipation.

Suddenly as he'd begun it, Turner broke their connection, fumbled for her hand, and drew her deeper into the night. He turned corners swift and silent, his free hand feeling along the tunnel wall.

Aiela followed, exhilarated and trusting, watching the soft colors emanate from him, the red glow around his hips that spoke of heat and passion. She laughed at the thought of his desire lighting their way as he rounded another corner, whispering for her to duck. Releasing his hand to put out her arms, she traced both sides of the cold rock earth closing around them, fingertips guiding the rest of her body. Abruptly they were in a small chamber bathed in shy light and she focused on the opening above that let in the moon's unsteady glow.

The sound of water lapping rock, of constant drips playing arrhythmic beats, told her much of the space they had come to. "What d'ya think Moon Goddess? I saved the smallest chamber, joost fer you."

She jumped slightly at Turners low voice so close, and felt the hair on her arms raise. "It's warm in here!" Suddenly timid, she moved toward the edge of the pool, a miniature of the one they had soaked in earlier. Eyes now adjusted to the moon lighting, she studied the chamber, and saw that water filled most of its conic shape. Large stalagmites rose up through the steam, some of them connected to the stalactites above, creating pillars that threw shadows like misshapen giants. Nooks and alcoves cradled darkness that the light couldn't reach. Crouching down at water's edge, Aiela dipped her fingers in, letting the hot water steady her.

Turner watched her intently. "I don' understand this cravin' for ya. Breath-takin' ya are... " He cleared his throat. "Ya want to, em, would ya like ta get..."

Emboldened by his earnest compliments, she stood to kick off her shoes, pulling her tunic over her head in one smooth move, followed by her pants. She'd waded in before he finished his question, loving the feel of water-smoothed stone under the soles of her feet.

"Right then!" he muttered with a laugh.

"Ohhh sooo warm" she breathed, sinking into the depths of the pool. Steamy water closed around her breasts, and lapping over her shoulders. It was only about three and a half feet deep and she relaxed against the nearest rock. "Did you bring me here to soak alone or are you coming in?"

"Always three steps ahead aren't ya!" He retorted removing his shirt and kicking off his own boots. Though he turned away, she caught a glimpse of his blatant desire before he hid in the water. He sank next to her, emitting a groan identical to her own, "It's loovly." Gentle ripples spread out to collapse against the walls of the cave.

"Pretty loud in here." She whispered. "We won't be heard?"

"The water masks things, an' any noises joost join all the other racket tha' moves through these tunnels. Da and I discovered this when I was but five mabbe. I've spent a lot o' time here."

She found his leg underwater and pushed it with her foot. "Ah, this is where you bring all your girls, you mean." He grabbed for her foot but she was already gone, gliding off into the water away from him, around the stalagmite she had been leaning on. "What's back here? Can we go farther?"

He followed her. "Ya can, sure, this whole pool is safe. It gets a wee bit deeper though." With a splash he grasped her waist and turned her around to face him. "Yer the first girl I've been here wi'. Doos it make ya 'mine'?"

His bold hope made her smile, his pillar-like arms made her want to run her hands over every inch of him. She started with his biceps and moved to his chest, grasping his thick shoulders to lift and wrap her legs around his waist, locking them together. Enjoying the feel of his body going from taut shock to hot desire, she stared into his eyes. Not just desire but raw tenderness poured from his eyes, his body, his aura into hers. Her breath caught in her throat. "The way you look at me..." It was all she could say, caught in a wilderness of unfamiliar energy, heat, lust, love. She slowly closed the distance between their faces and fitted her full lips against his, this kiss slower. Her dancing tongue tickled his lips and he opened his mouth at the touch.

He pulled her body even tighter against him and she felt his erection pulse against the inside of her thigh. For a moment she froze and he broke the kiss.

"Sorry, is it wrong? I canna hide it, I want ya Aiela—too much, but I won' do anythin' ya don' want too, I..." His words died as he felt her hand encircle him with gentle fingers.

"It's just...overwhelmingly...good. I'm trying to take it all in." She whispered. "I've never felt this much before." Her hands explored slowly. "You can touch me", she breathed in his ear before gently grabbing his earlobe in her teeth.

"Well, it's joost...I'm tryin' not ta...yer gonna make me come if ya keep doin' that!" One of his roughened hands left her waist and covered hers, stilling it.

She felt the urgent throbbing underneath. "Oh! is that bad?" Pulling up slightly in question and command.

"It isn't! Do ya want, I mean are ya alright wi'..?"

She moved his hand up to her breast. "Touch me here."

As his fingers closed around her silky firm breast, his penis convulsed and lunged in her hand, ejecting into the darkness of the water between them. He groaned, breathing fast as waves of sensation visibly washed through him.

Aiela unwound her legs from his waist and pressed her length against him, kissing him deeply as they sank under the water together. They rolled, now him on top, now her, and broke the surface gasping with breathless laughter and desire.

She pushed wet hair back from her face and floated next to him, bodies touching, then moving apart with the motion of the waves they had created. "How did you imagine this would go?" She reached out and ran a hand over his wide thick pectorals, "Do you know you have a decadent body?"

He captured her hand, holding it over his heart.

She could feel its strong fast beat, still calming from the intense orgasm.

"I didna think so far, I joost wanted ta show ya this, ta bring ya here. To be with ya at all is like a dream. Of course I want ya—terrible much. I just didna think about...we haven't talked about this at all." He touched her face, her hair. "From the moment I met ya I think I was in loove." He spoke thoughtfully now, pulling her in front, wrapping his arms loosely around her ribcage so they floated as one.

For a moment the only sound was the lick of water on rocks. Aiela relaxed completely in his embrace, into the feelings washing through her; safety, warmth, desire, and something deeper. Connection, completion. She wasn't sure she could find a word for it and it didn't matter. "I feel like I've known you my whole life", she admitted. "Speaking of dreams, you've been in mine for so long."

He explored her ribcage, the shape of her belly and sides, his fingers making her shiver despite the heat. "What do ya mean by that? Ya keep sayin' it but I don' know what yer talkin' aboot."

She laughed. "I'm sure it sounds...what's your word? Daft. Since I was a little girl, you've been in my dreams. Not all of them, but plenty. I feel like I know you already. You can't imagine what it's like to have a person who belongs in the dreamworld, suddenly show up in real life. I can't imagine what it might mean."

"Huh. Bit jarrin' I s'pose." His hands were still exploring, without hurry.

"I know we're mostly new to each other, but this seems *right*." She twisted to look at him, "Have you ever felt like this before? You've been with girls, surely, and did it feel like this?"

He laughed and kissed her upturned lips. "So direct ya are. I've kissed girls, fooled around a bit, but it was no' ever like this. The feelings I mean. Well the other too..." He pulled her hips back and she felt him hard again against her buttocks. "What's the Atlantean rules or...em, customs wi' matin' and love? Here, women generally choose ta handfast—or marry—before matin' because they risk pregnancy. Men aren't as picky o' course, mating wi' what girls will have them."

She circled her hips playfully against him, "Why aren't you? Hand-fasted, I mean. We're older than many when they marry."

He floated her on the surface, his left arm cradled under her shoulders to keep her afloat as he moved them in a slow circle. "Da taught me respect, especially fer girls. 'Women can be man's best friend or worst enemy son—it's all in how we treat them. We may be stronger but they're smarter. They give life an' all we can do is take it. Women are no' ta be crossed if ya want a long an' happy life'." He quoted in a deep voice. "Da said never take something that isna offered and I hadn't yet found an offer I wanted ta accept..."

He stroked her leg from foot to knee with his right hand, leaving a trail of chills as he moved slowly higher up her thigh. "Until now...but ya didna answer the question."

Aiela felt hypnotized by the water's luxuriant heat, combined with delicate sensual peaks he was building with his touch. His eyes roamed freely over her moonlit form, low voice cracking and smoky with desire. Her body rose to his touch, every cell imploring him never to stop.

"Atlantean rules? It's simple, we don't offer ourselves until we feel a deeper connection and bond of love. Sex is a sacred expression of love and freedom between two people who share a desire/love connection. It's not to be taken lightly nor misused. End of quote." She squirmed, "That tickles and feels divine at the same time. There's been few offers I wanted to accept." She echoed his earlier words and somehow it sobered the moment, stilled his fingers.

Something profound was happening.

She turned, sinking in the water to face him. "We're making a vow aren't we. I don't know how this works between our two cultures, or what to name it but I want you Turner, and it's not just my body that wants you. It's all of—"

He cut her words off with his mouth. This kiss intense, full with the emotions they couldn't yet put into words. Both a giving and an opening that for a moment, suspended them outside time and space.

"I am yours and only yours Aiela if ya'll have me." He whispered against her lips.

She pulled back slightly, locking her luminous dark eyes to his as she wrapped her legs again around his hips, very deliberately and ever so slowly, taking him inside of her.

They gasped together as she replied "I will have you Turner and be yours and only yours."

Sometime later when they could breathe again, when heart beats slowed, their passion temporarily sated and the silvered outlines of the cave had faded, Aiela whispered, "We made magic tonight. Did you feel it?"

His head rested by hers and he stroked her hair, sleepily. "I b'lieve my whole life has joost changed direction, set a new course." The moon had moved on, dawn was on its way and the cave had grown darker.

"We should go back before they wake."

Moving together to find their clothing, he embraced her. "My moon goddess, ya have my heart. Try no' ta break it."

Aiela's heart felt full to bursting, her body content as a milk-drunk cat. "It's an even exchange then." This night would eternally change them both. She felt sure of it.

16

THE GREAT MOUNDS

"The world is quiet here."

— LEMONY SNICKET

CARVER

*T*hey'd spent a day and two nights playing in salt-scented surf, and risking the tight blackness of cave tunnels to lounge often in the hot pools. He'd been careful with Ahna, unsure what might happen next, downplaying his feelings for her to Drommen and Lister, convincing them she was merely a passing fancy.

Lacking privacy, he couldn't really talk to her, despite ending up side by side much of the time, drawn together like silent magnets. Her quiet, pointed commentary made him laugh and he could tell she felt more comfortable with him than the others.

Spirits soothed after the brief, vicious battle with the islanders, their group returned to the mainland packed in rough and sturdy fishing boats. Even the teachers seemed buoyant and relaxed.

Over half a dozen warriors waited in Semias, bringing greetings from Meihal, along with a fresh supply of foodstuff; fruits, vegetables, grain and cheese. Carver helped repack and load the supply wagon, as glad as Turner was to have the extra protection. Eight tough and formidable warriors had ridden hard to catch up to them in the small town. Dressed for battle, and riding huge horses, they wore an aura of invincibility that spoke louder than their firm assurances to the group that no further harm would befall them.

Aiela directed the students in reloading their things, while Turner helped the Drivers get wagons and aurochs ready to move out. "Sure an' it'll be nightfall before we're at our next, em... destination." He promised.

"Ye'll join me briefin' the guards?" Turner asked.

"Sure." Carver nodded, pleased beyond measure to be asked.

Both took turns recounting how the islanders attacked, the forced killings including the part where Ahna had foreseen a different, more brutal outcome. Meihal's warriors listened intently, asking a few questions.

"Your Da'll be pleased with your bravery. In this case, it was good to act first and ask questions after." A large-boned woman with the mannerisms of a man spoke, nodding her approval. The rest of the guards heartily agreed, clapping Turner and Carver on the back, squeezing their shoulders. Proud smiles and admiration was poured upon them as deserving heroes.

This is what it's like to be part of a family that cares for each other, Carver thought, with a sense of wonder. Turner stood a little taller, being accepted as an equal by these warriors. "They're Da's best. His personal guard." He whispered to Carver, clearly in awe.

Dara, their leader, directed her words to Turner, "Your Da insisted you're to lead still. We're to follow you, same as the rest."

His strong, round face beamed then, wordless at this long range proof of his father's confidence in him. *He assumed his father would replace him, send someone more capable to lead.* Carver realized. Placing an arm around Turner's shoulder, he shared in his friend's relief. *Wish he was my brother.* The thought caught Carver by surprise.

Two of the guards rode in front of the wagon train, with two bringing up the rear and the others roaming alongside the middle. True to their word, they hung back and let Turner continue to give orders and guidance. Everyone relaxed into the added security of having these eight armed fighters surrounding them.

Aiela

On their way north, Turner and Carver again sought the twins out. The four of them walked for hours, preferring movement over the stiffness of riding in the wagons. Turner told colorful stories of how each of the men and women warriors had come to be one of his Da's personal guards.

Even while enjoying the tales of courage and sacrifice Turner had grown up on, Aiela wished only to be alone with him. To spend hours— better yet days—kissing and talking and exploring each other's bodies. Distracted by daydreams, fantasizing elaborate love-making rituals, she stayed uncharacteristically quiet, while Turner seemed tuned only to her. Trying valiantly to include Ahna and Carver in the conversation, his attention drifted back over and over to Aiela's face, his hands touching her hands, her arms, her hair.

"What's that word we use when someone's mind gets mushy with desire? Obsessed? No, that's not quite right... Besotted, that's it." Ahna teased her secretly, out of the other's hearing. "You've never been this immersed in anything—except maybe healing your animals. Something's shifted. What secret and wicked things happened the last two nights while the rest of us slept?"

"Shh. I'll tell you later." Aiela whispered, unable to stop smiling.

The caravan passed slowly through rippling hills with covers of alter-nating forest and grassland. They began to see more people dressed in roughly woven cloth or patched together skins, journeying in small groups or families. Most smiled, calling greetings in their language, and the students waved back. It didn't matter that they didn't know the other's words. These travelers exemplified the simple, earthy culture throughout Ireland that she'd been expecting.

"The farther north we go, the more populated it becomes." Turner explained, "Less roads, makes fer heavier use."

As dusk ousted an apricot sunset, they stopped to feed the aurochs and pass out hunks of lavar bread, wedges of hard cheese, and strips of salty dried fish. Everyone stretched their legs one last time before piling in the wagons for the last few miles of this day's journey.

Voices waned as the muted point of equal darkness and light made it difficult to identify shapes, playing tricks with their eyes, turning the landscape around them otherworldly. Stars began peeking through the hematite sky, as Ahna and Aiela laid back beside their handsome compan-ions, watching earth's galaxy come alive against its backdrop of the infi-nite. With no moon yet, the stars were bright and active.

Aiela pointed out constellations and Ahna told the legends associated with them, echoing Papa's tone and emphasis from a hundred nights spent listening to his star stories.

It was very late when they arrived at the Monastery. "The highest school in Ireland" Turner said. "Scholars, mystics and seekers come here from all ow'er the mainland—other lands as well—ta study the stars, seekin' ta unfold the mysteries o' earth an' what's beyond it."

A walled complex, large as any of Ireland's cities, safeguarded her greatest treasures; spiritual masters, art, and knowledge, cherished and passed down by brilliant minds from countless generations who'd inhabited these lands. Allowing foreigners in was a great honor that only such as Meihal could arrange.

Night watchmen were waiting, and waved them inside, then shut the gates behind them. The wagon-train passed neat rows of tiny homes already dark with sleep. Stone-laid lanes led them slowly up toward inner walls that ringed the great Monastery itself.

Monks with scanty pointed beards, robed in natural linen and carrying single-flame lanterns, opened the narrow inner gates. Tall and ornate with metal symbols of constellations, sheaves of wheat, and runes Aiela didn't recognize. Fearless of the giant aurochs, the monks led them by their harnesses to a part of the monastery reserved for guests. Quarters lit by hanging firepots cast friendly circles of welcome for the tired travelers.

Invited directly into the monk's long eating-room, they dined on soup made from potatoes, bone broth and leeks, accompanied by small cups of sweet honey mead which had them drooping into their soup bowls before long. Turner assured everyone their belongings were safe in the wagons, and good-nights were exchanged before the monks dispersed them to bare sleeping rooms. They would rest on tightly stretched canvas, padded with blankets tonight.

She and Ahna shared a tiny room, it's only furniture a bed barely big enough for two. Walls of textured whitewash surrounded them, lit by a single window filled with starlight that descended to the horizon.

"Gods, this blanket is itchy..." Ahna was already snuggling down under the sheep's wool bed-covering while Aiela sat beside her, still inside the dreamy daze, wondering if Turner might come knocking on her door, and where he might steal her away to.

"Alright. Tell me about it from the beginning and leave nothing out." Ahna turned towards her. "Abbreviate though, or I'm like to fall asleep in the middle." She let out a gaping yawn to prove her point.

"He took me to a smaller hot pool after everyone was sleeping. First, on the first night, we kissed in the tunnel and it was... magical. To soak, we took off our clothes, *all* our clothes, and the water was even hotter than the big pool. So we talked and then we started, you know, touching each other, which we couldn't seem to stop." Aiela glanced at Ahna to gauge her reaction so far. Ahna's eyebrows were higher than usual but her energy remained a calm deep. Aiela continued, "And then we made a vow, spoke an agreement to each other. I never expected we would go this far so fast but it makes complete sense. He's been in my dreams my entire life! Of course we are meant to be together."

Ahna smiled and stifled another yawn, propping her head on her hand, eyelids heavy.

"Then we… you know, I put him inside me."

"Really? You had *intercourse* with him? First or second night?"

"No… we *made love*, on the first night—and a whole lot on the second night. So much attraction intensity has been piling up between us, plus getting to really know and understand him these last many days, it all just came out. It felt an expression of the energy we've created between us. He's everything I want and more, I can't stop thinking about it. Maybe I'm addicted. Is that possible?"

Ahna shrugged.

"It was….exactly how I wanted it to be." Aiela watched her sister, hoping she'd understand. Somehow, she needed Ahna's approval, maybe for validation, maybe just to share this profound and unspeakable new joy.

Ahna flopped onto her back, hand to her forehead. "You've fallen in love in Ireland *and* made a vow to a foreign man." She looked at her twin, eyes wide and soft, reflecting back Aiela's wonder, holding with her the sweetness of this sexual experience born of young love. "I'm happy for you. He *is* exactly right. As good and strong and smart as you are." Ahna reached over to give her hand a squeeze.

Relieved, Aiela blew out their lantern then tucked herself into bed. Settling, before whispering "I wanted to tell you all day and just never could. You don't think it was wrong? Or foolish?"

"Not at all. The two of you seem linked, twined into each other's lives like two parts that fit perfectly to make a bigger whole. And I'm not talking about your bodies…"

Aiela smiled, inhaling the linen-scented promise of rest. Exhaling with sleepiness and more than a smidgen of longing.

BELLS RANG PRECISELY AT DAWN, clanging layers of singular notes that called Aiela from her dreams. She was still tired. The smell of freshly baked bread finally coaxed her out of bed.

Outside the window, starlight had given way to a splendor of colors as the sun's light crested a horizon of rollicking green. Waking Ahna, they followed their noses to find a hot breakfast being served to the resident monks gathered at long, polished, trestle tables in the peaked central hall.

The men were chattering quietly but paused to smile and welcome their guests with broad sweeps of their hands. Rumpled from travel and sleep, Ahna and Aiela bowed their thanks, gratefully eating oats stewed with wild berries, and topped with generous puddles of white laurel honey from the heaping clay bowls set in front of them. Creamy goat cheese with rosemary and chives was spread on long crusty rolls, then topped with tomatoes and tender shoots of asparagus.

Nirka settled down the table from Aiela, leaving plenty of space between them, his tousled hair the same color as the light golden honey. Sharing a mischievous smile, Aiela and Ahna moved to sit across from him. "I've noticed how well you lead your group." Ahna began.

He glanced at her and grunted but didn't stop eating to respond.

"And how strong you look. I was wondering where all those muscles come from?"

"Wrestling." Nirka mumbled around his food. "Winning. I'm the best wrestler of my age in High City."

"You're from High City? We've only been once, but we're both apprenticing there this autumn."

"You could come watch me sometime." Nirka seemed to be warming to Ahna. "I guess you can bring your sister, since you do everything together. I haven't lost a match in moons."

"Oh I'm not interested in wrestling." Ahna said. "But Nanat is. She was just talking about how its her favorite part of Poseidon's Jubilee. Wait until she hears you're a wrestler! She already thinks you're the most interesting person here."

"And most handsome." Aiela added. "All the girls talk, you know... "

"About me?" His chest puffed out.

"They talk about boys in general, all of the males on the trip. But Nanat, she mostly talks about you." Ahna shrugged. "Not sure why you two haven't paired up yet."

"Anyway," Aiela smiled brightly, "we just wanted to compliment you on your group. Oh look, there's Nanat now. How does she manage to look so radiant all the time, when the rest of us are covered in dust?" Once Nirka's eyes were fixed on Nanat, they slipped away.

The monks refused help with clearing soiled dishes and instead showed them to a row of individual bathhouses. Collected rainwater, stored in sun-warmed shallow tanks on the roof, flowed through an intricate system of pierced metal pipes, creating antiquated showers. The water, though tepid, was a sight lot better than the cold sea or lake-water they'd occasionally been able to bathe in. Balls of soap made from goats milk, wild lavender and sage, soothed travel-worn skin. They were given robes of the same natural cream-colored linen worn by the monks, ankle length, billowy and belted at the waist. A uniformity that blurred physical distinctions of male and female.

"Because they allow us inta their holy places, we dress ta honor them." Turner explained when the group was once again assembled, nourished, washed, and uniformed.

Their tour began with an elderly monk, lecturing as he led them through the stark and sturdy stone-lined corridors. Turner translated and Aiela missed parts of what he said, lulled by the melodic timbre of his voice.

"The large castle-like complex ya slept in is Ireland's foremost Abbey, constructed on a raised mound at least five-hundred feet in diameter. Ancient to e'en we Irish, it was built by three mysterious visitors froom the stars.

Legend tells o' one female an' two males froom another world who came ta teach the nomadic hunters o' Ireland how ta build wi' stone, when ta plant seeds, and methods o' using earth's energies ta heal our bodies. The visitors stayed long enough ta build three advanced structures: This Abbey—constructed wi' methods far beyond the times—was where the star people lived an' taught during their years on earth. The great Observatory, they used ta monitor all the movements o' the heavens day an' night, tracking seasons, predicting earth events, and eventually choosing the window o' opportunity ta return home ta their far-away galaxy. Lastly, our Great Mound funnels earth energy ta chambers that heal human bodies and increases mental energies. Effectively raising human intelligence, which in turn lessens the violent, survivalist animal-nature.

Our star people taught this knowledge in a language o' symbols ta the first monks o' this Abbey, leaving them ta carry it forward an' spread it across the continent. Since then, people froom far-off places were drawn here ta learn, continuing ta build on the knowledge, develop better technologies, and take it back ta their own villages."

Outside the Abbey's gates, rows of little homes stretched out neatly around the central mound. Built of baked clay brick or mortared stone, this entire city, according to the old monk, was dedicated to the study of the heavens, the movement of energy, and the powers of earth materials.

A half-hour's brisk walk in one direction brought them to a series of earthen mounds, varying in size. They started with the central one. Larger even than the one basing the monk's Abbey, the Great Mound was tall, its foundation a ring of stones, each one the size of an average cow. From these kerb stones rose a stone wall no higher than six hands and the remainder of the Mound's dome was carpeted in brilliant green grass. Designs and drawings carved into the kerb stones spoke of the hours spent here by many. Painstakingly etched by monks and students as a form of meditation, the carvings illustrated the wisdom and knowledge gained in this sacred place.

Three paces in front of the humble entrance stood three stones. The middle one was pure white quartz, irregularly shaped, and symbolized the female from the stars. On either side stood brown granite stones for each of the males. Pausing here, the monk finished speaking and waited for Turner to translate before moving on.

"These three stones were transported from elsewhere. Our legend makes no mention where the star people sourced them. We still hope that someday, some traveler froom another land might recognize them, perhaps have a legend in their own land o' three stones bein' mined and taken by people no' froom earth."

A few at a time, the students entered a short, rectangular doorway, passing through a long tunnel lined and capped with stones—many of them decorated with more meditative drawings. The tunnel ran in a straight line for what seemed an incredible distance before ending at a group of chambers under the apex of the mound.

Aiela's small group gathered in the big chamber. Beautiful stone work formed the corbelled ceiling—reminding her of Caoimhe's home in the mound village. The entire room, like the tunnel, was lined with rock fitted together without mortar. Careful selection and placement made them tight enough to keep dirt and damp from seeping in.

"This largest space is a healing chamber", the monks explained, "which utilizes earth's energy. Channeling and directing it through appropriate design amplifies the full potential of earth's meridians, creating enough power ta balance the maladies o' humans."

Rather archaic compared to Atlantis' advanced healing pantheons, it fascinated Aiela. She returned to the chamber a second time, feeling nurtured by the earthy comfort cradling her spirit in this womb-like pocket deep inside the giant earthwork.

The smaller chambers, little more than niches in the tunnel, were for raising the energy frequency in a subject, with the purpose of expanding intelligence. But like a machine, the Great Mound needed power. The power was sourced from Earth, so it waxed and waned with the moon and tides.

"Fer all of earth is a living being with her own rhythms and seasons, slumbering and waking. That is why the Observatory we will visit next is so important ta us." The monks explained through Turner who was tirelessly translating. "Because wi' it, we track those seasons and rhythms, so that we know when ta use this great gift ta mankind. Or when it is dangerously powered."

"Why is that tiny window over the door?" Aiela asked.

"It is the keystone." Came the reply. "On the first day of Spring when the day and the night are exactly equal, the first light o' the rising sun shines in this window. The doorway was aligned under it, the tunnel and healing chamber built at precise angles ta receive each precious ray o' light as it rose. The star people taught that all life on our planet comes froom our sun. So they honored the magical moment, here in this place, when the Season o' the Sun begins and reigns fer six and a half moons until the dark again takes ow'er at Autumn Equinox. Our legends say it took seven years o' observing, marking, building, readjusting ta get it exact, before it could be covered ow'er wi' earth. Seven years ta capture one very special hour out o' each year. And so it became our moost holy day.

We gather here, Spring Equinox Morn, ta remember and thank the star people who changed the course o' Ireland's humanity. We bring offerings, perform rituals in homage ta the Three and we celebrate fer seven days. One day honoring each year spent building."

Walking back to the Abbey, they ate a second hearty meal at high noon, then ventured out in another direction to visit the Observatory. A place described by Turner, as one of "high magic".

The monk guides lectured all the way, explaining the exact placements of the Observatory, the Great Mound and the Abbey. "A trinity formed o' body, mind and soul."

"Planet earth's ley lines, carry and disperse energy ta every live thing throughout the globe, like the arteries and veins in our own bodies. Where the lines intersect, a reservoir o' energy is created. It is on these energy points that the star people built, and all o' Ireland's greatest structures down through history follow suit. Our Observatory," Turner translated, "sits on a spot where multiple leys intersect, creating an extraordinarily powerful force".

Nothing appeared majestic about the circle of stones that stood like irregularly shaped, fossilized sentries in the middle of a field with no trees even to mark the spot. Rather unimpressive to these Atlanteans who came from eons of gilded beauty. Taught to equate beauty with power, they immediately doubted any power in this unremarkable grouping.

The High Priest had accompanied them here. A tall effeminate man with no beard and oversized nose and ears, he had followed silently, listening and observing until now. Gathering them outside the stone circle, he spoke, explaining in simple terms the very particular mathematical dimensions for each of the Observatory's stone pillar placement, and what each dimension represented. The measurements recorded distances between planetary bodies significant to the three star people, precise earth measurements, and the means to track every lunar and celestial body in the firmament.

"Sit, sit all of you." High Priest ordered. Speaking in fluent Atlantean, he gave Turner rest for his voice, grown hoarse from the morning of translating. "We must raise your awareness. So you can know the energy that is here."

He led them in a meditation focused on raising their minds to a spiritual plane. Then he allowed them to enter the stone circle.

"The Star People could have built a simple observatory anywhere. It does not take extraordinary energy, such as exists at this spot, to read the stars. So why, then, did they choose this particular crossing of the leys? What purpose is behind the careful alignment of these stones to the power center? I will give you all the ingredients, but you must decide for yourselves what it means. We have this greatest of tools, this stone structure to track exactly what the heavenly bodies are doing over eons of time. We have, there in the center—can you feel it now? See or hear it maybe?—an energy portal. A place where earth breathes in and breathes out, depending on the season—depending on the exact degree of relationship to its brothers and sisters of the galaxy. Again I inquire of you, why here? Why combine the two? What is it they were trying to tell us?" With that the High Priest left them there to contemplate, while he headed back to his home.

Some could feel the energy at the center. "It feels as if the air is denser there." Ahna tried to describe it. "Not a wind, more like invisible water—a subtle change in sensation." Blatant rushes of it lit up their energy centers, as if injected with caffeine. Aiela watched it happen.

She also saw the great influx of energy coming through the portal, flowing, pouring in from above and all around, in a spiral as though gathered from the universe into a funnel, it was white and pure and beautiful.

Ahna simply stood in it, eyes closed, unable to speak until later. "It felt cleansing." She sighed, eyes clear and glowing. "Like a sharpening of experience and clarity of mind."

Aiela nodded. "As though earth inhales here. I wonder when, or where, it exhales?"

THEY STAYED NEARLY two weeks at the picturesque monastery. Venturing out daily from this center, like spokes from a wheel into the middle-lands of Ireland, they found endless fields of flat grassland, occasional splotches of forest, wide, slow-moving rivers that emptied into Lochs, and scattered, rocky hills. They visited the clustered settlements and villages of simple farmers and herders, always welcomed by the people who seemed eager for these visitors from foreign places. They helped with all manner of chores, from sheep shearing and goat milking to building projects where they cut and carried earth blocks, mixed mortar and stacked stones into fences, or laid bundled thatch as roofing. Mingling with the country people, they shared meals and the ceremonies of Irish life, so very different from their own.

Evenings were spent in recreation at the monastery. Monks challenged them to games, some involving intellect, others physical skill. Sometimes these unpretentious men played music, and sang in lilting harmonies that seemed to weave the individual hearts of Irish and Atlantean back into one.

Aiela assisted Healer Lira much of the time, tending to the sick in the villages with oils, tinctures, teas and subtle energy work. They spoke with the few local medicine women and one man, showing better ways of healing. Aiela used her ability, touching each person in need of help, finding their pain, quietly describing the colors coming off their body which enabled Lira to treat them more effectively.

"We won't mention to anyone that you have these abilities. Their beliefs are different than ours. They'd make you a god or a devil," —Lira smiled—"it could go either way." Knowing the primitives were suspicious of foreign ways, Lira always brought monks with her to translate and reassure the wary traditionalists that her medicine was wholly good.

"I did not know the gap was so wide between us and others." Aiela remarked to Lira one day, after leaving the bedside of a child very sick with fever, caused by infection that had not been treated. "Why do we not share more of our technology? Or why do these countries not send their people to learn from us?"

Lira, who had made many of these trips with students to places around the globe, looked sad, "That is a complex question. The short answer? Because not enough Atlanteans are aware or care enough to disrupt their own lives to change it. I'd like to be able to fully answer you but I don't understand 'why' either. Perhaps that is something you can explore while you study in High City this autumn. You've rare skill already at your age—and with no formal training. Could it be this is the reason for your gift; using it to help those who have no access, or under-standing of higher healing?" Lira spoke with passion, "I've dreamt often of planting small schools around the globe, creating an easy way to take our knowledge to those who need it most. These people have no means to come to us. We'd have to go to them."

Aiela nodded, thoughtful as they went on to make an old man comfortable on his deathbed. He'd been lying unconscious for days and the village murmurs had turned to black speculations;

"Something is wrong with his crossing, the gods must not want him."

"He must have done something terrible to be imprisoned like this, stuck between life and death."

Aiela listened as Lira assured the tattered, withering body that death was nothing to fear.

"Have no worry of what's on the other side dear one. It is only returning home, a place of rest where those you love are waiting to rejoice over you. This life, all of *this*, was the illusion, a stage where you came to play your part, a role you agreed to act. What you are going back to is your real existence—your true, whole, boundless Self. There will be no judgement of your choices here, for they are only lessons learned. You are loved beyond measure, you can let go whenever you're ready and go home to that love. You can release any fear or worry that you're holding and cling instead to that love. This is the way.....all that you yearn for is in that next place."

The monk was translating softly into the old man's ear, every word that Lira spoke.

"I'm not even sure he can hear us." Lira whispered to Aiela.

But Aiela knew that he did. Holding his age-damaged hand, she'd sensed his consciousness still alert, even though his body stagnated in a coma. She'd felt the tiny sigh of relief as he took in the truths that Lira spoke over him. It wouldn't be long. Aiela asked the monk to speak to the man's family, "Tell them he won't be here much longer. He is ready. Any moment now, he will choose to be free."

THERE WAS scant time alone with Turner. It seemed he was needed every minute of the day by someone. Or she was; listening to a wide variety of complaints from disgruntled students, mediating between two boys who'd nearly come to blows over a misunderstanding, planning out who should go where for the next day. Several evenings they stole away from the group activities, exploring the monastery or its town. Finding private spaces to hold each other, they kissed and talked in equal measure, wanting desperately to further explore their love physically, yet reluctant to do so in a monastery.

"We're surrounded by *celibate monks...*" Aiela sighed, removing his hand from her breast again. "Don't you feel at all guilty?"

"No' a bit." Turner pulled back to grin at her. "They chose this life, poor bastards. Although, I bet if they'd known what they were givin' up, there'd be a good many less willing ta make such a sacrifice ta God."

ON THE LAST morning the monks fed them a hearty breakfast before the bells of dawn, helped them load the wagons and ready the aurochs, then bid them an emotional farewell. They'd grown quite fond of having these lively, young adults in their midst, injecting their normally monotonous days with spontaneity, investing tedious chores with fresh merriment.

Aiela, like her fellow Atlanteans, had accidentally fallen in love with the monks' sincere affection, their pure spirits and uncomplicated life-style. Each would miss the balance the other had provided.

"Why is it", Aiela thought aloud to Turner, "that we don't know the value of our experiences until after?" It was nighttime and they'd been travelling north the whole long day, but still the aurochs plodded onward, the place they would make camp still distant.

"I don' know what ya mean." Turner shifted to face her. They were laying side by side in a jostling wagon, philosophising about life and watching the stars flicker ceaselessly as if beckoning the moon up to join them.

"I appreciate things I've done—people and events—much more looking back on them. For instance the monastery. I treated it and the monks as though it were normal, just another mundane part of my trip. Now, I see they were an absolute treasure. Why is that? Why didn't I see that when I was there?"

Turner thought about it. "Maybe it's impossible ta capture *all* of each moment while it's happenin'. Maybe we're too busy experiencing an' respondin'. Right now, I'm listening ta ya, an' thinking about what ya say, an' speaking my thoughts, but there are a hundred more parts ta right now. The night sky; peaceful, constant. The joy of being beside ya, learning how ya think an' wha' ya feel—yer patterns. There's my relief ta have the guards around us as we travel so I don' have ta be vigilant. I hear talking an' laughter from other wagons, camaraderie, an' I feel satisfaction because I helped create it. The night is warm, without wind or rain…" he slapped at his forearm, "… an' the bugs are tryin' ta eat us like a cursed devil-plague." He turned his body to hers, wrapping the bulky length of himself around her, one hand straying under the blanket to stroke her stomach. "Each moment holds an entire world. I can smell an' touch ya an' we're covered in darkness, so there's anticipation in my moment—hope an' desire ta be closer ta ya…" his hand slid higher, as his head lowered to hers, "…sooo much happening…how could we expect ta experience it all?" His mouth moulded the softness of hers for only a second before parting, so his tongue could trace a slow line, tickling and light along her inner lip before rippling deeper. Passion exploded then, turning them both urgent and greedy.

When her lips were puffy and tingling, and every body part tremulous with satisfaction, they lay interlaced, watched by the stars.

"We'll be close ta stopping, hear the corncrakes call?" Turner commented sleepily, one hand buried in Aiela's mass of hair.

"Corncrakes? What's that?" Aiela was snuggled into his chest, wishing this night would not end.

"Ya hear tha' kritch-kritch-kritch sound?"

She nodded against his chest. It was constant and loud, similar to the cicadas at Aunt Charis' Old Forest home.

"They're birds, nestin' in these tall grasses. The males will call all night long when they're defending their territory or attractin' a mate. They get louder between midnight and dawn. It must be close ta midnight now, judging by the sound o' them."

Sure enough, the wagons slowed, then stopped, and Turner and Aiela crawled out to rouse the others. The Drivers were exhausted so Aiela insisted they rest, urging the students to work together. Slowly and clumsily they raised three large tents in the dim light of lanterns.

Spreading tarps over luggage in the wagons to guard against rain, they crawled into bedrolls, hunkering deep inside where the lowland bugs couldn't reach, to fall quickly asleep. No one had bothered to divide into boys and girls or teachers and students. Just locating an empty spot and bedding down in it. Normally, a night on the ground might have been shocking after the last two weeks in monastery beds, but at this late hour, no one laid awake long enough to complain.

THE SUN WAS high in the sky the following morning, before they stirred. Turner built a small fire to boil eggs. Goat-milk yogurt, beaded with forest berries and wild honey from the monks, was passed around with urges to eat it all "because if this heat keeps up, it will spoil today". Then they took down the tents and made to travel on.

"It's half a day ta the coast. We'll arrive before supper, stay the night, then ferry the crossing ta Balor's Island." Turner announced. "We spend only the day on the island, and return ta the mainland where we head north again. Finnegan's stronghold on Ireland's north point is a short day's travel and we'll rest there before crossing ta Scotland, and Benandonner's Castle. Load up!"

They skirted 'round the village they'd camped outside of, and the rest of the morning was sameness. Aiela walked for long stretches, swatting away hordes of flies and mosquitoes, wishing fervently for the little crystal devices they used at home for keeping bugs away. She spent time with the girls, who'd been complaining about the loss of her since she and Turner became a couple.

Turner was busy anyway. He, Carver and several other Atlanteans took turns driving wagons, giving the Driver's rest after their long haul yesterday. The sun had everyone sweltering, coaxing out increasing masses of miserable insects.

By the time they reached the coast, they were grateful for the fresh ocean breezes, strong enough to keep the bugs down. This shoreline was rugged, with no beach. Small cliffs and jutting rocks seemed to repel incoming tides rather than welcome them, as if the land and the water were at odds, engaged in an eternal battle that neither could win.

A mid-sized town bustled here with hardy people going about their business of daily life. Bearded men repaired buildings that the constant salt-tainted winds tore at, and hauled in the morning's catch from all sizes and shapes of fishing vessels. Stout women worked on stained boards set across rocks, stumps and posts, cleaning and preserving their food supply that was shuttled to them from the boats by a bevy of suntanned children.

Everyone stopped what they doing and stared at the large group of foreigners creaking through rough-cut streets in a train of wagons.

"Be friendly." Aiela reminded those with her, and they waved and bowed, smiling and calling out greetings they had learned in the native tongue as they trundled past. Their cheer spread rapidly until they were a festive parade setting the villagers to talking excitedly amongst themselves.

Their lodging for the night was the town's gathering hall. Multi-purposed, it was long and low, built of stacked stone fitted tightly together. It served as a court of law, a temple of worship, and a place where the community danced in celebration of the changing seasons.

An impromptu feast was set up and the whole town joined in roasting meat and breaking bread. Barrels of sour-berry beer were rolled out and after the foamy cups had been passed, musicians—grinning and guffawing—played high jigs, hollering at anyone who dared not to dance.

Arms threading together, forming circles that moved in opposite directions, they danced, kicking out heels, lifting knees high, until the fires ran out of light and the barrels ran out of beer and the players ran out of songs.

17

BALOR'S ISLAND

"We lived depravity and called it truth, silencing our dreaming, and our love, discarding things holy."

— JOHN DANIEL THIEME

AIELA

*L*eaving wagons and aurochs behind with their luggage, save small day packs of food and water, they boarded their ferry, a single large boat used for deep sea fishing. The sea—once away from its belligerent shore—rippled calmer than Aiela had seen it here in this stormy country.

"Gather roun', gather roun', "Turner was calling, "Pack in tight so ya can hear. We havena much time before we land. Colin here will tell ya the tale o' Balor on the way ta his namesake island."

Colin was one of the guardsmen who'd joined them in Semias. With great gobs of ginger hair flaming in all directions and a terrible unruly beard, he seemed as cheerful as he was hairy. His booming voice carried well over waves slapping against the hull as he began;

"Now Balor was a giant with a third eye. This eye wrought destruction when opened so it was always covered with seven cloaks to keep it cool.

When he took the cloaks off one by one, at the first, ferns began to wither. At the second, grass began to redden. At the third, trees grew warm. At the fourth, smoke came out of the wood. At the fifth, stone began to heat. At the sixth everything got red hot. At the seventh, the whole land caught fire.

After Balor grew to manhood in the sea—where he'd been raised by his mother's family—he returned to conquer the Spanish kings who had taken the land from the Tuatha De Danann; the people of Danu. Balor returned these lands to the people, to honor his mother, but found it all much too peaceful for his taste. So he gathered around him all the wandering outcasts and outlaws—the men who like to brawl and take what didn't belong to them, the wicked of this land and beyond. They became Balor's people, called the Formorians, and they lived on Balor's island when they weren't out causing trouble.

Now Balor had heard a prophecy that he would be killed by his grandson, so to avoid this fate, he locked his only child, his daughter Ethnui, in a tower on his island to keep her from becoming pregnant. One day, Balor stole a magical cow of abundance from the local Smith on the mainland and took it to his fortress on the Island. A young man named Cian, who was supposed to be guarding the cow for the Smith, followed Balor to get it back. That night, while Balor slept in his castle next to the tower, Cian entered the tower and found Ethnui. They mated, and from that night, she gave birth to three sons. Balor attempted to drown the boys in the sea, but one was saved and raised as a foster-son by Manannán, the sea god. The boy grew up and was called Lugh.

Eventually, Lugh became king of the Tuatha De Danann and he led them in the second battle against the Fomorians, who, incited by Balor, had been ransacking the mainland villages. Balor was disarmed during this battle—but he killed the brave warrior who'd managed to disarm him, with his 'evil' eye. Then Lugh threw a spear through Balor's eye. Trying to get the spear out, casting this way and that, Balor's eye destroyed most of the Fomorian army. Lugh then beheaded Balor, but the eye was still open as the head fell face first into the ground. Thus his deadly eye-beam burned a hole into the earth.

Long after, the hole filled with water and became a lake, now known as Loch na Súil, or 'Lake of the Eye'. Ethnui's tower still stands and you will find the inhabitants of the island not much different than the Fomorians were."

"That's right", Turner said, as Colin nodded at the group's applause. "The islanders will no' harm ya because they fear my father's retribution

—and because we've brough' them food an' gifts. But they are thieves and liars an' w'out a doubt murderers, which is why we left most belongings on the mainland, and why we won't be stayin' long. We go fer charity's sake. They are poor because they're lazy and would rather starve and live in filth than work ta grow food. Sure, many try ta help them but all have failed. It is sad and yet, no one can force them ta change. Stay in groups—just ta be on the safe side."

It was not a large colony but they were markedly more primitive than any of the Irish thus far.

"I hope we brought them clothing." Aiela whispered to Ahna as they walked in a clump from the landing dock towards the fallen-down fortress.

Only a few curious younglings came out to greet them, carrying sticks and shells that were their toys, every one of them paper thin, except for bulbous bellies, unsmiling, keeping their distance from these bright strangers. Stringy-haired adults lounged in front of haphazard structures, nothing more than rocks held together with mud, roofed with branches and tattered tarps—more shelters than homes. The people stared at these visitors with silent suspicion.

"Our cleaning rags are nicer than what they're wearing." Ahna whispered back. "Poor children, they look somewhere between hungry and starving. I'm glad we're bringing them food at least."

Turner and the Irish guards spoke to the islanders in their language, gesturing at the bulging packs each Driver carried. A few islanders began trailing behind the group and by the time they arrived at the castle ruins, they were a winding stream, eerily quiet, except for agitated whispers among the students.

Crumbling walls of varied heights were all that was left of Balor's castle. Weedy grass grew from what might once have been plank floors and the dirt spaces were littered with bones, charred fire remains and garbage. A few molting chickens pecking at the trash, squawked and ruffled away from the influx of people. Used as a gathering space for the islanders, a playground for the children, and parts of it a dump, this was not the castle they'd been expecting.

Turner instructed the group to remain at the ruins while he went to fetch the chief and explain why they'd come. The Island Chief lived in Ethnui's tower, a stone square that squatted, more than towered, next to the ruins. It was the only structure in sight that still had a real roof.

"Looks like something a monster would build." Aiela remarked.

Ahna nodded. "I wonder how long Ethnui was locked up in there?"

"We probably don't want to know."

The Chief was fat. Waddling his way over, all smiles beside Turner, trailed by a line of girls and women, his blubbery layers quivered and jiggled. Once in their midst, he began speaking, gesturing grandly, and Turner translated.

"Welcome! Welcome! Welcome! My friends from Atlantis. We are pleased to have you today. I am the great Chief here. My power is mighty, see this whole island is mine. These people are mine. On this beautiful day we will make you welcome with a meal." The Chief barked orders at the women who scurried to build a fire, some heading back to his tower home, presumably for food supplies.

Turner and the Guards and Drivers continued conversing with the Chief and eventually showed him all that they had brought for the islanders as "gifts of peace".

Word spread quickly and more of the island's hundred and twenty inhabitants started appearing from their scattered hovels. Keeping their distance, they made an effort to nod in friendliness once they saw their Chief's effusive acceptance of the visitors.

Turner directed the students on portioning the foodstuff to each person. There were bags of dried beans, grains, flours, root vegetables, hard cheeses and dried fruits. Bags of seeds were distributed too, in the hopes they might plant and harvest to provide for the future. There was candy for the children with a few small toys. Cloth for blankets could also be made into clothing. The people accepted all this bounty, still unsmiling, not meeting the Atlantean's eyes.

"Did you notice there are not many women? " Aiela whispered to Ahna.

"Most of them seem to be with the Chief."

"See that girl over there? Probably about our age, let's go be friendly. She looks sad."

The twins headed towards the girl who squatted in the dirt some distance away from the Chief, watching everything going on about her. She was bone-thin with dark auburn hair in a braid that reached her waist.

"Your hair is so long. Very pretty." Aiela knew the girl wouldn't know her words and was miming as she spoke.

The girl seemed to understand and ducked her head shyly at the compliment. Her face attempted a smile but fell just short.

"Do you like this?" Aiela touched the beaded headband holding her own shiny dark mane away from her face. It was many shades of blues to match the patterned tunic and leggings she wore today. The girl's eyes kept going back to it.

The girl nodded, "Leor." She spoke so soft it was hard to hear.

"Does that mean pretty? Leor?" Aiela and Ahna both settled in the dirt close to the girl. The girl did smile a tiny bit then, at Aiela's attempt at her language.

"Lee-ahrr". She said a little louder, rolling the r at the end.

"Lea-rr" Aiela and Ahna both tried to copy her.

She met their eyes then, taking in their beautifully tailored clothing, their simple travel jewelry and hair ornaments. Her eyes scanned over them slowly as if absorbing or learning their strangeness.

"Aiela". Aiela patted her own chest. "Ahna". She touched Ahna, then raised her eyebrows and reached over to touch the girl's arm. "What is your name?"

The girl looked blank until Aiela repeated the hand gestures, again naming herself and Ahna.

The girl's eyes lit with comprehension. She touched her own chest. "Brona". She pronounce it "Brro-nuh" rolling the r again.

Aiela and Ahna smiled with delight, both saying Brona's name several times until they pronounced it right. Next they set about telling her how old they were and asking her age, drawing tally marks in the rocky dirt to helped her understand what they were saying. She reciprocated by talking in her own language while she drew tally marks and brushed the worn grey linen on her own chest.

"She's only fourteen?" Aiela murmured to Ahna, "She looks older."

Brona stood, scooping her arm in an expression of "come with me". Pointing off across the island and saying the same words in her language over and over, an expression of expectation on her sharp, skinny face.

"I think she's asking us to come with her."

"I'll see if Turner can send a Guard or Driver with us, so we aren't breaking rules. You stay so she doesn't think we're refusing. I'll be right back."

Aiela made her way to Turner, who was still talking to the Chief, both groups milling around them. Squeezing in next to him, she whispered in his ear. "This girl, Brona, wants to show us something across the island. Could one of the Drivers come with us?"

Turner twisted to answer, "Find Carver. He may be able ta translate fer ya."

Aiela touched his back in thanks and threaded her way between the busy crowd of people. She found Carver still dividing food into small

333

woven bags. "Ahna and I made a friend and she wants to show us something...somewhere. Would you come with us? Maybe translate...?"

Carver nodded, his face lighting. "Yes! I've been measuring beans for the last hour. Drommen, Lister..." His ever present companions were lounging nearby, "take over for me. Do it like this; two scoops to each bag and then tie it. And keep eyes on this candy here. Those boys over there keep trying to sneak up, probably to take the whole bag."

"You don't want us to come with you?" Drommen looked less than thrilled.

"I thought this was a dangerous place. What if you need us?" Lister tried to arrange his chubby face as tough and protective.

Carver shook his head. "I'm armed. If we're not back in awhile, come looking." Carver slapped both their shoulders. "Thanks for doing the beans."

Introductions were made between Brona and Carver. She ducked shyly but managed a faint smile at him as they exchanged names and tried to communicate. Carver used a lot of hand gestures and finally told Ahna and Aiela, "Brona wants to show you a place that she likes....I think. Their dialect is pretty different so I don't understand a lot of her words. I may not be worth taking along as a translator, but I can provide some protection at least. These men would likely steal you both away if they could. Women are valuable property here, more coveted than the chickens and huts."

The four of them set off, walking the long, low island which had no trees but an over-abundance of rock. Scraggy grass grew heartily in the rich black soil, filling niches and cracks between heaps and scatters of broken stone in shades of gray-tinged white or black. The grasses looked gray too. A shadowed spectrum that contrasted oddly against the bright blue sky and white clouds above. Even lit by an exuberant sun, the whole island felt as if all color had been scrubbed from it. Abandoned garbage lent a putrid smell wafting between salty breezes.

"Brona, is the Chief your father?" Aiela asked.

Carver took a long time getting the question across, trying many words before finding the one she understood.

She shook her head, uttering one word with a sense of defeat.

"Husband?" Taken aback, Carver translated. "She says the Chief is her husband."

"Oh." Aiela was lost for words, not expecting this response. Then, realization hit. "Are all those girls his wives?"

Again Carver labored to translate. Brona nodded once, eyes never leaving the ground.

Silence allowed them to examine the island, with its uneven angles and layers of gray. *All the energies jangle and fray.* Aiela noticed. *Expressed musically, it'd be all minors with dissonant chords.* They'd walked straight to the coast before turning northward, following its crooked outline. Gusts of wind came in dashes and dots to lift their hair, flavored with seaweed musk and something ominous. Hopelessness maybe. Searching the horizons, Aiela couldn't see the land edges ahead, behind or to their right. Apparently this gloomy island was good-sized. Cloud shadows rolled overhead, turning the air from hot to chilly and back again. Every time the sun popped out, Aiela noticed the four of them instinctively raise their faces to its buzzing light.

They walked fast for a quiet twenty minutes before Brona muttered a single word and veered off towards the water, leading them to an outcropping of black rock expanse. It was sliced through randomly so that water lapped into its criss-crossed crevices every time a high wave flowed in. Shells, smooth polished stones, live crustaceans and all manner of sea-debris collected in thousands of dimples, dents, cracks and cuts of the rocks.

Brona stooped and began gathering things, handing Aiela a perfect sand-dollar shell and Ahna a small pink conch. Pointing out the smallest scallops, sea urchins and cockles swimming in the wider cracks, she named each item in her language, indicating that they should touch, examine and gather as well. It was clear this was her private wonderland. *Like my rocks or Ahna's hammock.* Aiela thought.

The black rock extended out a long way into the sea, and each of them became absorbed in this shallow display of living shapes and colors, brought here by lost or foreign waves. It felt like an oasis of life in this bleak place, and a cautious joy crept into the moment.

"Tell her thank you. Tell her we like it here very much, and thank you for showing us."

When Carver translated, Brona looked glad, almost carefree in this captivating place.

Thirst stopped them, after a long time of bending and squatting on the sun-warmed black rock. Even wading in cool water didn't help. Carver told Brona they needed to head back and she nodded, gathering her assorted treasures into the skirt of her dirty linen tunic, not noticing the wet that seeped through.

She led them back towards her home, hugging the coast closer on the return walk.

"What's that?" Aiela pointed towards a pile of massive black stones, rising high to the edge of miniature cliffs that fell maybe thirty feet to the rocky beach.

Brona shook her head, frowning and walking swiftly inland to skirt around. But Aiela headed straight for them wanting to investigate what seemed a landmark on this desolate flatness.

"This is a dark place." Ahna cautioned her sister. "I don't know this energy. It's slow and dense….and strong. I feel spirits…"

"I know. It's interesting. Let's see if Brona will answer some questions."

Hearing her name, Brona stopped, waiting for them to continue with her, looking expectantly at Carver. They exchanged many words, going back and forth, Brona stubbornly refusing to come closer to where the twins were climbing up the rocks.

On top of the pile was what looked like an altar, an irregular slab balanced on two natural pillars.

"Careful." Ahna watched her sister peer off the steep side of the altar, almost straight down to the craggy beach.

"Holy gods", Aiela breathed, "are those skeletons?"

Ahna maneuvered to a vantage point and her eyes grew round.

"There's so many. Maybe this is what they do with their dead? A sort of burial ground?" Aiela felt a chill, staring at the tangle of bones below, exposed and salt-washed, twined with seaweed.

"No. Oh noooo, it's much worse than that…." Ahna had touched the altar. Her eyes closed and face cringing in a mask of horror, "they've *killed* them! On purpose….children, babies, people they don't like. It's awful! Why would they do that? So many dead babies…" She jumped back from the altar and grabbed Aiela's hand to pull her, scrambling down the rocks. "No wonder Brona doesn't want to be in this horrifying place! Let's go."

Aiela let her sister pull her away, shocked at what they'd seen, but also interested. "Do you think she would tell us about it? Should we ask? Is that rude or wrong somehow? I'm just really curious. What's happening here and why?"

Ahna shuddered, "Doubtful she'll want to talk about it—but the worst she can say is no."

Carver was standing close to Brona, the look on his face showed plainly he felt the evil here. "Brona is very upset."

They walked so swiftly behind Brona they were almost running.

When she slowed, Ahna touched her arm, "I'm sorry Brona. We didn't know....we shouldn't have stopped there when you didn't want to."

Brona nodded, her eyes accepting the compassionate tone even while Carver translated Ahna's words. She replied, saying many words, with Carver seeming to clarify several times. Tears appeared in Brona's eyes as she stopped abruptly and sat down on the sharp gray ground, hugging her arms around herself, rocking. When she finished speaking, Carver turned to the girls, his face heavy with emotion.

"She wants me to tell you this story. I hope I understood it right....the Chief—she calls him 'husband'—says they must make dead people for the gods. That the sea gods don't have human bodies, so when human bodies are given to them, they are happy and make good weather and bring food to the people. She says the Chief insists the gods like children and babies better so most of the sacrifices they make are young ones. Her own baby was killed there a short time ago...."

Aiela went to Brona, sitting on the rough ground beside her and wrapping her arms around the skinny, mourning girl. "No wonder you're so sad. Probably forced to marry that ugly, rotten, fat man, have his baby, and then he took it away from you. Forever. No wonder everyone here seems afraid and angry. I'm guessing he does this to control the people. Especially the women." Aiela was rocking Brona gently as she spoke. Her soothing tone belying the meaning of her words. "Maybe we should sacrifice the goddamn Chief. Maybe then you'd have some peace."

"I take it you don't want me to translate that part?" Carver said. "You know, it's not a bad idea though..."

"I don't understand how people could believe in gods like that and still agree to 'serve' them." Ahna spoke softly but Aiela could feel her outrage. It mirrored her own.

Carver replied with a knowing bitterness, "I'm sure it's less about the gods and more about the people. The whole 'gods like children and babies' thing is probably just population control so the Chief doesn't have so many mouths to feed. So the mothers aren't preoccupied and can work more—do whatever he wants more. I'm sure Aiela's right too, about him controlling the women through this. If they do anything to upset him, he will kill their children. I've seen this sort of thing before. It happens more places in the world than you'd think."

"Do you think Brona believes it? Believes in these angry gods? It almost seems worse if she doesn't, to know that her baby died for nothing. I guess either way she loses..." Ahna faded off, shaking her head sadly.

Carver crouched down in front of Brona, speaking compassionately to her. She considered a moment before answering him.

"I asked her what she believes about the gods. She says;

'There must be something more powerful than us, something who controls the world and all within it, but I don't believe sea gods would demand suffering. I've spent my entire life by the sea and it is not evil or good, it just is. So I do not believe any sea god would be evil or good either. If these gods do exist—ones that don't care about me—if they are that evil, than I don't care about them. I vowed the day my baby died to never do another thing for the gods, and I don't care what it costs me. Still, you have come bringing food. And the weather is well, so who's to say?' "

They helped Brona to her feet, and Aiela took the headband from her own hair, carefully placing it in Brona's, who looked younger with all the wind-loosened strands pushed back from her face. The contrasting shades of blue crystal beads brightened her auburn hair and looked stunning with her pale skin.

"I wish I had a mirror to show you," Aiela said, "how very pretty you look."

Brona smiled at the gift. Touching Aiela's cheek in thanks and then awkwardly hugging her. Her body reminded Aiela of the flamingo she'd treated long ago. Long and light as air, barely there.

Carver stayed beside Brona, talking to her for a while as they walked back. Aiela could tell from her expressions that whatever they discussed was serious but Brona seemed to walk a little taller after they quieted and Carver dropped back beside Ahna.

They were in sight of the shanty village when Aiela asked Carver. "What were you telling her? What were you talking about?"

Carver hesitated a moment. "I suggested she must know of some poisons, living by the sea all her life, she must know what can kill a person by ingesting it. I told her that if she is ever to be free, she will have to free herself—choose to go somewhere else and make a good life."

"You told her she should kill the Chief??" Aiela was stunned. "But that is not the answer! More death doesn't solve anything! What if she gets caught, what would he do to her then? How can you tell someone that! And what if she actually does it?!"

Carver stared levelly at her. "Then she might get a chance to be something other than a fat man's slave. That's what." He stalked off, leaving Ahna and Aiela in various states of disbelief, unable to communicate to Brona how very bad this idea seemed.

338

18

DEATH COMES SOFTLY

9,972 BCE CANADIAN MOUNTAINS

"... this passing is no conclusion, only a portal—a transformation..."

— ATLANTIS BOOK OF THE DEAD

*I*t was the twenty-seventh time that week, Drey and Taya ended up in a tangle, this time giggling in the snow.

Deciding nothing says adventure like skiing a far northern mountain range in summer, they planned to be gone one week while the twins were in Ireland. Single-mindedly committed to make that week sizzle, Taya packed enough to stay away for a full moon including snowshoes, skis, food, and all the warm clothing they could find. They'd sleep in the Aero and go home early if they tired of the cold.

Extended solitude and total freedom felt strange. They played the edge like teenagers, taking risks, delirious with wonder and happiness. Camping in the Aero, they hiked up one of the white-capped peaks every morning and skied down, dreaming up elaborate—and sometimes peculiar—fire-cooked meals to concoct from their provisions. They reminisced about their daughters, trying to guess what they might be seeing and doing this moment. Making love, reacquainting to each other, they could barely remember the last time they'd had this much time alone together. It felt like they'd run away from the world. From their lives, certainly.

Landing the aero by a stream at the base of a mountain range, they discovered it stayed chilly even in the height of summer-day. Dotting the spongy, grey-green tundra, high mountain flowers, so delicately pink you'd think a puff of wind could carry them off, sprang joyfully from the rocky mountain plateaus. Fat brown marmots and auburn hawks chased each other. Dirty white mountain goats played around them when they came to the stream to drink. Once, they glimpsed a Woolly Mammoth herd far off in the distance trumpeting, on their ponderous slow path across the horizon.

At night, wolf packs prowled, their mournful hunting howls carrying for miles in the still cold air. Before dusk, they built roaring fires to huddle by. Twice, they woke to watch the northern lights pulse and swirl and dance across the sky. Like otherworldly air goddesses, the brilliant colors seemed completely outside earthly color spectrum, undulating sensually as if making visual love to both earth and sky.

Today had been almost balmy. Brilliant sunlight woke up the snow below like a million grains of rainbow diamond, while above them a sky of deep blue swirls hugged the earth with determined serenity, as if bent on introducing eternity into the earth's present moment.

They were at the summit of a smallish mountain, struggling on the ground, with Taya astride Drey, pushing his face into the snow with all her might. He'd deposited huge chunks of snow crust down her sweater front *and* back. Now she was trying to bury his head in it.

"Cold isn't it love? If I could get to it, I'd pack your bumcrack full. That's right, keep it up. Maybe you'll wake up tonight with your ass freezing and melting all over your bedroll! Hahaha."

Drey, weakened by laughter, still struggled faintly to dislodge his indignant wife. Once she got going like this, running off at the mouth, it was so comical he would get the giggles, unable to stop.

He pushed up suddenly with his legs, bucking her off and slamming his body down on top of her. Rubbing his cold wet face against hers, he kissed her until her writhing began to arouse him. She kissed him back until he began pulling at her layers of clothes.

"Drey if you think I'm taking my clothes off out here—" His next kiss stilled her. She pushed at him. "No! I'm cold and wet and hungry!"

He rolled off and helped her up. Finding their short wide skis, they strapped them on, still taunting each other, and raced down the mountain, stopping only twice to find better routes.

It was late afternoon when they reached the Aero.

Drey fed her first. Seducing her slowly and completely with nutty cheeses and soft bread, and spiced pear wine, until she grew as passionate and wanton as he was. Bringing her to the edge of desire, he cooled them both a little with a deep massage on her tired leg muscles, before they brought each other back again to that aching urgent need.

"Mmm, I love your body. It's... *luscious.*" Drey murmured.

"You mean largish." Taya retorted.

"No, I mean it's...savory", Drey said. I've fully enjoyed you at every stage." He wiggled an eyebrow and smiled a naughty sly smile. "I like it best like this. Muscular or gaunt seemed nice at the time, but that's only because I'd never experienced you when you're soft and full."

He truly had taken pleasure in every change that her body underwent through the years. There had been gawky early adulthood when they'd met, and then a muscular filling out during her twenties. The firm plumpness of pregnancy lasted only a short time while thirties were gaunt with muscle loss after having two babies with double the feeding, chasing and fatigue. She'd regularly forgotten to eat during that time, and had lost probably too much weight. Now, several changes later, she'd filled in a little, "in all the right places", Drey often commented, demonstrating exactly which places he meant with his fingers and lips.

Rogan

Two Mutazio were enjoying the show from their perch amongst the trees just above the aero. Watching the small man and his woman laughingly play together, and then physically love each other deepened the muta's pleasure of what was to come. Killing was bred into them. They couldn't help that it gave them a release. Fulfilling the commands of their master was another of the few pleasures they experienced.

The Mutazio had known only great abuse. Created to be slaves, their sole purpose was to fulfill man's darkest urges. They'd not experienced or seen love, it was completely foreign to them.

"Whad they do?" The taller one asked Rogan, forming awkward syllables in a nasally voice, like a child trying to pronounce complex words.

"They make love." Rogan responded darkly.

"Whad?" The two oversized men squinted questioning eyes at Rogan.

"Why. You mean to say '*why* do they do that?'" Rogan corrected. He was in no mood to teach these two the intricacies of human sexuality, but he did want to teach them better language. He'd spent too much time around Mutazio to think they were better left dumb, as Mardu believed. Rogan's muta camps were the most organized and peaceful of them all, due entirely to the fact that he built up the muta's intelligence. They loved to learn, and they showed gratitude for humane treatment by being eager to please their masters. The camps not under Rogan's command, suffered too many losses due to chaos, and violence. The sort of violence that happens when ignorance combines with boredom and begats meaning-lessness at epic levels.

"It feels good to them. Good like when you eat. Good like when you sleep in comfort." Rogan explained.

The Mutazio grunted their comprehension and approval. Eating and sleeping were *very* good indeed. "Good like kill?" The big one asked. They grinned at their ability to make their own example.

Rogan had brought two of the more intelligent mutas with him to complete this task, but he wasn't enjoying it like the nine and ten-foot-tall, numbered skinheads by his side.

It was a rare privilege for any of the Mutazio to leave their camps. Travel in an aero, seeing portions of the rest of the world, watching the ways of the strange small people, was an unimaginably bright spot in their dismal and harsh lifespans.

The three of them had been shadowing Drey and Taya the entire time they had been here,, waiting for an opportunity. "It must appear an acci-dent." Mardu had warned Rogan. "If the Oracles suspect it was anything else, they will examine it until they see the truth."

And if any Atlanteans learned the truth, there would be repercussions. There were strict blood laws signed by Onus Belial himself, about crimes committed between the two nations. If Sons of Belials took the lives of Atlanteans, the penalty was particularly steep. Portions of Belial land would have to be ceded back to Atlantis. Enough violations and the Belials would lose all rights to any of the land on the Atlantis continent. Rogan knew High City would not hesitate to enforce it. Atlanteans took murder to be the ultimate sin against their Law of One.

No, they must be carefully clever here. If anyone should discover this murder, they would have the Oracles digging tirelessly into the *why* until they'd likely uncover all the things Mardu needed to hide. That would ruin everything. Yes, it must look like an accident, even though no one was watching—especially since no one was watching.

The fashion of slaying was vexing Rogan. He couldn't poison them—Drey knew too much about plants for that to be believable—and he certainly couldn't strangle them. He'd thought about inducing a pack of wolves to attack them, or sabotaging their aero so it crashed on the trip home. But the wolf plan had too many variables and the aero-crashing plan could leave behind too many clues. Still, they were good backup ideas.

Avalanche conditions abounded here, certainly a most believable accident. They'd made two attempts already but the mountains had refused to cooperate. Rogan was starting to lose faith in his brilliant scheme.

"C'mon you two. Let's go eat." Rogan heaved a sigh, setting off for their sparse camp nearby. They'd need to get up early the next day to stay ahead of their targets.

Taya

Drey and Taya woke to another unusually warm day. Building a fire to boil tea, poaching the last of their eggs in the leftover water, and bundling up a pack of water and food each, took until the sun was mid-high. They had decided to trek up the tallest peak today, at least as far as was safe.

It was steeper—much slower-going than any of the other mountains but this would be their last run before heading home. They wanted to make it count.

"I wonder what the girls are doing right now—this very minute?" Drey panted, squinting into the bright distance. He wondered this aloud, at least three times a day.

"Probably trying new foods, playing games, maybe learning Irish—or kissing boys." Taya replied, smirking as her last remark instantly soured Drey's face. He hated to be reminded that they weren't his little girls anymore. She'd been trying to ease him into the idea that they'd eventually love other men, ever since the twins had started showing romantic interest in boys. That had been almost seven years ago. Taya was losing hope that he would ever accept any mate the girls chose.

"I should've gone on board and talked to every one of those boys. Told them what I'll do if they don't treat my baby girls with respect." Drey huffed.

"Mm, but seeing as how they're my *grown* daughters, it's much more likely you should've gone on board to *warn* those poor unsuspecting boys, give them a fighting chance to resist becoming the playthings of our sweet girls. They're not innocent or helpless, certainly less so than I was at their age and that's saying something! I have no doubt whatsoever they're having rollicking ventures." She paused to turn around and plant a brief kiss on his nose. "We've taught them well Drey—and they always have each other. That's what gives me peace. They've got way more advantages than you or I did."

"I forget sometimes. I just....miss them. I'm going to miss them too much when they leave to apprentice. It hurts to even think about it. I really think we should relocate to High City. I can work from *anywhere*. That's unusual you know, it's got to be a sign, there's a *reason* we're situated to be mobile and I think this is it." Drey said.

Taya shook her head. This again. He wasn't going to give up. He'd been trying to convince her they should move—should follow their offspring halfway across the country like those clingy parents who just couldn't let their younglings fly.

A pair of giant eagles with wing spans bigger than Drey's height, flew in graceful circles overhead and Taya stopped to watch them play and hunt. She stood still, catching her breath, her mind still on the twins so far away.

The air filling rapidly with snowflakes didn't register at first—and then the sound reached them.

Drey lept to Taya's side and they'd turned towards the mountain just in time to see the first fist-sized rocks falling at them. Followed by a hundred tons of snow.

They grabbed on to each other as the snowpack beneath their feet moved, and became a rolling wave under them. Face to face, arms wrapped tightly around each other's bodies, they were flung violently downwards, tumbling over and over—and then buried underneath a silent sea of white.

Still clinging tightly to each other minutes later, they died from suffocation. Their lungs unable to expand under the tremendous weight of snow, ice and rocks atop them.

Physical pain from the multiple broken places in their bodies registered, but already, it was quickly detaching from their awareness.

By the time fear might've settled in, their spirits were rising together, leaving behind the miraculous body-shells that had harboured, sheltered and grown them so lovingly for so long. They knew an instant of deep peace as in a flash, the mysteries of the universe were returned to their consciousness. Their last earthbound thoughts were of their daughters, their precious babies who were orphans now.

As the whole and magnificent eternal souls of Drey and Taya passed from this illusion, homebound to another dimension, they shared sadness at the loss their girls would feel. But much much more was the knowing— the surety, that everything was deeply alright. Perfect, complete, and good.

. . .

Rogan

Rogan sat with his simpleton giants amongst the boulder field for two full hours following the live burial of the targets. The view was spectacular up here. The sun, warm on their backs, called forth the mountains voice of booming pops and resounding cracks, as ice molded stone under the blinding snow.

He had to make sure the couple didn't somehow survive to dig themselves out. It would take more than a miracle for anyone to escape the rearranging of this entire mountainside, but his luck lately had been consistently irksome.

Their early morning hike up this mountain had been arduous. Having to stay out of sight meant taking a dangerous route and if it hadn't been for the inconceivable strength of the mutas, his plan would've failed a third time. He'd found a mammoth-sized boulder perched just right, but it had taken all three of their strengths to get it rolling. It bounced twice on the steep snowfields below and the ensuing chain reaction conspired with gravity to complete the rest.

Rogan congratulated them on their efforts. Kind words were the ultimate reward. Immensely relieved that it was finally done, he promised them sweets during the return trip, rendering them ecstatic. They whooped and hollered, galloping around him in circles, burning off the high of a successful murder, playing like great hulking children in the sun-bright snow. With no concept that they too would be dead in a few more hours. Their candy would be poison, then Rogan would drop them out the aero door into the churlish sea. Their great carcasses becoming feasts for some lucky sea-monster. Maybe he'd even wait until they were unconscious so they wouldn't be afraid.

Watching them discover and enjoy their expanded world these last few days had touched him somehow—no matter how he'd resisted or ignored it. He felt shame for this softness, so unexpected, creeping in lately. He blamed it on aging. What a nuisance, growing a conscience now.

It was really too bad losing these good Mutazio but there could be no evidence, no loose ends from these last few days. Even the aero he came here in would be destroyed so its travels couldn't be tracked. Rogan made himself return to his usual emotionless thoughts. Lethal cold, but thorough. The thing that made him Mardu's number one General.

LAND OF GIANTS

"Remember this when you think you are seeing giants, they may not be giants at all; perhaps it is you who is the dwarf."

— C. JOYBELL C.

AHNA

*T*hey'd entered a realm of verdant birdsong, brazen and bold, that competed with the cicada anthems. Each trying to drown out the other.

Aiela mused, "It's easy to imagine giants living here. Everything seems bigger. That lake back there—"

"Loch", Turner corrected.

"You say loch I say lake." Aiela retorted. "It looks like a giant scooped it out, then filled it with water." Aiela had always been imaginative. She curled beside Ahna in the creaking wagon, as they trundled towards Ireland's northernmost coast.

"Why would a giant have done that?" Carver inquired over his shoulder. He was sitting on the driver's bench, keeping Turner company and switching off driving the wagon.

"Probably had his buddy Balor broil it with his evil eye into a hot pool to seduce some girl." Aiela poked Turner in the back. He shot back a sly grin.

"Maybe he just needed a mirror to shave in." Carver absently rubbed sparse dark stubble on his chin, watching the loch surface reflect an aqua sky that peeked between clouds moving apart, then together again.

"Prob'ly joost wanted ta swim." Turner said.

"Or maybe *she* was beautifying the land around her home...and planted herself a garden—look at those huge flowering bushes. They're as big as the trees!" Ahna joined this conversation she'd been observing, still wrapped in her bedroll. Unable to sleep, she'd listened to raindrops pelt the tarp overhead for the last two hours. A rainstorm now faded to vapor with thin sunlight poking through.

"How much farther?" Aiela asked.

"Two hours mebbe. We're gettin' close. Soon ya should be able ta smell the sea. Shall we stop ta eat or keep goin'?" Turner conferred with Aiela as he always did when making decisions for the group.

"Let's keep going if we're that close. What do you think Ahna? Carver?"

"Fine with me." Ahna was still gazing back at the glossy loch, glowing pink reflections of the huge flowering bushes instead of the usual umber tones of still water.

"Do the aurochs need a stop? If not, might as well keep moving."

Carver was curiously relaxed, Ahna thought, studying his back, long and lean, shoulders flared like a soaring raven beneath the large-weave black tunics he wore. She wanted to touch the sinewed spread, randomly wondering how many years he was. He seemed experienced, older than apparent.

She wanted to ask him, but some questions just made him go silent and she was never sure what was neutral and what was part of his secrets. *Why am I attracted to such a complex person? And what is it about me that he can't or won't trust?* Her thoughts began to spiral, mind spinning stories, insistent on groping through all the unanswered questions. Why this inexplicable need to fill in the bottomless blanks in her understanding of who Carver was?

"When do you celebrate your birth day?" Ahna posed the question to both boys at once.

"My next will be August ten." Turner replied.

Carver said nothing so Ahna asked Turner, "And how many years will you be?"

"Twenty-one, although I don' much feel like it." Turner shook his head. "It's strange ta be this number in years an' still feelin' an ignorant child." He snorted. "Still actin' it too, accordin' ta Mam."

Ahna and Aiela both nodded in understanding.

"We've just passed our eighteenth birth day." Ahna was aware of how stiff Carver's back had gone, his loud, steely silence. Apparently this was not one of the neutral subjects.

"And you Carver?" Aiela had no such sensitivity to his secrets.

"Twenty-two. I'm not sure...." Carver was mumbling so soft it was hard to catch the words. "....be back later, need to find Dromm." He jumped down off the wagon, standing still to let each wagon behind pass him by.

"What'd he say?" Aiela crawled up into Carver's abruptly vacated seat, losing her balance in the swaying, jostle of a bumpy road.

"He said he's no' sure what exact date he was born, and that he will return after he finds Drommen." Turner shrugged, then beamed his delight as Aiela sprawled beside him. "Right bonny ya are t'day! Sure an' I'll teach ya how ta drive... "

Ahna went back to watching the passing foliage. The road was winding up and over hills, narrow—really just muddy wheel ruts in the overthick grass. More often than not, the faded road was lined with huge rocks colored a middle grey, sometimes carpeted with rich green moss. Stones were stacked into fences and cairns as if the surrounding grass-covered hillsides had been cleared for some long ago purpose.

So much for trying to fill in any Carver blanks. She sighed, digging the eggplant-colored journal Papa had given Aiela back in Armanth, out of her pack. They'd been sharing it, since hers now belonged to some pinch-faced boy who had to forage, scratch and steal to keep from starving. She'd written in it sporadically, not every day, mainly just the highlights of their travel experiences. But there were whole pages about Carver.

"Late morning, travelling close to the northmost point of Ireland.

Attempted to ask how many years Carver is. He said he is twenty-two, (older than I expected) but didn't know the exact day. Then he left. It must have something to do with his not having a mother. Why does he react so oddly to normal questions?

There's times I wish I'd never met him. It would be better than having this blistering desire. Better than this feeling of needing someone I probably can never have. There are moments of glory like teeny tiny islands in a sea of wanting more. Moments when I really see him and he connects to me and there is this enormous....something that we share. What is it? Passion? Love?

Those sound very cliche.

I know he is attracted to me. I feel the energy coming from him like a reflection of my grasping heart, but he refuses what he feels.

And why him? There are twenty-some other boys here. What is this mysterious force that dictates I must want Carver and the rest of them won't interest me a bit?

Everyone's grouchy—or perhaps it's just me. I'm wearied of damp and bugs. Mindsick of being with people constantly. Maybe it's the gloom and insanity of Balor's Island still clinging. Healer Lira said last night, while the girls were all bickering and sniping over who would sleep where, that every group reaches this point. That so much travel and foreign food and activity wears us down at a level we don't understand. I just know that I'm ready to be done.

Except then I might never see Carver again.

A bunch of the girl's menstrual has started, so that doesn't help. Aiela and I have at least another week before ours, one thing to be grateful for!

20

CARVER AND JAYDEE

"Three may keep a secret, if two of them are dead."

— BENJAMIN FRANKLIN

CARVER

*H*e was sick to death of hiding. Tired of half-truths and secrets. Hating the constant fear that these gallant, caring, light-hearted companions would discover things about him they wanted nothing to do with. What would they say if they knew they were the closest friends he'd ever had? He couldn't bear the thought of Ahna's pity. *I can't share even the simplest parts of who I am with her.*

At least he hadn't lied. He really didn't know when he had been born. His alleged age was based on what Orja told him. His father neither cared, nor kept track of his day of birth. Carver screwed up his courage and asked once, a very long time ago, and his father just looked disgusted. "Why would I know that? Your mother should be here raising you, telling you that sort of thing. Now you see the sort of selfish, heartless whore she was..."

Trailing behind the supply wagon, as far from the lead wagon, and Ahna, as he could get, He released some of his frustrations in the exertion of climbing, looping far up the hillside then back down, avoiding the twisting tracks rutted deeply in some places where water runoff took advantage of any place lacking vegetation. Lush green smells and the calls of unfamiliar birds soothed him and he rooted his attention into their safe haven. Anything that kept him from contemplating how torn he was between this unexpected opportunity to love and be loved, and the vile life that threatened even here, far away from home, to imprison and condemn.

"Carver. Youngest son of Dominus Mardu...." The voice was tawdry, mocking, and Carver's gaze jerked up in shock. Jaydee was striding towards him. He'd lagged quite some distance behind their convoy. Couldn't even see it any more.

"Wh-What did you say?!?" His voice held confusion.

"You heard me. I know exactly who you are—don't worry, we're on the same side. You are so much like your father..."

He knew she'd meant it as a compliment. The words curdled inside him like drops of vinegar in new cream. But he was a lifelong expert at hiding his reactions. "Who told you that and why would you believe it?" He made his voice sound light, even innocently baffled.

Jaydee fell into stride, lacing her arm through his as if they were long-time friends. "Oh Carver, there is so much you don't understand. What would you say to a little exchange of information? I've known your father since long before you were born. I know that you don't want your sunny little friends—especially that sweet thing Ahna—to discover your true identity. I know you were sent on this trip for a specific purpose. Tell me, was it to get close to her? Are you reporting back to your father on the twins? What did he tell you about them?"

Carver stopped, jerking his arm away so hard she lost her balance and stumbled to recover. Struggling to understand how a High City teacher could know who he was, he laughed a harsh rebuttal, "No! I've no idea what you're talking about. What is this, what do you want from me?"

Jaydee laughed. Tossing long, travel-greased hair in the breeze, strands stuck to her overly red-glossed lips. "Oh fine, I will just have to earn your trust. Since I know who you are and what you're here for, it's only fair that I give you the same. Besides, we might as well work together." She started walking and Carver did too, wary, mind racing with all the possibilities. Was she a spy for High City, who'd found out about him somehow? What else did she know? How was he going to keep her quiet? Mardu would be furious, demand to know how Carver had fixed this obvious leak. Would he need to kill her? It'd have to look like a convincing accident...

"Relax. I said I'm on your side." Jaydee was looking sideways, watching him as he sifted through dark thoughts, "Mardu sent me here on his errand as well. I've no idea why he thought there was a need for both of us, but then he is smarter than the two of us put together isn't he? And he was sort of right, I mean you have succeeded in wooing one of our little subjects within hours of landing here, and becoming brotherly with the other one—whereas I have nothing to show for the last moon of trying. Which is why it's time to reveal myself to you. You know how Mardu is. If I return to him empty handed....well, he can be rather stern I'm sure you know....I won't tell him how much you actually care about these whom you're betraying and you won't tell him that I failed in my duties." Her tongue darted to lips that didn't need moistening like a reptile's, flicking out to test the air. Her tone smoothed, "I am the only one here that you can trust but you *can* trust me Carver, that I promise. So. What have you learned about them?" She managed to sound malicious and cheery all at once.

"You were sent to watch the twins? Why? What exactly did my father ask you to discover?" Was she lying? If so, she was an expert deceiver, there had been no indications. He knew Mardu had spies in High City, but it certainly went both ways. Of course the Atlanteans would have their own networks of intelligence watching the Sons of Belials.

So which was she?

Jaydee was silent, deciding, Carver was sure, how to play this.

"I wasn't given details of why..." Her level eye contact told him she was speaking truth. "Mardu's instructions were to get close to the girls. Specifically, report how their relationship is with their parents and what the family secrets are. What they know of their parent's lives and how they feel about the Sons of Belial."

"How do you know my father? Why would a High City teacher spy for the great Dominus Mardu?"

"I think it is your turn to share information Carver. I've told you enough. Now it's time you report to me what you have learned—it's your father's command."

She was an amatuer liar after all. Breaking eye contact, body tensing, holding her breath, Carver knew she was bluffing with this insinuation that he was to report to her. Clearly, she had no idea what his real purpose was and assumed he was gathering information on the girls like she was supposed to.

At least now Carver had an excuse for having a relationship with Ahna. He'd simply tell Mardu that Jaydee was unable to gain their trust, so he had seduced Ahna—a seduction of total pretense of course. Mardu would believe that readily. He believed all relationships to be strategic pretense.

But why was Mardu interested in them? Carver's stomach clenched at this thought.

"You're a bad liar Jaydee." He said softly. "That's not how it works. If you knew Mardu as well as you claim to, you'd know this about him; there is no hierarchy, everyone reports directly to him and only him." Carver stared at her coldly, letting unspoken accusations accumulate on his face.

She stared back with narrowing eyes, knife-sharp words suddenly twisted with sarcasm. "You know, I could 'accidentally' slip, place just enough doubt into her pretty little golden head that her lover-boy is only using her. I know that you care about her, you can't fake it that well, and the way she looks at you? Well it would break her tiny stupid heart to learn that everything she sees in you is a lie. How would the rest of this god-awful trip be for you then? Losing these nice new friends you have....poor poor Carver—sent to do a job and ends up falling in love." Jaydee's threatening hiss turned mocking. She'd stopped walking and gripped his arm like a vise.

His logical brain knew she was bluffing again but the thought of her hurting Ahna—the thought of anyone hurting Ahna—blinded him with instinctual rage.

He snatched her hand from his arm, crushing the bones of her wrist, puffing up to full height, looming over her. His other hand had wrapped her throat. He could strangle her right here, right now. Eliminate the threat that she was to him and all that he loved. End this dark confusing game she was playing...

He watched, detached, as her face turned slowly to purple-red. Her body odor fouling the air, discernible even over the sharp lilac perfume that assaulted the nose of anyone within three rods of her.

First she squeaked through her constricted throat and kicked him. Then she panicked, started prying at his hand to get free.

Only when her body weakened and stopped responding to her frenzied fight for air did he finally let go. He flung her away so hard that she crumpled, wheezing in the grass.

He stalked after her. His tone grated low and harsh. "Don't you EVER threaten me! We do things my way. If I so much as see you talking to either of those girls—if I even suspect you've said a word about me to anyone on this trip, I will make sure that you never return to Atlantis. I am the son of Mardu! Cross me in any way and I will have you hunted down. I will ensure that you and anyone you ever loved will suffer..." Carver's face was inches from hers. He knew she believed him from the way she cowered. A single tear trailed silently down her cheek as she raggedly sucked and gasped for the air he had deprived her of.

He stood up, slowed his breathing, willed his rage under control. "You can tell my father that the twins know nothing. That we've talked days and hours and they know nothing that concerns us in any way. That's what I will report because that's the truth. If our reports don't match, he'll think *you're* lying. Do you know what Mardu does to liars?"

The look of terror that flashed in her eyes before she managed to veil it, revealed much to Carver. She was Mardu's spy, and she knew exactly what he did to liars.

He turned and jogged to catch up with the wagons, shuddering at how precisely he'd echoed his father, how he even thought like Mardu. He wished he had more time to process this, to sort through all the variables and decide what to do next, how to stay one step ahead of them. But all he could think about was getting to Ahna's side. Protecting her from Jaydee's evil manipulations—which really meant protecting her from himself...

He swung up over the wagon side, landing breathless beside Ahna. Her surprised smile welcomed him back and he touched her sun-warm hand with icy fingertips, heart jumping around like it always did when he was near her. He traced the scar curving down her face, healed now to a faded garnet line. "I was thinking, since you just had your birth day, I shall have to give you a gift. It might take time but I'll come up with the perfect idea..."

Ahna reacted slowly to him, making him realize how intense he was being. He didn't care. This girl made him want to change everything about himself. Be the man she deserved—someone she could be proud of. Someone who wasn't expected to betray her love.

2 1

AHNA'S GAMES

And who could play it well enough, if deaf and dumb and blind with love?
He that made this knows the cost,For he gave all his heart and lost."

— W.B. YEATS

AHNA

*I*t was concerning. Carver's energy felt off when he arrived back panting—completely different than when he'd left. Like anyone, he had a definite scale of moods, but this seemed off his scale. She connected to him fully, laying a palm on his knee, meeting his eyes. His nearness combined their energy fields and she concentrated on what his felt like; confusion-edged anger, black fear. Intensity.

"What happened back there?" She eyed him baldly, directly addressing what she felt.

He shook his head and shrugged, his hand dropping from her face, not meeting her eyes.

"Something did, I feel it in you." She pressed.

"Nothing important." He lied, turning away to watch the distant mountains. She registered lies as easily as changes in temperature. The energy of it felt like walking into a wall. Why couldn't he trust her yet?

355

But still he held onto her hand with both of his. Ahna could feel emotions warring in him.

Sighing out frustration, Ahna spoke quietly, "Let's walk awhile. You don't have to answer questions. I promise not to pry."

He nodded, stepping over the wagon edge to land heavily.

Ahna made to jump off but he lifted her slowly to the ground. They were face to face for just seconds but when their eyes met, something in him tore at her, like the keening of a lonely death song.

They walked for a long time in silence and he almost clung to her hand, no longer seeming to care if everyone saw their affection.

She broke the silence to point out patterns the lichen made on rocks, some yellow as mustard, others pale silvery green, as if sea foam had pooled and dried into images, animals or faces.

Carver reciprocated by pointing out how the distant mountains resembled giants, snoring on their backs. "They probably just got old, laid down on beds of gorse and bramble to sleep forever. After the alders and birch and hazel trees grew up over their great carcasses, no one thought to search beneath for the bones of giants who never left this land."

His imagination was like a child's, Ahna realized. Challenging her to believe that everything was possible, like she used to when she was younger.

Falling into easy, conversational rhythm, they stayed in sight of the last wagon but far enough away from the other students who had spilled out around the convoy.

His energy calmed in increments and she relaxed into the midday sunshine and its warm business of drying out the liverwort and sedges and wood-rushes.

They shared what their expectations had been for this trip, versus the reality of it. Wondered about the oddities and talents and futures of various trip companions and teachers. Safe subjects, Ahna noticed. Nothing that might lead to his personal history or homelife. *Maybe it's the fact that he's a Belial and I'm Atlantean. Is that a much larger obstacle to him than it seems to me?*

Carver plucked a tiny blue wildflower, presenting it to her.

Inhaling deeply, she sighed, "Ahhh, I smell the sea. We're almost there." They both strained, shielding their eyes towards the horizons ahead, but no roiling movement, no watershine reflected back yet.

"Close your eyes," Ahna took his hands, dancing mischievously in front of him. "Trust me to guide you. Now, tell me everything that you hear." She led him, blindly describing the bouquet of sounds he perceived.

Next came scents. Admiring the gentleness of his voice as he described how the world smelled to him, she guided him with only a few stumbles, along the flattening road.

He insisted she do the same, expanding the game to include tastes in the air and sensations on her skin, going beyond those even, exploring her ability to sense the energy or emotions in his aura. He seemed fascinated by this, asking her many questions about how she used her additional sense.

By now, her earlier caustic mood had passed. After all, this was what she'd wanted most, just to be with him. It felt like regular joy multiplied—or squared.

Seagulls screamed their shrewd demands long before they rounded a hill to find the ocean straight ahead, closer than Ahna anticipated, bringing the horizon to sparkling life as the water's eternal motion winked hope at them.

Everyone spilled from the wagons, excited to explore this new destination.

ALL THROUGH FINDING the massive stone fortress where they would sleep tonight, organizing teams to unload the wagons, carrying bags, and preparing food, Carver never once left her side.

THE GENERALS

TEMPLE CITY, BELIAL

Power is not a means; it is an end. One does not establish a dictatorship in order to safeguard a revolution; one makes the revolution in order to establish the dictatorship. The object of persecution is persecution. The object of torture is torture. The object of power is power."

— GEORGE ORWELL

MARDU

*M*ardu wore tyrian purple, its red undertones commanding the attention he was due in a room of uniform black.

Newly painted battle scenes covered the walls in shocking colors, and slim-fitting side tables held collections of their newest weaponry displayed as thoughtfully as fine art. Sword-shaped crystal sconces with intricate hilts and brightly lit blades, cast long, sharpened light pools at intervals around the room.

"General Rogan will lead the land troops, consisting primarily of our muta army. General Pompeii will lead the seaward attack." Mardu said. His great black head swiveled to address the statuesque young man who stood at attention, refusing to sit or lounge like the older Generals. Pompeii kept his hair trimmed short, his body a model of discipline and his manner an odd blend of arrogance and absolute devotion to the cause for which he fought.

"Of course, General Pompeii, you will wait until the Grecians are focused on—fully engaged with—the land battle. They will be forced to leave their shores lightly defended in order to stop the Mutazio, allowing you, with our own Belial warriors, to overtake their capital city."

Pompeii bowed curtly as Mardu's gaze swept down the long table, studying these dozen men he trusted most. His elite. They would carry out his commands, leading the Belials to victory and a glory long dreamt of. Power hungry and smart enough to follow whomever could hand them more, he'd chosen only men who shared his vision.

"Once their rulers are at our mercy, I will express that we don't care over-much about ruling Greece, we simply ask their army to back up ours when needed, and their allegiance to Belial instead of Atlantis. They will be so relieved at our simple requests and merciful terms, they will end up welcoming us to celebrate the successful end of such a brief war." The men laughed and nodded at each other. "It is this image that I want you to sear into the minds of our warriors; they will soon be drinking, eating, dancing and perhaps one day fighting, alongside these Grecians we go to conquer—so go easy, do only what is necessary to overcome them. We go not to wage war, but to earn their respect and allegiance. The battle will be staged only as a neces-sity, to convince Greece of our power and the wisdom of allying with Belial."

He pointed. "General Pompeii will now acquaint us with his maps of Greece, then General Rogan will outline his plan of attack." Mardu sat in the high-backed, ornately carved chair at the head of the table, and motioned at the man to his right to refill his brandy.

Inhaling the smoky sweet aroma, he sipped, watching with satisfaction as the erect and slightly regal Pompeii touched points on the maps spread across the table. Explaining in great detail the locations of Grecian border defenses, the coastal bases, and how long it would take the soldiers to travel from point to point, thereby creating advantage if Belial was strategic in their initial attacks.

This battle room lay deep under the General building, another layer of precaution against their plans leaking. Every one of these men were sworn to silence until the opportune time. They would spend the next few months making final preparations, and no one else—not even their own warriors—would know what was happening until they were en-route.

Pompeii was the youngest of them. Driven by some internal force that

Mardu hadn't quite decoded, he had come to Mardu while still a hoarse-voiced boy, begging to be trained and allowed the honor of protecting Belial's greatest leader. An immigrant from Greece, Pompeii had wanted more than the hardscrabble life his family offered. Believing he was meant for greater things, he'd abandoned home young, to seek his destiny and build his fortune. Mardu had put him under the care of General Hercule, also from that continent, and by the time Pompeii was a man, he did indeed become part of Mardu's personal guard. He worked so hard, training and fighting, Mardu soon reassigned him, loathe to waste or curb the potential of such dedication. Now, it had all paid off beyond measure. Pompeii had left behind extended family, spread across the land, and he eagerly exploited those ties, gaining intelligence. Information that would render a merely successful battle, into an easy—even simplistic—one.

"General Rogan, I defer to you." Pompeii finished speaking and bowed, stepping back to attention again, while Rogan stood to speak.

When the planning was complete, the Generals broke into pairs or threes, conferring privately on related matters.

Mardu leaned in, speaking softly to the man on his left, "Rogan, anything to report concerning the matter I asked you to see to?"

Rogan nodded. "It is done."

"Excellent, and you've no want I can further provide for?" Mardu enjoyed acting the magnanimous leader, seeing to every desire of those under his care.

"All is in order, thank you Dominus." Rogan bowed his head in respect, face neutral, even though Mardu knew the assigned errand seemed a bothersome pettiness to him, a task that someone else could have completed.

"News from the muta camps? The vaccinations are working?" Mardu was sometimes perturbed that Rogan didn't offer much. You had to ask the right questions.

"The news is mostly good; no new outbreaks and the Mutazio are battle ready. Sending our warriors to spar with them has not only eased the restless troops—both man and muta, but is honing skills. Any weaknesses the Mutazio have, we address, adjusting their training." Rogan stood to leave. He didn't socialize and his business here was complete.

Hercule, Pompeii and Hercule's own son, (a flaccid, unremarkable man who liked to boast of adopting Pompeii as his younger brother) moved in to speak with Mardu.

"Oh, before I go," Rogan turned back, interrupting the trio of Generals, "did Jaydee find anything with the daughters?"

"No. We've no worries from them. Sounds like they've got their heads in the clouds, concerned only with shallow dramas of romance and pretty baubles." Mardu replied.

Hercule's son inserted himself into the conversation with a snort. "That describes Jaydee herself, real good. I wouldn't trust that bitch's word on anything. You're sure we shouldn't have sent a better spy to judge that situation?"

Hercule and Pompeii blanched as the puffy-chested son blundered on, continuing to peer at Mardu, whose neck was slowly turning the color of his tunic.

"Are you *questioning* me?" Mardu's volume rose, drawing the full attention of the room.

"No Dominus, of course not, I'm questioning Jaydee. She's made too many unwise decisions, remember the time she—" Mardu's fist stopped the offensive words, smashing the unbearable man's lips and nose in a burst of bright blood-splatter. He flew back against the wall, stunned first, then angry.

"I said I'm NOT questioning you..." Hercule's son shouted, defiant with pain.

Mardu hit him again, vicious fists connecting in rapid succession with both temples. Ending with a powerful open palm, he broke the man's nose, head slamming against the wall so hard it bounced violently off, and the man ended on his hands and knees at Mardu's feet. Mardu kicked the blood covered face, flipping the body onto its back. His booted foot pressed on the man's windpipe.

"Mercy Dominus, mercy, he is my *son*." Hercule whispered, eyes bulging in fear and despair at what he knew he could not stop.

Mardu waited until he had made eye contact with every man in the room, excepting the one gasping and flailing at his leg in terror. The rage was still coursing through him, blending now, with the familiar surge of absolute power, the anticipation of doing anything he wanted with the life he held under his boot.

So frail life always seemed in the end.

He paused, not just to make sure each of his men internalized this lesson, but to enjoy this build-up towards the ultimate climax, a thrill that nothing else compared to.

His foot was a blur when he finally lifted it, stomped down with most of his considerable weight. The flaccid man made the funniest noise, a sort of high wheezy scream, then went limp, before the inevitable stink of releasing his bowels.

"Clean it up." Mardu said softly to Pompeii. Then to Hercule, placing an arm about the old, weakening shoulders, "Come old friend. Let me comfort you in your grief."

Orja

"It may've been too far...do you think Hercu...cu...Hercu-EL will turn on me now?" Mardu was slurring, slow and sloppy-drunk as Orja helped him into bed. This dance happened only on days he questioned himself.

"Of course not. You can't allow your men to doubt you. You know well what to do about Hercule, a gift may be in order, something extravagant. Perhaps a luxury home and land...on another continent?" Orja knew that Mardu would remember none of this conversation in the morning, just like she knew exactly which hangover remedies would be required to get him back on his feet.

The older he got, the more he seemed to value her. Life had gotten better over the years and she'd wondered often, while raising his brood of sons to adulthood, and running his household for over two decades, why he was kinder to her than any other woman. Why he hadn't ever tried to rape her.

"Do you know what happened last time I let some'un dish-dish...dishrespect me?"

"Tell me." Orja climbed into the middle of the enormous bed, sitting with her back against a solid orichalcum headboard so shiny it reflected the plush room like a red-lustered mirror. She arranged Mardu's large messy head onto her lap. He didn't like to fall asleep alone when he got like this. "Tell me what happened," she smoothed back the thick black hair that spilled over his face. The story came in fits and pauses.

"They all loved me y'know, in High City. Wherever I went, they followed, sh-shurrounded me, everyone wanted to be my friend...or my lover." He leered dramatically up at her but then his face collapsed from the effort. "They said I was charming, wise, beautiful...meant for great things...capable of anything... could have the whole world if I wanted it. They loved me." He heaved a big nostalgic sigh.

"Then *he* spoiled it. He was jealoush of me. Threatened. Thought he was always gonna be the only male Ruler. After I declared for Head of the House of Foreign Relations, that same night he took me aside and bawled me out. Just 'cause I was young and had come so far so fast. S'cause I was smarter. He knew I would become more powerful than him. I shoulda

362

dealt with him right then, that night. Things would have ended differently if I'd taken care of it then."

"Who?" Orja asked, as he flopped restlessly, shaking the bed.

"Ziel." He spat the word towards the ornate ceiling. "That stupid little man who calls himself a Ruler. I will not call him by that false title, never. He doesn't deserve it!"

"He said I liked control, that I was thirsty for power and just wanted people to serve me. He went on and on about Atlantis Rulers being servants to the people, making sure that power is distributed evenly, being willing to serve the greater good." Mardu wagged his head slowly back and forth, one hand covering his eyes. "Such offal. It was *him* that took it all away from me. He said if I didn't overcome this ash-ashpect of my character it would keep me from my dreams. From leading Atlantis, but he was just trying to stop me." Mardu's words came slow and tired now. "He was just a scared, birdshitty little man...and I hate him. I hate him...."

His voice faded, more asleep than awake, his head falling to the side. "You remind me of my mother...you're jus' like...jus' like..."

Orja waited several minutes to make sure, then waved off the lights and slipped away to her own bed. He'd wake early, despite being so drunk he couldn't manage going to bed without help. And he'd be surlier than a camel in heat. She'd need to be up even earlier to prepare.

A GIANT'S COTTAGE

"A little nonsense now and then, is cherished by the wisest men."

— ROALD DAHL

CARVER

Finnegan's Stronghold commanded the summit of a bramble-covered hill, overlooking a natural harbor from which the giant's bridge sprouted, like a womb with the umbilical cord still attached. Set a good distance outside the quiet harbour town on Ireland's northern-most coast, the stronghold was a square block built of boulders the size of aurochs. Hunched against relentless salt-crusted winds, its walls were severely weathered, but structurally sound, due to the massive girth of the stones. Built like one might expect a giant to construct a cottage for his family, it would house the entire group comfortably inside its single, four-cornered space.

"How long has this been here?" Carver nearly had to shout across the table to Turner. The din of so many people echoed off stone walls and floors, filling the dust-blanketed room with conversation and laughter. They sat along benches at crude plank tables eating leathery strips of dried fish, slender pale parsnips and lavar bread.

Turner shrugged, "No one knows. Finnegan's stories ha' been handed doon fer generations. Elders in the village claim their great-great-grand-parents knew Finn's children before they vanished along wi' the rest o' the giants. Somewhere around five hundred years I'd guess. Tonight Kinny will tell us the story." Turner resumed chewing, his eyes searching out Aiela who was, as usual, centering a knot of adoring friends.

Carver made room for Ahna, who arrived with a handful of the slender, pale parsnips.

"Looks like it took an entire forest just to make the roof." Carver observed between bites, studying it. Whole oaks and alders, bigger than any he had seen during their travel, were lathed and fitted together to cap these impervious walls.

"And there's no hearth." Ahna noticed. "Guess giants don't get cold."

"And ate their food raw." Carver added gnawing mightily on the salty thick sinews of jerked haddock.

After the meal, Turner sent two Drivers into town to procure a ship that could ferry one aurochs team and wagon, containing their luggage. From here, the group would cross the six-mile-long Giant's Bridge on foot.

"...a path much too uneven fer wagons", Turner explained. "We'll each carry daypacks fer food an' water. The rest of yer belongings'll be ferried across ta Benandonner's Castle. Sorry aboot the dirt in here, this place is used only fer ceremony and holi-days by the villagers, so it's rarely cleaned."

Carver saw cobwebs thick as wool in the corners. They'd had to sweep an impressive variety of dead insects and rodent droppings from the tables before eating. An abandoned giant's home would take all of them working together to make habitable—even for one night.

Aiela organized team chores before they broke from the tables. "Which team wants to sweep the floors?"

Surprisingly, Nirka stood first. "Mine will."

Nanat simpered up at him with a sickly sweet expression. They'd become quite attached during the last week, which distracted Nirka from the sour looks and nasty comments he frequently gave Carver. Mostly it had been easy to ignore, but a couple times Carver thought Nirka might push too far again. Then he'd have to teach the large, golden boy a lesson he wouldn't forget—which would be problematic because the Atlanteans got so bothered by something as simple as a fistfight. Not like at home where most arguments ended in one.

Aiela nodded. "Thank you Nirka. Which team will gather firewood?" Another team leader stood. "Bring water from the well? We'll need the trough outside filled for cleaning—the barrels in the wagon too, for cooking and filling water jugs. We'll need two teams to clean this place. One to prepare supper." On it went until they were all busy.

In the midst of this mayhem, the Drivers took their leave. They would resupply in town before driving the empty wagons back home.

"How long will your return take?" Carver asked one of them, proud to have expanded his Irish vocabulary so much during the last few weeks.

"Only five days. With empty wagons on a direct route, it is not far." Came the answer.

Carver had helped Turner track each place they were on the crude maps that he kept rolled under the seat of the lead wagon. He'd brought them, intending to add roads, towns, and other missing—or new—features they encountered. Navigation had been mainly asking the locals which roads to take between destinations.

The teachers selected gifts, presenting them to each departing Driver. Atlantean items would hold great value here. Both students and teachers lined up to speak thanks, bowing or even embracing these rugged, simple men who had worked tirelessly, and with great patience.

They're surprised just as I am, Carver thought, *at this fondness that's crept in after weeks of shared meals, hardship, and travel both monotonous and majestic.*

"And so the great goodbye begins..." Ahna muttered beside him as they watched, and he felt a small heaviness born, deep in his heart.

Supper was an abundant and varied mixture of fresh seafood. Brought back from the harbour town by the guards, they'd roasted or boiled it over open fires outside the stronghold. Chores completed, everyone gathered around the leaping flames, mesmerized by the view—a stunning expanse of wild beauty in all directions. Markedly more cheerful now, they watched the sun set while they ate. Its colors burned from mandarin to vivid violet before shrinking in thin bands of electrified gold on the horizon. A genial breeze still swept round them, calming as evening rose, keeping down the bugs that had plagued them during travel in the lowlands.

The girls and female teachers had taken lanterns and buckets of water inside to wash with. A much longer process than the males, who simply stripped in the semi-dark beside the long water trough, and washed off travel grime as quickly as possible, returning to the fireside to dry and enjoy the brisk feeling of being clean.

While the sky completed its transformation from day to night, Carver sat between Drommen and Lister, listening to the guards sing their native songs around the fire. Wishing he had thought to bring out his dulcimer, he hummed along to learn these melodies which ranged from plaintive to bawdy.

No longer distracted by constant activity, Carver's mind returned to the confrontation with Jaydee. Initial shock long gone, he ignored an overshadowing fear of why his father was spying on Ahna and Aiela. Shutting emotions away, he let his mind sort through possibilities and solutions. Being raised at the center of a nation's worth of intrigue had trained him well. He remembered no mention of the twins before leaving, nothing had been said about Jaydee either. He tried to let the worry fall away, planning to extract full explanations from Mardu later.

The girls rejoined them, pillowing waves of citrus flowers, eucalyptus, and mint into the air currents. Circling close to the fires, they combed fingers through damp hair in an attempt to dry it completely before it was time to crawl into bedrolls.

Leaving Drommen and Lister, Carver searched for Ahna, finding her on the far side of the second fire. He set a log on end and settled quietly behind her, watching as the breezes and fire heat worked together, drying and fluffing her shoulder length strands.

She was listening, and occasionally responding, to the girl chatter around her, but directed a smile towards him, aware of his presence at once. Sitting with his face shadowed from firelight by the layer of female bodies, he was free to admire. Her choppy layers of blonde hair glowed subtly in the dancing light, but it was the lines of her body that drew his eyes. Wearing clean sleep clothes, baggy—until the breezes plastered them against her, he could plainly see her curves silhouetted against the bright flames. Beneath her travel leathers, she appeared girlish, small and slender, but tonight he saw a woman's body. Hips curved out from the indentations of her waist. Buttocks a round bubble, cleft so alluringly down the middle.

As if on cue, the guardsmen began singing again, crooning in rich baritone harmony. Ahna, like the other girls, began to sway. She turned her back to the fire, facing him now, hips moving to the slow beat of an irish love song. He felt her eyes fasten on him, her enjoyment of performing this sensual dance while he watched, knowing full well how his body would respond.

What was a slight and pleasant rising became a fierce, raging throb. Thankful for the cover of a moonless night, Carver exhaled slowly. *Perhaps I should enlighten her. Tell her exactly how many nights I've gone to bed aching.*

At the close of the song, Aiela and the team leaders urged students to their bedrolls.

Turner announced mysteriously. "Tonight we've an especial bedtime story, but Kinny willna tell it 'til we're all tucked in. This story is best told midst the night."

Further instructions faded as Ahna crossed the brief space separating them, reaching both hands out to pull Carver to his feet. He rose to her, pressing her against the length of his body in one smooth move. Gratified when she gasped, he kissed her still parted lips, not bothering to hide the surge of passion. She tasted of hazelwood smoke and sweet cream. He kissed her hard and thorough, almost laughing at her shock as she felt his raging desire. This time he felt no shame. She had deliberately contributed and deserved to know just how effective she had been.

He kissed her until most of the group disappeared inside, trying to be more tender after that first searing assault, but she seemed as aroused as him now. Pulling his head down so she had better access, finding his tongue with hers, urging him to explore her mouth. When she began gently suckling the tip of his tongue, he pulled back abruptly, eyes wide.

"Ah, come on! Now I'll be lying awake for hours!" Inside the veil of night, he slid his hands down to her round little rump, igniting the charged air. Tenderly caressing, then pulling her against him tight, his lips hovered on hers, light as the flutter of moth wings.

She almost moaned. He could feel her swallow it.

"Sleep well white-haired vixen", he whispered fiendishly in her ear, glad to have gotten at least a little revenge. They walked into the stronghold side by side as if everything was normal. As if they weren't both overheated, and unsated.

Tarps had been hung to divide female and male sides of the room. Still, Kinny's voice carried easily to the four corners of the giant's cottage. Pulling a tarp back from the north wall, Kinny sat on a high trestle table, boots resting on the bench so both sides of the room could see him. He waited until the rustling settled, calling for the lanterns to be extinguished. Then he lit a single lantern, turning the restless flame up high so that shadows bounced and quivered dramatically across the walls and roof beams.

Carver was still trying to slow his heart rate from the provocative encounter with Ahna, when the story began:

"Finnegan's real name was Fionn Mac Cumhaill. Which means son of Cumhaill—the winemaker—but ever since he was little his father called him Finnegan because he had no interest in making or drinking wine, being more a beer man, you see. Now, Finnegan grew up to be the biggest giant in all of Ireland. Probably because he was the result of a love affair between his father and a Scottish giant maiden. Of course, Scot giants were a quite larger race.

As a young man, Finnegan married a giant lady named Oonagh (OH-nuh) and together they built this very house we're in, complete with a cradle for the giant babies they would make, and a rocking chair where Oonagh could sit knitting booties and caps in the evening. It was only just a cottage to the giants, but regular people call it a Stronghold because it's sheltered humans many times against warring clansmen invading from Scotland and strong-nosed tribes sailed down from the north. But those are stories for another day....

Not long after Finnegan and Oonagh settled here, a giant named Benandonner built his castle on the Scot shore, just across the way. Benandonner liked to host gatherings for all his giant friends over there, and let me tell you, that many giants romping in the ocean and fishing, created waves so high, they washed far inland on this shore and kept destroying Finnegan's barley fields and Oonagh's flower gardens.

Finally Finnegan had enough and shouted to the giant Benandonner to please romp and fish farther north so the waves could just wash out to sea.

Benandonner hollered back a flat refusal—a blatant insult to Finnegan.

So Finnegan challenged Benandonner to a fight. If Benandonner lost the fight he would move north but, he insisted, the fight must be here in Ireland.

The problem was that Benandonner did not know how to swim and there were no boats big enough to carry the Scottish giant without sinking. So Finnegan set to work building a bridge between Ireland and Scotland. As he was finishing the Scotland end, he caught a glimpse of Benandonner, who had only been a voice shouting across the sea before, and realized this was a giant so massive as to dwarf him. He didn't know that he had challenged the largest of all Scotland's giant men.

Feeling afraid now of the imminent battle, Finnegan fled back home, unseen. That's when he heard the huge giant Benandonner, headed across his bridge, causing the earth to shake with every step he took.

Finnegan was in a panic. How could he win against this Scot he had so foolishly challenged?

Lucky for him Oonagh was smart, quick and sly as a crow. 'Off with your clothes and into the cradle Finn!' (Kinny used his best female voice here, much to the amusement of his listeners)

'But I will not fit, my legs will hang over!'

'Precisely!' Oonagh replied. She swaddled Finnegan's head and body with their bedsheets so that only his face peeped out, surrounded by lacy ruffles, and his legs—which hung huge and hairy from the cradle down to the floor. Then she fashioned booties from two blankets tied onto his feet.

'Suck your thumb and do not wake up until I tell you.' She commanded her husband.

KNOCK KNOCK KNOCK at their door. (Kinny stomped both feet so hard on the bench, the 'knocks' boomed across the room bringing forth shrieks and squeals.)

Oonagh opened it. Smiling with welcome to Benandonner, she invited him sweetly inside. 'My husband Finnegan is out hunting the five stags he eats for supper each night. Would you like some tea while we wait his return? Shhh. We must speak quietly for our wean is sleeping. Would you like to peek at her? She's the wee image of Finn and may grow to be as big as her daddy someday.'

Benandonner came quietly to see the baby, staring in dismay when he saw the size of her. If the baby was this huge, how big was her daddy?

'Come. Let's take tea outside so we can chat without waking the baby.' Oonagh said. Pointing to a round porcelain tub that she usually bathed in, she added, 'You can use Finn's teacup. I'm sure he won't mind.'

Again Benandonner was taken aback. He could barely lift Finn's teacup using both arms!

As they sat in the yard by the fire, waiting for the water to boil, Oonagh pointed out a pile of whole pine trees which Finnegan had peeled to build a barn.

'There's some of Finn's throwing spears. He leaves them lying all over! He likes to see if he can throw them far enough to reach the other shore. You can play at that while you wait if you like? Or, those boulders down below. They're but pebbles to my husband. He likes the splash they make, far out in the ocean's deep.'

Benandonner's eyes grew wide, thinking how mighty this giant must be, as he peered at the enormous boulders piled at the hill's base. Shaking his head, he got up, speaking for the first time.

'Thank you, wife of Finnegan, for your kind welcome. If you will, please give this message to your husband: Tell him I have moved north and cannot honor our appointment.'

Then he bowed and clomped his way back across the bridge. True to his word, Benandonner built another castle far to the north on Scottish shores.

Finnegan and Oonagh celebrated their victory—and their dry gardens and fields—for many years. They had five children who soon began to create tidal waves against the Scottish shore as they grew and played in the sea.

Regular people had moved into Benandonner's abandoned castle and the tidal waves were washing away their gardens and fields. They crept across the bridge one night to see what could be done. Seeing the family of giants they were very very afraid to find their neighbors so close across the bridge were giants! Probably human-eating giants who would steal their children and terrorize the land! They decided there was only one solution.

They tainted the well where Oonagh rose early to draw water for her family each day. Her children found her dead beside it, a drinking ladle fallen from her hand. Finnegan buried her under the boulders at the base of this hill and moved south with his children, rather than risk losing more of his loved ones to an unknown adversary so vicious and deadly.

The townspeople say that Oonagh's ghost still roams this hill, weeping for her lost family. They say that no one can sleep in this cottage because if they do, she will come a knockin', rousting out any who try to stay. You see, ghosts have no concept of time and she believes her family might return someday...."

Abruptly, Kinny's lantern extinguished, plunging the room once more into thick blackness. Something outside began to wail, faint at first, fast growing louder and closer. A high-pitched shivery noise keened and screeched, mourning an incessant loss.

Around Carver, the boys sat up craning this way and that, trying to see through the dark, holding their breath in spite of themselves. All went dead still for a moment and they heard the huge door creak open very slowly, felt the gusts of cool air blowing in. A hazy light shown outside the open door and a shadow loomed, moving across the ceiling overhead. The giant shadow of a woman.

"Get oot! oot! OOT!" The shadow shrieked in a familiar falsetto.

Well played Kinny, well played. Carver was grinning as lanterns suddenly bloomed around them on both sides of the tarp walls.

The adults threw disapproving looks at Kinny instead of the applause he'd no doubt expected.

Shrugging, he untangled from his cloaked woman figure and called in his noisy cohorts, who proved to be three of the guard.

The lantern-wielding teachers moved among students, calming them, urging them to "go to sleep now" and "this inappropriate display will be dealt with in the morning".

This should be interesting. Carver thought. *They don't know Atlanteans censor entertainment. Poor Turner. He won't see it coming.*

I wonder what Ahna thought?

GIANT'S BRIDGE

"Let me not pray to be sheltered from dangers, but to be fearless in facing them."

— RABINDRANATH TAGORE

AIELA

She sat at the longtable in Finnegan's Stronghold, watching the faces of her group as Turner addressed them. Each expression told a story; interest, excitement, distraction, a yawn, dreamy staring at someone, uncertainty, hyper-focused, uncomfortable. A telling collection of emotions.

Bedrolls and luggage had been packed into the one remaining wagon, which was currently enroute to the harbour town to meet its ferry.

The night's fast had been broken with the usual pasty hot porridge with berries.

Each person had prepared a small pack they would carry, with drinking water, jerked fish, and leathered fruit mash. Turner, the remaining two Drivers and the eight guards, also carried rope and weapons respectively.

"Sure an' all six miles are no' equal." Turner was reminding the group. "These miles are uneven ta the point o' havin' ta climb ow'er sections o' columns. It'll be slippery wi' sea plants—some parts under water. Instead o' handrails, this bridge is edged wi' ocean—vera vera deep in places. We'll go slowly an' wi' care. We'll rest when needed. We'll ask each other fer help an' be cautious fer one another. Many ha' been lost in this crossing because they went alone. Have ya questions?"

Their faces echoed Aiela's own. Equal parts trepidation and bravado.

SOON AS AIELA woke to the loud racket of coastal gulls at dawn, Helena had taken her aside, voicing her concerns about the ghost story and accompanying antics that Kinny had staged last night.

"There are reasons we censor our art and entertainments. I'm sure no harm was meant, but they must be told of our ways. I thought, given the relationship you and Turner have, you may prefer talking to him rather than having the teachers do it, but it is your choice. If you do not, we will."

"But we are not in Atlantis!" Aiela countered, aware her frustration was spilling. "Aren't we to follow the rules of the land we abide in? We do not demand to eat Atlantean food, nor to live in the same luxury as we do in Atlantis. Why should they have to tailor our entertainment? And where does that end? Must they then censor any frightening part of every legend? What about the darker parts of their history? Are they to cut that away too?" *As we have.* She wanted to add, but didn't.

"Please lower your voice." Helena requested evenly.

Aiela saw the other girls casting curious glances their way, talking little amongst themselves, the better to overhear her loud side of the argument.

Helena continued earnestly, "We cannot control all things, people or events—that is true—and last night was a good example. But we can control what we choose to take in. Just like at home, we should choose carefully with intention. As much as possible, our environment must be only of the light. Purity, beauty, wisdom, that which will enrich us. Fear is one of the most powerful emotions on earth. Naturally occurring, it is a useful protective device. Used improperly, such as for thrills in entertainment, it becomes a darkness we do not want to toy with."

Aiela waited a beat to answer. She'd not understood how vastly different Atlantis' laws were until now. Being here, where artists in the markets painted pictures of someone weeping or screaming—even of evil as they imagined it—was altogether new. Stories that created drama from things like jealousy, threats, fighting, and other lower energies, were not tolerated back home. Which was why, Aiela thought, no one knew how to react to the electrifying fright last night, making it novel, tinged with danger, exhilarating—even though they all understood it was artificial.

She exhaled in an unwilling puff and met Helena's eyes. "I will talk to Turner, make him aware of our views. I will not, however, demand that he or his people change their ways for us. That is not fair or right."

Helena absorbed this, turning it about in her mind, finally nodding. "Alright. If that is what you believe is right for us, the other teachers and I will not interfere. I do understand your position although some of us would handle it differently." She smiled at Aiela. "You've learned well the essence of government, seeing all sides, finding compromise, understanding that you will feel strongly in opposite ways than the person next to you does. You are a good leader Aiela, sensitive, sensible and strong." She rose from the bench, bowed and turned to face the day.

AIELA WALKED beside Turner down the sedge-lined lane spiraling the hill from Finnegan's Stronghold. From its base, the cusp of the giant's bridge lay just to the north, close enough to watch the high sprays of wayward waves that broke against it. The sun beamed brightly, ignoring its darker horizon to the south, where clouds were building leisurely.

"Wi' any luck, we'll make it o'er before the rain hits." Turner glanced at the far off storm. His tone hinted at worry. "At least we've a calm morning."

"How dangerous might it be. Really?"

"Depends on the strength o' the storm. Wi' normal conditions, the danger is low...*if* everyone pays attention. Add in rain, wind, waves, lightning and sure, it could become life-threatening. If we wait ta go, we take the chance o' no' being able ta cross 'til the next calm day. Sure an' you've seen our weather patterns, it could rain an' blow fer days. I do think we'll be crossed before the worst o' it hits. That storm's a long way off. Could even go in another direction entirely."

"Alright. I trust your judgement. If we wait and get stuck here, we may miss our opportunity to see Scotland at all. We'll just keep everybody moving. What a beautiful morning!"

Exclamations grew loud behind Aiela and Turner as they reached the wide, choppy stone swath that was the giant's bridge, and began the trek across. It was made entirely of tall stone columns fitted together.

"...thousands of them! Hundreds of thousands!"

"Such irregular shapes, different sizes, yet perfectly matched."

"I wonder how tall the columns are?"

"Look how black and smooth they are."

"What really made them?"

"Are they all hexagonal?"

"No, see that one has five sides, and there's one with eight. Most are six-sided, but there seems to be a variety of polygons."

"Wouldn't they be better described as prisms?"

Progress was slow as everyone studied the columnal stepping stones comprising this strange land-bridge.

Mostly the path was choppy, the columns stepping—not always gently —up and back down again. Two places, the group snaked single-file around a veritable column mountain, stepping gingerly, feet soaked to the knees. Cold water lapped over the lower pathway of stones that took them around.

Then they came to a place where there was no "pass". Turner sent two of the guards up first. "Better climbers than me." He explained. Fixing knotted ropes, they brought up three people at a time, helping them descend before hauling up more. It took well over an hour to get the entire group over. The column path grew treacherous in places, slippery with ocean algae, the black rock worn smooth and slick where waves constantly polished the surface.

Turner urged them to drink and eat as they walked, not wanting to stop and risk the storm catching up.

Aiela sifted back and forth among the long winding mass of people, encouraging her charges when they wearied of the constant vigilance it took, to tread without slipping or stumbling.

AHNA.

"My feet hurt! I think I'm getting blisters...and look at my hands!" Nanat had been lagging behind all morning. Her hands were scraped red and she picked at the tiny-slivered aftermath of climbing a splintery rope.

Ahna arranged a compassionate expression. "I'm sorry. Might help to think of it as having fun, having a once-in-a-lifetime experience. Did you see the whales that passed awhile ago?"

"They weren't as big as some I've seen... too loud when their blow-holes spouted. No, I'm *not* having fun...Nirka's upset with me." A whine crept into Nanat's tone. "I didn't sleep well last night on that hard stone floor and," she paused to look around and make sure no one else was listening, "I kept hearing noises. They were *frightening* after Kinny told us of Oonagh's ghost. I kept thinking what if she really did come in to make us leave? When I finally fell asleep, I had nightmares about being stepped on by a giant. Then I woke and just lay in the black being afraid."

Ahna squelched a smile, carefully maintaining her sympathetic face. "You could have woken me. I would have helped you out of fear."

Nanat brightened. "Really? I didn't think you liked me. It seems like most of the girls don't like me much, except Felicia—but she's my cousin so she has to. Not like you, everybody's friend."

This rather shy confession surprised Ahna. Nanat's self-awareness had been considerably less, bordering non-existent, on the voyage over. "I think it has more to do with connection. If you focus on others and learning more about them, they will like you just fine. People want to be known as much as they want to know you. I'm no expert—you probably notice I avoid people more than I engage them—but friendships seem a balance of talking and listening, giving and receiving, wouldn't you say?" Rain began as Ahna talked. Sprinkling at first, it was soon pouring in sheets. The Scottish shore had looked near, and now she couldn't make it out at all.

Nanat stumbled in the sudden downpour and Ahna clasped her arm, steadying both of them in the turbulent wind, intently blowing rain in their faces.

"M-m-my eyes are s-stinging." Nanat shivered in her light dress, designed solely for beauty, now soaked and clinging to her body. Her eyes, always intricately lined and painted with carefully chosen colors, were pools of smeared black, big as a racoon mask.

Ahna almost felt guilty to be this comfortable inside her practical pants and tunic. Sure, she'd been too warm when the sun was beaming down on them this morning, but that hadn't lasted long. She'd assumed everyone would consider the fact that they were crossing miles of ocean on a ridge of columns. Surprisingly, many of her companions had not worn appropriate footwear, much less dressed for the constant wet. Perhaps because they hadn't grown up beside a northern sea.

Stepping closer to Nanat, she wrapped an arm around the taller, shaking girl. "We're not that far from shore. Keep going my friend. We'll be in front of a warm fire before you can say 'shivering shark shit sank south of the seashore.'"

"Sh-sh-shivering sh-shark shit..." Nanat began between chattering teeth.

Ahna smiled as a plan formed. She sent a mental picture of the entire group linking hands or arms—everyone connected to each other—to Aiela. And felt the fluttery feeling of mind to mind response in the affirmative. She grabbed Nanat's hand. "There's something we have to do. I'll need your help. Come with me."

It worked. Compassion, and distraction from her own small miseries, had not just hurried Nanat along, like a tiny miracle, it turned her into a helper of others. Working together from the back, they soon had the group linked, pressing forward as one mass, enabling them to move faster by catching one another when they slipped or blew off course. "Don't let go of each other." Ahna and Nanat instructed the students and teachers.

From the front of the line, Aiela worked her way back, doing the same.

Near the middle of the group, Ahna caught up to Carver conversing with a guard, gesturing at the molting clouds and the bothered sea. "Ask the guards to sing. Teach us one of their songs." She half shouted now, to be heard over the magnified hiss of rain hitting water.

Carver nodded, and the guard obliged them readily. Before long, everyone had joined in, butchering the foreign words, but following the melody until they rivaled, then rose over the noise of the wind and rain.

That's when the first wave hit.

No one was looking behind. No one saw the watery mountain rushing across the surface.

Screams erupted as it hit and like a giant amoeba, the back half of the linked group washed into the sea.

"Don't let go! Pull! Get them oot o' the water! Move oot th' way so we can work here. Felicia's washin' away, Kinny, get her!" Turner shouted commands over the hub of chaos, surrounded by an anarchy of storm fracas. Seeing Ahna, he thrust a long coil of rope into her cold hands, explaining what he wanted, roaring over the pandemonium.

She nodded and immediately went to work, splitting the sopping students into sevens and eights, "Here, take this rope and tie it around your waists, like a chain. Go on ahead. Keep moving as fast as you can and watch for another wave. Get to shore." She sent them off, lashing themselves together with the ropes.

Turner and the guards were pulling the last of the students from the water.

Carver dove in, rope coils slung about his torso, stroking hard towards Kinny who had swum out far in the growing swells to find Felicia.

Ahna watched the sea behind them nervously, knowing the next wave could be bigger, realizing with a shock that she hadn't seen Aiela—didn't know where she was. "EL! Aiela!" She shrieked with her mind and her voice, turning this way and that in growing panic.

Then Turner was at her side, face frozen in worry. "She wasna wi' one o' the groups going on ahead? Where was she before?"

Ahna felt the blood leave her head when she remembered. "She was heading towards the back. Said she wanted to check on the whole line when I passed her in the middle. I think with Felicia..."

"Tie this off on somethin'." Turner shoved another coil of rope at her and lashed one end around his waist, diving into the boiling water.

Ahna could barely see Kinny bobbing in the distance. He had reached Felicia, keeping them both afloat but struggling to swim back—losing against the raging swells.

Carver was not far from them now, his rope played out. Ahna could feel his indecision, whether to cut himself loose and help Kinny, or hope Kinny could battle the short distance to him and a tie to safety.

Colin, the huge red-bearded guard was at her side then, taking the rope from her, securing it around a protruding column. He was calling to the other guards, two of them swimming out to help, taking with them inflated leather balls they called bobbers.

Relieved they had taken over, Ahna studied the water. Her eyes moved methodically back and forth farther and farther out, straining to see anything resembling a floating body or a bobbing head between the rollers. *El, where are you? Are you here?* Ahna closed her eyes, concentrated on feeling her sister.

Nothing. As if no connection existed at all.

And then a sudden surge of energy. Panic. Struggle. Cold. *Where are you? How can I find you?*

Kinny.

Ahna strained to see Kinny. Turner and Carver had reached him, towing him and Felicia back towards the bridge. The guards beside her hauled in ropes as fast as they could.

Ahna held tight to the stones and the ropes tied around them, as another wave crashed over the bridge.

Then Kinny was close enough to clearly see his face. It was not Felicia holding onto him, but Aiela, clinging tight to Kinny's shirt with one hand, holding a bobber in the other arm and trying to kick with her legs.

She was alive and almost back. Ahna wanted to sob with relief.

They reached the lower stones underwater and climbed, coughing and sputtering, dragging their exhausted bodies up to collapse onto the bridge. Ahna reached for her sister, who was coughing heavily, trying to pull in breath. "C-can't believe I almost lost you. I didn't know what to do...."

As Turner, Carver and Kinny sat, streaming water and catching their breath, guards roped them all together, watching the water warily. Monster waves roamed the sea, breaking against the bridge behind them, or in front.

A chilling wind relentlessly pushed from behind as if hurrying them over the uneven stone walkway. Turner and Carver led the way. The guards and Kinny came behind a violently shivering Aiela, who hadn't let go of Ahna for a second.

The rest of the group had made it to shore.

Everyone except sweet, shy Felicia.

Aiela

Aiela needed to cry but it was stuck deep inside her belly, refusing to surface, held under by some ponderous force.

"I let go of Jai's hand when the wave hit—or maybe he let go of me... I don't know. But I held onto Felicia and her head must have hit... something. When I surfaced, she was already unconscious. I tried so hard to hold her up—I'm a good swimmer—but her weight kept dragging me under. Those waves were pounding us every which way... mostly down." Even to her own ears, Aiela's trembling voice sounded wooden. Monotone. But Ahna didn't shush her or tell her to wait and talk about it later. They hadn't quite reached the shore and Aiela wanted to get this out. Needed to share it with her sister before others started clamoring to know what happened.

"We started sinking and I had to let her go so I could come up to breathe, but I went under to grab her again, then I couldn't find her and it was harder to get my head above water and then I couldn't see where she was. Didn't even know where I was... " Her unshed tears clogged a weary, raw throat.

"It's alright El, you did everything you could." Ahna spoke these words of assurance over and over, but Aiela couldn't seem to take them in.

Finally, their somber group was ashore. Underfoot, the bridge's hexagonal columns spread up towards a castle that appeared built from the same long black prisms. It towered above them like a shadow, displacing the downpour.

Everything was off kilter, either cuttingly loud and bright, or blurred, like pieces chipped from a dream. The castle fit perfectly into her surreality.

I lost Felicia.

I let go.

Felicia's gone—washing farther and farther out to sea.

Thoughts marched like a drumbeat round and round inside her head as someone wrapped a rough blanket around her, speaking words she couldn't understand.

Some force was pushing her up, and up, until they were at the castle entrance. It was still raining and she stopped to look up at the sky's tears dripping on her face. At least *it* could cry over poor, drowned Felicia, but why was there no thunder? Storms at home always had thunder. The strange lady on her left, holding the blanket round her, spoke rapidly, pushing to get her moving again, uttering sounds that had no meaning.

"I don't know what you want. What are you saying?" Aiela looked to Ahna, still close beside her. "What's she want?"

Turner glanced back at Aiela, "She j-just wants ya ta keep w-w-walking. We need ta get inside so we can warm."

Aiela let out a hysterical laugh. "Your lips are BLUE! And Carver's are PURPLE. I've never seen purple lips...." She clamped her own lips shut over the lunatic sounds escaping.

The castle seemed enormous inside, and full of people.

"People everywhere!" She croaked loudly, while Ahna steered her in the right direction.

Ahna was pulling her up a staircase with ridiculously huge stone steps that wound around a turreted wall. The strange lady was still pushing from behind.

"We can get out of our wet clothes, get warm. Maybe they'll have some tea..." Ahna sounded as exhausted as Aiela felt.

There was indeed a fireplace with a smoky peat blaze giving off delicious heat. Several girls and healer Lira were in the room, and came to help the worn and soaked sisters out of their wet leathers. Warm hands stripped her quickly, seating her close to the fire with a soft blanket taken off one the oversized beds in the room. Aiela stared into the fire, the movement of smoke mimicking the waves she had so recently been trapped in. Her body began to shake in huge unstoppable shudders.

Lira, who had been listening to Ahna's recounting of the short story, sent two girls downstairs. "Find my small green chest from the wagon and we need hot water. Tell Turner wine or anything else we have. Not beer. Strong wine or brandy would be best, and their healer if they have one. Aiela, I want you to drink." She held her water skin to Aiela's lips, one hand steadying her head to still the waves of tremors.

381

Aiela tried to dodge it. "N-n-not thirsty." Her stomach heaved at the thought.

But Lira simply grasped her chin firmly and started trickling water into her mouth.

She had to gulp—and promptly began vomiting, retching into her blanket again and again. Surprising, the volume of liquid that poured out. Finally, the tears started. She went from throwing up to heaving with sobs. As if the salty water that had bloated her stomach was no longer there to stop up her grief.

"You swallowed a lot of seawater. Lay down now, it's going to be alright, it's not your fault." Lira seemed to know about the thoughts still marching in fog-bound cadence through her head. "Losing Felicia is *not* your fault, Aiela. I will say it as many times as I need to. It would've happened whether or not you were with her."

When she was settled and the sobs slowed, Lira helped the castle lady clean up Aiela's mess, unwrapping the soiled blanket, rebundling her in a fresh one. She lay there for what seemed a long time, listening to movement and murmuring around her, letting the tears leak from her body, slack with exhaustion.

After losing Felicia, she had felt herself drowning a degree at a time, the monster waves pushing her under again and again. Terror had penetrated every cell. Each time the water sucked her in, she had lost which way was up, until it surprised her if she managed to surface for a few precious seconds of air. She'd accepted that she was going to die by the time Kinny got to her.

Ahna didn't leave her side. Rubbing her back in light patterns to help release the trauma, she helped Lira apply oils and balms to both of their heads, chakras and feet.

"I've some tea here whenever you can stomach it." Ahna leaned in, speaking softly.

Aiela nodded, slowly sitting up to sip the intense warmth which tasted of berries and lemon. It reminded her of Auntie Sage with all her potions and brews at home.

She heard Nanat crying now, curled in a ball on one of four massive beds. Three more girls huddled around her, talking quietly, weeping with her.

"Poor Nanat. She only told me this morning that Felicia is her cousin....was..." Ahna whispered. "I imagine we'll hold a remembrance for her instead of the party we'd planned..." Seeing Aiela's face she stopped. "It wasn't your fault—that would have happened, even if she'd been alone."

Aiela nodded, unconsciously rocking back and forth, trying to make the words sound true. A tear trickled down her cheek again. "I want to believe that." She whispered, "But I don't yet. It *feels* like my fault. I let go... I didn't save her."

"*Couldn't* save her." Ahna corrected firmly. "There's a vast difference."

Voices grew loud outside their room and Lira went to see what was happening. Before she got there, the great oaken door banged open.

Turner came in first, with big Colin close behind carrying a dripping mass in his arms. "Yer no' going ta believe this." Turner's voice was vibrating with gladness, "They found her! Felicia's alive..."

Aiela's mind couldn't grasp much else he said as Ahna got to her feet, making room for Colin to lay his bundle in front of the fire. The castle's scottish healer was with them and Turner set about translating the rapid exchange between the stout middle-aged woman and Lira.

Felicia's skin was paler than the cloudy whitefish they ate here, but she was breathing.

Aiela's relief intensified, and a surge of energy revived her as she joined in, holding dry blankets for the women who were undressing Felicia, trying to warm her.

The Scots healer went to fetch things they'd need.

Turner and Colin left, knowing she was in good hands.

Even with Felicia still unconscious, with unknown injuries from her fall against the rocks, a quiet jubilant spirit took over the room. Felicia was not dead, not lost to the sea. They had her back!

Aiela gladly accepted a tiny cup of ginger wine from the tray sent up by their hosts. Rich gold in color, she breathed in its tangy, unusual scent. Smooth sweetness clung to her tongue at first taste, a burst of ginger heat followed, growing fiery after she swallowed. Warming her throat all the way down, it instantly soothed her misused stomach.

"This may be the best drink I've ever had!" Ahna remarked, sipping from her own clay cup, watching Lira and the healer examine the gash on the side of Felicia's head.

"I have to know." Aiela said to Ahna. "Let's go see how they found her." She glanced at Lira. "Do you need us?"

Lira shook her head. "No, but send up food. I'm famished." Spying the wine, she tossed back a cup in two gulps, then frowned at Aiela. "Are you feeling well enough? You should be resting."

Aiela nodded. "Much better! Tired... will Felicia be alright?"

Lira shrugged. "I can't say until she wakes. Her breathing is shallow but her pupils look even and there are no other injuries I can see except the gash. It's hard to say yet. Her indications are positive." She smiled kindly. "Go ahead, I'll take care of Felicia. Be easy on yourselves. You've been through quite a lot today. "

Both girls headed down the broad winding staircase. Torches mounted on stone walls lit the way, emitting a faint, oily smell. They could hear rain stinging the high windows, shuttered to keep out wetness, one of them banging slightly in arrhythmic intervals.

Following a far-off clamor of voices towards the back of the castle, they wound through a maze of tall, dimly lit corridors, peeking into rooms with high-soaring ceilings.

The kitchen was a smaller expanse. Warm and humid, it was quite stuffed with their group, and their host's extended family, come to meet the Atlanteans. Tables lined every wall except where the hearth was.

Everyone was gathered around several bearded men speaking in their own language, while Turner translated. Most held short pottery mugs, filled from a keg, and were straining to listen to the Scot's tale.

"...so quick it was, the sea got rough! Our boat bein' too small fir those waters, we turnt ta head back...an' that's when we saw 'er....fallin' out o' a gigantic wave just off ta port....we sent Gawain in since he swims like a sailfish....he almost didna find her again.....then 'ere he was hollerin' fir us ta take her so he could climb back inta the boat before the sea smashed them again' it or carried them away....she wasna breathin' o' course but I know the breath o' life from my gran, healer in our town.....the lassie didna take ta it fir quite some time. Ach, I almos' gave it up wi' the boat pitchin' an yawin' somethin' fierce—we needed all hands ta hold our course....but then she burped a mite an started coughin' water up an I knew, the gods had given her back...."

Carver came as soon as he spotted the twins in the doorway. Offering his mug to Ahna, asking them both, "How is Felicia? Will she be alright? Did she wake yet?"

Ahna sipped, passed the mug to her sister before answering. "Still unconscious, but Lira says it looks good. Who are those men?"

Aiela tasted the cider beer. More sour than sweet, it was very fizzy.

Carver still looked damp. "Fishermen from a village up the coast. They brought Felicia here because they were close to the castle and knew there was a healer. They said it's likely she would've washed ashore eventually if they hadn't found her. Tide's coming in tonight."

Aiela felt a shiver go through her at this mental image. Carver noticed her reaction and said, "There's food over here. You should eat." He led them around the back of the crowd towards the orange glow of the hearth. Built into the brick wall above it were ovens where cooks took out round, ruddy loaves, and replaced them with swollen, speckled ones. Pots so large that Aiela could have sat in one, simmered over open flames. They watched a bony, white-haired man dump double handfuls of pale langoustine into the boiling water. It seemed only minutes until he used a round wire scoop to lift them out again, turned a shocking coral and white, and heap them onto platters.

The nearest tables, crowded with food, gave off scents so hearty they almost fooled the belly into thinking it was being filled. The cooks noticed the three of them salivating, and invited them with smiling gestures to help themselves.

They fixed bowls for the healers and girls upstairs too. Simple fare; bread with soft whirls of steam rising from the broken crusts, and langoustine with scoops of buttercream melting over them, fragrant with wild garlic and herbs. It tasted like something fit for angels.

Eating as she stood, Aiela watched the mill of people asking questions from Felicia's rescuers, cramping the room's space. They needed to be organized.

"Carver and I can take the food up to Lira." Ahna said beside her. "You stay and help Turner with this—if you're not too tired."

Ahna

"You went into the ocean to get her." Ahna stopped halfway up the broad stairs, turning to face him, recalling how Carver reached Aiela only moments after Kinny—and that he was deathly afraid of being in deep water. His own surprise registered in both expression and energy.

"Yes....I hadn't thought of it. Guess my father is right. You can do anything with the right motivation."

"Your father's a wise man?" She continued climbing stairs, knowing this mention was a slip.

"He's smart..." Carver hesitated. She felt his indecision. "But not a good man. Neither are my brothers." His words were almost too soft to hear.

"How many brothers?"

"Four. I'm the youngest. No sisters. We're a merchant family sort of like Turner's...among other things." He'd anticipated her next questions perfectly.

They reached the room then.

"For you. It might be the most delicious meal I've ever had." Ahna

385

handed bowls to the healers who had finished suturing Felicia—bundled now, on a pallet of blankets close to the fire. Carver gave bowls to Nanat and the other girls sitting vigilant by Felicia.

"Any change?" Ahna touched Nanat's shoulder softly.

Nanat pulled away, shaking her head, hard eyes refusing to look at Ahna. "Not that you care. Go back to your sister."

Ahna wanted to defend against the unspoken accusations. Instead, she took the green jug of remaining ginger wine from the tray and left the room. Nanat's resentment felt like stinging barbs being lobbed at her. Blame that needed a target.

Carver followed her out and sat beside her on the top step. "Nanat's just punishing you for her shock and worry. Ignore her. It'll pass." They ate in silence, sharing from the single bowl of food they'd kept, before he spoke again. "You want to go back to the kitchen? Still hungry?"

Ahna shook her head. "Not really. I feel like I've been run over by two full wagons, then trampled by aurochs. Too tired to be around people. You?" She took large swigs from the bottle, appreciating its glowing bite more and more. It blunted the burdens and fears of this day.

"Same, but my twin's life wasn't in danger. You're shivering. We could look for a fire...with no people."

She nodded, tried to smile gratitude at him. Cramming the last langoustine tail, slick with congealing buttercream into her mouth, she washed it down with ginger wine before heading down the hallway, swaying with overstimulation...and maybe the wine.

Carver placed their empty bowl by the staircase before catching up with her. "Ahna, just follow. Let me lead, for once."

She gladly dropped back, trudging behind him as he knocked and peeked inside closed doors. They searched inside all five doors on the second level, finding only dark spacious rooms with cold hearths.

Taking her hand, he gently pulled her up the stone staircase that led to the third floor of the castle.

Ahna couldn't remember the last time she felt so sleepy, ready to curl up anywhere at this point. "If the rest of you's as warm as your hand I don't need a fire... just you." Should she have said that out loud?

The first door they tried, opened to a room directly above where Felicia was. A wave of warmth hit them, its fireplace smoking cheerfully.

"Anyone here?" Carver called. Three empty beds were arranged against the wall. Chairs and wardrobes were scattered throughout the rest of the space. Going directly to the fire, Carver crouched, feeding chunks of dry peat to waning flames, blowing to encourage more fire, less smoke.

Ahna pulled folded blankets from a bed, curling onto her side behind him on the tufted hearth rug. She was half asleep by the time he had the blaze to his satisfaction and moved to wrap his body behind hers. Her last thought was how gloriously warm she felt. The fire hot before her, Carver's solid safety behind, the pleasant weight of food and wine in her belly....

Carver

Carver woke when a group of students, full of food and probably healthy amounts of the cider beer burst into their room. Chattering loudly, they were led by Jai.

He sat up to keep the boys from tripping over Ahna in the darkened room. "What are the sleeping arrangements? Where should I put her?"

Jai smiled dreamily down at Ahna who hadn't even stirred. "Girls on the second floor, boys on this one. But I'd keep her if I were you...she's like a little goldfinch isn't she?"

Carver smiled at Jai's affection for her. Yawning and stretching he mumbled "Save me a bed, I'll go tuck her in." Heaving her up, blanket and all, he headed down the stairs, going slowly so as not to trip over trailing blanket ends. She turned into his chest, startling awake at movements he made to balance her.

"You don't hafta carry me." She whispered sleepily. "I can walk...probly heavy..."

He snorted in the shallow pools of wavering torchlight. "You can't weigh more than a good-sized stone. I won't drop you, but if you don't trust—"

"I trust you." She interrupted, "You're always having to tote me places like some poor helpless—"

"I know you're not helpless." Stopping to sit carefully down on the steps, he cradled her against his chest. Now that she was awake, he didn't want to take her back just yet. She didn't move away and he wished they could stay inside this moment. It felt good, taking care of her, and then she pressed her lips against his neck, her hand creeping around to twine in his hair grown longer than usual.

"I haven't said thank you, for going in the water to get El. Sorry you keep having to save us. Real glad though..." She was whispering, sitting up in his lap, blanket falling around them, exposing bare shoulders. She kissed him, soft and bold at the same time. Tasting of wine tang and butter, she held his face firmly, opening his mouth with hers, pushing her tongue inside, taking what she wanted without asking.

His body responded violently, and his mind stopped working. He kissed her back with the passion she stirred in his most secret corners and untamed edges.

She squirmed, trying to get closer, hands roaming everywhere they could reach.

He touched her neck, skittered finger pads across her collarbone, tracing slowly down inside the blanket, to close loosely over her breast. Small and firm, it was infinitely soft in his palm.

She made a tiny moaning sound as she broke the kiss to breathe in. "Mmm that feels...ahhh" She pressed into his hand just as another group of students reached the bottom of the stairs, their conversations preceding them.

Carver pulled his hand away, feeling guilty. Unsure why, he wrapped the blanket back around her.

Her green eyes pooled with wanting. "Let's find another room with no people. It doesn't need a fire this time." She kissed him again before he stood with her.

He continued down the stairs, brushing past the ascending boys who stared openly at them. He'd admired, liked, even wanted girls before, but this, how she absolutely consumed him, was new. His mind processed options, willing to search the castle carrying her, for as long as it took to find that empty room.

Then he remembered she'd had a fair amount of ginger wine, and half his cider beer, and probably wasn't accustomed to alcohol.

He sighed and turned towards the girl's rooms at the bottom of the stairs.

Setting her lightly on her feet, he touched her face, whispering, "As much as I want to continue this... I don't think now is the best time." It was painful, forcing himself to say it.

"Why not?" She stretched up to fit her lips against the hollow of his throat, too short to reach his mouth unless he looked down, allowed her access. Molding her body against him, she moved her hips slightly, rocking them.

Holy bleeding gods! Another uncomfortable night trying to fall asleep!

Or he could just give in. Surely they could find some sort of privacy in a place like this.

NO. It wouldn't be right. What if she regretted it in the morning? He couldn't face that.

Her lips and tongue flickered against his collarbone, hands moving rapidly downwards. She seemed oblivious to the talk and laughter coming from the girls rooms, or the group of teachers coming up the stairs.

Moving them gently apart, he trapped her hands and towed her to the room just past where Felicia and Nanat were. "I will see you in the morning, green eyes. Go back to sleep." He kissed her one last time.

The first few steps away from her felt impossible, going against everything he needed most. Like forcing yourself not to breathe.

He turned to look back at her, "You're beautiful. Do you know that?"

Her answering smile was saucy. "I'm going to find a way to keep you. Do you know that?"

25

<hr />

THE BANQUET

"First you are named, then you are called, and your calling becomes, not just a noble purpose, but your sacred contract with life."

— ATLANTIS BOOK ON DESTINY

TURNER

*T*urner woke beside Aiela when sun rays poked into the turret attic where they'd slept, bathing the tiny stone chamber in liquid gold like some whimsical alchemist come to practice there. Stretching, he basked for a moment, noticing an alarming amount of dust, crusty with ancient bird droppings on the edges of the room. Invisible last night it was, outside their circle of lamplight.

She slept still, whispery snores puffing from the huge tangle of midnight hair; all that he could see of her above the bedroll. He smiled, thinking of their tender night, falling asleep when they both wanted to be doing other things together.

Last night after everyone had eaten, and the excitement of Felicia's dramatic rescue had worn down to relief, he'd waited for her, knowing she would see the others fast asleep before coming to him.

A first cousin on his father's side lived in this castle, so he had been here often, knew every hidden space, corners, attics and cellars of the giant's legendary home. He'd known exactly where he and Aiela could find privacy. *And we've two more nights here!* His heart expanded at the thought. *We won't be so tired tonight....*

He dressed and headed down rickety ladder stairs.

It was a day without agenda. Everyone was set free to rest or explore the castle and its grounds. Most went out to enjoy the rare, brawny sunshine, and the sea with its small waves licking innocently at the rocky shoreline, as if erasing the raging beast it had been yesterday.

The Atlantean Healer Lira came to find him, to report personally. "Felicia began stirring just before dawn, waking shortly after to complain of a vicious headache."

A weight eased from his shoulders at this news. A pressure he hadn't realized was there.

"There is definitely a concussion." Lira continued quietly. "I'm worried about her brain swelling, but at least I can keep her quiet and comfortable until we're home to our healing temples where damage can be assessed and fixed."

That night over another boisterous meal, everyone rejoiced by toasting Felicia's waking. Recounting to each other the minute details in their memory of the dangerous crossing, the group seemed grateful to be whole, safe and soon home.

Earlier in the day, while Aiela was occupied collecting flowers for the banquet, Turner had cleaned their little turret hideaway until it sparkled, adding pillows and candles, pilfered from the huge castle estate. All day he anticipated a romantic evening with the most enticing girl in the world.

Indeed, their breathless lovemaking was as wondrous as he'd imagined —if rather shorter than hoped. They talked late into the night while thin streams of new moonlight bloomed, then flowered over them before it slowly moved on. Frequently, they punctuated their conversations with periods of sex, as sweet as it was intense.

"I will find a way to be with you." Aiela promised. "In just two moons we go to High City to apprentice. If I study hard, I could convince them to post me here in Ireland as a teaching healer. Maybe even soon—a year from now!"

"Or in Greece? I'm ta 'prentice wi' my uncles, learn weaponry an' cartography. They make the finest blades in the world fer the Grecian army. Their company supplies weapons an maps ta elite forces...maybe the entire army, no' sure, but my eldest uncle works wi' the commanders ta improve an' design their weapons. Our amharu blades came from them...." He paused, gauging her response to this gory reminder of the triangle palm blades she'd used against their attackers. But she said nothing. "They update an' produce maps o' Greece an' surroundin' areas."

"Interesting combination." Aiela was slurring with drowsiness.

"It is. The maps were joost an interest or...em, talent one o' them had, a recent addition ta their business. So, you could come ta Greece as easily as Ireland?" He shifted up to ask this important question, propping his head on his hand so he could look at her. His excitement was high at the thought of having her forever in his life. He didn't mind waiting—however long it took—if it meant not losing her.

But a snore pushed apart her lips.

He lay back down, carefully snuggling closer to this girl who seemed to fill up his whole world, rejecting the coming parting, the return to days with less color or meaning. Life without Aiela now seemed unthinkable.

PREPARATIONS BEGAN at dawn their second morning in Scotland. Food had been bought, gathered, hunted, baked, foraged, and brewed, all prepared by the castle families. Blossoms, rushes, vines and branches were cut and fashioned into garlands, punctuated with enormous bouquets. The castle's great hall was turning into a fairyland that looked as if magical creatures should sporadically roam through it.

The Atlantean teachers had sequestered much of yesterday, preparing the Cartels; the official calling forth of each student into their adulthood.

The students had spent a portion of the previous day preparing their finery; their best garments and body adornments brought along for tonight's banquet. Today, they would complete their masquerades. They would create elaborate costume masks to hide their identities from each other.

Aiela had explained it all to Turner last night. "It's our tradition. At the end of the trip—which is really a trial to see what hidden talents come forth from a student—the teachers determine who that person is at their core, based on their observations of behavior. Also, they take into account interviews conducted one-on-one with us, before and during our travel. They've been carefully watching our choices, our interactions, who and what we gravitate to. Their recommendations hold quite a lot of weight with our placement in apprentice programs, and eventual positions after our formal education is done. The 'Cartel', meaning 'in agreement', is a ceremony wherein the child-self in each of us is honored, completed, and the adult-self called forth. It marks the final rite of passage, officially ending our childhoods."

"And why the masks?" Turner was fascinated. Irish culture had no such ritual as this.

"We enter the banquet with our true identities hidden to signify that we could have become anyone we chose. All through our childhood we practiced, trying on different persona's. We enter the celebration anonymous and leave a fully realized, unmasked individual, just like in life. You could say it mimics the transformation into our true selves."

"I will know ya, no matter what yer masquerade." He'd said confidently, kissing her eyes, her lips, minute by minute down her neck, to the very tips of her breasts...

Aiela

Her nipples tingled at the memory and Aiela stood, stretching to bring herself back to now.

"Focus El. You seem sleepy. Long, busy nights lately, hmm?" Ahna teased. "You *think* I stay asleep all night after you've left..."

Aiela dropped back down to shush her sister. "We can talk about it later."

They were constructing their masks along with three other girls that slept in their room, all of them spread out on the floor. Extra blanks, the basic masks that everyone started with, were piled beside her and she grabbed another to start over. She'd cut the last one too much and now it was lopsided. Feathers and paint, fabric and lace scraps, filigrees and tiny crystals littered the floor planks.

"I don't think he *will* recognize me." She muttered to herself. "He hasn't ever seen me in a dress."

This morning had started full of sunshine, languorous and fresh as a world made of daffodils, worn slowly away in the afternoon by another incoming storm. With practiced eyes on the horizon, their hosts once again battened the castle's oversized shutters.

Excitement ramped up as the students separated into their rooms, bathing, dressing, helping each other with hairstyles, face paint, and intricate costume details. She and Ahna were dressed long before time for the banquet to begin.

"Come on." She pulled Ahna towards the door. "Let's go watch the storm come in."

They ran downstairs, along dim hallways that felt honeycombed and foreign. Passing through the great hall, laid and ready, they stopped to breathe it in deeply.

"It's like a symphony of garden flowers."

"Heaven couldn't be prettier."

Heaving together against a great oaken door, stubborn to open against a rising wind, they tumbled out onto the balcony. The expanse of quarried stone slabs spread all the way to a cliff top overlooking the sea. Thunder rumbled constant music in the distance, sounding closer every second.

They ran together towards the railing and stood watching the sea angrily charge at sheer black cliffs that dropped from their feet, down down down. The cliffs seemed indifferent, stoic, ignoring each wave that crashed against them, spitting sprays of frustration high in the air.

Aiela inhaled the electric rain-fresh wind, carrying stories of salt and death. A perfume that spoke unknown endings and infinite beginnings.

"Small prelude of what's coming." Ahna murmured, her queer expression telling Aiela that some memory had registered in her psyche.

Tarnished silver clouds above them tossed lightening back and forth, the sound of it a far-off grinding from one horizon to the other and back.

"Not long until full dark." Aiela observed, "when we'll no longer be able to see what's coming toward us."

"I saw all of this. Years ago...." Ahna waved her arms to encompass their surroundings, the queer look still on her face. "It's in my journal." She began quoting: "We are beautiful, my sister and I...the gown she's wearing tonight has only thin strands crisscrossing her back..."

Aiela glanced down at the silky gown clinging to her, in a purple so deep it looked inky in the storm light.

Ahna was still quoting, "...showing muscles better defined than most men's....seeing her like this, framed by nature's raw emotions, I understand that she intimidates most people. Why have I never noticed that?"

Soaked wind slammed into them as lightning reached greedy fingers closer.

"We grab hands like we've always done" Ahna narrated, reaching for Aiela, "leaning together into this assault that tastes of seawater and change. Looking at each other with wild smiles, we raise couraged faces towards the storm and begin a cacophony of long, mournful howls. Half challenge, half approval, mostly just celebrating our naked joy in this moment. It's something our Papa taught us."

They did howl then. Cupping their hands around their mouths, they tried to outdo each other and the dissonance of storm and sea breaking together. They ended laughing, whooping and breathless.

"Papa would be so proud!" Aiela said wistfully. "He'd love this."

"C'mon, let's go dry out." Ahna looked down at her emerald green gown spattered with raindrops.

Ahna

Ahna stood looking into the mirror. The other girls had gone down already. She knew they were late now but didn't care, too entranced by the image they made. Side by side in glamorous masks that covered most of their face with elegant filigree patterns, gems twinkled back the torch-light. Even their eyes were changed, outlined in thick strokes and whirls, colors sweeping out to meet the generous mask eye holes. Long silk gowns, embroidered with tiny flashing crystals, draped their bodies, turning every curve graceful and abstract.

"We look like something birthed from the stars." She whispered.

"Two parts goddess, one part warrior..." Aiela agreed.

"Do you think Carver or Turner will know us?"

"Maybe. We are sort of wearing our favorite colors."

"And no way to mask our voices..."

Echoes of laughter and music greeted them before they entered the great hall. Stepping inside, its exquisite beauty came to them in layers of dancing flamelight. Long tables took up the far end, laid with feastware, filled down the middle with candelabras connected by purple and yellow heather flower garlands. Instruments were set up in one corner, flutes and pipes, drums and lyres. A middle-aged lady dressed in white, played cheerful tunes on a variety of flutes. The rest of the great hall was lined with bouquets of colorful flowers taller than Ahna. Garlands scalloped down from the rafters and twined around stone pillars. Lanterns, torches and candles were everywhere turning it all utterly romantic.

In High City, this banquet might have been rustic, but after a moon of coarse living and travel, it seemed downright sumptuous to every Atlantean here.

They separated to find seats at the crowded tables. The feast had just been served.

Ahna squeezed in beside Helena, dressed in her finest, unmasked like the other adults. On her opposite side was a boy wearing black and gold, his mask a jaguar complete with ears and triangular nose. Paw-like gloves covered his hands. He smiled and she knew immediately that it was Jai.

He entertained her with a running monologue on the charades in the room; who each character might be, outrageous theories on why they chose their particular masquerades. All throughout the lavish feast, he kept up the commentary, making her hiccup with laughter.

After the food was cleared, wine was served. First a glossy white elderflower with delicate layers to cleanse the palate and aid digestion.

Aiela stood, raising her cup to begin the toasts—the Atlantean act of blessing someone who deserved recognition or gratitude—in this case, their Scottish hosts. "On behalf of every Atlantean here, we honor your magnificent home, which you've welcomed us into. Your hard work, in order that we might eat and sleep like royalty. And most of all your constant, cheerful hearts which have touched our own with friendship. Good health and abundance be with you always and may your friendship be echoed back in a thousand ways."

"Slainte!" Everyone chorused, raising their cups in the direction of the castle families, before drinking heartily.

Next, Helena toasted Aiela for her leadership, and then the Matron of the castle toasted the Atlantean travelers for bringing joy, and a reason to celebrate. Light wines were always reserved for female toasts in Atlantis, and the Scots caught on quickly.

A deep-as-shadows purple bramble was poured next, its rich and untamed musk intoxicating the nose. A male teacher toasted Helena for her oversight during their trip, Turner raised his glass to the bravery of those who'd saved Felicia, and the Patriarch of the castle families spoke proudly of his grandnephew Turner, the pride and joy of Ireland who had managed to bring them all safely—more or less—to journey's end.

Ahna wondered if any of them, besides her and Aiela, could feel or see the powerful energy of these spoken blessings multiply as each person drank to it. This energy felt both warm and invigorating, multiplied tenfold by every person who agreed with the beautiful words, until it was a tidal wave of love, centered on the receiver of the blessing.

The percussionists struck up a beat while flute players gathered, and just like that, the dancing began.

Jai toasted Ahna privately. "To my alluring dinner companion who understands even my oddest moments. If I were a girl, I'd hope to be you." His smile glowed like a crescent moon beneath his glossy mask, playfully whiskered like a jaguar should be.

She kissed his whiskers, taking his hand and swinging into the best rendition they could remember of an irish dance.

She danced with all manner of mysterious male creatures, fierce birds of prey with pretentious wingspans and talons, a mesonyx, an armless titanoboa snake (how did he eat?), a smilodon and assorted reptiles. A grey, ghoulish looking boy with flashy lightning streaks was meant to be a stormcloud. There were intricate designs made from color combinations and geometric shapes, some simple, some exceedingly artistic. After spending so much time together this past moon, the costumes lent an air of otherness—even when she recognized someone behind their mask—as if they had all been reset, gifted with anonymity.

The dances were as varied as the costumes. A traditional "greeting" dance, very formal with stiff steps and partner changes, officially began all celebrations of this sort in Atlantis. Others were free-form, meant for individual expression, letting the body interpret the music. There were three consecutive female dances where the girls flaunted their femininity; wild, chaotic, flowing. The boys watching wide-eyed in the face of this baffling magic. At the last female dance, each girl invited a male to be her partner. He was to mirror her movements, learn her ways.

Ahna found her way to Carver, lounging against the back wall. Bowing formally, she beckoned him to join her. He was dressed in silky black shirt and pants, cut precisely and trimmed in black embroidery, accented with swirls placed to draw the eye to his wide-set shoulders. His mask was half white and half black with musical notes contrasted in the opposite color, as if he was of two worlds, two ways of being, the only constant being the music. She had recognized him early in the evening— would have known those hands anywhere—but they had not yet danced together.

He stepped too close to her as the music began, whispering into her ear, "There you are. I should have known you were the one I couldn't stop looking at."

She backed away from him, hips swinging to the slow beat, an invitation to follow her lead. He complied, his eyes never leaving hers save when she turned, backing against him, her body compelling his to mimic every sensual movement. At the end, she pulled his head down, kissed him lightly and left him standing there.

The male dances were bolder, structured like a conquest, designed for displays of might, agility and speed. The girls weren't chatting or giggling as usual, eyes magnetized instead to these young men, caught up wholly in their blazing strength. When it was time for the males to select part- ners, Carver came to her at once. Sweeping her off they fell into steps meant to resemble a flamboyant mating dance. With movements simple and nuanced, the girls were held, twirled and lifted at times by their more muscular counterparts. At its conclusion, Carver stepped back, breathing hard, bowing to her as she had to him.

It was time for the ceremony.

They took their seats, noisy with anticipation, thirsty and hot from the vigorous dance. Ahna filled her cup and Carver's, from water pitchers flavored with lavender and mint, and they took seats together.

Helena began. "Tonight, on the final eve of our journey together, we celebrate the adults you have become. It is my privilege to have been with you in this final transformation, to come to know each one of you. The teachers and I spent much time considering your personalities, the behaviors that tell us what is in your heart, and of course, your own dreams and desires which you indicated during the interviews. Most—perhaps all—of your evaluations have morphed and grown, changing from the impressions we began with. And that is how it should be, for your outward persona is as different from the inward, as your child-self is from your adult maturity. We have done our very best to accurately contract each of you. Our full evaluation notes at every stage are here for you." She gestured to a large basket holding scrolls that stood on end.

"The order will be random, determined by the scroll I draw." Taking a scroll from the basket, she called out "Jai Talmon of Venuska, come forward."

Jai rose and walked to stand before Helena.

The seven teachers formed a semicircle wrapping him, backs to the students, creating a wall between them and Jai. In tones so low they barely reached a whisper, the teachers began chanting "Zatoz nire seme-alaba, eraldatzeko garaia da". *Come my child, it is time to transform.*

The actual conferring of Cartel was private. As was the act of removing the mask.

Short moments later, the teacher's chant changed, "Azaleratzen hazi bat eta gurekin." *Emerge grown one, to join us.* Parting in the middle, the crescent of teachers were smiling, applauding Jai as he appeared, a wide grin now decorating his unmasked face.

The students came to their feet, stomping in applause and approval. Being the first to contract was an especial honor.

Jai bowed to them and re-took his seat.

Again and again Helena called out a name and the conferring was repeated. It was close to halfway done when Helena called "Ahna Argiaren (are-JIH-rin) of Chiffon come forward."

Ahna's heart pounded a staccato as she walked forward, eyes searching out Aiela, who smiled support before she disappeared behind the wall of teachers, chanting their whispery prelude.

Helena's energy felt at odds, as if resigned to some unspoken dread as she consulted the scroll, beginning with a gentle smile. "Ahna, we had some trouble seeing you well for you keep your true self hidden more than most." Her expression became solemn. "It is time to step out from this hiding. Shyness and conforming are no longer needed to keep you safe. Do you agree to give up these childish things?"

Ahna nodded, "Yes, I do." She gulped at the sudden feeling of exposure.

"Repeat after me; I honor the majesty of childhood and agree to keep its tenderness in my heart always."

Ahna repeated the traditional refrain.

"Now I call forth in you, your adult-self: Abundant but weighty wisdom—which your world will depend on. The courage to speak that wisdom boldly. Consistent faith in your own power and its importance to a greater plan—no matter the circumstances. This is the cartel I offer, do you accept it?" Helena watched her closely.

Ahna felt that weight closing in around her, wondered what might happen if she refused. If she said no to this rather ominous agreement about to settle on her shoulders. "I accept." She whispered, bowing as Helena touched her forehead.

"I bless your adulthood with ten-thousand blessings, that you may learn what you came here to learn, and give to the world what you came here to give. By now removing your mask, you signify readiness to step into life as your true self."

Reaching up, Ahna took off her mask, wondering if she was removing the last barricade against all that was coming.

TURNER

"...your restless impatience is to be overcome. Do you agree to give up these childish things?"

Turner nodded, unsure what protocol was correct in this strange Atlantean ritual. He was still surprised that Helena had called his name at all. Hadn't thought he might be included.

"Repeat after me; I honor the majesty of childhood and agree to keep its tenderness in my heart always."

He spoke the words, but in his own language.

Helena smiled in approval. "Now I call forth in you, your adult self: The strength to lead many in their time of greatest need. The will to sacrifice, so that you can serve a higher purpose. An endless joy in experiencing life, which can sustain you and those around you. This is the cartel I offer, do you accept it?"

Her words were puzzling, yet he could feel the wisdom of them flowing into him as he replied, "I do accept. Thank you."

Helena blessed him. Removing his phoenix mask, he rejoined this group of new friends.

Aiela

Aiela thought at first that Helena might hug her, such a rush of warm colors engulfed her as she stood in front of this quietly mighty woman. Instead, Helena began.

"There was too much we all wanted to include for you. Your potential is limitless! We had to choose between many possibilities..." Her face sobered then. "Though charming, your charisma must be tempered with intention. Retain the charm if you wish, but channel it, wield it only for unselfish purposes. Do you agree to give up your childish tendencies?"

"Yes." Aiela nodded, "Yes I do."

"Repeat after me; I honor the majesty of childhood and agree to keep its tenderness in my heart always."

Aiela said the words, aware she was bouncing slightly with exuberance.

"Now I call forth in you, your adult self: The power of love that is spread by your very presence. Courage to choose the light, no matter what the cost. Discipline to steady you in the midst of chaos. Faith in yourself, knowing you are always enough. This is the cartel I offer, do you accept it?"

Aiela was already nodding vigorously, "I do, I do, I accept, yes." She threw her arms around Helena then, and received the traditional blessing.

"Take off your mask Aiela." Helena reminded.

Carver

"...you can no longer afford to be a victim—or go along with things your soul disagrees with. Will you forego these childish traits?"

"I will." Carver was infinitely glad this part of the ceremony was private.

"Repeat after me; I honor the majesty of childhood and agree to keep its tenderness in my heart always."

He said the words, even though majesty and tenderness had hardly been a part of his childhood. He considered if there was anything he *would* want to keep.

"Now I call forth in you, your adult self: Enigmas, with which you will serve those you love. Steadfast light, no matter how small it seems in comparison to your darkness. Acceptance of who you are and your importance to a greater plan. Trust in the goodness that you find. This is the cartel I offer, do you accept?"

Carver took in Helena's words, feeling shock at being seen for the first time ever, and a bit of suspicion. Had Jaydee said something to these teachers about who he was?

"Yes, I accept." He received her blessing, removing his mask, emerging to applause and Ahna waiting for him.

26

LAST NIGHT

9,972 BCE SEA SHORE OF SCOTLAND

"You only need one man to love you. But him to love you free like a wildfire, crazy like the moon, always like tomorrow, sudden like an inhale and overcoming like the tides. Only one man and all of this."

— C. JOYBELL C.

CARVER

*E*lbows leaned on the broad stone railing, feeling its gritty strength, Carver listened to waves shatter against cliffs below. Too far down to see in the night, their monody soothed his soul. Tiny bursts of moisture ruffled the air around him, and he inhaled the scents, exquisite as any flower.

He couldn't help admiring the solemn rituals practiced and revered by his almost country-mates. Belial only bothered marking milestones, celebrating a birth or marriage, as an excuse for eating and drinking to excess. Social entertaining was as much a competition as a distraction from boredom in Temple City. It was hard to imagine any Belial parents or teachers caring enough for their young to mark the ending passage from child to adult. He felt privileged to have been included without a second thought, in this ceremony.

Something pressed his back and he jumped like a cricket, thoughts interrupted.

"Sorry. I didn't know if speaking or touching would be less intrusive." Ahna looked up at him, her face painted in shadows.

"I needed space and it stopped raining..." Why did he always feel simple around her?

"Look there, the moon is coming up." She pointed to a glow on the night horizon. "Deep thoughts?"

"Belials don't have a Cartel ceremony, I was thinking that I liked it."

"How do you mark your adulthood?"

He gave a bitter-tinged laugh, "We don't. Everybody's too self-absorbed to care about what the young are doing. We just...grow up."

A group of students wandered out, talking and laughing, exchanging bits of what had been conferred on them in the ceremony. It suddenly seemed extraordinarily loud.

"You want to walk up the beach with me?" He hoped it hadn't sounded as desperate as it felt. This was the last night he'd have with her, a small dying inside, something integral finally found and soon to be snatched away.

"Yes! I've had too much people...not that you're not people...I'm just done for tonight. But not with you...uh, not what I meant to say."

He smiled, glad that she was awkward too. They left by way of the great hall, threading through groups and pairs of students, some eating again, some swaying to music that would continue as long as dancers lingered, others reading the scrolls given to them by Helena.

Winding through the deserted hallway, he dashed up the wide stair-case, calling behind him, "Be right back." Borrowing two blankets, he settled one around her before they stepped outside the towering castle into the night. Ambling beside her over odd-shaped columns of rock, angling down towards the shoreline, Carver's thoughts drifted.

"I was scared that..."

"Still can't believe Felicia..."

They spoke at the same time.

"You were scared that....?" Carver walked closer, until they were nudging each other.

"We'd never know where Felicia ended up. Coming down here brought back how it felt, her being 'dead'. I couldn't imagine what I would say to Nanat. How awful it would be for Felicia's parents when we returned without her." Her pause stretched and Carver didn't rush to fill it, easy with quiet, and comfortable with empty.

"Just remembering, that's all. You were saying...?"

"Same thing...hard to believe Felicia was found and lived through that. Big ocean, crazy storm. That fishing boat just happening to be in the right place, spotting her even while trying to not drown themselves. A miracle I guess."

"She's definitely not done here." Ahna's voice was sure.

"How do you mean?"

"You know, whatever her soul wants to accomplish—whatever her mission is to this world...she must not be done yet."

"You think we don't die until, what, our soul decides to?"

"There might be times we can't help it, like when someone kills us, but I think usually, we've predestined our own end."

"So, sickness or 'natural' causes, like falling off a cliff or being eaten by a bear? What are those?"

"I'd think those are squarely in the category of our soul's choice, the doors we program in to exit life. Think of all the people like Felicia who 'escape' death narrowly when they should have died—yet didn't by some 'miracle' as you said. Then there's those who die in such bizarre ways it couldn't be recreated if they tried. When a hundred things had to come together—like lightning strikes, or a meteor falling." They had reached the beach, and she stooped to remove delicate gold sandals. "If our soul plans out our entire life before we come in, surely attention is paid to the circumstances of our departure."

"Do you always dissect death with your...friends?"

"Yes. And then they leave, typically at high speed." She stared at him pointedly, tripping over a rock. "Ouch!"

He grinned. "You'll have to do better than that if you want to run me off. I have more questions about death, about life, about you."

"Well, I guess this makes us friends... now that we've had the death talk."

He laughed, taking her hand to steer her left. "This way. Can you see the path? It goes to a very nice beach. Found it yesterday morning— missed the sunrise but it was still nice."

They stood at the wet-line, watching water rush towards them over the dark sand, before retracting in obedience to its mysterious master. Carver wished he knew what to say, how to turn off the tide of emotions rushing in and out, like the sea at his feet. He'd been sent on this trip for one insignificant-seeming errand for Mardu. Certainly he'd not expected to make friends, have adventures alongside them, fall wildly in love with this backwards country, meet a girl who made him believe in angels, in himself, in the possibility that life is inherently *good*.

He moved behind Ahna, needing to touch her, hold her, just be with her.

She leaned against him when he wrapped his arms and his blanket around her, and they stood watching a waxing crescent moon rise over the solemn sea.

"I feel like I'm losing my heart." He said into her ear, needing to express how important she'd become to him. How he felt when he was with her.

She turned just her head, kissing the underside of his jaw. "I know. Me too." Her chest rose and fell in a sigh. "I'll be apprenticing in High City by autumn, is there any chance we could see each other? What are your plans for apprentice? I don't even know where you live or what—"

"I can't." He interrupted, "I know you have questions, but the answers won't make any difference. Believe me, I've thought of it so much, worked it through in my mind over and over...there is no way...I'm sorry..." She stiffened in his arms, made to step away, but he held tight to her, clinging to every moment he still had.

Her voice hardened, "Your reactions to being touched tell me more than you think. I feel the strength of your attraction to me. I feel how overwhelmed you are when we're together. I know when you speak the truth and when you....don't."

It was his turn to stiffen. She knew when he lied? With no idea how to respond to this, he simply waited for her to continue.

"It just hurts," Both hands fisted at her chest, clutching her blanket like she was trying to pad her heart, "knowing exactly how you feel, yet you're entirely willing to let it go. Won't even try..." Her tone turned bitter.

"No," he stepped from behind to face her, to make her understand.

"I'd do *anything* to be with you. I would give up my miserable existence right this minute if I thought we could be together even just awhile."

Have to give her some of the truth. Can't let her believe she means so little...

"It would bring harm to you Ahna—your sister, your parents. I wouldn't just be risking what I love, I'd risk everything that you love. You don't know who I am and the mess I'm in..."

"Then *tell* me! Why does it need to be secret? Do you think you can't trust me? Tell me the mess you're in! I know very powerful people in High City. Ruler Ziel—do you know who he is? He's like a grandfather to me. They would help you, they would give any Belial refuge that needed it. They'd consider you as much Atlantean as themselves..."

He thought about it. The urge to spill everything right then was overpowering, to share all the darkness, the fear. Having this girl assuage his loneliness was more than he would've thought possible.

Then images filled his head. Mardu beating him bloody at even the smallest disobedience. Screams coming from behind closed doors for days when Mardu punished a traitor. Mardu ordering death after death to those he imagined had conspired against him. But never swift or clean deaths. His genius was in creating terror, bringing as much horror to his victims as possible before they died, letting them, and everyone else know they were being punished according to his power. He had spies everywhere. Carver had not one doubt that Mardu could get to him no matter where he went, would kill him if he left. Not that he cared too much about dying. The bigger problem was that Mardu would go after Ahna. Bring her as much pain as possible, simply because Carver had cared for her, because she aided Carver's betrayal.

And then there was Mardu's plan to take over High City, Ahna's soon-to-be home. No, the only chance of protecting her would be from right in the middle of it. He could figure out a way to keep her safe only if he stayed involved in Mardu's plotting.

"I can't." He had turned to watch the waves again, unwilling to look at her in case the despair overwhelmed him. "You'd be in constant danger if I left Belial. I wouldn't care what they did to me, but you—no. I will not risk you. Just knowing that you're alive and well and happy, that is worth giving you up." He felt tears form. The frustration and hopelessness of ever having such simple things as love and joy and safety brimmed over a drop at a time. Immediate shame at his weakness followed.

Ahna moved to embrace him, and though he swallowed again and again, trying to force them back, the tears still rolled down his face, their tracks chilled by sea breeze. Why did it hurt so much to be loved?

Her gaze was steady on his face when she brushed at his tears and then her own with the edge of a blanket. "I'm sorry Carver. I didn't—don't understand your fear. I can see it's very real to you. Whoever that black-haired man is that terrifies you so, he is evil and I'm sorry for all the things he's done to you."

Carver held his breath a little. Oh gods, what had she seen? He certainly wasn't going to ask. Couldn't bear the thought of talking about those things with her.

She laid her head against his heart, arms tight around him until the urge to sob had passed, and his tears finally dried.

They broke apart to wander up the beach. Silent at first, they eventually discussed the party tonight, the parts of the trip they'd always remember, the interesting bonds between their fellow travelers. Stopping, they admired a burst of moonlight when it rose above remnant storm clouds retreating on the low horizon.

"So bright for just a sliver." Carver was watching Ahna's expressions now as she turned to take in the beach and cliff lines around them. They were in a small cove. The Castle lights in the distance, shone like extra big stars.

"I wish it was warmer so we could go into the water." Ahna smiled suggestively, bringing an immediate image of them naked together in the water that he tried to push away. Surely that's not what she meant. She wouldn't want that with him now that she knew they had no future together. Probably felt, at the most, pity for him. Still, his body responded.

She spread her blanket on the sand, "Sit. You're too tall to kiss when I want to..."

He settled with her, face to face, draping his blanket around both of them and she kissed him light and playful, drawing his lips with hers, as her hands wandered to his hair and face and shoulders.

Her kisses deepened suddenly to hunger and intention. She slid her gown up bare thighs so she could scoot in and wrap her legs around him, forming her body into his, her crotch fitted tight against him.

He let go.

No will remained to control the fiery demands of his body. No more reasons to deny meeting her dainty lust with his own.

He tried to be careful with her. From that first night in Ireland when he'd picked her up, bleeding and limp, she'd reminded him of the Atlantean instruments crafted from blown glass and crystal, infinitely beautiful to look at in their fragility, making the most exquisite music when played according to their unique design.

He kissed her with all of the intensity built between them, running his hands slowly down her body, starting in her shining hair. Her face felt like sun-warmed flower petals covering bone. Skimming her neck, corded with delicate muscles, his fingertips found her shoulders, bare above the bust line of her long silk gown. Bringing both hands together, he paused at her breasts. Breaking their kiss he watched his own hands touch her, spread like a butterfly, thumbs together over her heart center. Her shape mesmerized him. So perfectly rounded, pliant, breathing. He fumbled for dress snaps, found a row of them lining her side. Glancing at her face as he pulled them apart.

She was watching him with interest, letting him do what pleased him.

She helped him push the fabric down, baring herself to the waist, and he realized he was holding his breath as his hands played over and around the curves, touching her every way possible, rolling her pale puckering nipples between his fingers. "Are you cold? Sorry…"

She was shivering. "Take off your shirt." She already had it open, was pushing it off his shoulders, rising up onto her knees, disregarding his attempts to pull the blanket up around her.

The feel of her nipples brushing his lips nearly brought him to orgasm. Leaning back to slow himself didn't help, seeing her full torso alluringly pale in the moonlight.

"Stop." He held her waist, keeping her still. "Just….give me a minute…let me look at you."

"I wish I was an artist. I'd sketch you, sculpt you, paint you from a thousand angles, just as you are right now. I'd decorate a castle with only you and live there content for the rest of my life…."

She broke his grip, pushing him onto his back on the blanket with a little laugh. "Pretty words from a pretty man. I have some words for you…take off your pants, I want to make love. I want all of you touching all of me, around me, inside me…"

He willed his body to wait, filling his mind with anything that might distract, sliding out of his pants as she wriggled out of her dress. The air was chilly, the sand all bumps and rocks pressing into his back. He tried to concentrate on that as she straddled him, hovered above him, looking at, then touching his penis.

"Mmm. So….silky." Abruptly she lifted up and slid him inside her.

He convulsed, registering her heat and slickness just barely, before he gripped her thighs as the orgasm shot through him.

His awareness returned slowly. She was perched still, unmoving, grinning down at him, then stretched out on top of him, covering them both with the blanket, their sexes still connected.

"This…this is what I wanted…what I've dreamt of too many nights since I met you. This." Her body seemed so small and light draping his, her skin cool against his heat.

Moments later he rolled her onto her back, meaning to warm her, but exploring her instead. Asking questions, learning exactly where and how she liked to be touched, he tuned to her movements, breaths, and tiny sounds.

She cried out when she climaxed, and he made a silent vow to hear that sound as many times as possible before the sun came up.

They made love again and again, bodies warming each other as they dozed to nature's perfect watery music, lulled between bouts of wanton passion or languorous and tender coupling.

HE WOKE her to watch the sunrise, their limbs still tangled between the blankets, gritty from inevitable sand straying into their seaside bed. "We've become ocean creatures. You taste like the sea and you feel like a sand woman I once knew."

She cocked her head at him sleepily. "A sand woman?"

"Moon spirits come to earth to guard and guide the oceans. Sometimes they covet the human female form—who wouldn't? So they mold sand into a body and inhabit it to dance on deserted beaches. I caught one once. She was dancing with her eyes closed and didn't know I was there. I snuck up and touched her before she could dissolve. See, while a human is touching them, they can't change forms—Look! You're missing the colors..." He interrupted his own story, pointing to the elaborate eastern sky.

Ahna had been watching him, her hair stuck out in messy angles, jade green eyes wide. At his words she rolled to watch the sky change minute by minute, as shades of just ripened raspberry touched iris purples before melting, surrendering into a lustrous molten glow. The colors faded just before sun tips spilled their blinding newborn light.

"A sand woman." Her eyes narrowed.

He nodded solemnly, touching her nipple lightly with one finger, instantly distracted by its dusty pink shade.

Her tone was confused, "The odd thing is, it feels like you're telling the truth."

"Should we go back?" He was trying not to stare at her body, amazed at the pastel shades of her. He'd learned over and over the shape of her throughout their long lusty night but seeing her in full morning light, colored, tousled and chilled was a whole new kind of erotic. He rose, shaking out his shirt and pants to dress, holding her gown out to her as she raised eyebrows at his prominent erection.

"We could...I'm only a little sore, I'd like to...one more time."

But he was almost fully dressed now. His breath caught when she stood and dropped the blanket to step into her gown.

She dressed slowly, provocatively, entirely aware that his eyes followed every move.

"I'm going to make you a bath." He announced, with his most devilish smile. "Can't risk getting sand in your...delicate parts."

She laughed. "And all the people up there at the castle...?"

"...were up late. No one will wake for hours yet."

He was right. No one was about as they crept into the deserted kitchen, as he filled and boiled pots so large he struggled to lift and carry them to the little bathing room adjacent. He filled the wooden tub with steaming water and Ahna carried in buckets of cold to mix it to the perfect temperature.

He barred the door, undressed her and sent the sand swirling away under soapy hands. The room was dim, unreached by early light. He bathed her in silence, gently washing out her hair, awkward and timid with this unfamiliar task but enjoying it all the same.

When he finished, she stood to wrap in a towel. "Now you." Making him sit she soaped him, washed his hair grown halfway to his shoulders, her face going from solemn to sad.

They were both drying off when he saw her wipe away a tear. He stopped to wrap his arms around her, pressing her head to his naked heart. "I'm sorry. I shouldn't have done this....it's not fair, being this intimate, when I can't give you the rest of me...can't be with you. I'm sorry Ahna....I shouldn't have..."

"She looked up at him, sniffling, interrupting with a finger on his lips, "I don't regret one single minute. If this is the only part of you I get, it's completely—all of it—worth it. If this is the once in a hundred lifetimes we get to love each other, it is enough. I will miss you for a very long time...will always want more of you, but please, don't be sorry. I'm not."

Doubt and regret disappearing, he lifted her up and she wrapped her legs around him. Balancing her against the wall, he moved inside her, slowly at first then harder and deeper as she rocked her hips to meet him, head leaned back, eyes locked on his, fingers digging into his shoulders. He stopped a few times, trying to prolong it, wanting her to climax first. When she did, he let himself go too, and they ended panting and gasping, foreheads resting against each other.

"I love you too." He whispered. "And I will try...understand that it wouldn't be soon...may not be ever, but I will try to find a way to come to you. I love you...I do. Maybe you are my one shot at a good life, at happiness. I'd be a fool not to fight with everything I have to keep you."

"That's all I ask Carver..." she cupped his face, "that you try."

27

HOMECOMING

9,972 BCE ARMANTH, ATLANTIS

"...but Destiny chooses blindly and Fate plays childish games, while on this side of the veil we dance to their music, because Understanding seems too far out to grasp."

— ATLANTEAN BOOK ON DESTINY

AHNA

*A*iela's midnight hair streamed behind her on the wind, pointing back like an arrow at the seamless fusion of blue sky and sea that had swallowed the Scottish shore they left behind two days ago.

Ahna leaned beside Aiela on the sea cruiser's smooth, teak rail, watching the aqua water speed underneath. But her mind was on other things. Clad in travel leathers, now sea-weathered and adventure-stained, their torsos reached as if to hasten their homecoming to the familiar land approaching rapidly on the horizon. After a choppy night of sea travel in the cramped cabins below, everyone had spread up here to the decks, soaking in the early sun warmth of a new day.

Students repacked travel bags, scrambling for ways to stay in contact with the heart friends they'd made during the last moon in Ireland. Thirty-three wild days had bonded them, as only shared heartaches, hardships, survival and play will do.

411

"It's over now."

Ahna strained to hear Aiela's unusually quiet tone.

"I don't know whether to laugh or cry. Feels like *everything's* changed in a way I can't quite take in." A gust of wind pushed her slate gray, embroidered hood over her head as she glanced back towards the emptiness behind them. Impatiently, she pushed the hood down only to have her hair take its place, swirling around her angular face in a dark fury of tangles and exclamations.

Ahna nodded at her sister in understanding and pulled a purple hair tie from the smallest pocket of her mantle, handing it to Aiela. "What do you think Papa and Mama will say about all that's happened? They'll be surprised we *both* found love. The colored caves, sweet old Caoimhe—"

"And your scar," Aiela interrupted, "you *look* different than when we left! Hard to believe it was just thirty days ago when that boy..." She skimmed a finger over the slightly puckered line that ran from Ahna's high cheek to her chin, tucking a strand of fine, white-gold hair behind her twin's ear, "Not to worry, the Healing Temple can erase it completely. Then you'll forget and I'll have to remind you that it even happened!"

Ahna's green eyes turned grave. "That's not why I'm worried. My scar is easy to vanish—unlike the fact that you had to kill, how do you think they'll feel about *that?*" She touched the now familiar ridge marring her softly tanned skin, then pulled her hand away from the memory. As the land grew large above the bow of the boat she turned toward stairs that led below. "We should get our bags."

Aiela

A crowd of people waved, smiling and shouting "welcome home!" from the dock as the seacruiser nudged against it.

Just as when they'd departed, a wall of students packed against the railing trying to see the families who'd come for them. Talking raised a chaotic swell of sound, as they ignored diligent instructions from the Teachers, too excited to see the warm faces just below.

Aiela hung back, an aura of anticipation both tight and bright around her. The moment had come. The imminent goodbyes she'd been pretending away until now.

Turner's wayward brown curls glinted ruby highlights in the sunshine as he held her so tight inside his rippled arms that she could not draw breath all the way in.

"At least you got to be with us sailing home. Something to be grateful for..." She buried her face in his neck, matching his desperation at their parting. Determined that she would not spend her last precious moments with her first love weeping, she breathed in the tangy sea-salt and fresh-pine smell of him, filling her sensory memory full of all things Turner.

Turner stared into her eyes as he spoke. "I *will* find a way ta be with ya. That's a vow. We're bound now, an' no matter wha' it takes, I will honor that....honor you."

She knew he meant it, and everything in her yearned to believe him. The possibility that she might never see him again was too much to bear. So she reigned in her breaking heart, willing into existence the truth that they were only parting for a little while.

Carver

He forced himself to smile at Ahna. Despite the hollows of impending loss he soaked in her tenderness, so life-giving, imprinting each detail to draw on later.

Slipping into her hammock last night he'd held her as she fell asleep. Letting the rocking of the waves outside soothe them both, he wished he could whisper the unnameable feelings she'd woken in him over these last weeks; feelings he hadn't known existed before meeting this wispy girl who somehow had soothed the ragged holes in his soul. Spying her little journal when he'd woken early to relieve himself, he took it. Spent the next hour in his own hammock, writing out to her all the things he hadn't said, hoping to give her something she could remember him by. He returned it to her bag when she wasn't looking, five pages full of words poured from his heart.

28

MISUNDERSTANDINGS

"The single biggest problem in communication is the illusion that it has taken place."

— GEORGE BERNARD SHAW

ZIEL

I had brought only two guards with me—more protocol than actual precaution. Sans uniforms to avoid attention, each of these men were Captains of their own battalions. Men who'd been around long enough to have fought, trained and studied their way to the top of their profession.

Focused on finding the twins, I realized I hadn't seen Ahna and Aiela since they were sixteen. Would I still recognize them? *Thick grief haunted, clouding my senses, consuming my energy, trying to bury me at every turn. I pushed it back again, determined to see the girls home before giving in to grief's inevitable embrace.*

"There." I spoke to the large men hovering on either side, pointing with one brown-clad arm, shooting a straight line fifteen degrees to the right. "I believe that's them. To the left of the deck cabin, talking to boys. The blond girl in tan and the tall dark one in blue."

The men nodded, confirming they saw as they moved forward.

"Wait. Give them time." Something inside resisted yanking them out of their carefree world any faster than needed. "It'll be easier if some of these people clear out first anyway."

The Atlantean Guards scanned the crowd. A quartet of rough looking men gathered around two travelers who were talking, gesturing loudly and laughing. I watched as Aiela kissed a stout, curly-haired boy passionately, then ran to catch up with Ahna, waiting to debark.

A tall, black-haired young man stepped to Ahna's side and took her hand. As they walked down the gangplank, fingers intertwined, my Guards moved forward to meet them. That's when they saw the four men also striding towards the couple. Just before they met in the middle, my Guards recognized them as Belials.

"Mardu's men are here! Weapons! Guard Ziel!"

The Belials reacted to the aggressive shouting of the Atlantean Guards, moving rapidly towards them, pulling weapons free of their belts as they came.

Aiela

Aiela still hadn't seen Papa or Mama anywhere. They'd searched from the boat and then were too busy with goodbyes and gathering their things. Everyone else had debarked when Aiela, tears blurring her eyes, followed Ahna and Carver down the wooden walkway.

The crowd had dispersed until only two straggler groups remained. A few men had gathered around Drommen and Lister, awaiting Carver, to transport the three Belial boys home.

"I wonder where Papa is?" Aiela muttered, mostly to herself.

"Probably woke up late or found some irresistible new plant. I'm sure he'll be here soon." Ahna answered. "What's th—!"

Carver shoved the two girls behind him as men below suddenly ran at each other, shouting, then all out fighting.

"Hey those are my people.... no, NO DROMMEN, LISTER! STAY BACK!" Carver yelled as his friends stepped into the fray, trying to assist the Belials. Dropping Ahna's hand, he ran down to them.

"Let's get out of here! GO!" Aiela pushed the stunned Ahna into action and they ran, skirting edges of the miniature battle. A body bumped into Aiela almost knocking her over. They dodged accidental fists engaged in brutal play, trying to get away from the escalating scene that threatened to engulf them.

And then Ziel was there. "This way. *Run!*" He clutched both their arms, pulling them off to the right, urging them faster.

All three kept running until they reached a narrow street and a waiting dock Trolley. Out of breath, confused, the girls climbed inside with Ziel right beside them.

"To the Aero." He panted at the driver.

"Ruler Ziel?? Why are *you* here! Where are we going?"

"Who was that fighting back there and why?" Aiela's questions stumbled into Ahna's, as they fell back into the plain wood benches. The trolley lurched forward, and around a corner, picking up speed.

Struggling to catch his breath, Ziel answered. "I'm bringing you to High City. Your Aunt Sage is there and you're needed." He kept looking back towards his men, visibly anxious.

Ziel

"I can't fully explain until we're with Sage—I swore to her...and I'm not sure yet what danger my Guards saw back there."

Something told me that the more I said, the more questions these girls would ask. I felt winded still. My body struggled to keep up with all the demands I was making, my awareness still at the docks trying to see the brawl I'd run from.

"Where's Papa? He was supposed to meet us—are they in High City too?" Aiela's voice was insistent, her wide blue eyes searching mine while her sister sat studying me.

I felt Ahna prying into my mind, trying to read me any way she could, determined to get some answers. *She knows something's very wrong. They both do.* Blocking her easily, I concentrated fully on now, neutralizing my apprehension, especially the grief. We had a two hour flight ahead and I couldn't afford to reveal any more without telling them the whole damn story.

They were so beautiful, these girls. They'd grown into strong women already, resembling both Drey and Taya in opposite ways. This thought made me want to weep, so I pulled away from it, forcing my face into a blank as I spoke with great calm. "Please don't worry. My Guards are perfectly adequate. Are you hungry? Tired? How was your trip? It's been much too long since I've been to the Green Isle. I'd love to hear about it, all that you saw and did—what happened to your face child?!"

"My face? You just abandoned your men and you're asking about my face? If we're hungry?? Carver is *fighting back there!* We should go back.

You need to sort out whatever that was! If he gets hurt I will not forgive you." Ahna's reddening face was furious, probably at failing in her rather untrained attempts to probe my consciousness.

I took two long deep breaths, knowing they would subconsciously mirror my energy state. Young adults experience stimuli at three times the intensity adults feel it. It was time to slow everything way down. Time to just breathe.

We arrived at the Aero pads just then. Few other aeros were here, most of them smaller than ours, for short distance use.

"Go back to the docks. Bring my men here." I spoke to the trolley driver.

We exited the boxy little transport cart and I urged the girls to climb quickly into the Aero, while I turned back to the driver. "See if you can find their luggage."

The driver nodded to me and pulled away, while I followed the girls up the short stairs into the silver, bullet-shaped Aero that would take us home. No one else was around but still I closed and barred the door.

"What of our luggage? We didn't get our large bags." Aiela was the first to notice.

"The driver will bring them if he can. If he can't, I will replace your clothing and other things, once we get to High City." I continued to breath long and deep, settling into the seat nearest the food and handing Ahna a jug of lemon water, speaking kindly. "Your friend—Carver is it?—will be fine. Our Guards would not let him get injured. Surely you know this. At worst, the Belials will be stunned for a bit." I paused as a thought occurred, "Why did Carver run into it? Was he thinking to help our Guards?"

The look she gave me was almost condescending, reminding me of how she'd looked at me the first time I met her, just days shy of three years old.

"Those were *his people*. They came to take him and Drommen and Lister home. Why were they attacked?"

Understanding dawned then. For all three of us.

"You thought the Belials were a danger to *us*." Ahna accused.

"Your Guards were protecting us? From what?" Aiela demanded.

"There were Belial students on the trip?" I sighed.

417

29

HIGH CITY FUNERAL

9,972 BCE HIGH CITY, ATLANTIS

"You will lose someone you can't live without, and your heart will be badly broken, and the bad news is that you never completely get over the loss. But this is also the good news. They live forever in your broken heart that doesn't seal back up. It's like having a broken leg that never heals perfectly, but you learn to dance with the limp."

— ANNE LAMOTT

AIELA

*B*y the time Ziel's guards made it to the aero, solemn and silent, she knew something was disastrously wrong.

Ahna became frantic, picking up the guard's energies. They didn't know how to block the sympathy and anger they were feeling.

Landing two hours later at Poseidon's Palace, Ziel took them immediately to Auntie Sage, who was sipping tea and crying in his apartment.

She rose to fold them both inside her arms saying very simply. "Your Papa and Mama are gone. Passed on from this life. They'd been skiing...were buried in an avalanche."

Looking to Ahna for help, Aiela couldn't quite comprehend the words.

But Ahna only returned the same sort of blankness.

They sat down, right there on the intricate carpets, crossing their legs like they were preparing for a childhood class.

Auntie Sage sat too. "When they didn't return from their trip, I contacted Ziel and he had their aero tracked. It took two weeks to locate and dig their... b-bodies out." She stopped to let the sob out. It shook her for a few silent moments. "Ziel was adamant they be found and brought home, so I went to identify them, to bring them here." Auntie Sage's voice faltered away into another bout of tears before she continued. "At least it's confirmed now and you were spared the agony of waiting to know for certain. We arrived late last night—which is why I wasn't there to meet you in Armanth."

TIME STOPPED. Everything was muted from the time Aiela heard those unfathomable words,

"Your Papa and Mama are gone, passed on from this life..."

As if invisible blankets were draped, layer upon layer between her and the rest of the world.

Ahna agreed, "It's like being underwater where everything moves slower, muffles sound, dims color, blurs shapes. As if the world beyond my immediate surroundings has ceased to exist."

The worst part was waking up each morning. That first moment coming out of sleep was the only time left—one single moment—that didn't weigh a thousand pounds before she remembered and it all came crashing in to bury her again.

ON THEIR THIRD DAY BACK, Auntie woke her with tea. "Aiela it's late. Ahna is eating—trying to at least. Won't you get up and join us? We need to make plans. I know it may be the hardest thing you've ever done but I want you to have a say in their funeral. It'll be the day after tomorrow..."

Ziel had spent the last two days in preparations to honor them. Aiela was only vaguely aware of all this, unable to take in or sort out any extra details beyond the fact that her parents were gone.

"I just wanna go *home!*" Aiela rolled her face into the pillow, the tears starting again. "I'm so tired of weeping!" She looked up at Sage, "When will it stop? How long until I can go five minutes, an entire day without crying?" Her whole body ached from the torrential tears, like eventually she might just dissolve into a river, perhaps join the canal water on its journey back to the sea. She sort of wished it, really.

Auntie Sage set the mug down and sat, reaching to cup Aiela's face, smoothing her hair back, tears dribbling silently onto lightly wrinkled cheeks as her shoulders lifted. "I don't know. It's different for everyone but it *will* pass, I promise you. I've too much experience at this sort of thing and each time, I think it's too much, that my body can't possibly contain such heavy, voluminous sadness. Truthfully, it can't. Which is why we cry, why it's so important to let it all go, and be patient and trust your body's wisdom. Because it knows what to do even when you don't."

They both looked over as Ahna appeared in the doorway, clutching a steaming mug.

She leaned against the door and tried to smile at her sister. "Good morning, it was nice outside when I got up at noon. We should get something pretty to wear for...we need to pick out flowers, see the paintings Ziel is having m-m-made...." Her voice broke and her face crumpled.

She looks ten years older, Aiela thought, rising immediately and picking up the mug of fragrant tea Auntie Sage had brought. This demanded her continued strength. She had to be there for Ahna. It's what Papa and Mama would want most; them to help each other through this relentless grief. If there truly was a "through"....And so she choked down the foods Auntie set in front of her, tasting too rich after Ireland's bland fish and root vegetables.

They eventually left the palace accompanied by Ziel, squinting at the shock of bright afternoon sunlight. The startling colors and pristine layout of the city bombarded her with overstimulation as they walked. "Everything's too perfect here!" After Ireland's wild countryside this felt like a painting, an over-arranged, over-decorated facade. "It's all just...stupid."

Ahna nodded in agreement. "I wish we could go back..."

The noise and bustle of the marketplace seemed offensive too. People all around were laughing, buying things, eating and playing as if nothing had changed.

Craftswomen and merchants called to them.

"I've the next fashion in shoes, come look pretty ones, you'll fall in love..."

"Stuffed figs! Twenty flavors..."

"Cloud chairs here, sit a spell, you'll want one for every room!"

Ziel led them to the clothing section but there were too many choices and they just stood there, side by side, staring blankly around.

"Could you bring them a selection of nice outfits to try on please. Something formal." Ziel instructed the helpful woman, as Sage shepherded them to a fitting room.

"What I really want is one of the dresses Mama made me. Why can't I have one of them brought? I don't want something from here, they look silly and uncomfortable!" Aiela knew she was acting childish. Didn't really care.

Ahna chose quickly for both of them. Rejecting every fancy, overly designed outfit that was shown to them without trying even one on, she insisted quietly, "I know what we want, I will show you."

The dress woman sighed, clucking at their mutinous faces and poor choice of such simplicity, when they could've had layers upon layers of fabulously styled, jeweled, color-morphing gorgeousness. Instead, she brought them identical long gowns that wrapped their bodies loosely in a light fabric, leaving one shoulder and arm bare. Buttercream colored.

"It's the exact color of the linen robes at the monastery in Ireland." Ahna whispered.

Next they were supposed to visit the flower fields, but Aiela questioned why they needed to go see all the flowers that were available. "Can't we just tell you their favorites? I only care that we have what they loved most. I'm just real tired..." She'd only been awake a few hours and already felt exhausted again.

"Make sure there are plenty. Mama loved flowers." Ahna's voice was flat.

Sage looked at Ziel who nodded, seeming weary himself.

"Alright. What flowers do you want?"

Aiela sat down in the shade. She had wandered away from the markets and stopped at a spot beside the east canal where the bank was lined with old wisteria trees. They had come here only two years ago, pausing to eat midday meal under these branches whose vines had touched the ground then, heavy with blossoms in every shade of lavender and violet. Aiela remembered her delight at the scent, the wonderland of being in an endless tunnel of flowers. Now, the grass was littered with remnants of withered, dried-up blossoms. The branches and vines had sprung back to normal height, dripping seed pods here and there, with no other trace of the glory that once was.

"...definitely blue lotus, the really big ones. Papa always brought one to Mama. What else El?"

They gathered around her, a parody of the family of four she'd last been here with. Ahna, Sage and Ziel, settled on the ground beside her.

"Did you say roses? Papa liked red roses." Aiela spoke in a monotone, forcing herself to participate, trying to care.

"Yes, I said that already, and white peonies for Mama, purple phlox." Ahna frowned at her with concern.

"Sorry, I guess I didn't hear you. That's all I can think of…"

"Blue lotus, red roses, white peonies and purple phlox?" Ziel's words seemed soft and rounded.

Both girls nodded confirmation and Auntie Sage added, "Beautiful choices to honor your parents. The first time Drey ever saw Taya, he gave her a blue lotus. Did you know that?"

Ziel shook his head as both girls nodded.

"Yes, but tell us again. Please?"

Aiela felt a little focus return as Auntie Sage retold the story they'd heard so many times before.

"It was quite large and wilted see, and Taya didn't know what it was because she'd never seen a blue lotus—or any lotus—before. So she looked at Drey, very puzzled and said 'What is this, a dead bird? Where's its head and what is wrong with you?' Then she dropped it like a live coal. Drey replied 'Oh, well the answer to *that* will take the rest of the day. We better go sit down…' "

Aiela felt the muffling blanket lift just a little when they all smiled and Ziel chuckled.

"Then Drey knelt to pick up the flower, and proceeded to tell Taya all about the trip he had just returned from, how he had fallen wildly in love with this new flower and brought back as many tubers as he could. How he planned to plant them all over Atlantis and would now do so in her honor, because he had never seen a woman so desirable. 'Your hair turns blue in the sunlight, your eyes match this flower perfectly, your tattoos are even silvered blue! This is most certainly your flower. Perhaps I will rename it the Taya. The people I got it from say it symbolizes eternity, that the plants themselves can live for a thousand years. I'd like to spend eternity with you pretty Taya, starting right now. I give you this flower as a promise, that I will stay with you for a thousand years if you'll have me.' He said all of this, gazing up at her from his knees, mind you. And having never met her before!"

Sage chuckled at the memory, "She came home and told me how she met this boy who was absolutely crazy. That she was going back to him at sunset and may not be home until sunrise because he was her kind of crazy, and she needed to know everything about him. She figured that would take all night because he'd been just about everywhere in the world. Drey was only supposed to stay in Chiffon a week, brought in as a consult on some of the plant plagues we were having. Instead, he stayed three moons, until she agreed to be his mate. He dug a special pond, with an island just big enough for two in the middle, and planted every one of his tubers in that pond. They wouldn't set a date for their vows because he didn't know how long until the lotus might bloom, and they were determined to make vows to each other surrounded by those flowers."

"I've never heard that story." Ziel said. "And did not realize Drey originated the lotus' transplant to our country—how very extraordinary. Is their pond still there? Still blooming?"

"Oh yes!" Sage smiled a sad smile. "It blooms all summer and half the autumn, doesn't it girls?"

"What would you think of having a sculpture of them made, to put by their pond at home?" Ziel asked softly.

All three of them nodded, teary-eyed at his suggestion.

"It doesn't have to be now, but when you know the stone or materials, what exactly you would like, just let me know. I'll make sure it gets done and sent to you. Perhaps I could deliver it myself."

Sage touched his hand in appreciation, as they gave him watered down smiles—but smiles nonetheless—and rose to continue this heartbreaking day.

THE PAINTINGS WERE GIGANTIC, towering above a stage overflowing with musicians and flowers. Aiela gazed up at them, pleased at how well they'd been done. Mama was depicted from the "tattoo side" as Papa always called it, and her laugh looked real enough that it seemed odd not to hear the accompanying sound. A wave of homesickness tore through her, as if she could just go home and maybe Mama would be there, looking exactly like this. Papa was in a lopsided stance with the distracted look he wore when he was pretending to pay attention to what you were saying, but really his mind was working through something else entirely.

Holographic images played by the far wall, flashing through the contributions made to Atlantis by Drey and Taya. Mama's fabrics—more than Aiela had ever realized—were listed and shown. Teacher Mia spoke of the rapid growth of Chiffon from the increased production, and the products developed from Mama's fabric blends by designers across the country. There were Papa's plant and stone discoveries brought back from across the world, incorporated into Atlantean gardens and lives.

Many many medicines. Growing methods that increased food production. Even relationships to other cultures, forged because of his help, given freely while he worked in those far-away places.

Aiela felt over-styled—even though their gowns were much plainer than any other woman here. Auntie Sage had let the beauty people get them ready this morning saying, "Everyone is very sad for us. They just want to help and this is a way they can contribute."

So now their hair was twisted into some new fad, and their faces painted so that they barely recognized each other. It had actually made all three of them laugh—once they were safely alone behind closed doors, and wouldn't hurt anyone's feelings. They'd pointed and giggled at each other, growing more hysterical when they saw themselves in the mirror.

Auntie Sage had invited them to join her in drinking a large glass of wine, (but only after they ate something) before being escorted here. "You'll need the little bit of relaxation, the little bit of dulling, as much as I."

There were thousands crowded into High City's largest outdoor venue. Many came all the way from Chiffon to attend. It felt good to see familiar faces, have the villagers they'd known all their lives hugging them, laughing and weeping alongside them, even though the crowd flowed out so far she couldn't see its end.

Auntie Sage had explained, "Many will come to honor Ruler Ziel. He's claimed Drey and Taya as his family. Thousands upon thousands are mourning his loss with him, so great is their love and respect for this man who has led them, longer than they can remember."

Aiela noted the touch of pride that crept into Auntie's voice and wondered at it. For the first time it occurred to her to question what the connection was between Ziel and Sage.

Funerals were a celebration of not just the life that had ended, but also everyday joys in the experience of being alive. And so everyone dressed in their best, surrounded with beauty and the warmth of connecting with each other. Musicians would play for hours while refreshments were served. People would dance and filter by to bless the family and friends left behind. Later, Ziel would take the stage to talk about her dead parents, telling their stories, honoring their lives from beginning to end.

I wish Turner was here. The thought caught her unaware. Usually she only thought of him once she was alone with nothing else claiming her attention. Some of her tears were from missing him, although it was hard to say how many. She wondered, would he come to her if he knew that her world had just shattered?

They'd opted for neither of the traditional body arrangements.

Long ago, Atlanteans offered their dead to the skies. After the soul had left, its empty shell was returned to the nature it belonged in. Bodies were placed on the nearest mountaintop, offered back to the elements, the predators, the earth herself. A year afterward, the bones, picked clean and washed by storms, would be retrieved, painted with red ocher and laid to final rest in a tomb. Spirits would sometimes hang around their vacated bodies for a period of time. A full year gave the spirit time to let go and return home. Special ornate temple-like body altars at the highest points around the country still stood, but were rarely used now.

Cremation was most popular, the ashes made into jewels, vases or even statues in the likeness of the deceased.

But Aiela and Ahna wanted to return their parents to the sea they'd both enjoyed so. Ahna had said it first, startling Aiela and Auntie Sage. "I think Papa would want to go to the fish—Mama too of course."

The more they talked about it, the more sure all three of them were that this was the perfect solution. It wasn't unheard of. Pretty much like the ancient mountaintop ritual, except they'd be floated out into the ocean when the tide went out, and there would be no need to retrieve the bones.

Once the sun went down, they would mime the floating out ritual here, but the bodies wouldn't really be on the pallets. All three of them were adamant. Papa and Mama's bodies must be taken home, floated from the dock they'd lived and loved each other on for over twenty years.

30

MOVING ON

9,972 BCE CHIFFON-HIGH CITY, ATLANTIS

"I know you love that part my sweet, but we won't find out what happens next unless we turn the page."

— DREY

AHNA

*E*xactly two moons later, Ziel sent a piloted aero to Chiffon, to collect her, Aiela and their belongings for the move. They'd opted to leave most things behind, not yet ready to disassemble their childhood home.

"I need to preserve Papa and Mama's memories a while longer I guess." Aiela said while they packed.

Ahna was relieved, "Me too. It feels too final, too big of a change at once, losing them *and* everything here. Even if it's just illusion, we need a place that holds us together still."

Tears leaked out as they absorbed more of the enormous loss, as they chose items they each wanted to take. Besides clothing, they packed only one box apiece, favorite mementos of parents who had cherished them.

Auntie Sage insisted on coming along "to get them settled in". For two moons she'd been relentless in making them face their new independence. Comfortingly firm, she'd refused to shield them. So it came as a surprise when she became abruptly protective again.

Deciding to travel through the night, they departed as dusk veiled the countryside around Chiffon. All three of them pressed faces against windows, watching the clouds turn cantaloupe colors, the glow of white-washed buildings fading slowly beneath them.

IT WAS EARLY, not yet morning when they approached High City. Gentle rain tinkered against the aero. It would stop soon as the sun started to rise —Atlantis had been regulating the weather for quite some time.

Ahna was thinking of Carver. Remembering damp moments during the Ireland trip, wrapped with blankets and drowsing against him in a wagon, while rain thumped on the tarps overhead, laughing around campfires in the evenings, damp sand by the sea under a crescent moon. It was lovely to be back in Atlantis where the sun shone almost every day, after living in Ireland's soggy green. But whenever it rained now, Ahna thought of Carver—wondered if he had the same association. She missed his solid presence and quiet caring, his earnest questions, his imaginative stories.

"What's happening inside this pretty head?" Auntie Sage smoothed Ahna's hair back from her cheek. She leaned into the touch as Sage settled into the bright plush colors of the seat beside her.

"Good morning Auntie. I thought you were still sleeping..." Ahna smiled faintly before looking back out the aero window, watching as they moved through slow splashing rain. Sage continued to caress her hair, waiting to listen in case she wanted to talk.

She exhaled slowly, "I was thinking of Carver. It was rainy in Ireland, so this makes me think of him." Ahna traced the little water streams, flowing horizontal across the glass, with her finger.

"Ah, you miss him. Tell me about this boy...." They'd been so busy grieving their parents and preparing for the move, there'd been little time to talk about those they'd met or relationships formed on their trip.

"He smelled like earth after a storm. You know that slow, fresh smell?" Ahna glanced sideways at Sage. "Did I mention he's Belial?"

Sage nodded. "I remember that much, but what does he look like? I don't think you told me that."

"He had nice hands....big, well shaped. He's tall, with black, longish

427

hair and blue eyes like a frozen lake. He plays the dulcimer really well, and played for me... I think that's why I liked his hands, the way they moved when he was playing. And the way they felt..."

Auntie Sage was smiling. "He sounds handsome!"

Ahna raised her eyes up to the aero roof, "Yes! I wish you could have met him. He's quiet until he gets to know you but everyone listened when he talked. He can be charming, but really, he didn't care what they thought of him. He was shy with me—I don't think he had much experience with girls—and he didn't want to be touched at first."

"Why was that?"

"I don't know. He never wanted to talk about his family or where he's from. There was so much he wasn't telling me."

"Frozen eyes and secretive, but yet you trusted him?"

Ahna nodded slowly, feeling doubt. Her own and Auntie Sage's.

"He rescued me when my face got cut. He's gentle and kind, always looking out for others. I know his heart is good—but I don't think he knows it. Anyway, it doesn't matter. I won't ever see him again." Her eyes watered and she turned back to tracing the window streams.

Auntie Sage caressed her back. "How do you know that?"

"He refused. Said once we got back to Atlantis he could never be with me. That it was to protect me. He told me never to contact him..." Ahna tried to stifle the tiny sob bubbling up. She was so tired of crying. So tired of losing people she loved.

Auntie Sage hugged her tight from behind. "Oh little one, let the tears come. You loved him, I can feel it. Someday I will tell you of the boy I loved and lost. You've lost too much, too fast. Your whole world is changing. Here's something I know; whether you ever see him again or not, this love you have for him is a bond. It's as real as the nose on your face. Those bonds have a way of pulling people back to each other. But if that never happens, you had that time with him. You got to feel exquisite emotions, and experience someone your heart wants. Treasure that. Hold it. And then one day, you may be ready to let it go. Just know that the time will come when all of this won't hurt so much, and you will want to turn the page and see what happens next."

Aiela was still sleeping soundly after they landed atop the thick white wall surrounding High City. Ahna rubbed her sister's arm lightly. "El wake up, we're here. Ziel's people are waiting outside for us. They want to carry our things..."

Aiela sat up, coming quickly to life as usual, no matter how deep her sleep. "That was fast! Seems like we just left home...." She yawned, stretching both arms in a V shape, hair sticking out in strange ways and Ahna smiled, trying to smooth it a bit.

"I slept most of the way too. We must thank Ziel for sending such a comfortable aero. Come on, I'm starving. Maybe he has food ready."

ZIEL

"*Feeling lost, crazy and desperate belongs to a good life as much as optimism, certainty and reason.*"

— ALAIN DE BOTTON

ZIEL

"It's been lonely without you here..." I embraced each of them in turn, noting the twins seemed more interested in the food spread on my table than in greeting me. "Let's eat. No need to wait."

We all sat and to my surprise, Ahna blessed the food. To hear my own traditional refrain coming back at me was rather haunting, and I could feel Taya's laughing presence. *Stick around.* I told her. *I don't know how I'm going to teach them all that I need to....*

"How was your trip?" I inquired automatically, though there were infinitely more important things we needed to discuss.

They nodded at me. Mouths full and chewing.

Sage swallowed first. "We slept. So nice to have a pilot."

"Thank you for sending a comfortable aero, I've never been in one that nice." Ahna added.

Aiela was bobbing her head in agreement, mouth perpetually full.

"You're welcome. I'm pleased you liked it and were able to rest. We

430

have a very full day ahead and I have rather monumental things to discuss with you. But first, I'd like to hear—if you're willing to tell me—how was the ceremony in Chiffon? How is your grief journey since you left here?"

They all stared at me for a minute, waiting for another to answer. I knew these were big questions, but I was about to throw their lives even more off-course, so I figured this was no time to avoid the hard things. I needed them to trust me deeply with their inner and outer worlds—as I was about to trust them.

Aiela swallowed and didn't take another bite, as if the subject instantly suppressed her appetite. "It was beautiful" she said, her expression somber yet soft. "We waited until your statue arrived."

I'd commissioned it before they'd left High City after the funeral. A life-size figure carved from amazonite, of Drey and Taya waltzing, memorializing the way they had danced through life together.

"We decided to place it as part of the ceremony." She paused to let Ahna or Sage chime in but they sat watching her, their silence urging her on.

"The blue lotus were blooming like we've never seen, as if they knew it was a special occasion. We put it on their island in the center of the pond. Some of the villagers didn't want it there permanently, but it's their rightful spot. If it wasn't for Papa and Mama, the lotus pond wouldn't even be there. Then we went out to our little dock at sunset—as many villagers as would fit. Lots of people had to stay up on the cliffs. Mia, our childhood teacher who was such good friends with Mama, had the idea of setting fire to Papa's fishing boat that we were floating the bodies in, so that it would eventually return them to the sea. And we did. Each villager brought something to put in the the boat that reminded them of Mama or Papa. They filled it with hemp stalks and llama wool, cotton, bamboo, flax, dried herbs, flowers and leaves. Ahna and I put a torch to it before the tide took them away..." her voice broke, and she fell silent with faraway eyes.

Ahna and Sage reached across to hold her hands, and I could picture it as it must have been in their minds, two bodies wrapped in white hemp muslin, soaked in flower essences, laid side by side on a floating wooden vessel filled with tributes. Set aflame by these two daughters whose world had become colder. Sadder.

Sage pulled something from her pocket. "Mia was Taya's best friend. She wrote this for the funeral. I kept it because it's such a comfort." She handed me the scrap of paper.

Already There

I'm already there where you're going,
Though human me weeps in the gap.
There's a hole here you left but I won't stay bereft,
I'm filling in memories and laughs.
Till it's full.

I'm already there where you're going.
Awake from this dream of confusion.
The part that's still dreaming, absorbing the meaning,
knows losing your love's an illusion.
Pretend.

I'm already there where you're going.
Master Time only rules us now.
You're done with this strife, while I finish my life.
When I miss you, in silence I'll bow.
'Cuz I know.

I'm already there where you're going.
Without even missing a beat
we're sharing our pain and the love that we gained,
planning for the next life we'll meet.
Doesn't end.

You're already there where I'm going.
Awake from the dream we made.
Like a new breeze at dawn, our souls carry on.
Time rules a grand charade.
We're eternal.

We sat in silence and tears, letting the farewell wash over us.

Ahna finished the telling. "We wore the cream dresses from the funeral here and I remember thinking how strange to have our entire family dressed in white this last time together. Because when we said goodby in Armanth, before Ireland, we all wore so many colors. I don't think any of us *owned* white clothes 'til now. It was exactly what we wanted, sending their last remnants off together, into the deep beyond."

I smiled at her poetic heart, even as I wiped at my eyes. I wondered if these girls might ever reach a point of letting me father them when they needed it. I hoped so.

"I'm sorry I missed it." I'd already sent my excuses along with the statue. I'd been busy with new intelligence on the sudden movement of Mardu's army, compounded by a certainty of what I must now ask them. Clearing my throat I plunged in. "Pardon my abruptness. There's no easy way to say this so I'm just going to blurt it out. Aiela, I need you to apprentice in the House of Rulers."

She frowned at me and shook her head. "No, it's all arranged already. I'm to apprentice in Healing. I don't want to be a Ruler, don't care one bit about any of those positions. It sounds boring and I would hate it! I'm a Healer—it's set!"

"It's all she ever wanted...why would you change it this late? And without consulting with her at all? It doesn't seem fair." Sage spoke as if unruffled but her eyes had narrowed. She was preparing to do battle.

I looked at Ahna expectantly, inviting her protests too. Might as well let them get it all out. Then maybe they'd listen to my why.

But she just sat there drumming her fingers on the table, eyebrows raised in silent question. Wearing the exact expression I'd seen on Drey countless times.

"Ah, reading energy are we? And what does mine say?" I inquired pleasantly. Blocking nothing.

"That what you're about to tell us matters more to you than anything else. So it doesn't matter what we say."

"Very good. Except what you have to say *always* matters because if you're unwilling, my plan won't work. You do now—and always will—have choice with me. Do you understand Aiela? I will explain myself to all of you and at the end, you can choose. Regardless of what you decide, will you vow to me that you will never repeat or reveal what I'm about to tell you?" Making eye contact with each of them in turn, I gathered their nods, then began. "Your mother programmed our three power Crystals—which she named the Heart of Atlantis. Did you know that?"

Ahna and Aiela looked at each other and slowly shook their heads, looking confused. Sage refrained from any response.

"Do you remember the time she was gone for a moon? She came here, designed the programming, and physically carved the surface of each Crystal herself. A sort of encoded map among other things. Should our knowledge ever be lost, it can be regained by those of high enough vibration, and the crystals activated for various uses of power. Currently, our grid needs only a fraction of the power generated by just one of the Crystals. It is my desire to eventually share our grid, our power source, with the rest of the world. More importantly, the power of the Crystals is a weapon —and now there are four of us that know this. Your mother was not just the designer, she was my Keeper of the Crystals. That is, she was my backup as the last line of defense should Atlantis ever fall to those of darkness. Anyone who would use all that we have and all that we know for evil purposes."

I paused to gauge their reactions. Drank some water, waiting, but they seemed puzzled, not alarmed, so I continued.

"It is true that Atlantis has the highest trained army and most advanced weaponry in the world, but we also have weaknesses. Chief among them being everyone's certainty that no other would dare to come against us. Our longstanding peace has led us to believe we are no longer susceptible, no longer threatened, no longer vulnerable. Foreign Relations has prepared in every way possible, despite their secret belief that I am just a paranoid old man. Our army is ready, our spies continually report back from their far-flung posts. We have layers of strategies, yet I am sure we are overlooking something." I stopped and leaned forward, looking each girl in the eyes before I continued.

"I need you, both of you, to take your mother's place as Keepers of the Crystals. Apprenticing as an Oracle and a Ruler are covers for having you housed here in the Palace where I can train you, prepare you for what I believe is coming. Your parents," I hesitated only a second while I glanced at their Aunt, "and Sage were, are, the closest to family that I had. And now you are the ones I'm choosing to place my ultimate trust in. No one else knows of this—and no one will. Should all else fail, we are the last defense, the failsafe in protecting our people, our history, our country and all that we stand for."

Ahna spoke slowly into the growing uncomfortable silence my words had produced, "You believe something, or someone is coming against us. What have you seen? What are you preparing for?"

"The Oracles visions are many and ominous, but as you know, the future is never absolute. There are simply too many variables created by free will. Yet increasingly, the dreams and visions deal with attacks against Atlantis." I anticipated her next question. "Coupled with the intelligence we have of Sons of Belial armies being built and trained in huge numbers, I strongly believe they will move against us. It may be far off or may be soon, but it Is coming. They are weary of their overpopulation problems. They resent being dependant on us for their food supply. They have no moral reason to let us keep our peace. The Sons of Belial are my number one concern, and the only ones who have the technology, the knowledge and power to do us harm." I turned to eating, having imparted all I was willing to right now.

Sage looked to Aiela and Ahna with a heaving sigh. "Well. This certainly turns everything on its head. I will support you in whatever you decide." Their answer came more quickly than I expected.

"I'll do it." Aiela stared at me with bold, determined blue eyes. "Of course, I will be your Keeper of the Crystals."

Ahna nodded. "If Mama did it, so will we."

"I realize it is not what you wanted or planned and I won't ask it of you forever." I was humbled by their quick, sure responses. Their willingness to join me in giving their lives to something they understood only a little. And they did not yet know of the prophecy, or their part in it. Was I being deceitful not telling them?

I caught Sage watching me, and knew she was thinking the same thing. Likely, she would corner me and demand full disclosure. Oh but she grew fiery and irresistible when she wanted something!

"Thank you for saying yes. I'll tell you this—now that it won't pressure you; I didn't have a backup plan if you'd said no."

They both grinned at me, eating quickly as if energized by this new adventure.

"I've already arranged your rooms. When we're done here, there are older apprentices who will show you around, get you oriented. Oh! Aiela, I almost forgot. There is a young man waiting to see you..."

"Who?"

"I've no idea. I accepted a message for you last night, and advised him to meet you in the main eating room at noonday meal." I glanced at the sunclock. "Plenty of time to get settled in before you see who it is and what he wants. Now, what other immediate questions do you have?"

3 2

AIELA'S VISITOR

"All the beauty that's been lost before wants to find us again"

— U2

AIELA

She smelled food before she entered the sunbright eating room on the first level of Poseidon's Palace.

Commotion greeted her in the clatter of dishes and the hum of voices. The large room flowed outside, breezes softly stirring the everyday robes of young men and women, eating with newly-met fellow apprentices, or getting to know their advisor. Several teachers were circulating through the low tables surrounded with floor cushions, no doubt assessing their newest crop of charges.

Ahna was still on the Oracle's level unpacking, and Sage was presumably with Ziel somewhere. They were all to meet for early supper at Ziel's suite this evening.

Her eyes scanned the overflowing crowds, trying to find anyone familiar, curious who had come searching for her. She assumed it to be one of the boys from the Ireland trip, or perhaps someone from Chiffon. Her childhood friends were many, and the students from the Ireland trip might want a recommendation from her as their leader—or perhaps just to reconnect.

Then she saw him.

Leaning against the wall near the opposite entrance. Still as a stone save for restless eyes roaming the room, and that mass of springy curls swiveling slowly.

"Turner!" She shouted across the noise, oblivious to the heads turning her way, running towards him along the room's periphery. "Turner!" He heard her that time, started towards her, colliding in a lavish embrace. "It's you! You're here, how—"

But he was kissing her then, with his smile and laughter wrapping around them.

"No way can I go a year wi' oot ya, I barely made it this long! Sure an' I've made a bargain wi' my Da." Turner didn't let go of her as they moved outside searching for a quieter space. "Da was glad enough ta keep me in the family business, he agreed ta any terms an' now I'll be on every one o' our ships deliverin' ta High City. He said I did a fair job leading the Atlanteans so I might as well keep makin' connections an providin' services. I'm ta build the business wi' more runs, transportin' goods an foods from other countries ta yers, an' I'll be here at least twice a month— e'en more during summer."

Aiela literally vibrated with delight, grabbing hold of him and twirling them both. "I can't believe it! We really get to be together!"

When she stopped, a new thought came. "What about Greece? That was your dream…"

"Greece'll always be there an someday, if ya want, we can go t'gether. I've a new dream now." He pulled her down onto sun-warm grass. "Tell me what's happening wi' you."

Her smile faded along with her voice, "My parents…my Papa and Mama have d-died." She had to whisper it this first time, speaking those flimsy words, so inadequate compared to their reality. Fresh tears welled as she narrated all that had happened from the time she'd kissed him goodbye on the seacruiser in Armanth.

He held her hand, and then the rest of her, tightly, as if he might press all her pieces back together. Listening, his face looked stricken at her loss.

"I'm sorry my love, so sorry. I wouldna know what ta do if I lost my parents. I cannit make it better, but I can be wi' ya in grief, an' in yer new life here. I'll be wi' ya…"

CARVER'S VOW

9,972 BCE TEMPLE CITY, BELIAL

"Murderers are not monsters, they're men. And that's the most frightening thing about them."

— ALICE SEBOLD

CARVER

When Carver had arrived home from Armanth, mute with despair from the abrupt loss of Ahna, Mardu was in his spacious library.

Lined with cases brimming with books, scrolls, codices, crystals, maps and artifacts, this room held a lifetime of hoarded knowledge. Bought, bartered and stolen from around the globe, some of it had even been smuggled out of High City; a fact Mardu liked to boast of. He tapped a booted foot behind his desk, its base a dragon skull dipped in illumine, the thin slab top elaborately formed from pyrite.

Carver, leading the Belial guards and Drommen and Lister, found this picture oddly beautiful; his father sitting impatient and proud—as if he were an extension of the stone desk he treasured. Beautiful in the way that a lightning storm is. Or a lion. Magnificent power, if you could ignore the terror and death that was its nature.

The sun had long ago sank to its rest, leaving black shadows in the library.

Carver motioned for Mardu's men to report on the skirmish with Ziel's guards in Armanth.

"They attacked us...too close to use blades...sound lasers knocked every one of us out except the boys here. They had to carry us to the transport." The guards were speaking overly loud, still recovering from the intense beam of sound decibel that had incapacitated them.

Carver watched Mardu's face turn the color of eggplant—sure sign of his effort to control the rising rage.

Mardu kept his voice carefully level as he pointed at the men, "Go directly to my healer and have him see to your eardrums". Giving in then to the anger, he pounded both sizeable fists over and over on the desk so that everything on it jumped and skittered. "They think they can do whatever they want! Attacking my men unprovoked!? You should've killed them!! We could've claimed self-defense..." He subsided into tense irritability, sending everyone away except Carver.

"What of Meihal's ships?"

"He accepted, but the price he demands is high." Carver stood at attention, knowing better than to cower. He was one of the few who refused to, and Mardu showed him a certain respect because of it.

Eyeing his largest and quietest son for a moment, Mardu snapped, "You negotiated?"

Carver shook his head. "He refused to bargain. It was yes or no, and the yes only came on his full terms. He's...intelligent, more than we thought."

Again a long silence. Mardu's way of dominating any conversation. Carver remained quiet, waiting. Finally, heaving a great sigh, Mardu leaned back in his chair.

"Alright. Tell Ramon whatever it is that Meihal wants and get it done." He waved a hand back and forth, "I don't want the details right now, it's been a long day already. I lost eight dozen soldiers last week, outbreak in the muta camps—had to pull my best scientists off their projects to figure it out. One of my ships went down outside Asia, losing the cargo of jewels and girls I'd promised to Greece's border patrol regiment. That was our way in, and now, because of that and the soldier losses, I'll have to delay the attack. My overseer of food imports from Atlantis is suspected of treason, selling our secrets to them. I've sent Balek to deal with that, but I need to appoint someone to replace him. Someone the Atlanteans will want to deal with...I may send you to see it's done well."

Mardu look old to Carver for the first time. "What else do you have for me? Jaydee says you romanced one of the girls."

"Yes. She was naive and childish, a spoiled Atlantean princess as empty-headed as the rest of them. She did like me though! She shared it all if you know what I mean..." The insinuating laugh Carver threw out soured his stomach. He forced himself to continue. "What specifically do you want to know about? She wouldn't stop talking...I'm not sure where to begin."

Mardu raised an eyebrow. "Fucking to get information. Good for you. Now I know you're my son. Did she speak of her parents?"

"Just that her father is away most of the time and her mother gardens and does something else...what was it? Oh yes, weaves I think. She didn't seem particularly connected to them and can't wait to leave for a High City apprentice this fall. I got the impression they weren't close—barely mentioned them." Carver lied smoothly, expertly sprinkling convincing details.

Mardu snorted. "Well then, it won't break her heart that they're dead."

Carver's breath hitched. He turned to feign studying the cityscape outside the window, fearing his eyes had widened as he felt this shock.

Orja bustled in, bearing platters of Mardu's favored late-night snack, veal fried crisp in its own fat, with mountains of onions, sauteed to pearly, opaque strands.

Carver hated onions. Their smell and taste and texture would forever remind him of his father.

They waited in silence till she left.

Time to put on a show.

Sighing, he shrugged lazily as if to say "well, sometimes things happen", hoping Mardu hadn't caught his intense reaction. Managing to sound bored he asked, "What's our concern with them?"

"Nothing really. Her father knew too much about the Mutazio, had a run-in with Balek years ago—which Balek failed to contain. A loose end I needed to tie off before we take Greece. No longer a concern. Get something to drink while you tell me the rest."

Mardu's mood improved as he downed glass after glass of apple brandy, his current passion.

Carver tried to stomach some food, inventing truth-based lies big and small about the twins, until he'd painted them to be harmless fools that he'd taken advantage of. "...and now you've orphaned them too." He clucked, mockingly shaking his head at his father. He continued the tales: his friendship with Turner, their bloody killing of the islanders, even the entertaining legends of Balor, and Kinny's staged farce of ghostly giants. Mardu seemed to enjoy the stories, particularly his son's chilling condescension in the telling.

Knowing Jaydee would—perhaps already had—relate anything she deemed significant, Carver left nothing out. Putting his own spin on the people and events, he hoped Mardu would consider all of it a huge waste of time. Except perhaps the expensive but successful bargain with Meihal. Carver knew better than to ask questions about that. The less he showed interest in his father's schemes, the more Mardu told him.

It was late when Carver finished, aching to be alone, to vent the internal combustion threatening to spill out, to escape the claustrophobic stench of onion, to rest and figure out what, if anything, he could do for Ahna.

He needed to process his deep horror that his own father had killed the ones she loved and depended on most. The Papa she spoke of in every conversation. The parents who had been her world.

His father had taken hers away. Forever.

"Ruler Ziel is like a grandfather to me" Ahna had said. It echoed over and over in his mind while he sat watching Mardu scratch notes in his record book, then lock it away.

This could be the connection. I could avenge her parents, give her the information needed to disrupt Mardu's plans, curb his power, eventually break him. The idea sprouted and took root, growing rapidly in a swirl of thought crowding his already weary mind. Solidifying finally, it became a vow. *I will bring him down, for Ahna, and her Ruler Ziel.*

Mardu was starting to slur as he went to a locked cabinet, removed a handful of small, leather-bound books, and tossed them into Carver's lap. "Drey's. Read them. Bring me anything of value, then destroy them."

Black as death looming, he stood over Carver, reeking of the slimy onions that Carver detested from the depths of his being.

Swirling the last of his apple brandy in the smoked teardrop glass, Mardu was deliberate in savoring its nuance. "Was it fun? Fucking the little orphan whore?" His half-drunk, leering voice was curious.

Carver tasted bile rising as he stood to look straight into his father's soulless eyes. "Most fun I've ever had."

The End
(to be continued in Book Two)

Dearest Readers:

First of all, thank you for reading!

Because we did so much research, we want to share some probable realities of Atlantis that aren't portrayed in the books. We left out certain abilities, traditions and underlying belief systems that have little relatability—rather than write an entire book of explanations.

- Atlantean writing was comprised of many *sigils* which made their written language overly complex. Symbols represented a large concept like a legend, or doctrine, and were used more often.
- Geographic locations in the story bear the current day name to avoid confusion. "Merika" is one exception. Atlanteans named the American continent for a star, long known as "Merika", which presided over the huge landmass to their west. Keep in mind, the continents were shaped quite differently then, with lower sea levels and different climates.
- It is likely the magnetic poles were reversed.
- Atlantis used a complex calendar with a "moon" (month) starting and ending at the new moon. Their days were a 24 hour cycle but they placed emphasis on the differences of the three eight-hour periods.
- Many of their customs were similar to "Shamanism" or "Druidism", closely tied to earth powers and rhythms. Astrology informed everything they did.
- Atlanteans were incredibly advanced because they perceived energy via fully developed pineal glands, providing an actual sixth sense. Working with the famed "third eye" is modern humanity's attempt to restore this sense.
- Some Atlanteans could levitate, fly, communicate telepathically and with animals, change molecular composition of matter to reshape or move it, and defy pretty much all the laws of nature or physics if it served them. They communicated with other planets and species. They travelled in space and certainly, all over Earth. They were the world power.

Instead of sticking strictly to chronological events or cultural paradigms in Atlantis' final "Golden Age", we remixed bits and pieces from earlier times. It would be comparable to telling a story set in 2017, but including things from say, the 1950's, the 1800's or even earlier. It's all indicative of Atlantean culture but it might bother those who know. We know you're out there.

We chose the "Golden Age" as our setting, rather than the horror of machines and inhumanity Atlantis became by the end. They were shifting from the light cycle into dark. We are now shifting from the dark cycle back into the light.

It is estimated that over half of the souls on the planet today lived a life-time (or many) during the Atlantis Epochs. If this story resonates with you, you're perhaps one of those souls. With awareness, we can choose different paths this time around. May it be so.

"There is a day in the past and another in the future which mirror each other, and the same events repeat. The past can change the future, and the future heals the past." -Cosega Search

ACKNOWLEDGMENTS

Many thanks to those long-suffering souls who read early drafts, and helped us make it better.

Many thanks to Jason for his support of Diana's life shifts toward fulfilling a lifelong desire to write. Eternal gratitude to Roy, Logan and Cole for cheerfully excusing Donna from the role of spouse and mom whenever she was on a roll, or needed a writing retreat, or just ignored you because she was lost in the story. You set us free. And that's true love.

Thank You to Readers

Hands together at the heart, we offer a deep and flourishing bow to each one of you, our beloved readers. Without you falling in love with the heroines and heros, imagining the splendor of Atlantis, despising the black-hearted villains, and wondering what'll happen next, this story would only be words on a page. Our sincerest gratitude for bringing it all to life.

If you enjoyed this book, please leave us a review on Amazon, Goodreads, and anywhere else you purchased it. Your rating and words have a powerful influence on potential readers, and the mysterious algorithms of online marketplaces.

We would love to connect with you. Visit us at www.ddadair.com.

BIBLIOGRAPHY

Though we read every book and article we could find on Atlantis—or any other ancient advanced civilizations that might relate to Atlantis, the following were the most impactful, with data points that repeated. These are the books or articles we'd most recommend.

Andrews, S 2004, *Lemuria and Atlantis; Studying the Past to Survive the Future,* Llewellyn Publications, Woodbury, MN.

Andrews, S 1997, *Atlantis: Insights from a Lost Civilization,* Llewellyn Publications, St. Paul, MN.

Cannon, D 1992, *Jesus and the Essenes.* Gateway Books, Bath, UK

Cannon, D 2001, *The Convoluted Universe: Book One,* Ozark Mountain Publishing Inc., Huntsville, AR.

Cannon, D 2005, *The Convoluted Universe: Book Two,* Ozark Mountain Publishing Inc., Huntsville, AR.

Cannon, D 2008, *The Convoluted Universe: Book Three,* Ozark Mountain Publishing Inc., Huntsville, AR.

Cannon, D 2011, *The Convoluted Universe: Book Four,* Ozark Mountain Publishing Inc., Huntsville, AR.

Cannon, D 2015, *The Convoluted Universe: Book Five,* Ozark Mountain Publishing Inc., Huntsville, AR.

Cannon, D 2014, *The Search for Sacred Hidden Knowledge,* Ozark Mountain Publishing Inc., Huntsville, AR.

Cannon, D 2012, *Keepers of the Garden,* Ozark Mountain Publishing Inc., Huntsville, AR.

Cayce, E 1968, *On Atlantis,* Hawthorne Books, NY, NY.

Donnelly, I 1882, rev. 1976, *Atlantis: The Antediluvian World,* Dover Publications Inc. NY, NY.

Hancock, G 1995, *Fingerprints of the Gods,* Three Rivers Press, NY, NY.

Hancock, G 2015, *Magicians of the Gods,* St. Martin's Press, NY, NY.

Michell, J 2013, *The New View Over Atlantis,* 3rd Edition, Hampton Roads Publishing Company, Charlottesville, VA.

Santesson, H.S. 1972, *Understanding Mu,* 2nd Edition, Coronet Communications, Inc. NY, NY.

Tyberonn, J 2010, *AA Metatron Channel: 'Revisiting Atlantis: The Crystalline Field of 10-10-10',* https://atlara.wordpress.com.

Wilson, C and Flem-Ath, R 2008, *The Atlantis Blueprint: Unlocking the Ancient Mysteries of a Long-Lost Civilization,* Delta Trade Paperbacks,

Wilson, S and Prentis, J 2011 *Atlantis and the New Consciousness,* Ozark Mountain Publishing Inc. Huntsville, AR

ABOUT THE AUTHOR

Sisters Diana Adair and Donna (Adair) McMurtry were trekking up Colorado mountains or soaking in hot mineral springs while they plotted the Golden Age Series. Atlantis, and other periods of "lost" history, have been a long-time obsession and over 10 years of research went into their first series. Luckily, being Quantum Healers who specialize in past life regression hypnotherapy, they can access history first-hand—so there's many more stories to come!

They both live in the wild west. Diana has built her own tiny home in the mountains with her partner and two big hairy dogs. She loves trail-running and climbing fourteeners. Donna writes, hikes, and plays in her own mountain paradise with husband, two nearly grown sons, and two dogs.

Together they're known for hugging trees, constantly plotting future stories, and occasionally podcasting. (thespiralpath.podbean.com)

To contact them, visit ddadair.com. Follow them on facebook for the latest announcements and upcoming events.

ALSO BY DD ADAIR

- **"Shadows of Atlantis"** Golden Age Series: Book 2
- **"Atlantis Moirai"** Golden Age Series: Book 3

Continue reading for an excerpt from *"Shadows of Atlantis"*.

Ruins and Spirits
The Crystal City, Atlantis

"... he is to instruct them about all the periods of history for eternity ... and in the statutes of the truth. Anticipating the time, dominion passes from Belial and returns to the Sons of Light."

— "THE COMING OF MELCHIZEDEK", FRAGMENT OF THE
DEAD SEA SCROLLS

Ahna

"Why would there be a door three hundred feet above the ground?" Aiela's exotic, angular face squinted with incredulity, straining to peer skyward on this relentlessly sunny morning. One hand swept back strands of blackberry-colored hair, escaped from her mass of braids. Wind gushed and stilled in a rhythm only the mountain folds understood.

"I'm not sure it's *three* hundred feet. Ziel will know." Ahna's gaze roamed the valley below, trying to spot Ziel and Auntie Sage in this deserted ruin, overtaken by high mountain forest. She could see faint movement of spirits as they bustled to and fro in their own time, unaware of visitors. Unaware that their city had become a monument, an uninhabitable place where the veil was too thin to fully separate time dimensions. Like catching movement from the periphery, they were here and gone before her brain could translate what exactly it saw.

Her teeth chattered, not just from the cold. "What's taking them so long?"

Aiela shrugged and turned, thin sunlight catching the pale blue tattoo, a double spiral running along the left side of her long neck. "Auntie Sage has never been here. Ziel's likely showing off for her. His colors get brighter when she's around..."

"... and hers get softer." Ahna finished. They smiled conspiratorially.

No one had lived here since the third Epoch. For one thing, the energetic frequency was too fast to stay more than a few hours. The four of them had prepared themselves all week; eating only liquid and raw foods, meditating hours a day, applying essential oils, and tuning their chakras with crystals twice a day. They'd stay here only a short time.

Originally, Crystal City was Atlantis' treasure vault. Their entire collection of knowledge had been stored and maintained here, for it wasn't metals or jewels, not beautiful art nor any rare substance that Atlantis valued most. It was knowledge. The accumulation of all that had been experienced and learned in millions of lifetimes, since souls first began inhabiting human form on planet Earth.

Here midst a mountain range of quartz, the Ancients had built an entire city from crystals—some left whole, much more, ground into a cement that could be cast in molds or friezes, then designed and embellished in endless ways. Such high frequency had been all the protection needed. It was rumored those of low frequency could not physically see the city, and few could enter without intense sickness or mental distress.

Ahna and Aiela, one light, one dark, waited on a worn flat spot, perhaps a balcony once, hewn into the mountainside. Bare, jagged peaks jutted out in all directions. Crumbling remnants of this once holy City, littered a bowl-shaped valley below with broken walls and toppled columns.

"If only we could fly like our ancestors!" Ziel panted as he and Sage appeared in the arched stone doorway, gasping from their climb. Dressed alike in creamy linen tunic and pants, with light-reflecting cloaks of gold thread streaming behind them, they looked a perfectly contrasted pair. Shoulder-length silver hair blew across his fine-boned face, the color of burnt sugar. Light cerulean eyes gave him an almost alien look. Auntie Sage's skin was as pale and welcoming as butter. Her features were soft, almost blunt, topped by long hair turning from gold to cream and currently piled into a messy bun.

"There you are, we wanted to ask you about that." Aiela pointed to the curious round door, glinting high above where they stood.

"How's everyone feeling? Alright so far?" Ziel glanced at each in turn, concerned they not stay too long in this high ancient place.

"Symptoms are comparable to oxygen deprivation at extreme altitudes", he'd explained to them over and over. "You may feel light-headed, or hyper-focused as your brain works overtime in an environment that uses more of it. You will tire quickly because your body struggles continuously to adapt."

"We're fine." Aiela answered.

Ziel tipped his head back, gazing at the weathered door. "That was for the Priests and Priestesses of this original Temple of Knowledge. You had to be able to levitate to enter. It was once Atlantis' most sacred place—where the wisdom of the universe was kept—both a vault and a test that contained the understanding of where we all began. Some of it was brought to us by visitors from the stars."

"I thought *everybody* could fly back then." Ahna puzzled.

"Not everybody. There were those who carried the ability, the innate understanding of levitation—unbinding gravity's force—and also plenty who didn't. It's the same today; we have natural talents and abilities that differ widely from each other, such as the ability to draw a perfect likeness of what we see, or the ability to flourish fields of plants, or engineer complex technologies based on mathematics. It only *seemed* that everyone could fly, because those that could, helped transport those that couldn't, by touching them, or levitating simple objects. A carpet often carried those people and objects gravity-bound on their own. It's said the energy used was the same frequency as a child playing. That sort of joy and pure imaginative state the brain enters when involved in play. We are all capable of it—even still today—if only we tuned in to the exact frequency."

"At the time this city was constructed, Atlanteans believed those with such powers were holier than others. So they were named Priestesses and Priests and became regarded as set apart—a higher or more advanced sect. This ability of flight was gradually lost, like many psychic powers after the third epoch's calamities destroyed much of humanity. Fewer and fewer of the remaining gifted ones procreated—so it was not passed down in DNA structures."

"And that door was for those who could fly." Aiela still squinted at its faded gold luster. "What's inside now?"

Ziel shook his head. "Nothing. Everything was relocated. No doubt we've lost a bit. What's left is in the Hall of Records. Our 'Book of the Dead' was written here you know, along with some of the books and prophecies from the first two epochs."

Atlantis' 'Book of the Dead' was said to have been written by souls who'd passed on. Returned to converse with the living, they assured humanity that death was not to be feared, describing in great detail the process of leaving a physical body, crossing to the "other side", and deciding what came next.

Ziel continued, "This was also home to the 'Seers', those who could see forward and backward in time as easily as you and I see the present. The Seers searched through future possibilities until they found what seemed the best outcome and Atlantis followed their suggestions. As humanity has fallen in frequency, those abilities disappeared. Snippets of visions and dreams are all we have left."

"Does the sun seem incredibly bright here, or is it just me?" Ahna's eyes hurt.

"It is bright at this altitude—stronger." Auntie Sage shivered and pulled her shimmering gold cloak around her, the breezes playing with her hair. Even with intense sunshine, the air's chill was piercing.

Ziel took Sage's hand. "Let's go inside. I will show you the things we came to see."

"It feels strange to see people alive in another time, doing daily things in the same space we're walking through now. I can't quite wrap my mind around it." Ahna spoke in hushed tones inside the crumbling building. It looked like the air itself took shape and moved. *What might they think*, Ahna wondered, *of being observed thousands of years after their time.*

Auntie Sage's eyes followed traces of movement around the room too, even in mid-air above. "The Space/Time continuum gets tangled in our understanding." She murmured. "Time seems a sequential straight line, because that is its movement from inside; A perspective quite different from the reality seen from without. Really, it's all happening at once in a spiral-like movement. Ascending rings of events take up the same space, separated only by time dimension. It's like time is really an infinity of space... or multiple spaces layered by time in the same space..." She stopped with a small laugh, "My mind understands it but when I use words, it sounds confusing!"

Pausing to think, she squatted in the gloomy dust, drawing a line the length of two hands. "Space makes time possible." She crossed it with an equal line. "And time is what multiplies space, or makes it infinite. Where the two meet, is the hallowed place." Her fingertip dimpled the center of the equidistant cross. "Herein lies the present moment—which is all we really ever have." She straightened, eyes tracking the ghostly movements again. "Because the energy is so special here—much higher frequency than most places on earth—the dimension membrane that normally separates time rings is thinner. That's why we catch glimpses and echoes. Scents are the strongest, can you smell the people walking by? The incense they burn here?"

Ahna stood still and closed her eyes, inhaling. "Sweetgrass, rose, pine resin, myrrh, and something else... it's familiar but I don't know what."

The four of them wandered, dream-like and abstruse, examining large interior halls with walls that were deteriorating, broken down by centuries of mountain trees and grasses slowly digesting the rubble humanity left behind. Each step they took grated with broken crystal shards, ground to loud dust. Interior surfaces had been glazed with plasters made from ground quartz, and the ruins still sparkled beneath earth's reclamations, when touched by sunlight.

They gathered by a bank of hollow windows where sunbeams touched the floor, turning its forgotten carpet of grit to flashing stardust.

"It may have been this very spot where our ancestors first conceived The Order of Melchizedek." Ziel began as they huddled in the scant warmth of the sun. All four of them gazed across the picturesque valley.

"There had always been a Melchizedek; One of great personal righteousness who devoted his or her lifetime to gathering, organizing and protecting humanity's knowledge. As you know, the experience of each and every lifetime is significant. Sacred to our collective path, each serves as mile cairns, maps, caution signs and 'place of interest' markers to those coming after.

Because knowledge of all our truths begats abiding peace, male Melchizedeks were called the King of Peace. Understanding and living according to our vast experiences begats a rightness or wisdom, so female Melchizedeks were called the Queen of Righteousness.

Portions of texts are missing that might have told what event or events caused the Melchizedek to become an Order. What we do know is, at some point, someone realized a time was coming when all knowledge must needs gradually be lost. That Someone wrote;

> *To enter the shadow is humanity's fate. To journey in darkness, our greatest hope. This choice shall wear the mask of doom, shall burn all truth. But ignorance begins our winding path home, to glory."*

Ziel finished quoting, and glanced at the shivering forms around him. "Come, let's hydrate and warm up. We've perhaps an hour left, and there's more I want you to see." He continued the story as they picked their way down stone steps, decaying in damp semi-gloom.

"The Melchizedek who led this city at the end of the third epoch, was faced with a riddle; she knew that humanity would eventually destroy, change, lose, or reject every bit of truth they possessed, yet they would need to regain it once the lessons of darkness were learned."

"What lessons of darkness? I don't understand." Aiela asked, as they stepped into sunshine again and headed towards the shiny, egg-shaped aero they had piloted here.

Ziel quirked an eyebrow. "I don't fully understand either. Perhaps it speaks of times past. Those long descending cycles away from the Source of all that is." He sounded doubtful. "More likely, it is the long darkness still to come. Because we are born of Divine Source, we already know the light—indeed we are the light. It is the darkness that holds our greatest lessons."

Aiela nodded. "And spiritual darkness, by definition, would have to be void of truth."

"Yes." Ziel paused to study her, a gaze both affectionate and sad. "You are very like your mother, Aiela. So very like her…" His eyes were moist when he shook himself into motion again.

Auntie Sage passed out thermoses in the plush warmth of the aero. They drank spiced plum tea, fragrant and steaming, while Ziel finished his tale.

"The Melchizedek who conceived the Order was female, but her plan depended on a male. She selected her successor, trained him with explicit instructions, then tricked him into taking her life, binding him into the duties and powers of the Melchizedek.

Following their plan, he encoded Atlantis' knowledge—the entire collective story of humanity—into his very DNA. For the first time, the knowledge became biologic, known as 'Body-gnosis'. It had been kept in many forms: written texts, symbols and images carved in stone, even geometrics and mathematical equations communicated through architecture of buildings. Eventually of course, it was encoded in crystals, as it is to this day.

Over a span of many and more years, hundreds of women from all over Atlantis came here to literally birth the Order. They were known as the 'Divine Feminine'. They came here, to the great Crystal Pyramid of all knowledge, to be impregnated with Melchizedek's seed. A process known as 'immaculate conception', because there was no mating or sexuality involved. It was all done clinically and spiritually.

As per the agreement, the Divine Feminine spread across the world, and the resulting 'virgin-birthed' babies grew into women who carried our universal knowledge, and passed it to their own daughters. On and on it went, down through generations. The Order of Melchizedek was established in the very bloodlines of we who must walk through a great 'era of wickedness'."

Ahna squinted in the over-bright afternoon as they emerged from the aero. City ruins flashed around them but the spot they stood on was empty. "I don't see Crystal Pyramid ruins, what happened to it?"

"I was wondering the same thing." Auntie Sage agreed. "You'd think it would have partially survived, structurally sound as pyramids are."

"You tell me." Ziel looked intently at Ahna. "I think if you concentrate and ask the question, you could discover the answer. Try. See with your inner eye, listen with your ear of knowing."

Ahna and Aiela both closed their eyes, opening awareness to this strange place, as high mountain winds played sonatas through a thousand empty tree branches. Nature's melodies rushed frantically to and fro, as if there were only this one moment of life. Arrhythmic and overlong pauses, highlighted bird voices singing odes to utter freedom, and arias to nature's bliss.

"I see it!" Ahna turned in slow circles, eyes shut tight, smiling in wonder. "We're standing inside... it was here on this very spot!"

"Yes! Yes it was!" Ziel clapped his hands together. "Describe what you see."

"It's huge! Just... enormous... made entirely of crystals. The pyramid walls are not smooth but formed from thousands of crystal clusters that spike out like fur standing on end. Both the exterior and interior surface in fact! It sparkles in the sun, so bright I can barely look. Most of the inside is filled with crystals, and there is a small chamber where only a dozen people could fit, in the upper third of the pyramid. Clear panes are laid as a floor, but other than that, it is only crystals... there must be millions! El, you're here... I see you here with me!" She reached in Aiela's direction, catching her sister's hand like they had as little girls, facing their large, strange world together.

Aiela laughed with delight, "I *am* here with you. Look at this place! It's incredible, and the altar! There are crystals forming all the moon phases."

"I wonder what it was for?" Ahna mused.

"I think it's used for the 'initiates'—what they call the women who come to form the Order. They go through an initiation called 'The Welcoming'. It's basically the process of impregnating them on a waxing moon night. They return on the next full moon to bless the conception and go through a ritual which attunes the mother's frequency to that of the embryo, so the DNA coding is less altered by her own." Aiela laughed again. "I don't even know how I know all this! I just feel it…"

But Ahna knew. They were born of this line—through Mama. Standing here in this thin place, the spirals of time overlapped, and she felt oddly split between realities.

"What else do you know… or see?" Auntie Sage asked.

"Only women were involved in the entire process, from beginning to end. Melchizedek's priestesses take the mothers through the initiation… because the divine feminine is to carry the knowledge… and the masculine is to protect it… because it will not be safe for a long, long time."

"What do you mean, the knowledge will not be safe?"

"It will be used by those negatively oriented, those addicted to power, those who seek to destroy beauty, or what is innocent and expansive. The knowledge will become weapons that control…" Aiela's voice lapsed into tones of horror.

Ahna had felt the rush of knowledge downloading into her awareness, saw the images her sister had spoken. There was more coming in so fast she could only focus on bits and pieces. But it was enough to complete the story. "Ohhhh. This pyramid, all these Crystals held the knowledge. This chamber was built specifically so Melchizedek could encode his own DNA within it."

Aiela was walking around in their luminous, fog-like dimension, examining things. "There is a beautiful, jeweled dagger on the altar, used to draw blood. After the conception, a tiny thimble of blood is taken from the initiate and poured into the earth… but I don't understand the significance…"

And then a moment later, "Of course! It's a covenant. A trinity of trinities, see? Crystal, blood, and feminine. The earth crystals correspond to the crystal matrix of the human body, which is a microcosm of the crystalline universe. The moon cycles correlate to feminine cycles which tell the story of universal cycles. Women bleed. Blood carries iron which interacts with earth iron, binding them like magnets, one to the other, signifying the covenant between humanity and this planet. A trinity is the strongest number there is and this particular trinity, this pact, ensured the DNA would be carried a long, long, looong time. They knew some bloodlines will end and others will be tampered with, diluted, but some must remain strong and pure to the end."

"To the end of what?" Sage asked.

"To the end of the 'Era of Wickedness'. They used the trinity of elements and energies to ensure the Order of Melchizedek will endure until humanity needs its knowledge back. Until those that live, perhaps, millennia in the future, are ready to have their history returned. Only then can they step from the shadow, made stronger by surviving their darkness." Aiela paused.

Ahna opened her eyes to see if Ziel and Sage understood. "It's the truths of Source. The Light of wholeness. We have to *understand* the light. We have to experience all possible darkness, before we can enter the higher realms of wholeness." She finished.

The four of them stood silent, each absorbing, what had just transpired.

Aiela, ever the inquisitive one, thought of one more question. "But where did it go? There should be remnants, a mountain of shards at least. It was so big! Why's there nothing here?"

Ziel looked pointedly at her. "How should I know? Get your own answers."